THE SUICIDAL GOD

Ylisa Ebert

THE SUICIDAL GOD

DOUBLE DRAGON

DEDICATION

This book is dedicated to Rebecca, who knows the ending to another story. And to Ernie, whose magic is clumsy and beautiful.

PROLOGUE

After a three and a half billion year relationship, all Thom had to say was, "fuck you," as he tried to prevent the three-inch dagger from sinking any further into his stomach.

Edmund smiled. "Don't swear, Thom. It's rude."

Thom grunted and started to pale under the blood loss. Then, his eyes widened as a new pain seared through his gut.

Edmund's smile widened. "Like that one, do you? A friend helped me whip it up. Lethorsum. Smells of apricots and is completely harmless unless it comes in contact with your blood. In that case, even a single drop is enough to ensure death. There is no antidote. Not even lifeblood can cure it. And the more liberal the application of the poison, the more painful and horrifying is the death." Edmund tightened his grip on the blade and chuckled. "Can you guess how much I used?"

Thom spit blood onto the ground. It was shiny and frothy. His fingers were becoming slippery with his own fluids and it was now harder to keep his grip on the knife. His words were bitten off in anger and pain, but also in grim satisfaction. "It's too late to kill me. Time is up."

"Kill you?" Edmund's mouth quirked. "I never want to actually kill you. Incapacitation, yes, torture, yes, painful and horrifying near death, yes. Actual death? No, not at all. Why do you think I waited until this late to use the poison? It gives the troops morale when I painfully disembowel people,

7

and if the person in question just happens to be in possession of cosmic powers, all the better. But I don't want to kill you. What fun would it be if there was only one god?"

Thom shook his head in anger. "The blood is dying. The mortals . . . your playthings . . . . We'll be alone again if you don't stop this madness. We are not meant to be in this world and we are killing it."

Once more came that deep chuckle. "My dear Thom, always the pessimist, now aren't we? Right, then. See you in four hundred years."

And with that, Edmund thrust the blade through the last of Thom's resistance to put an eight-inch long gash into his lungs. His scream of pain was interrupted when both he and his assailant disintegrated into a fine dust.

CHAPTER 1
RYNNA

Rynna was born with the desire to kill herself the way some people are born with webbed feet. Although where healers can take small knives to free the individual toes of those unfortunate cases, Rynna's problem was one of the mind, not of the body. It is rather more difficult to cure afflictions of the brain. Not that they hadn't tried, though.

The girl's earliest memory was of the man holding the cup to her lips. The man was telling Rynna to be a good girl and to drink a burning liquid that she was later to identify as brandy. After the ineffective sedative, she remembered another man, this one with clear blue eyes. He was holding onto her neck with one of his hands and in his other was a straightened fishhook. His smile was so sweet. She thought her father was only napping on the floor and that her mother enjoyed the kiss the strange man was giving her.

Then the blue-eyed man was squeezing her neck and bringing the hand with the fishhook closer. The white-hot pain that followed blurred the rest of the memory. Rynna's right ear leaked blood for two weeks after the incident and she did not regain the hearing on that side.

In her next memory, she was four. Rynna's mother was wearing a wide brimmed hat for Trinni, the planting festival, and she was humming as she put up the laundry. Linens fighting their pegs for freedom trailed her progress through the air. Rynna remembered those dampened fabrics because they took longer to burn. Hidden in the back wood lot, the girl and her mother watched the flames eat their house and all their pretty things, and then travel to the small shed where the clothesline was attached. Eventually, even the wet shirts and pants were consumed, and it was then that Rynna and her mother quietly snuck away with their lives.

In her third memory, Rynna was alone and waiting at the kitchen table. It was late and when her mother finally came home, she was smiling tightly and holding a small, stale heel of bread. The bread tasted simultaneously of triumph and inadequacy.

It was these dark recollections that began Rynna's consciousness. The fleeing and gradual poverty. The fires, screaming mobs, and thrown rocks. Her mother slowly becoming a night lady, because at least that way she'd get paid for the rape.

And yet, curiously, that aspect of her which one would assume to be most damaging, emotionally and physically, was not among her earliest cognizance. Just as most small children do not remember every instance of tying their boots as a child, Rynna's mind discounted her repeated efforts to end her own life. They were too frequent an occurrence to be of any importance. After all, she didn't mean to keep trying to kill herself. It was something that happened when she wasn't paying attention. Like how some people twirl their hair in their fingers, or bite their nails. In Rynna's case, it just so happened that if her mind wandered when she was practicing her letters, her hand would migrate the sharp quill to her temple and start ripping a hole there.

Her first suicide attempt happened when she was two, when her father was still alive and she could still hear from both ears. There was a little fire made of some twigs and leaves. On toddler's feet she waddled over and calmly stood in the middle of it. Her father spotted little Rynna first, standing there giggling while the skin on her toes blackened. He scooped her out, doused the flames, and then immediately rushed her to the healer's where they paid ten coppers for a salve that still left her bereft of toenails.

Next it was the creek behind their little wooden hut, too small for even a toddler to drown in unless you specifically moved rocks to make a hole at the bottom. Rynna's mother found her face down and only just managed to breathe air back into her lungs.

It didn't take Rynna's parents long to figure out that they not only had to keep their precious bundle of joy away from the typical dangers to small children like loose blankets, sharp instruments, and heights, but that they also needed to keep her from being alone with more innocent things like small puddles, piles of laundry, and her dinner.

The other children noticed. The other parents, too.

Mothers and fathers did not want their sons and daughters playing with a girl who might pour boiling water onto them without a moment's notice. And of course they didn't want their children getting any funny ideas, as if Rynna's problem was small pox or a bad cold which could be caught. And these were the more rational minded ones.

Other members of the community thought that she was a demon or a changeling and needed to be killed, or in the very least removed from the village proper. It was the result of this thinking that left Rynna and her mother constantly without any possessions or money.

It was the same no matter where they went. Welcoming neighbours to a widowed mother and her cute daughter became suspicious conspirators within months. Rynna and her mother were always relocating. Place to place, town to town, movement was the general state of the girl's youth.

Although her suicidal impulses had no cure, Rynna and her mother developed ways to fight them. So long as Rynna never allowed herself to be thinking absently or get distracted, they could be avoided. She learned to watch herself at all times and never allowed herself to be idle. It reduced the number of 'incidents,' as her mother began referring to them, and made them less noticeable to the community.

Rynna helped knead the dough, but not cook it nor slice the ensuing bread. They ate soft foods: soggy crusts, liquid cheeses, soups, and things boiled for so long that it all became a mush that could slide down her throat easily.

She also learned other skills. At age six, she knew basic first aid and could construct a splint for herself with nothing more than fallen branches and her own hair. She knew how to dislocate and relocate all of her joints. She could smother most flames in less than five seconds.

It never really helped in the end though.

As a three year old, Rynna had been attacked by people who wanted to fix her to save the village. Years later, Rynna was never sure whether they were trying to get rid of her condition or simply get rid of her, period. The end result was the same. Rynna and her mother respectively left a father and a husband along with most of their personal possessions, and had been nomadic ever since. They would stay in one spot for six months or a year at the most, and then Rynna and _____ would be moving on. Sometimes it was voluntarily, but those times were seldom. No matter where they settled, the two always kept a small traveling bag packed, just in case.

CHAPTER 2
THE LOVELY LADY SHUTBA

Shortly after Rynna turned fourteen, her and her mother had been staying in the same village for two years, which was a record of sorts, if there was anybody paying attention to these sorts of things. It was affectionately called Dompt by those who lived there, and they didn't really get enough visitors for anybody else's opinion to matter much.

Between the small village and its surrounding farmland, the place managed to stay afloat by exporting sheep, wool, and potatoes. The general level of intelligence of the townsfolk ranged from stupid to an almost average. The usual pastimes for the adults were procreation and inebriation, with the tedium only being interrupted by Trinni and the harvest festival, Mong.

The youth, on the other hand, had another pastime. Her name was Lady Shutba. 'Shutba', in the local slang, meant more or less 'cuntface' and had originally been grafted as a joke, but it had stuck, and then caught on, and eventually even the adults began to address the old hag as such.

The children and young adults of the community had been throwing rocks at Lady Shutba for decades. It was a coming of age ritual of sorts for the boys. For causing a light bruise, your voice lowered, for breaking a bone, you grew pubic hair, and if you actually managed to knock the old hag over with the force of your blow, your testicles dropped and all the village virgins would proceed to swarm you.

The most vicious of this generation's attackers was Fik Tucker. He sported red hair, a square jaw, and a nasty temper. So naturally, he was the most socially sought after boy in the entire village by both males and females alike.

The young girls in the town, either too timid or too aware that the hag had to have been a small girl like themselves at one point in time, never participated in the stoning. Instead, they would sit on the sidelines chanting their rationale for the abuse,

"The only good witch 'sa dead witch.
Buried in the back ditch
Hot fire and black pitch.
A good witch 'sa dead witch."

They would then proceed to rush up and fawn over the successful attacker with batted eyelashes and compliments about bravery. For after all, they did not want to end up as groomless hags themselves, and the best time to look for a husband was a firm 'now.'

Nobody knew much about Lady Shutba, neither of her name nor of her origins. She had just shown up, already old and senile sixty years previously. She hung around on the edges of town and down by the lake where she had a hut, but other than that, did not do much else. Sometimes she would disappear for a few months at a time, but she would always come wandering back eventually.

There had been much speculation as to the woman's past, but people didn't speak of said theories too often. No explanation really fit and the whole situation was unnerving. If she really was insane as some people claimed, then she should have died from eating poisoned berries or a fetid piece of meat long ago. If she was just an aborted Oceo Tolok project from centuries past, why would she put up with abuse from the prepubescent boys in the neighbourhood? And if she was a changeling, as was sometimes whispered, biding her time until the devil's return to power, then why had she not at least eaten a few of the local children to slake her evil appetites?

And the weirdest thing of all: why did the butterflies follow her? Wherever she went, there was always a plethora of brightly coloured, fluttering creatures trailing her every move. Why, they asked, why?

The old woman didn't speak any known language, and instead just shuffled around making grunting, coughing, and wheezing sounds. Whether she had forgotten how to speak or simply lacked the human organs was something much debated, but as a result by and large the woman's life remained a complete mystery.

Rynna had never liked how the children treated Lady Shutba, nor the benevolent amusement with which the adults looked down upon the situation.

"We should stop them. You and I both know how it hurts. We can't let them keep doing it!" Rynna would argue with her mother. But her mother's answer always left the bitter aftertaste of truth in the air.

"There is finally somebody stranger than us. You will let the abuse continue because it means they will be too busy watching her to notice you."

Rynna, as always, obeyed and did not draw attention to her mother and herself by interfering with the children's activities. Instead, she would walk down to the hag's hut, wait until she left, then leave bundles of warm clothes and blocks of cheese with bread.

It was on one of these trips that Rynna discovered the hag's corpse on the forest floor.

"Lord of Salvation," Rynna whispered, nausea and fear creeping through her limbs. She had never seen a dead body other than her father's, and that she couldn't remember well.

It was a pitiful thing that lay on the ground. Small, mostly. Small, frail, and lifeless. Rynna walked towards the body slowly, and then carefully knelt beside it. There were no live butterflies circling the woman now, just a few crushed ones littering the forest floor.

So that was it, then. One of the boys must have gone too far this time. They had actually killed the innocent hag. Just a lonely old woman with nobody left in the world except sadistic kids. Rynna wondered if once the woman had been sane and happy. She hoped so.

Rynna imagined Fik bragging about it for weeks to come and she felt a knot in her stomach. The feeling was made worse because deep down she didn't know if it was the senseless murder that bothered her or the fact that without the distraction of the hag, the villagers would search for someone else to make them feel secure about their own lives and normalcy.

The girl frowned in a sad sort of way, then shook her head and placed her bag to the side. Abandoning Dompt was a discussion her and her mother could have tonight. For now, she felt she owed something to this woman who had given her two years of security.

Rynna reached out to awkwardly touch the body. She thought that she should hold Lady Shutba or do something to give her a last ounce of human affection. The young girl tried to stroke the woman's forehead, but the moment her fingers came in contact with the skin her hand recoiled. Wrong. There was something wrong. There was no resistance under that flesh.

Her fingers had left a depression in the skin where she had touched it. An indent that meant that there were no bones, no organs, and no muscles under there to support its shape. The thing was only skin. The girl may not have been familiar with dead bodies but she knew for sure they weren't supposed to be hollow.

Rynna gagged. She had visited the tanner in town to see him at his work before. Leathers of all shapes and sizes being cured, shaped, and eventually stitched. Rynna had also seen the butcher skinning the cows and sheep after they were slaughtered. It amazed her how efficiently creatures could be broken down into their parts, although she had never liked the floppy, fleshy bit that was the animal's hide. Why someone would do that to a person . . . how someone could do that to a person brought bile into her throat.

Feeling sick, but surprisingly less angry than she ought to have been, Rynna weighed her options quickly. Only shaking a little, she picked up the fleshy remains of the old woman and walked along until she found a peaceful spot under an elm tree.

There she started to dig a shallow grave with just her hands. Mud dug into the flesh under her fingernail as she scraped a hole. An unmarked tomb that nobody would ever know about let alone place flowers on. This would be just a small old woman disappearing quietly. She had no plans on informing the mayor or anybody remotely official. Justice would not be had by accusing the residents of Dompt of indiscretion and scandal. Justice was a bit of a fickle bitch.

When she finished, Rynna wiped her hands off on the coarse material of her plain wool skirt. She then returned to the path, picked up her bag, and began the walk home. The girl felt tired and culpable for all the things she was not going to do.

Two minutes.

It was exactly two minutes when Rynna heard the strange noise. It was a deep, angry rumble. A frustrated roar of a volume and calibre that it could be felt through the forest floor for miles. It was like a mountain with a herniated disk threatening the cosmic healer. Or a very large, and very incensed beast who had just discovered something unpleasant.

When Rynna heard the sound, she began to walk faster, unease mixing unpleasantly with her earlier emotions. As the sound kept repeating itself and seemed to get angrier, the young girl went faster still, unease blossoming into something more panic-esque and less rational. However, she didn't really start sprinting until she felt the booming echo of large footsteps coming quickly in her direction.

More heavy pounding, more horrific roars, and suddenly Rynna was pinned to the ground by a large, livid beast.

"Where is my human suit?" the creature growled overtop of her.

Rynna didn't know what a human suit was. She also didn't know exactly what the beast was. All she knew was that there was a twelve-foot, grey-green monster towering above her.

"Tell me where my human suit is or I will eat you!" the creature threatened.

Rynna was still stunned and now had started to cry panicked tears. And all she could do was tell the truth.

"I don't know!"

"You lie!"

Rynna sobbed and shook her head. It had all happened too quickly. No response would come to her lips, not even to plead for her own life.

So the beast ate Rynna.

It was a very fortunate thing that she tasted terrible. The creature immediately spit out the girl and proceeded to gag for a few minutes before running its tongue all up and down the rough bark of a nearby tree.

"Dear Salvation, human, you taste terrible. Have you never bathed before?" The creature shuddered and then once more scratched its tongue along the serrated bark.

Rynna did not answer. She had been spit out headfirst and hadn't been able to cushion her landing. Pain flashed through her and a large bruise could already be felt on her back and right shoulder. Small cuts from where the monster's teeth had begun to graze her were beginning to bleed, and the creature's caustic spit was blistering into a rash on her exposed skin. It was a wet, painful feeling of terror.

As her mind was not quite functioning, the young girl could only manage to get herself away from the beast in a weak crawl. Knees and hands cut themselves against the rough forested earth in her frantic efforts, and the broken skin burned when dirt was ground into her wounds.

The beast watched the pathetic escape attempt emotionlessly for a few minutes. Then, he calmly extended his foreclaw, sliced through the meaty section of her leg, and dragged the girl towards him. Rynna shrieked in pain as she was pulled across the ground, grabbing at scraggly grass along the way.

The creature lifted the girl's body in the air with the same claw. Rynna felt important veins and muscles ripping apart as her own weight pulled the cut deeper. Her screams were jagged.

Then, as if the beast was a lady delicately nibbling on honey cakes, the creature bit off three toes from Rynna's left foot. Blood leaked from a new source. Rynna kept screaming.

The creature spit out the three toes to the side and shuddered once more, while simultaneously sliding the girl off its claw the way thick mutton slides off a roasting spit.

"Definitely one of the worst things I have ever tasted in my life. Listen, human. Apparently I cannot eat you, but I have no qualms about ripping

21

off all of your extremities and leaving you for dead. I can find my human suit by its scent alone, but that would take time. It would greatly increase your lifespan if you were to tell me where it is."

Rynna had not stopped screaming and the girl had actually gotten louder as she was now desperately clawing at her foot, trying to stop the blood flow.

The beast swung its large tail around and hit Rynna in the side of her head. A loud thump was followed by silence. Spots danced in front of Rynna's eyes and her hands went limp.

"I will ask one last time. Where is my human suit?"

Rynna could only shake her head in ignorance. She had this funny tilting sensation.

The creature once more brought its tail around to hit Rynna in the head. Its sharp scales smashed into the soft flesh of the girl's face with a sick thwack.

Then, somehow, Rynna was lying on the ground far from where she had been before. Why was she lying on the ground? Everything seemed unfocused and she was covered in a wet, messy substance. Things seemed to be frozen in a static buzz around her.

From a distance, she could hear what sounded like a bee. An angry bee. It was speaking to her. When Rynna concentrated very hard, she could almost make out what it was saying.

"Human! Human! Wake up, human!"

That's nice, she thought. Then Rynna passed out.

CHAPTER 3
THE DEAD VISITOR

She woke up, which was surprising in the way that milk left in the sun for a week and still being potable would be surprising. Granted, her head was pounding fiercely, and more skin was bandaged than was not. But still, she was awake.

Rynna recognized where she was. She knew well the feel of the lumpy mattress below her legs and the sight of the knotted wood on the ceiling above. Usually they lived in one room hovels but luck and bribes gave them a bedroom for the first time in years, the same bedroom she found herself in now.

"_____," she called, her voice rasping through a bruised throat. She winced and the pain in her head increased significantly. The young girl called for her mother again, but this time, the words were whispered and tapered off in a whine, "_____?"

Rynna's mother entered the room with a box of fresh bandages and the haggard face of poorly concealed worry. "How are you feeling?"

The girl tried to smile, but it hobbled out crooked and weak across her lips. 'She would live, wouldn't she?' the expression implied.

Rynna's mother's reciprocating smile was stretched over cheekbones that lacked the padding of consistent meals. She had once been beautiful and the remnants could still be seen: the blue eyes that would radiate were they not ringed and sagging with dark circles; the blond hair that would glow

23

were it not greying and thinning with stress; the alabaster skin that was flawless but for the scars that traced the record of her angry clients across her face.

Rynna's father had once made a sketch of her mother from charcoal and it was one of the few things that had been repeatedly salvaged. Rynna had cherished her mother's lost beauty as other girls cherished love letters. It was lost what . . . two, three towns ago?

The young girl's body did not share her mother's lost grace. She was thin. Not the svelte thin of cinched waistlines and dainty ankles. It was the haggard thin of beggars and invalids. Her hair was a dull, matted brown, more fit for a rabid bear than for someone on the cusp of womanhood. And rather than her eyes settling on one clear colour, they were a hazel similar to the shades seen on a bloated, gangrenous limb.

Rynna's mother began changing bandages. As she worked her way across her daughter's body, she began to hum a familiar melody: a half remembered ditty that was half popular half a lifetime ago. It was now cacophonous 'C' sharps and 'E' flats that jarred the ears and set teeth on edge. There were never words that accompanied it, just a corpulent melody. It was an ugly, mutated song which Rynna immediately understood.

Sometimes when Rynna's 'incidents' happened they were almost laughable in their weak ineffectiveness. Other times, the wounds were more serious, but still nothing overly concerning: a broken collarbone, a fractured wrist, a concussion. But a few times, Rynna was lucky to be alive.

Miraculously lucky. And it was then that she heard the song that her mother hummed now.

Rynna listened and watched as her mother shifted to the other side of the bed, checking wounds and applying cheap ointments. It was not until she had finished a complete inspection of her daughter that she spoke with dull words.

"I found the food you left for Lady Shutba. You shouldn't try to befriend her. You shouldn't be around people, period, for that matter. That's when your incidents get noticed. You know this. I should think that you wouldn't want these things to keep happening where there are witnesses."

The young girl did not come to her own defense. She did not go into a grand story of a beast, a skinned hag, and a lonely forest path. She stayed quiet and avoided meeting her mother's eyes. _____ was right. Rynna shouldn't have been going to visit the old woman. She knew better than that.

"Soup's ready on the table, if you can walk. If not, I can bring it to you." With that, Rynna's mother left the young girl alone to test out her limbs.

Rynna pulled herself upright with difficulty, grunting at the throb that continued to burn into her temples. She then clumsily shifted her legs until they swung off the edge of the bed. Carefully, she applied pressure to her feet.

Sore, sore, but not broken.

The young girl put more pressure on her legs and stood slowly. She felt nauseated as the dull pain increased behind her eyes. Sore. She gritted her teeth and continued. Arms, hands, neck, and knees.

Sore, sore, sore, sore, but not dead. Rynna smiled grimly. It was enough for her.

She slowly made her way out to the kitchen to join her mother. There was a silence between the two of them, but not an angry or even a disappointed one. Just the weary silence of exhaustion and inevitability. It was only broken when Rynna told her mother about Lady Shutba's death, and that night _____ added a few more items to the bag in the closet.

Rynna had lost three days to a near coma-like state following her rescue, and it took another two and a half weeks before the young girl became useful around the house. At first, her bed to the kitchen table to the privy outside were the limits of Rynna's strength. But as she regained most of her skin, she was able to start help kneading bread and cleaning once more.

The girl never brought up the beast to her mother. They had survived as long as they had by keeping their heads low and purposefully ignoring key details of their lives. The truth of this time not being the result of an incident did not matter. In her mother's mind, once the bandages came off the whole thing had never happened so blame was a moot point.

However, these weeks were marked by paranoia and an extreme aversion to the outdoors on Rynna's part. Her volatile childhood had early on dispelled any notion that a small town represented safety, and considering that their house was on the outskirts of said small town, the danger was even worse. A twelve-foot animal with a grudge could easily walk into their backyard, kill them both, and walk away without any notes of alarm being raised. So she stayed inside on the off chance that at least if the creature was not a figment of her mind, maybe it didn't know where she lived.

Had the situation continued, perhaps _____ would have grown concerned. Perhaps she would have taken measures to cure her daughter's supposed agoraphobia, like extended labour or maybe a mild beating. Perhaps she would have even talked to her daughter, and explored the ever-dangerous topic of emotions in their household. It was, after all, a fairly drastic change in the girl. However, this never became necessary because something unprecedented happened.

The two received a visitor.

They had never had social callers before. Never had friends, or even neighbours who needed to borrow sugar and the like. Her mother's clients always met her in other places, or else snuck in through the back door late at night. Other than during the initial optimistic month when they had first arrived, the doorknocker had never sounded since they had moved into the place. Which is why the clacking in and of itself was enough to cause alarm. That hollow KNOCK KNOCK which announced the stranger reverberated in Rynna's heart.

From the bedroom Rynna listened with a coil of disquiet in the pit of her stomach. The next words she heard transformed that coil of disquiet into something worse, something that clawed its way through her veins, paralyzing her with terror.

"Lady Shutba?" came her mother's surprised voice.

Rynna bolted for the back door. The last time she had seen Lady Shutba was when she had been burying her corpse. Something that died and came back to life could only mean one thing. Changeling. A living nightmare. Rynna had always thought Lady Shutba's eyes had been dark brown, but she must have been mistaken. They must have been black all along.

This was worse than a beast with a grudge. This was the Prince of Dusk's assassin. So she got the fuck out of there as all sane country folk did when there was even the smallest hint of underbeings.

Rynna heard a loud thud which meant a body had just hit the floor. After that began a series of slow, uneven thumps heading towards her. This soon became a series of very fast, uneven thumps as Lady Shutba began the pursuit in earnest. Rynna was now halfway to the trees behind the house, scrambling as quick as she could through their small garden.

Sadly, it was not fast enough. Rynna had only gotten another eight paces when she felt thin fingers tighten around her shirt in an iron grip. The girl was brought up short like a drunken man who had forgotten to unhitch his horse and fell hard in a gasp that knocked the wind out of her lungs.

Lady Shutba moved her grip from Rynna's shirt to her neck and proceeded to haul the girl to her feet. Fingers dug into the flesh around Rynna's spine. The butterflies that usually flew about the old woman were flitting about intensely.

The captured girl made a brave attempt at nobility.

"You better not have hurt _____ or I'll . . . I'll .
. . ."

Rynna stopped. Lady Shutba had begun to smile at her. The hag had no teeth. Her gums were a dark black colour and there was brown ooze dripping out from under her top lip. The sagging skin buried the ends of her smile, and you could only barely see the grin's cracked edges.

The expression did not reach the hag's cold eyes. Even now those eyes were pretending to be a simple, dark brown. What little courage Rynna had mustered, promptly slipped away.

"Don't kill me, please. I promise I won't tell anybody that you're a changeling."

Lady Shutba's smile turned to a deep scowl. Instead of making any sort of reply, the old woman licked her. The tongue left a burning trail of slime along the side of Rynna's face, starting just above the chin and finishing on her temple.

Then, the old woman's face contorted with disgust. She hiked the speechless girl over her shoulder and started walking towards the forest, butterflies keeping up with them at a lazy pace.

CHAPTER 4
HOW SHE TASTES

Being dragged off into the forest by a surprisingly strong hag who you buried over three weeks ago tends to lead to certain inevitable doom. Rynna did her best to fight it. She kicked, punched, bit, and did all she could to hinder her abduction. It was in vain. Lady Shutba simply closed one hand around the girl's throat and let the lack of oxygen take the fight out of the girl.

When Rynna was finally dumped onto the ground, she was exhausted, frightened, and mostly convinced she was going to die. This was only compounded by the fact that Lady Shutba had taken them deep into the forest, to the edge of a little cliff. It was a place Rynna had never been to before. A place that would swallow any protesting screams as easily as a river does a stone or a child does a lie.

It also didn't help that it was at this time that Lady Shutba chose to peel her skin back.

The old woman grabbed onto a loose fold of skin at her neck with her right hand. Then she pulled upwards, stretching her face. It began to part along an invisible seam, and slowly the old wrinkled hag fell away while scales began flashing through the edges.

Finally, the beast from three weeks ago stood before her, holding onto the sagging flesh of Lady Shutba by the neck.

Rynna's worst fears were realized. The creature was a changeling. The young girl began to scream.

"Quiet, human, or I will make you be quiet," the beast hissed, then raised his tail ominously. Rynna remembered the headache she had nursed for two weeks the last time. Her cries quieted to a low whine.

"Good. I hate screamers. And before you ask, yes, your mother is alive. She will wake up in an hour and suffer no lasting side effects. She is fine, which is more than I can say for you."

Rynna's mouth tasted too dry and her breath came with difficulty.

"Are you going to eat me, changeling?"

The creature's great eyes, the same colour that Lady Shutba's eyes had been, narrowed to slits. Its throat began to swell, reminiscent of the way a cat arcs its back. It was a physical warning that to continue pursuing the present course of action would be dangerous.

"Changeling? You think I am an underbeing? That is the second time you have landed that accusation. Worthless excuse for a piece of sentient flesh . . . . I am not a changeling. I am a dragon, you fool!"

Rynna frowned and shook her head, confusion momentarily dispelling terror. "You're not a dragon."

If anything, the creature's eyes only narrowed further and his neck swelled larger. "Do you actually have the audacity to deny me my own species, human? Do you really want to make that mistake?"

"Dragons are just stories. Like unicorns or giants or fairies or . . ." Rynna trailed off. The realization that somehow she was making the

31

already bad situation worse was seeping into her mind. She spoke very hesitantly. "Dragons are supposed to be noble and heroic and . . . not grave robbers. I buried that old woman nearly a month ago. And your eyes are . . . they're black."

The dragon backhanded her. A solid smack across the face, which was less damaging that being crushed by its tail, but still painful. Rynna clutched her cheek and shrunk away from the dragon. The beast's terrifying form reared up before her.

"Listen and listen well, human. My eyes are a deep golden brown when in the light, and a darker burnt brown in the dark. I am not an underbeing. I am the mighty dragon Darlan of the clutch Lal. My kind can change forms by wearing the skin of others, but we cannot change our own flesh form unless we want it to be permanent. We get one great change because we are a people of dedication. Dragons do not shuck between one body and another like underbeings.

"And this, here in my hand, is an earth beast suit which I liberated over a hundred years ago. It was after the old woman's soul had already departed and before she was eaten. Dragons do not unearth the dead. Your kind forgets sacrifices made when your great-great-greatparents were not yet born. I will not allow you to insult my people when we died in the thousands for a memory you no longer possess. So I warn you now. If you insult me or mine again, I will tear out your heart."

Tears began to slip out of the young girl. She was trying not to cry, not to scream, and not to make the dragon angrier than he already was. But gods, he was scary. Her eyes were red rimmed while a trail of snot was running from her nose.

"What are you going to do to me?"

The large beast contemplated the pathetic creature before him. Pity and disgust bled out his anger somewhat. His neck shrunk visibly and his voice, if still not pleasant by anybody's account, was less rough when he spoke. His tail started twitching with mounting tension.

"It is not what I am going to do to you, it is what has already happened."

The dragon produced a small cloth bag from about his person and poured the contents out onto his reptilian hand. Wet, black rot, and stench. What rolled onto his foreclaws were three little pieces of decomposing meat. The young girl looked at them uneasily. Upon closer inspection, Rynna realized that they would fit perfectly onto the end of her foot. She started to feel sick again

"Those . . . why did you take them?"

"Because I could not eat you, of course."

"But . . . . Why- why did you try to eat me?"

"Because, you hid my human suit, and I was angry. But that is beside the point. The point is I could not eat you. And it was not for lack of trying, either. That is why I bit off your toes. I thought if I had you in smaller portions, I could choke you down, but no. You are simply disgusting. Green-bellied pot snakes taste better and they breed in chamber pots. And then there is your scent, too. It's horrendous. If I had not been so angry at the time I would have realized it immediately. It was not until I had calmed down later in the week that the truth presented itself to me."

The dragon was pacing now, a back and forth motion of tense energy. It was like watching a panther's tail before a kill or lips before a kiss. He turned to her once more. "Do you know what this means?"

Rynna stared at him blankly, still sniffling a little from before. She was completely overwhelmed at this point. The beast's words washed over her in a vague way that increased her nausea and just made her want to close her eyes and be home. The girl's eyes found the dragon's expectant form and she shook her head.

"This means you are not human!"

Rynna's face paled at the news. It was whiteness so complete that meant only one thing: all her life, the mobs had been right.

"Or at least," the dragon continued, "you are not just a human. You taste like something that I have only tasted one other time in my entire life."

There was a silence at that. A painful silence which lasted until Rynna's quiet voice asked the only logical question.

"How do I taste?"

The dragon cringed in remembrance.

"Like a god."

Rynna paled even further, her skin now tinged with the colours of death.

"And how does a god taste?"

"Much too salty."

CHAPTER 5
THE OVERDUE GOD

High Priest Oshar Lemin sat quietly at the table in the Council Room, which was primarily used for meetings between the priests when the Council of Three was not in session. The temple in Lavanor was one of the most lavish buildings in the entire city. But the room he was in now was simple and mostly unadorned. The man didn't need distractions. He certainly didn't need riches. What the high priest really needed was to find a god.

Oshar felt old. Mossy tree stump old. Ancient and tired and growing on the side of a dead giant. His heart creaked with arthritis and his spirit had cataracts. But he wasn't that feeble, not really. He hadn't yet seen forty years and his body was still powerful and healthy. But sacrosanct failure had aged him prematurely.

As high priest he had many responsibilities. However training priests, leading the religion of three races, settling morality disputes, advising kings and elders, and relaying orders to lieutenant-generals all means nothing when you can't find the one person your people worship. Particularly when you have been failing to find Him for fourteen straight years. The high priest's confidence was now hunchbacked and his resolution was saggy.

On the table were the three stacks of parchment all littered with Xs scribbled in different hands. Each piece of parchment was headed with the name of a community. He lifted a few sheets off the first stack. Lavanor was there of course, along with Port Algin, Lot, and Dall. The main human and human-mix dwellings in the northern continent had all come back with resounding negatives.

In the southern continent, Fisherport, Syrr, and Stonewell were the same. Watchtower and Ta'ao were 'no's. Almost every boy on Minder's Isle seemed to have been tested by the number of names on that sheet. Knotte, too, had a long list. They must have sent priests along the fishing villages of Lett's Strings. Webbed and shaky letters had been angrily crossed off that parchment, with some parts of the sheet scratched through in defeat.

There were still more towns and cities which had undergone testing, but mostly just the ones with temples and priests permanently stationed there. The plethora of hamlets and villages that comprised the center of the human kingdom were for the most part missing. The first stack was only partially complete at best.

The high priest riffled through the second stack and frowned, a deep furrow creasing his brow. Dwarves. What an infuriating bunch. The human lists were incomplete, but at least they had tried. Who had the dwarves tested? Royalty. Mysterious deaths and abductions were rampant throughout the kingdoms and all they test is Tolm's bloodline. Black eyes were killing travelers, murdering farmers, and the Gate was writhing with activity while the miners played at politics. Never mind that their god was missing. Never mind the widespread terror.

But then again, he thought, if two entire races stood between my people and the Pit, maybe a succession would be the top priority as well. Tolm should have had thirty children instead of thirty cousins. For that matter even one child would have been good. Six wives and no offspring. Either the bowstring wasn't taut or the arrows were bent and either way, the squabbling got worse the closer to the grave King Tolm grew.

The high priest glanced towards Cully, a rather podgy dwarf who was chatting quietly with Lo, another miner. They were among the dozen medial priests in the room who had been gathered to reach a decision regarding which course of action was the best to be taken. Cully was currently relating a story to Lo, who had begun to chortle amicably.

Oshar wanted to slap the two of them.

The list they had brought back was a joke. They had been candidates for high priest themselves. They knew the severity of the situation. During the last rebirth, even with the full force of the free races united under the Lord of Salvation, the changelings had decimated the Ice City along with most of the people along the Old Road. Moad pottery was worth a fortune now that the city and its people were extinct. Dyed lace from Meryl Lake cost almost as much.

The high priest shook his head at the pair of dwarves chuckling together. Oshar wished it was possible to turn them over to Stewart for a couple of hours to shake some sense into them. But no, that was ridiculous. If priests could be tortured it would probably be his own name submitted for punishment first. As it was there were rumblings. Not all high priests passed the Eye on freely. It could be ripped away if it was decided its keeper was corrupt, deficient, or unworthy. Ten medial priests and two kings or elders were all it took.

Oshar closed his eyes and felt the pulse of the Eye. His connection with the Lord of Salvation. Silent for fourteen years now. The high priest shook his head again and returned his attention back to the lists.

The high priest pulled out a fresh piece of parchment and began writing out his mandate in clear words. The two dwarven priests would be sent back to the underground kingdom with fifty gallons of sacred resin and instructions that every stone in the Ull Mountains was to be turned over and tested.

A hundred soldiers and a recruiter would be sent with them as well. Thirty cousins brought to Lavanor as soldiers and advisors might settle Tolm's court a little. An heir would do a better job, but there was only so much that one religious man could do.

Oshar finally looked at the third stack of parchment. The elves had as usual tested the blood of every Tree Dweller and Water Weaver. The names of everyone from newborns to deathbed residents, male and female alike, were neatly written in columns with precise ticks beside each one. A laughable practice in the past and it had been seen as a waste of both time and resin.

Efficiency and thoroughness had been unnecessary because the Lord of Salvation always found them first. The search was more a bragging rights thing than anything else. Some small, backwards temple would get to shine in the spotlight for a century if they discovered Him. Now though, the elves were the only ones who wouldn't have to have priests sent through them again for further testing. The Weavers and Dwellers were going to be particularly smug about it.

Of course the scriptures, which he and every other priest had read upon initiation, had foretold the complications of this rebirth. Presumably, He would have been born without memory of His previous lives. Still, Oshar had never dreamed things would be this difficult. He had thought there would have been something that would have revealed their god's identity.

High Priest Lemin began to fidget in his seat. If the attack did begin . . . if the changelings did come pouring out of the Pit and they hadn't found the Lord of Salvation . . . . Well, then they would still have one course of action left. It was an option that had been abhorred universally, but there it was, still available, a last resort quietly waiting. Oshar shivered. The Oceo Tolok were always waiting.

Another thought briefly flitted through his mind. The bargain. If it was to be believed, they wouldn't have to search for Him at all. Bleak laughter rattled in the high priest's head. Dusty bones could not fulfill a pact. Extinction tended to get in the way like that.

With those dark thoughts the Xs marked all over the parchment leapt out at the High Priest. They mocked him, hackling at his lack of success. He gritted his teeth again. Somewhere they had to find Him. The Eye, ever silent, pulsed loudly and hotly in his head. He cleared his throat and his voice boomed through the little room.

"Let's begin. My fellow priests, it's time for us to decide how to find our hidden Lord."

The medial priests quieted at those words, conversation dying as they took seats around the room and turned their attention to the high priest.

Oshar took a deep breath and tried to sound the least desperate as he could.

"Any ideas?"

CHAPTER 6
SUBMITTING PROOF

"So, I taste like a god, what does that mean?" Rynna's face was uncomprehending and pale.

"Are all the humans this stupid, or is it just you?" the dragon hissed. "It means you *are* a god, you fool!"

"I'm not a god."

That was when the dragon licked her. It was a rough, greasy tongue that burned against her skin and traced the same trail that Lady Shutba's tongue had taken.

The dragon, after tasting her, immediately began to gag and cough.

"Of course you are," the dragon eventually hacked out. "I could never mistake that horrid taste anywhere. You are a god, or I am not a dragon."

Rynna shook her head and turned away from the dragon. She looked out over the side of the cliff towards the woods to avoid the creature's gaze. As she thought about his words, she absentmindedly picked at her dull, matted hair and scarred skin.

She remembered Master Flint's Inn. Another innkeeper in another town where she and her mother had once lived. On the wall in the inn had been oil paintings of the last three Lords. One, a gallant elf, had had wide shoulders and a charming smile. The second, another elf, had had a pale complexion, but warm eyes and perfect bone structure. The third, a dwarf, had been holding two axes, deadly but with a merry grin and a jovial face.

They had all been beautiful in their way. And they had all been male.

"The gods have always been reborn as men. I'm not completely ignorant, and history is very clear on that point at least."

The dragon made a vague gesture with one of his foreclaws. "No matter, human. Forever is a long time and written records only last for so long. Who knows what form the gods took when the world was new?"

"I don't have any memories of being a god. Even if I could be born as a girl, shouldn't I know everything that I have done since the beginning of creation? And I don't have any extraordinary abilities either. This is impossible."

Once more the dragon shook his head.

"No matter. We are what we are and you are a god. That is all that is important."

Rynna finally took out the last argument that she had in her arsenal. One that she was reluctant to admit, but one that was nevertheless applicable.

"I also . . . keep . . . accidentally trying to kill myself." It suddenly occurred to Rynna that this was the first time she had ever told anybody about her affliction rather than them deducing a version of it on their own through observation. It was strange explaining the truth. "Repetitive suicide attempts don't seem very god-like."

The dragon rolled his eyes.

"Enough of this, I will prove it to you."

He swept his tail around and once more knocked it violently into Rynna. This time, it hit her midsection rather than her head. With a muffled 'ugh' Rynna was thrown backwards six feet through the air, which was just sufficient to put her over the edge of the cliff.

She fell.

At first, too shocked by the lack of solid earth below her feet, Rynna dropped quietly. Then, as the implications of the approaching ground began to sink in, she began an ear-shattering screech of mortal terror. And although there was nobody close enough to hear even the echo of her scream, the earth itself cringed at the sound of her landing. Blood gushed, spewed, and pooled along with crushed organs, bone fragments, and shattered lungs.

The dragon, peering over the edge of the cliff and watching the abusive landing, began to have serious doubts about his taste buds.

CHAPTER 7
THE BLOOD LULLABY

She was bare except short pants, a sword, and the cloth wrapped around each individual foot for traction. She was also perfectly still. There was a quiet in the room unbroken even by heavy breathing as she only drew the shallowest of lungfuls.

Six thousand bells were strung across the room. The floor, the walls, and even the air were full of tiny, sensitive chimes that could be triggered by far less than a sneeze. The last test of the Warrior Clan's training. Flawlessly perform the three hundred battle poses while crossing the room. You were allowed to fail only once. The second failure meant a forfeit of all your forms.

Movement. One. Two. Three. Shift, shift, shift.

Quick progression through the stages of the swordplay and she was frozen once more, only now three paces to the left of where she had been previously. The position of her feet was also slightly different, and her sword was raised a little higher. A perfect, quiet harmony of movement and stealth.

You could see the strain in the muscles across her shoulders. The wait is just as difficult on a body as the battle. More difficult. The battle can be sustained by adrenaline and emotion. The wait can be sustained by nothing but self-control, something which must be schooled into the limbs for years.

For four and a half hours she had been crossing the room now. She was only twenty paces away from success. Another forty five minutes at most.

She took another shallow lungful of air as she prepared to move again.

"Oh, Eeeeeeeeeeerin," came a lilting voice that she knew well. "Catch!"

An entire drawer of cutlery poured down from the balcony above. Forks, spoons, and dull butter knives clattered down through the room, crashing and tinkling their way through hundreds of bells to land squarely on top of the previously still woman. She instinctively cradled her head with her hands and crouched down until the barrage stopped.

"Oops. Guess you fail again, sir."

Erin sighed as she stood and looked up at the balcony towards the perpetrator, a haughty little elf shaped creature. She was surprised to see the warrior, as she hadn't been informed of the other woman's return. The last Erin had heard, her littermate had still been in the south. When the sound of mocking bell song finally calmed, she called up to the other woman.

"You know Seina, I could have you killed if I wanted to." She pushed away her short blond hair which had fallen into her eyes, and then smirked. "Or, I could just kill you myself right now."

"As a dwarf? I doubt it. You are always weak in the miner form. But even if you were human, I would still beat you. If you can recall, I actually had to pass the trials. Also, if you apply your assault grease well, your hair doesn't come loose like that. Some of us aren't spoiled in the Menundra all the time and actually use the stuff regularly, you know."

She smiled. "My, my. So boastful this morning. Usually you need to have eaten a few humans to get that pompous. Tell me, do you have a reason for the visit other than sabotage?"

With those words, the slim elf form sobered. "Have you received the report from Yyati? The free races are still looking for their god."

"This is old news, dear warrior."

"Yes, but Lemin's new decree isn't. Starting today there will be mandatory testing. Every child under the age of twenty, male *and* female. You know what this means."

Erin paused at those words as she tapped one finger against her cheek.

"Interesting creatures, these humans, dwarves, and elves, aren't they? So convinced that their god would be proud of them and go chasing as quick as can be to lead them to their deaths. And now that they are desperate, they are finally making decisions that should have been made fourteen years ago. They have always been weak species, and now with the blood's advanced stagnation they become stupid, too. No matter though. I do believe this means I have a mission."

"And that is?"

The dwarven features smiled once more. A hint of wolfish canines could be seen peeking out from under her lips. "I am going to hunt a god. Find Him before the free races do with their tests."

"Hunt," Seina hissed softly between her teeth. "Are you mad? He would incinerate you before you even came within ten feet. He will not allow Himself to be captured."

"Relax, Seina. The scriptures have some interesting footnotes about the twentieth reincarnation. This one was to be different than any other. Possibilities and impossibilities have been altered. Do not concern yourself about me. Simply tell Dreadpriest Thorren I will need five legions. The first five legions specifically."

"Five legions . . . . Do you plan on just killing everything you come across until something doesn't die?"

Erin's words were particular and cold.

"And if that was my plan, would you have a problem with it?"

Seina's face grew smooth and her eyes found the floor.

"No, sir. I apologize."

"At ease, warrior," Erin broke into a genuine grin. "You never did reveal the time frame of my imprint kill. I guess a little impudence on your part is deserved even after all this time. And I don't plan on killing my way to the god, I have something much more destructive in mind."

Seina also grinned, "Yes, sir," and then saluted.

"Now," Erin raised her voice in command, "help me clean up this mess before Trial Master sees it."

The warrior threw back her head and laughed. "I have my own preparations to make. Happy hunting, dreadpriest."

Erin smiled as she watched her go. Reckless Warrior Nakao is going to lose herself a form, she thought. Then she looked at the mess around her and frowned. It would take a while to replace all the bells which had fallen. But still, there was the hunt to look forward to. And she did love a good hunt. The dwarf shaped creature bent down and began picking up utensils. As she did so, she sang the blood lullaby:

"Fresh blood, warm blood, red blood,
Please, please, please.
Plump helpless mammals
With their backs to me.
Thirsty, hungry, tasty,
Drink, drink, drink.
Into furry bodies,
My sharp teeth will sink."

She kept humming as she finished with the cutlery and then began to slide silver bells back onto strings, which in turn were tied into place. It was a methodical practice that required a pleasing amount of concentration.

Erin's thoughts only strayed from the task once and that was to wonder mildly, a small smile touching the corners of her mouth, how the god's blood would taste.

CHAPTER 8
WANTING TO BR-

Rynna did not so much wake as transcend from a painful, unconscious death to a painful, conscious one.

She hurt. Hurt badly. Hurt everywhere. Except the lower part of her body. That didn't hurt, but that didn't feel like anything at all. She was completely numb from the waist down. But more importantly, she could not breathe.

She could not breathe, she could not breathe, she could not breathe.

Rynna tried to suck air into her lungs, but couldn't because her nose seemed to be crushed, and something was being dripped into her mouth.

The girl coughed and she could barely make out a black substance spew out along with her spit.

"Swallow, human," was the rough command.

That voice. Rynna vaguely remembered it, but did not care at the moment. The black substance had not stopped dripping over her mouth. She was still trying to breathe, and still unable to get any air into her. She tried to suck in oxygen through the thick black stuff, but just began to choke instead as the gooey substance trailed into her lungs.

She was going to die. There was too much of the liquid, and she was going to drown. Rynna began to struggle away from the source of the substance and free her mouth to get air.

She felt pressure as her shoulders were pinned tightly against the ground, quelling her resistance.

"Be still."

Again it was that same gruff voice, but Rynna still didn't care because now she had a new idea. If she drank all the liquid, if she got rid of it all, if it came to an end, then she might be able to breathe. So she swallowed. She drank and drank and she still couldn't breathe and she kept swallowing, hoping she could stay conscious long enough to just get even one, small gulp of air.

She couldn't though. Her vision blackened and the last traces of her struggle ceased.

***

Rynna was in the clearing, only she was alone. No, not alone, there was a voice.

"We are afraid."

It was a beautiful voice. So pretty and delicate. She wanted to help that voice, protect it. "Where are you, voice?"

"Please, help us."

"Of course, little voice! I will help you, just tell me where you are!" Rynna turned around in a circle, searching for her voice but still, she was alone.

Wait, there was something. Something in the distance. It was a soft, pink light. The tiniest, softest little pink light she had ever seen.

"Please let us in. We are so afraid out here alone."

The pink light hummed in unison with the words, and a warm glow emanated from the small being.

"Of course you may come in, little voice!"

The pink light came closer and finally landed on her head. And then Rynna realized that it wasn't a pink light at all. It was a pink butterfly. A beautiful pink little butterfly with delicate round wings.

"We are coming in now."

Rynna smiled love and acceptance.

That was when the butterfly began to slowly crawl down the side of her head. It went incrementally at first, and then slightly faster, tucking its wings in as it began to scurry. It was skittering towards her ear quickly, and finally it squeezed itself into the small opening there and wriggled its way in.

Rynna screamed.

She dug her finger into her ear where the thing had entered but it was to no avail, the butterfly had already gone too far. The girl could feel small hooks digging into the soft tissue of her inner ear and it hurt. Rynna screamed louder and dug harder at her ear as the butterfly wriggled its way further.

And now those small hooks were digging into the other soft tissues, and she screamed again as the butterfly went deeper and deeper.

Then the little voice spoke one last time, and when it did, it was full of gratitude.

You are delicious.

***

Rynna was in the clearing, only she was alone. No, not alone, there was an old man sitting there. A terribly old man. A creature too ancient to be alive, but still breathing in thin, haggard strokes.

Age had obliterated identity and left in its place an emptiness. His face was a web of deep wrinkles stretched over a decaying skull. His ears were thin and brittle. His hair was the whiteness of absence and sterility. The man's hands were wizened and crippled with arthritis. Thick veins protruded all the length of his arms, and knuckles had swollen with cartilage.

He was in pain. Not just physical pain, but there was other pain too. His eyes looked hollow, as if somebody had bled out all his hope.

Around his wrists were rusted manacles. The ancient creatures' emaciated wrists could have slipped their bonds, but no desire of this seemed evident. Instead, he stared blankly.

The old creature was wearing only a pair of long pants. Had he been standing, they would have slipped his wasted form. The material was of a surprisingly good quality, and was by far the newest and youngest thing about the man.

There was a dry hissing sound that at first seemed to have no source, but then slowly it became clear. It was the old man. He was trying to speak but his vocal cords were dead. All that remained was the sandpaper cracking of dry muscles.

It didn't matter though. It was unnecessary. His request was simple and transcended language.

'Kill me.'

***

Rynna opened her eyes and felt odd. There was something about a dream she had just had. A something with a dream and a little pink glowing . . . an old man? Rynna opened her eyes. Or did she do that already? She was facedown and covered in blood. How peculiar. She looked around and saw the dragon. Only, he was not as terrifying as he had been before. Actually, he looked quite funny. With his large tail and wings. In fact, the more she studied the dragon, the more hilarious he seemed. Like a big lug with teeth hand-claws. A talking beast.

Rynna snickered.

"Hello!"

The dragon, hearing this, turned. "Good, you are awake." The creature's words were laced with both amusement and annoyance. A rough and grumbled sound.

Rynna found this humorous too, and giggled again. But it did not politely stop after a few moments. It grew and mutated into a full-blown laugh, one that started at the girl's toes and reached to the end of her eyelashes.

Everything was fine, everything was good, everything was great, and Rynna had never felt this wonderful in her entire life. In fact, everything was more than wonderful. It was adjectives so elaborate the Rynna had not yet learnt them. But she would. She would learn everything and everyone, and it was all so funny.

She looked at the dragon again. "Did you know that you don't have ears?"

Rynna laughed some more and laughed some more, and she was laughing so hard she began to cry. And it was still funny, but then it hurt a little bit. And she was still laughing and still laughing, but it started to hurt a lot and the laughter and pain were mixing in horrible quantities.

Now the situation was not funny at all. Rynna's head felt thick and heavy. The clearing was spinning and a painful pressure was building in her mind. Nausea churned in her gut while Rynna continued to laugh.

She began to gag.

Doubled over, the young woman vomited all over the clean grass. Rynna coughed up black, thick ooze as her stomach heaved and sides hurt. She stumbled to her knees as her body emptied. More black ooze sprayed on the ground, and thick hardened balls were being choked up as well. Bile and acid seared Rynna's throat while hardened chunks chipped her teeth.

Finally, Rynna was able to collapse on the ground, sides heaving with residual pain and her body's attempts to breathe normally. The deep ache that had begun in her head was now an obese migraine. The girl gritted her teeth and gripped her forehead between shaking hands in an effort to reduce the pain.

The dragon had watched all this with little emotion. Patiently he waited for Rynna to achieve her foetal position before approaching. He did not speak, but rather delicately used a claw to rip open the girl's blouse and undershirt to reveal the naked flesh of her back. Rynna flinched at the contact, but was in too much pain to resist, and so instead, merely gritted her teeth harder.

The dragon gently ran a claw down the length of her, pausing to circle it around every individual vertebra. He took particular consideration on the girl's lower back, inspecting the bones there exquisitely. Goosebumps raised where the breeze teased her skin. Only after a thorough investigation did the dragon say anything. And that was a demand.

"Move your legs."

Rynna obeyed, moving first one, then the other. She seemed to vaguely recall that this had not been possible only a short while ago.

"Now your feet."

Once again the girl complied and shifted both of her feet back and forth, moving them quite easily.

"Your toes."

All seven wiggled satisfactorily. The dragon grunted with approval and then lazily moved to where the girl had vomited, seeming to inspect the mess.

"What happened?" Rynna asked through clenched teeth from her position on the ground.

The dragon did not respond right away. Only after thoroughly searching her bile did he speak, and then there were notes of satisfaction ringing there. "Sleep, now. We will discuss it when you have awoken."

The girl did not want to sleep. She was confused and frightened. But exhaustion is the best sedative of all, and the girl quickly fell into an unconscious recovery.

CHAPTER 9
WHAT THE VILLAGE DECIDED

Rynna woke up alone with the moon blinking cheerfully above her. So, it was night. How much time had passed? Hours? Days? The dragon had claimed her mother would wake within the hour. _____ would be worried if she thought Rynna was still alive. The girl was less certain of how her mother would feel if the woman thought Rynna was dead. She hoped relief would not be the dominant emotion.

So much drifted through Rynna's mind. The dragon, the fall, the dreams, how once again attempting to tell the truth had not boded well for her health . . . . Rynna shut her eyes against the complexity of it all and instead, thought it best to assess her current situation.

She was loath at first to get up. She remembered being hit over the edge of the cliff clearly, but everything afterwards was almost a complete blur. If something was irreparably damaged then she wanted to delay that knowledge as long as possible. Rynna didn't feel any immediate pain, but that did not mean that her body wouldn't just collapse when she tried to move.

Finally, she slowly sat up to test her body's wounds and have a look around her. Curiously, there was still no pain. She was a little stiff but this was not even the stiffness of expended muscles. It was the stiffness of clothing caked in almost-dried blood. Too much blood for her to be alive right now. Puzzlement did not last long before she recalled the black substance. A thought struck her. After all, the beast claimed he was a dragon. Could it have been . . . ? But no, that was ridiculous. Still, the most damaged things about her now were the ripped clothing.

Her stomach growled loudly and Rynna became aware that she was hungry. And not just the normal skipped-one-meal hunger or even the more pressing hunger of when her and her mother had survived months on just bread and cabbage. This was something different. It was a loud obnoxious demand from her body that food was needed now or there would be dire consequences. It was a kidney-eating-liver hunger.

The girl got unsteadily to her feet to the purpose of finding some sort of nourishment. Which was when the dragon returned. The dragon's eyes did not even register his charge, but rather the beast simply dropped a large burlap sack at her feet and sauntered to the other side of the clearing.

"I brought food. Eat," he said while pulling a small leather pouch from somewhere about his person. Rynna wondered vaguely if scales had pockets. She shook her head.

"I'm not hungry." After what had transpired in the last . . . well, after what had transpired since Lady Shutba had kidnapped her, she certainly wasn't going to trust anything the dragon was offering.

The beast, for his part, finally deigned to look up at the defiant girl. An impatient frown decorated his face. "Suit yourself, human. But if you lose consciousness from hunger, I will not be to blame."

He then began examining the contents of his pouch, seemingly without a further thought for the girl.

Rynna was torn. On one hand, taking food from something that had already tried to kill her twice had stupidity written all over it. On the other hand, she did enjoy having an intact liver.

Finally, in a series of thoughts based entirely on the smells emanating from the food bag, Rynna figured that it couldn't hurt to look. So, she tied two sturdy knots in the pieces of her shirts to make them wearable again and opened the sack.

Inside was an entire loaf of bread, two blocks of cheese, a cherry pie, three bulging waterskins, and an entire cooked chicken. After a little of this and a lot of that, in the end it only took the girl twelve minutes to polish off every scrap of food and drink every drop of water the dragon had brought. Her resolve to refuse gifts from the dragon had lost against her hunger, and now a snug, full feeling made the girl heavy and sleepy.

It was then that she remembered she was supposed to be afraid. The dragon had tried to eat her, then had kidnapped her, then had almost killed her, so the least she could do was run screaming away from him as quickly as possible. It was difficult, though, to be afraid of something that had just fed her so thoroughly. She finally understood why Hansel and Gretel from the story had fallen into the witch's hands. Sated is a terrible state in which to be on the lookout for danger.

So since she couldn't properly be scared, Rynna thought that the least she could do was find out as much about the dragon as possible to better prepare herself for future encounters. Reason placated,

Rynna silently approached the great beast to investigate what he was doing.

It seemed simple enough. He was sorting black rocks into three piles. There was no rhyme or reason to the division at first, as they all looked identical. Only, upon closer inspection, the blackness of the rocks weren't all to the same pitch. After some staring, it seemed that some were a dark purple, others has a greenish cast, and the third pile seem to have an almost amber glow. It was quite strange, for when Rynna shook her head they all looked to be the same shade of black once again.

"What are those?" she asked.

The dragon quickly scooped up the rocks, placed them back in the pouch, and tucked them into his scales before speaking. When the dragon did, it was not to answer her question at all.

"I assume you do not have any pets?"

"No. But what does that have to do with anything?"

"It will be easier that way. Come human, we are going back to your house."

Although Rynna was delighted to hear those words, she was suspicious.

"Why?"

"To collect your earthly possessions and for you to say goodbye to your mother. Personally I would prefer to leave directly now, but you humans do seem quite attached to worldly goods. And one cannot leave without proper ceremony with one's mother. Blood calls to blood, and though it is in a weakened form in earth beasts, the Blood Call still beats strongly."

Rynna was taken aback. "Leave where?"

"To Lavanor. We go to see your priests. They will be able to help guide you through being a god better than I can."

Lavanor. Capital city of the free races. Where there were lords, ladies, a king, a queen, elves, dwarves, magic, parties, and pretty much everything that an unhappy teenager thinks would make life better. Escapism at its best and brightest. Nobody was stupid in Lavanor. Nobody was bigoted, untalented, or plain either. If you believed the travel brochures, in the capital city everything was, is, and will be perfect.

Lavanor was, in fact, all that and a bag of chips. All that and a bag of brand named chips.

But Rynna didn't care about the capital. She didn't want to visit any place where there were more people than trees.

"Listen, dragon, there's no way I am going to Lavanor. I'm not a god. My trip off the side of the cliff should have proved that. Gods can only be killed by other gods. So, if I was really a god, I shouldn't have almost died when I hit the ground back there."

The dragon did not respond to the claim because he was busy putting his human suit back on. It was a queer sight to see. First he used his foreclaws to squish both sets of his hindclaws, first lengthwise, then widthwise. Next, he stuck his shrunken hindquarters into Lady's Shutba's feet, like a fat woman squeezing into leggings.

Then, rather than flattening his wings on his back, the dragon wound them around himself, and did the same with his tail. In the process, the dragon had somehow halved his body's size. The creature crushed its maw against its face and then threaded its own arms through Lady Shutba's, as if putting on a coat. Finally, he fit Lady Shutba's head over his and tucked in all her edges.

The whole process made Rynna feel queasy. Watching the twelve-foot dragon squish into the body of a four-and-a-half-foot old woman was more than her senses could process properly. It made her logic hurt and the insides of her eyes feel too big.

"Well, you didn't die, did you?" The beast spoke through Lady Shutba's mouth, but it was odd. Not only did the pitch and tone differ from what one would expect of an old hag, but his voice had a pressed, echoing quality. It was a hollow, faint speech that did not sound human at all. Rynna could understand why he had never spoken as Lady Shutba in front of her village before.

"History says nothing about gods not suffering," the dragon continued in his rough way. "For all you know, gods almost die all the time."

"You were the one who healed me. If I was a god, shouldn't I have been able to heal myself? I'm not a god, I tell you! I am not about to let you-"

Lady Shutba grabbed the girl with strong arms, and hefted her over her shoulder. Then the hag simply began to walk away. It effectively ended any further verbal argument, and the debate continued at a physical level.

For just as the last time she had been whisked away by the old woman, Rynna began to kick, punch, and bite whatever she could gain access to. The dragon did not cut off her air as he had before, but rather, let the abuse continue. Maybe it was because the girl's weak efforts really didn't hurt him

61

at all. Maybe he felt guilty for throwing her down the side of a cliff.

Or maybe it was because he knew something of what was going to happen.

It was when they were about a five-minute walk from the village that they first smelled the smoke and saw it curling heavy and grey among the trees. Thick, dark, odorous smoke. Lady Shutba froze in her steps when the smell reached her nostrils and Rynna likewise tensed at the scent. The smoke did not smell singularly of clean burning woods. It smelled of other things, too. Of curtains and bed sheets crisping. Of shoes and yarn scorching. Of pots and cutlery blistering.

And worst of all, underlining everything else was the smell of human flesh roasting.

"Mom."

Lady Shutba dropped the girl without a word, and Rynna took off.

No matter that it was too dark to see clearly, Rynna ran. At first, her arms and legs pumped with a purpose, but the closer she came to her little village and the stronger the awful smell in the air became, the more her sprint broke down into a flailing, desperate charge. Faster and faster she went, oblivious to the branches that snagged her clothes, scratched her arms, or slapped her in the face.

When the girl finally burst from the trees in her own backyard, the view was terrifying. Crowded around her home were about forty men holding lanterns and makeshift weapons. They were a ring of bodies exuding a sense of accomplishment. The air had a sinister, inebriated quality.

The house itself was barely recognizable as such. Fire burned on almost all surfaces and had completely eaten the roof. The doorway was a mess of flames, and even from her position, Rynna felt uncomfortably warm. Those standing closer to the house were dripping sweat off shiny faces.

The young girl was too afraid to react. There were so many men and her mother was inside. Her legs began to shake and the ground seemed unsteady. She could not move. Not to rush ahead to save her mother, nor to run towards the safety of the trees. Rynna could do nothing but stand mutely in horror and just watch the house continue to burn.

She did not know how long she had been staring at the flaming wreck when she finally did hear a noise beyond that of the fire and popping wood. It had probably only taken seconds, but every moment of watching her house destroyed was its own special eternity.

Later when Rynna looked back on the noise she could only describe it as barbaric. A deep growl that rumbled its promise of retribution through the earth. It was a heavy, feral noise of outrage, hatred, and vengeance. It was the sound of an incensed beast who was coming, coming quickly, and coming to do violence.

The gathered villagers tore their eyes from their purifying bonfire, and instead stared in terror as a monster flew out of the trees towards them. Here was the dragon, only a horrific thirty feet in length. A colossal beast of death. Cruel teeth and claws had tripled in length. Powerful wings beat against even stronger back muscles that strained with the coiled spring of anger. Scales did not reflect light as they were no longer smooth enough to do so. Now they had the dull, misshapen surface of ancient rockfall.

The dragon flew down and lashed his tail against a wave of villagers. Six went flying to land with arms and necks at unnatural angles. Some rushed to help the fallen, but most of the villagers began to run around, screaming.

One man had gotten a hold of a vicious looking blade and was rushing towards the dragon. Without hesitation, the beast reached out a foreclaw and crushed the oncoming man's head. A loud, wet crack could be heard, and then the man collapsed, his face now a pulpy mess.

After that there were no more defenders. The villagers scattered completely, scrambling over one another, pushing one another down in their attempts to get away. The dragon did not take up the chase. They were merely an obstacle, not his goal. As soon as the majority of the men had scattered, the dragon walked towards the house. Carefully, he pushed his way through the closest wall and edged inside.

After a few minutes, he withdrew, cradling something delicately.

Then, the beast was gone. He only paused long enough to scoop up Rynna on his way before flying away.

That was that.

The abandoned home continued to burn while men sobered up and women patched up the wounded. A scared group of farmers with axes and bows were sent into the woods the following morning, but no trace of the creatures could be found. Truth be told, they didn't look very hard.

A small statue was erected to commemorate the Battle of the Great Beast. After everyone had either died from or been healed of their wounds, it was decided that it had actually been a heroic affair. Those who had witnessed the battle were worshipped for months to come. Drinks, backslapping, and a pig slaughtered for the party. The town was rid of its demons! Huzzah!

Nobody made the connection between the appearance of the monster and Lady Shutba's permanent disappearance. But it would be a year, two months, and five days until anybody dared approach the charred remains of that house again. And then it was only because stampeding straight through that ruined home is the quickest way for two hundred people to reach the cover of the woods.

CHAPTER 10
THE LIFEDEBT

Rynna was dropped to the ground as the dragon came to a violent halt. They had not gone far into the trees. You could still faintly see some lights of the village winking in the distance. The dragon only cared that they were out of direct view, and didn't waste time going any further than that.

He laid Rynna's mother down gently on her back. The young girl pulled herself to her knees and whimpered at the sight of the woman. She did not recognize the naked creature before her. The flames had given the corpse a foreignness of blistered skin and blackened flesh. She was no longer even recognizable as human. A dwarf, elf, human, or even a changeling could have been lying there on the forest floor and the girl would not have known the difference.

Blond hair was gone. The scalp which remained was covered in skin ranging from an angry red to a dark, mottled brown. Along her mother's right leg the flesh was seared down to the bone. A sickening blend of colours and smells assaulted Rynna and all she could do was make small pathetic noises of uselessness.

Because the worst thing of the whole scene, the most traumatizing thing of all was that her mother's chest was ever so slowly rising and falling. She was still alive.

The dragon was not frozen into inactivity. He quickly moved his forearm above the damaged woman. You could just make out the faint outline of a scar marring the pattern of his scales, and it was that same spot that the dragon now ripped his teeth across.

A black substance began to seep out of the dragon's arm, which he overturned over the woman's mouth. The beast rhythmically clenched and unclenched his claws, and soon a steady stream of dark liquid began to flow.

Rynna's lips parted with a small gasp. Lifeblood. It *had* been lifeblood which had healed her earlier.

The moment the dark blood came into contact with her mother's lips you could see the change. Blackened, withered skin began to slough off and a healthy shade emerged underneath. Human lips, identifiably so, shone through in the most beautiful of ways.

The healing process continued down her throat, the dead skin flaking away to reveal living tissue. In fact, all throughout her mother's body, ruined flesh was falling away, damaged tendons were healing, and in some cases entire muscle groups were forming anew. The woman's leg became whole while the blisters on her head receded, then disappeared leaving shiny, healthy skin.

Her hair did not grow back, but other than that her body was healed to a better state than it had been in before. The look of eternal weariness was gone from her mother completely. She looked younger than she had in ten years. Although her old scars were still there, they puckered fresh, glowing skin rather than the defeated rough flesh that had previously enveloped the woman.

After no further changes seemed to be taking place in the girl's mother, the dragon used his claws to pinch the wound on his arm closed. Several seconds later, it was once again just a small scar marring the pattern of his scales.

Rynna had begun to cry at the beginning of the transformation and was now weeping openly as she crawled over to her mother. When she reached the woman, Rynna placed her mother's head in her lap and tears kept slipping down her cheeks as she stroked the bare head.

"Thank you . . . thank you so much, dragon."

The dragon's eyes were hard. "She will not live."

Rynna's fingers froze in their caress. "But- but you saved her. Look at her now. All the damage is gone! You used- you use . . . well you saved her," the girl finished inadequately.

The dragon's voice was quiet, and now it was tinged with pity.

"I understand your passion, human. Among my kind the only other being more important than a mother is a greatmother. I to this day lament the loss of my own. But still, she will die.

"Lifeblood can heal any new wound except lethorsum, and a broken spirit. When lethorsum is used, the body is poisoned beyond anything we can do. And when the spirit is broken, the soul departs. A person cannot heal without a soul. Your mother has a broken spirit. She has given up, human. She does not want to live."

Rynna tightened a grip on her mother she did not even realize she had made. It was the possessive grip of disbelief. "You're wrong. Of course she wants to live. She loves me."

The dragon did not reply to the fervour he heard. Rather he simply stated. "We are leaving. I don't know how long it will take the villagers to gain courage, and it would be bothersome to have to kill them all."

"I am not leaving my mother."

"Fine, human. When the villagers have finished mutilating your body, I will come collect you. We will still go to Lavanor, only I will let you heal on your own to remind you of the follies of indulging futility."

Rynna wouldn't hear it. Not this. Not her mother. So she hid from the dragon's words in the sheltering distraction of accusation.

"No. Don't take me away again. If you had never taken me away in the first place, if you had never come to this village, this wouldn't have happened. We would be happy still. She would still be . . . she would be . . . she . . . ." Rynna could not finish the words, could not say them out loud, but the unspoken 'what if' hung desolately in her eyes.

Rather than argue the faulty thought process, rather than defend himself, and even rather than pointing out the obvious fact that two women against forty drunk, determined men were just as susceptible as one woman against forty drunk, determined men, the dragon conceded.

"Fine human. I accept the blame of this woman's death. For that I owe you a lifedebt. By the two gods, by the Lord of Salvation and Prince of Dusk, my life is yours until the debt is repaid. A life for a life until the sun dies." The dragon touched a claw to his forehead, his heart, and then finally his maw before pressing that same claw against Rynna's mouth. Five seconds it took to do something completely unimaginably. Her lips tingled where the claw had brushed them.

"Come human, we must leave." The words were a rough gentleness. "Your mother breathes her last. She goes to the golden fields."

It was true. Rynna held her mother even tighter and watched as the woman's chest fell and did not rise again.

The girl had no tears left. She didn't wail in horror or pity or grief. The only sound was the quiet rustling of leaves by a friendly breeze unaware of the tragic events taking place.

The dragon began to dig a small hole. He lifted off the top two inches of soil first, preserving the vegetation so that it could be replaced at the end to better disguise the grave. There would still be a mismatch, but better than blatantly upturned earth.

Firmly, the dragon lifted the girl's mother from her arms. Rynna did not resist and let her fingers slide away as numbness shunted her fifth sense one inch of flesh at a time. She watched the dragon lay her mother in the hole. Her mother. Perfect but for an exhausted spirit. Beautiful but for an exhaustive child.

"I have nothing now," she whispered finally.

"Wrong, human. You have Lavanor. You are a god. You can do anyth . . . ." The dragon's words trailed off. That obnoxiously happy breeze tiptoed through the trees again. The beast could think of no way to finish the sentence so instead stalked off to

70

retrieve his human suit, leaving Rynna to stare at the small patch of not quite matching grass.

CHAPTER 11
THE ROADS

They walked. They walked and walked and walked and walked. Rynna did not notice the miles, leagues, days, or weeks pass by. She lived in a daze. The numbness which had come over her in the clearing had not dissipated with time. If anything, it was entrenched and the girl became listless and silent. Other than to the briefest explanation of her condition, the girl did not utter a single word after her last unanswered statement.

Instead, she had a puppeted existence.

She walked when she was told to walk, stopped when she was told to stop, ate when she was told to eat, and slept whenever she could. Her body began to suffer as a result. She became gaunt, her hair thinned, her monthly courses stopped, and even her bowel movements came irregularly and were painful at that.

She didn't go with the dragon because she even remotely believed his claims that she was a god. Simply put, Rynna travelled with the dragon because she really had nowhere else to go. No welcoming family or friends to care for her, no neighbours on whom she could impose, nobody but the dragon.

And so they walked. Sometimes they passed through towns. They did not linger long in these but instead shuffled through quickly and silently. Once in a while they would stop to buy supplies and fresh vegetables, but for the most part they ate hunted meat and foraged wild plants which they then boiled down to a soft mush.

When they passed through villages, mothers pulled small children in off the street, and even called in their older ones. The two travelers often received glares. They were a ghastly sight. Although the dragon had dunked Rynna in a lake a few times to clear away all the blood and had bought her new clothes, the girl was still a bedraggled mess. An old, butterfly followed hag and her listless, dirty waif were no playmates for respectable youth.

Normally, they would have been treated better despite their rogue appearances, but the farther north they travelled, the more uneasy people became. These were troubled times. War was impending. Most families had at least one member who had been recruited into the war against the abominable changelings and their god, the Prince of Dusk.

That titled hissed and weaved through gossip. Lord of the Underbeings. The Devil. The Prince of Dusk. It was spoken in terror no matter where they went.

Had the troops of the free races been strengthened by the will and presence of their own god, maybe the attitude would have been different. But there was a noticeable absence of the Lord of Salvation. Emissaries from Lavanor had been sent into every place where the free races lived to double-check all boys and (can you even imagine?) girls under the age of twenty. The search was thorough and tinged with a desperation that debilitated the morale of the civilized world. The more cities and villages with no positive result, the more the global scales of confidence tipped towards despair.

Although the fighting had not yet begun, all knew that when it did, it would be devastating. No member of the free races lived who remembered the last rebirth of the gods, but very detailed accounts had been made of the deaths. The horrible, agonizing, countless deaths. And in every town and village, the locals, dust-ridden travellers, and wayward beggars all had the same question.

Where is our god?

Still Rynna and the dragon walked. Sometimes they rode in the back of wagons of kind farmers and were then offered a barn to sleep in. These times were rare. Mostly, it was by their own feet that they travelled, and they slept outside, deep in the trees so that the dragon could take off his human suit.

The whole thing became a ritual of sorts. The endless walking that stiffened hips, legs, and ankles until any movement was painful. Then, the finding of a suitably sized clearing. The dragon's killing of every butterfly that hovered around Lady Shutba's head and then the peeling away of the human suit. The dragon going to hunt, leaving Rynna behind because she scared off the game, then returning to cook and to make sure Rynna ate. Then the sleeping and the waking and the walking once more.

It was part of this that finally ended Rynna's silence. Not their route, nor their destination, nor even the fact that she was allegedly a god. It was the dead butterflies.

"Why do you kill them?"

The two, the girl and the dragon, were sitting across from each other with their fire burning in between. Rynna's legs were drawn up to her chest and she was resting her chin on her knees, watching the flames. Her voice was quiet and weak. It had been months since she had spoken last. Even now, no trace of curiosity could be heard in her words. The syllables were uttered in a monotone of indifference as her eyes continued to trace the movement of the fire.

The dragon did not reply. He was sprawled out across the ground, wings folded snugly against his back. His eyes had the almost closed look of two minutes before slumber. The fire crackled loudly.

Rynna let the quiet stretch on for a bit before frowning. Her voice still lacked expression, but now when she had to repeat her question, mild upset could be seen flitting about her face.

"Why do you kill-"

"Why do you kill wolves around a village, human?"

The dragon's lethargy was gone and replaced with a creature on the brink of pouncing. Eyes were open and alert. The muscles along the beast's back were strained with tenseness. Rynna blinked a few times before answering, surprised at the transformation.

"So they don't eat the sheep."

The dragon's snout twitched.

"Precisely." He then immediately relaxed into his earlier pre-slumber pose. The only difference now was that there was a deep rumble coming from the dragon's chest.

Rynna blinked again. She thought about the dragon's answer and suspected that there was another meaning she was missing. Her stale mind tried to wrap itself around the response but failed.

"What do you mean?"

"Dragons are sheep, butterflies are wolves." The dragon settled even further into his comfort and that deep rumble got louder.

"They eat you?" Rynna looked at the crushed insects that littered the ground. Harmless and pretty.

"Yes, but it is not our flesh they are after. They burrow under our scales and inhale our minds. Once a butterfly gets in, a dragon is doomed. We will scratch and scratch at our scales, gouge out our eyes, and rip holes into our bodies, all in the effort to extract the butterfly. But it is never any use. We always die.

"It is a terrible death for my kind. This is why they are the only creatures that we dragons fear."

Rynna was still looking at the dead insects on the ground and her tired thoughts could not absorb their supposed threat.

"You wear Lady Shutba. You fear the free races."

The dragon snorted. "The free races. Most leave us alone. But the ones that do pursue us are not a bother. Your brethren are noisy and impatient. Earth beasts who hunt my kind only for the sale value of our lifeblood. Only the very stupid or very sick are in danger from elves, humans, or dwarves. I wear a human suit because it is annoying having to cut down every poacher who thinks to make a profit from my blood.

76

"Besides, your kind have seen dragons so rarely that the surprise of my presence usually gives me plenty of time to either incapacitate them or leave if they have violent intentions. Mind you, even the most surprised still know that I *am* a dragon when they see me."

Rynna ignored the teasing, and her voice quieted as she spoke her next words. "You don't fear the changelings either?"

The great beast slowly stretched his claws, digging small troughs in the ground below him. The stars paled and night became lonelier for the mention of the creatures. The dragon hunched his massive shoulders and chose his words carefully.

"It is difficult to end an enemy that takes three deaths to kill, but not impossible. One underbeing is manageable. Ten thousand are not. My fear of them is somewhere between those two numbers and at which one depends on many different factors. I have been to the Gate and back and still have my breath. But would I go willingly now? No, not without very good cause. But at least the underbeings remain grounded. Out of arrow range and they are more earth beasts who can be avoided as easily as the free races.

"The butterflies though . . . the butterflies are different. They are earthair beasts granted access to the currents we ride. They find us in our caves and hidden homes. They hunt and follow and do not give up until either they die or we do."

Something about the whole situation had been bothering Rynna. Something terrifying but hidden, repressed, or just too complicated for her grief-drowned mind to consider. Something about butterflies. Something about a pink butterfly to be specific.

Rynna's apathy thawed slightly as she remembered the dream.

"Can the butterflies hurt humans?"

The dragon shook his head. "No. The rules are different for earth beasts. They cannot simply enter a human's mind. But for us dragons . . . I am surprised my fear has not been bleeding into you. The butterfly is horror."

Another pause before she gathered the energy to ask a question. Butterflies were one of the few constant things of her childhood. They fluttered, pollinated, and spun cocoons no matter which small village her and her mother had been refugees in.

"How are you supposed to kill them all? Butterflies are everywhere."

The dragon's eyes seemed to become particularly attentive at the question. That rumble from his chest deepened.

"It is not all the butterflies that threaten the dragons. Just the bel butterfly. Every butterfly has inherited the distant memory of our taste, and so they follow as well. But the bellanus butterfly is the only breed that can enter and eat.

"What they lack in speed they make up in stealth and patience. Once given the scent of a dragon, butterflies do not give up. They chase and chase, and even when they die their offspring will continue the pursuit. I kill all butterflies because even harmless ones can spread the word of my existence and bring down a real danger."

The dragon inadvertently glanced around furtively for death of the fluttering variety, then shuddered lightly in their absence. He continued carefully.

"Besides, we are not helpless. Earth beast suits are impregnable. And as long as you kill all butterflies before you remove it, it takes hours for new butterflies to find the scent. And I do not rely solely on Lady Shutba's nightly massacres. When dragons bathe, we weave water into our scales. Earthair beasts are denied access to water. Like covering bowstrings with an oilcloth to keep them dry."

A soft 'oh' escaped the girl's lips, and then nothing else. Rynna became quiet. She did not ask any more questions, and the dragon did not provide any more information. They just sat silently while that same deep rumble vibrated from the dragon. Rynna finally thought blandly that it was like how a contented cat purrs. Then she fell asleep, the conversation and sudden energy having drained her completely.

It was another two weeks before the girl spoke again, and then it was only to complain about the lack of variety in their diet. Afterwards she was silent for another fortnight, and then broke it with a request for new boots. Another week and then she uttered two sentences consecutively. Then it was every two days that the girl said something. And finally, one chilly morning at the sight of a farmer completely covered in mud chasing his naked two year old son around their yard, Rynna laughed a warm, bubbling laughter that made Lady Shutba reluctantly smile herself.

That was the turning point.

Still thin and still dirty, but no longer living death. Rynna chatted, complained, and smiled. If it was not as often or as liberally as a normal girl of fourteen, at least it was something. There were still days of pained silence and quiet crying, but they were no longer Rynna's constant state of being.

And with her spirit, came conversation. Real conversation. For, as the months dragged by, and their feet died slow, painful deaths of aching muscles and worn soles, Rynna and the dragon began to talk. Days were spent quiet for the most part as there were many travellers, and Lady Shutba's voice was still hollow and distinctly inhuman. But evenings around the fire were spent in discussion.

The dragon questioned Rynna on every detail of her childhood, both mundane and extraordinary. Her mother, her home, the towns in which she lived, the few details she knew of her father. They talked about Dompt, the last days, the first days, and all the days in between.

Rynna especially liked when they talked of her mother. It helped to discuss her. To explain about her eyes, her smile, and that special way she would hum when she was trying out a new recipe. How she could always get a garden to grow, no matter how much or little rain there was, nor how poor or rich the soil. The way the hala smoke curled around her mother's head as she smoked deeply and blissfully in the evenings.

Rynna talked about hiding under her mother's bed during thunderstorms, pretending to be afraid even though she had never been just so her mother would hold her tightly. Waiting for her mother to come home from an engagement so that she could feed her sweets and make sure she was safe. Good memories, bad memories. It was all discussed and made alive for the dragon. The beast listened attentively the entire time, asking questions here and there, extracting every iota of information about the girl's life that he could.

When Rynna led the conversation, she asked about the world, the history of the free races, and everything else she had never had time to learn about during her tumultuous childhood.

And of course, she asked about dragons.

"Can you breathe fire?" she asked one night. Rynna was propped up against a tree, while the dragon was splayed out lazily on the ground. They had both eaten too much. The dragon had caught a stag and had declared that Lady Shutba wasn't going to carry all the extra meat around with her, so they should eat as much as possible tonight. Rynna had the sneaking suspicion that the dragon was actually fattening her up, but still ate with a vengeance. Now, both felt slightly sick and had no inclination whatsoever to move.

"Bah," the dragon responded from his prone position. "Flamebreathers are the most common of our kind. I am rarer and more powerful than most." He paused here to let the suspense and momentum build, "I am a waterbreather."

"A what?"

The dragon frowned. "A waterbreather, human. Did your stories tell you of nothing but nobility and flame?"

Here the great beast slowly rolled himself over and then Rynna watched as his neck constricted tightly for a few seconds. There was a clicking sound and fog began to seep from his nostrils. Tendrils fell to the ground and a pool of mist formed. Then, the dragon opened his maw. Perched inside on his tongue was the most curious thing. A small, icy figure sculpted in exquisite detail. It was a young woman. And if you looked closely, you could see her small crystalline eyelashes, as well as her little toes. Rynna counted and there were only seven on the figure.

"It's . . . beautiful." Rynna got to her feet and hurried around the small campfire. Although the details had already begun to melt, the young woman carefully picked up the ice sculpture and held it close to her face. A tiny mirror image of herself.

"All water is my domain, human."

When the figure was nothing more than an unrecognizable block of ice, Rynna placed it on the grass. She watched the dragon's throat constrict again. That same clicking sound came and the same fog, too. Only this time when he opened his maw, water poured out. It was clearer and fresher than any stream, lake, or river that the young woman had ever seen. She smiled as she trailed her fingers through it.

The waterbreathing lasted several nights before the thrill of it waned. After that, they moved on to discussing the capital city.

"Lavanor . . ." Rynna tasted the word nervously, like an illicit drug. She pictured hoards of people staring at her and whispering. "What's it like?"

It had been one of those rainy days of the downpour variety. A soaking day where water seeps through every fibre of your clothes and drips further down your back with every step. To make it worse, the colours and the cold temperature of late fall had been especially evident that day. Although the rain had finally petered out, there was a damp quality to the air that prevented a body from properly drying itself.

The dragon snorted his reply to the young woman as he attempted to find something remotely dry under which to sleep.

"Lavanor is just a big city. Most of the glamour I heard described in Dompt is the fantasy of bored farmers. The capital does not hold a festival every night. The entire city only celebrates together at Trinni and Mong, same as any other place. The only time the city differs from anywhere else is for the Godnaming.

"Lavanor celebrates the event with the most preparation and biggest budget. Just wait until we arrive. The feast they will throw for you will be enough to sate your social appetite for years. The welcoming fires and smoke lit around the city are laced with hala, and wine flows through the streets as thickly as the people do.

"More impressive," the dragon grumbled, "are the other aspects of the city. Other than the ruins of the Ice City, it is one of the most beautiful places built by earth beasts. Also, art, history, and culture actually exist there. Lavanor is the only reason why your species is not still banging rocks on top of the heads of small mammals and eating grasses to survive."

Rynna did not respond to this description and instead wondered if culture and civilization meant that the city would be less suspicious of newcomers. Once again in her head she saw the eyes. Not the dozens of sets that glared from small villages and towns, but the hundreds of thousands that would skulk the busy streets of the most popular destination in the world. She shook her head doubtfully.

Sometimes, and these were very infrequent, Rynna asked about his allegations of her being a god.

"What . . . what is going to happen when we get to Lavanor?"

The dragon did not respond right away. Fall had made its inexorable death march into winter and now snow lay thick on the ground. The dragon was trying and failing to get a fire lit. Trying and failing, trying and failing, and he was getting angry. The tinder was all damp. The flint was also failing him. Other than pathetic smoke, the wood would not catch. After one disastrous evening when Rynna joked that she wished the dragon could breathe fire because then they would always be warm, the dragon had made it his mission that the young lady should never go cold.

As such, he had traded a small vial of lifeblood for more money than Rynna had ever seen (although the dragon still growled at how they were cheated) and used some of it to buy a fur lined coat, as well as thick blanket rolls that Lady Shutba carried on her back during the day. The dragon always lit a fire first thing and would not let Rynna help despite the fact that she was competent at arson and handling flame, having had so much practice in her childhood. Tonight though, it seemed he wasn't going to accomplish his goal.

The dragon did not hear the young woman's question, and she had to repeat it several times before he finally responded.

"I have told you before. We go to the priests," the beast grunted as he once again struck his claws against the piece of flint while blowing gently and encouragingly on sparks.

"But . . . we have no proof that I am the Lord of Salvation except your word. I won't be able to pass any tests that require me to put on some kind of display of power."

Rynna had stopped trying to convince the dragon that she wasn't a god. She wasn't a complete idiot. She knew that the reason why the dragon interrogated her so thoroughly on her childhood was so that he could discover some trace of cosmic abilities, or a set of repressed memories that would span since the beginning of creation. But there was nothing. Whenever she tried to point this out to the dragon he always just reiterated how badly she tasted and left it at that, as if his taste buds were enough for any sceptic. Which is why she had given up. In the end it really didn't matter what the dragon thought she was.

The priests on the other hand, were a different story. She knew that if she played at being God, eventually the real one was going to show up and the religious leaders would realize she had been lying. She doubted they would take kindly to learning they'd been duped. It was this that worried her. The condemnation and the fleeing. Not that she wasn't accustomed to those things, but just because you've had chlamydia before doesn't mean you go to a two copper whore house looking to catch it on purpose.

The dragon cursed loudly. Well, Rynna assumed it was a curse. It was a harsh, unrecognizable word preceded by the dragon slicing his palm open with the flint. Black blood began to seep from the wound and the dragon angrily pinched the wound together, sealing it once more.

"Dragon? Did you hear me? I said, there is no way I will be able to pass any tests. Why should they believe me?"

The beast growled, "It is truly atrocious that the free races allow so many lies to be sustained in its peoples."

"Lies? But I've heard the stories and-"

"And?" the creature exhaled sharply through his nostrils, the tip of his maw frosting over with the word. He waited five long seconds before continuing. "Exactly. Display of power. There are no trials or magic involved at all. It is a blood test. I do not know what hallowed ritual has been brewing in your mind, but that is it. Just some Oceo Tolok concoction that they will apply to a sample of your blood to show in ten seconds whether or not you are a god. They say that both sides developed them generations ago.

"Gods are given power, wealth, and respect by virtue of being born. People have done a lot worse than pretending to be a god to attain those things. And rather than have to spend the first five years of their reigns killing off usurpers, the gods came up with formulas for their followers.

"Simple, right? But your priests with their secrets, pomp, and ceremony . . . they probably enjoy people thinking their work is grand and mysterious. Knowledge is not hoarded so among my kind."

The dragon took a deep breath before continuing. His words were now rumbling like a brook rather than raging like a river.

"Do not worry yourself, little human. The date of the gods' rebirths is predicted to the day. The priests do not choose at random. So as to be certain, any child born within one year surrounding that day is tested. It is a great honour to be born the same year as the Lord of Salvation, so there are never any repercussions for failing the test. However, with this recent news of all earth beasts less than twenty years of age being tested . . . . Well, let us just agree you will be welcomed enthusiastically."

Rynna relaxed a bit at this and she took a somewhat calming breath. Blood tests. They would know right from the start whether or not she was a god and Rynna wouldn't have to worry about sustaining an elaborate lie. But of course, there was still the other side of things. What if the dragon was right? What if she was a god and she showed up and they were excited and . . . . Rynna frowned again.

"Okay, so let's say I am the Lord of Salvation. What then? I've had fifteen birthdays and my biggest accomplishment to date is not dying. I don't know anything about war. The people we've passed are desperate. How can I help them fight thousands of years of terror?"

The dragon paused in his efforts to look at Rynna seriously.

"You are a god. You can do what you want. It is my duty to see you to the priests. After that if you care to have all the firstborns in the world killed in your honour, they will be lining up to offer you the dead bodies. Were I you, I would see to ending this war in which the free races are constantly tangled. More souls have been lost to this fight than have been lost to simple age."

"And how do you think I can do that? The changelings are monsters. If it were that easy to kill them and end the war, it would have happened already."

The dragon watched her carefully and shrugged. "Maybe. But then again, I am not a god. I am a dragon. We dragons do not have war. We have the skies and breath."

"This is your war, too. Aren't you fighting for the Lord of Salvation as well? He is the god of all that is good. I thought the dragons sided with the free races. Besides, you're helping me."

The dragon appraised the young girl and fog seeped slowly from his nostrils as he considered his reply.

"We dragons have our own god. He is called Maulo. The Father of Greatfathers. We keep our involvement in the gods of earth beasts as small as possible."

Rynna had never heard of a third god before. There had only ever been the Lord of Salvation and the Prince of Dusk. Was there a third supernatural youth walking around, searching for the dragons? The thought occurred to her that a dragon god would probably be incarnated as a dragon.

"So have you found this Maulo yet, or do the dragons search like the free races do?"

The dragon cracked his maw and snorted a few ice crystals to the ground. Whether it was amusement or outrage, Rynna was unsure.

"The Father of Greatfathers walks among the stars, not the worlds. They say he will come one day. The Brood Mother claims he will walk this plane but whether it will happen during my lifetime or in ten thousand years from now is unknown. Maulo is not scheduled so neatly as the gods of earth beasts."

Rynna tried to picture this Father of Greatfathers but could only imagine a larger version of her dragon.

"Besides," the creature added. "Maulo's coming is said to be an ending. Whether it is of us dragons or life itself, I am not sure, but I am not opposed to living a little longer. It would weigh heavily on me if I entered the golden fields still owing a little godling a lifedebt. Not to mention how amusing it will be to witness the priests discovering your gender. A female god is something I do not want to miss."

Rynna knew that the situation wouldn't be as simple as the dragon described it. The ifs and buts of her being the Lord of Salvation could fill an entire temple. But then she closed her eyes and smiled a little. If she *was* the Lord of Salvation, she would have Dompt destroyed and the people dispersed. She relished the idea of Fik and the batting-eyelash girls adopting the nomadic lifestyle of her childhood. The thought amused her as she watched the dragon return his attention back to the flint.

The beast wasn't able to make a fire that night. Instead, the furiously disappointed dragon, who was then a manageable seven feet, reluctantly curled up beside her in a blanket roll. Hissing that her death of cold would be a failure of his lifedebt and grumbling about her stench, the dragon let his body heat leach into her. The morning saw him grumpy and awake much earlier than usual.

And so it went. They walked and walked and walked some more. Rynna had begun trying to kill herself again into their sixth month, and subsequently tried four more times, the second last time being exactly a week after the dragon's failed bonfire. Every incident but one had been thwarted immediately, with the most recent attempt only resulting in a minor wrist sprain. And as the roads continued on, everything became something of a normal. If they weren't exactly happy, they weren't exactly sad either. Both viewed their situation as a solid okay. And it was with this compromised optimism that the two entered Ta'ao.

CHAPTER 12
TA'AO

The city was underfed, dirty, and sleazy, with just a hint of fanaticism to round it off nicely. Or at least, that is how the dragon described it to Rynna. But the dragon had sounded more annoyed than anxious as he spoke.

"When we get to the city, we need to be discreet," he had insisted. "Were we able to catch a ferry from somewhere else on this side of the coast, I would avoid Ta'ao altogether. If it was possible for me to fly and not be shot to the ground I would simply carry you over the water. I would fly us the whole way.

"Ta'ao is notoriously known for its harsh dealings with suspected changelings. This city breeds paranoia the way your village did sheep. It is a conscious, annual effort. More than one body has been burned alive never to rise a second time, let alone a third. Strangers are suspects by existence. Given your past and your incidents, we do not want anybody looking at us twice. The cursed butterflies finding me will draw enough attention as it is.

"Things are different here," he continued. "You think that your childhood was harsh, but at least you and your mother got the benefit of the doubt for a few incidents before being driven out. That would have never happened in this city. The first incident would have seen you hung, if you were lucky. If you were unlucky, you would have been tortured for a couple of hours first, and then hung. The blood here is much staler than I have encountered elsewhere.

"And then of course, Ta'ao has actually seen underbeings. The local lord pays ten gold coins for the head of every changeling brought to him, and they say his manor is ringed with dozens of the creatures' rotting faces on pikes. Where your puny village had stories to scare children into being polite little humans, Ta'ao has night patrols around the city walls and frequent abductions. The Kral Mountains can be reached by a seven-day boat journey across the open sea. A suicidal trip if you ask me, but the changelings have never asked my advice on attack strategies."

The dragon's words had done nothing to ease Rynna's fears and, as they approached, she adopted a progressively grimmer outlook on their chances of success.

It was mid-morning by the time the city came within their sights. From a distance Ta'ao looked like a squatting crab. Rather than a discernible road system culminating in a palace, a large park, or even a religious edifice, there were just the same mismatched buildings crisscrossing everywhere. It was as if it had been a small town who had been too busy with the day-to-day of its life and just woke up one day to realize that its population exceeded its definition. And rather than adjusting, rebuilding, and making road signs, it thought 'fuck it' and kept on going. It was now a jumbled mass of browns, greys, and off-whites that was people, animals, and buildings going about their business in the bedraggled city.

Surrounding Ta'ao was a large fortification that seemed to have been tacked on as an afterthought. Cracked stones rose fifteen feet into the air and curved around in a wide arc, only interrupted by the open gates they now approached.

The broken wall was a match for the soldiers marching along its length. Youth and strength had been drafted and were training somewhere for battle, leaving the dregs to fill out the city watchmen. Limping, coughing, and squinting, the rusty men who lined the wall and manned the gates were glaring at everyone who approached their city. They sifted meticulously through those wishing to enter, double and triple checking each man and woman carefully before admitting them. It was this line of people that Rynna and Lady Shutba now joined.

The conversation of those who were waiting was brisk and the closer they came to the gates themselves, the more it petered out. For the final five feet, those wishing to enter were completely silent, waiting with their hoods and hair pulled clear of their faces. Rynna gathered her brown locks and braided them behind her back, while the dragon likewise gathered Lady Shutba's frayed and graying hair at the base of her skull with some twine.

Entrance to any free race community was easy enough. There weren't any secret handshakes, passcodes, nor identification papers. It was your eyes that affirmed or denied your species. Green, blue, hazel, mauve, or golden and you went about your business. If your irides were brown then you were detained a little longer and dark brown, longer still.

Rynna thanked Salvation everyday that her own eyes were not a dark brown. There were no second looks or double takes when she met somebody's gaze. Dark brown eyes were too easy to be confused with black, changeling eyes. Rynna pitied those who had lost their eyes in an accident or a battle. For, if your eyes were missing entirely you were always held and questioned for weeks before being allowed to go about your business.

People were rarely killed as a result of these checks though. Mostly because changelings were too intelligent to enter through the front gates in broad daylight. They knew their black eyes meant execution. When they entered cities it was tunnelling under, climbing over, and sneaking through the cracks both literal and metaphorical. Meaning that these security measures were mostly pointless except the illusion of safety they gave. But Rynna didn't complain. Nobody in the line complained. They held their cloaks tightly against themselves and waited for their turn to be checked.

Rynna was passed through immediately, but the guards took turns looking into Lady Shutba's face carefully, turning her this way and that. Finally with a grunt, they caught the gold glints in the hag's eyes and ushered the two past them without further comment.

When they cleared the gates they quickly found themselves standing in the main thoroughfare of Ta'ao. It was then that the noise smashed into Rynna like a wet rock to the face. She grabbed Lady Shutba's arm compulsively and shrank against her as much as she could. The sound was terrifying. Hisses, hoots, hollers, hackling. If a thousand peddlers had come to Dompt there would not have been as much to see and hear.

Men were chasing women with squealing giggles, discussions were being held with passion, animals were braying, clucking, and whining intermittently. Homes were crammed on more homes which were built hastily above shops. Small alcoves too small to house a donkey were supporting entire generations of families. So many people doing so many things in such a small space. Her left ear was simply inundated and for the first time, she was almost glad she couldn't hear out of the right.

Everywhere she looked people had swords, daggers, knives, axes, or other weapons strapped to their waists. A community used to defending itself frequently. She wondered if it meant their threshold for attacking someone would be higher or lower. Regardless, everyone seemed dangerous. It was almost too much to take in.

Equally overwhelming were the types of people. Rynna's childhood had been spent migrating from small human farming community to small human farming community. Other than pictures and the one dwarven merchant that visited Dompt, Rynna hadn't been exposed to the other races before. She had never travelled to the Gossamer Forest, the Water Weavers' Lakes, nor the Ull Mountains. And she had never been to any city before, let alone a mix one such as this.

She saw tall bodies with delicate bone structures and pointed ears stepping out of inns. She saw squat beings with thick beards and wide shoulders eating food bought from a vendor. She heard high lilting voices plying wares and deep basses bartering. And she was not immune from their interactions. The hawkers circled her, their weapons dangling from their sides.

"Does the lady need some hala leaf? Flavoured with crystallized honey. Just five coppers and you'll have enough for your afternoon dinner party!"

"Some coloured jewels to brighten your beautiful face?"

"Tea! One copper for a tea!"

"My laaaaaady, this oil of jasmine. It will bring in the men. Net you a nice husband. Would you like two vials or three?"

Rynna shook her head at the unending stream of elven, dwarven, and human street hawkers and merchants, all the while squeezing Lady Shutba tighter and tighter. The ancient creature let out a deep growl and shook her arm to free herself of the young woman's grasp. Rynna let go reluctantly but still kept herself in the hag's footsteps, stepping on the back of the old woman's boots as frequently as not while she waved away the goods being pushed onto her. Finally, Lady Shutba stopped with a hiss.

"Human," the dragon's flattened voice growled quietly. The words were only just audible to the young woman as he tried to maintain their anonymity. "If you step on me again I am going to slice open one of your tendons to slow you down. I am not a doorstop."

"I'm sorry, it's just . . . a lot."

"Deal with it. The less you cower, the faster we can get to the docks and onto a ship."

Rynna reluctantly took a few steps away from Lady Shutba.

"Better?"

Lady Shutba grunted and then began shuffling along once more. Rynna, for her part, decided to stare at the ground and track the old lady by her shadow. She pushed her way through the throng and tried to ignore everything except the dust stirred up by her feet and the hunched form leading her way.

It was for this reason that she didn't notice the woman with whom she collided until it was too late. Although the other woman kept her balance, Rynna fell to the ground at the feet of a blur of silk, lipdye, and skin.

Before the dust had time to settle, two burly arms grabbed her by the shoulders and hauled her to her feet. Fat fingers pinched against her collarbone and sent little tendrils of pain along her back. The grip only loosened when a woman's voice broke the tension.

"Charles, release that poor bumpkin. Does she seem like a threat? You are to protect me from thieves and unpaying clients, not beggars and peasants."

It was the silky, lipdyed figure speaking. Upon further inspection, Rynna concluded that the woman was beautiful. Shimmering hair the colour of coffee cut in an oval along her face. Cheekbones dusted with the browns and reds of a crisp late summer afternoon, which exulted and sharpened her features. Her lips were a sultry maroon, dark with promise. Not just beautiful, she was stunning.

There was too much showing for this person to be a proper lady, though. Delicate ankles and calves flashed under the violet dress. The neckline was low enough that too deep a breath would bare nipples.

She was a peacock in her own flesh and a woman on the prowl: a human lady of the night who probably cost more in an afternoon than her mother had in a month.

She then noticed something else about the woman. Her thick eyelashes framed eyes that were white, tinged with only the palest of pale blues. Blue was the most coveted of eye colours. They say woman had tried to mimic it by pouring dyes into their eyes and drinking concoctions sold by hedge doctors. Nothing had succeeded as far as she had ever heard, but it didn't stop the fools from trying. A blue-eyed night lady would retire a wealthy woman.

Rynna's thoughts were interrupted by a gruff voice.

"Mistress, this little rat could be holding a knife." It was Charles, presumably. He had the thick voice of hired protection.

"I'd doubt if this one was holding her bladder. Let her go."

The hands retreated from her back. Rynna clenched the muscles in her shoulders and rubbed her neck in relief. The night lady addressed her softly.

"Forgive my bodyguard. He is sometimes too eager for his own good." Her eyes were steady, and Rynna wanted to lower hers. She coughed awkwardly and did a little head bob before answering.

"No, I'm sorry, it was me. I should have been watching where I was going."

Rynna tried to duck away quickly, but the woman caught her before she could escape. The night lady brushed her hand along Rynna's cheek, studying the young woman. During the process, her mouth was smiling in simultaneously the most sinister and sensual way Rynna had ever seen.

"You are clearly new to this city. One thing you must learn is to never apologize. You are not beneath them." The night lady moved her hand away from Rynna's face and rubbed together the residual grease on her fingers. She asked her next question softly. "What are you called?"

In light of the growling bodyguard, the answer came quickly.

"Rynna."

"Well, then. Always remember that. Also, try not to go banging into people. There are many eager people in this city. And not all are as restrained as Charles here. But I must be on my way." She slipped a finger behind the belt that cinched her waist and withdrew a coin. She pressed it into Rynna's hand intimately. "Safe travels to you."

The night lady smiled for a final time then gently laid a hand on her bodyguard's arm. With deliberate speed they headed off into the crowd, the woman trusting in the protection of her hired man. The two were a bright patch of confidence and beauty striding off among the people.

Rynna breathed deeply in their absence. She was glad the interaction had not lasted long. The coin in her hand was cold and she opened her fingers. A silver. A fortune for a beggar. Nothing to her and the dragon with lifeblood as a bartering tool. But, of course, the night lady hadn't known that. She had deemed her a peasant. A poor country girl who had just been given a fortune.

Worry and gratitude tussled in her chest, but mostly it was relief that won out. A successful interaction in this city had not resulted in thugs dragging her away. With a strange sense of satisfaction, Rynna tucked the coin into her pocket then turned to Lady Shutba-

-who was not there.

The shuffling shadow she had been following had shuffled away. Leaving her. Surrounded by strange people. Alone.

They had only been in the city for what . . . half an hour? Forty minutes at the most. A ringing sound started to whine in her ears. Her vision began to whiten at the edges and her breath came shorter and shorter. Ah, consciousness . . . that capricious beast was leaving her to dance with another partner. She felt it slipping away and shook her head repeatedly while digging her fingers into her palms. Where had the hag gone? The young woman's eyes slid from face to face in the crowd searching for crinkled skin and colourful insects. Neither could be seen in any respect, and the beginnings of something bad started to grow in Rynna's intestines.

There were people all around her. People everywhere. Too many armed people everywhere. Where was the dragon? Not here. Somewhere going towards the docks but where she was and where the docks were was not known to the young woman. Rynna was immediately and painfully aware of the fact that she had no money, no supplies, and no people skills whatsoever. Oh wait. She had the silver. The lonely silver for the peasant girl.

"Hot meat pies for the lady?"

"Cheese! Cheese! Cheese to put some colour in your cheeks!"

"A scarf for your sweet neck is just what you need!"

The hawkers with their too big smiles circled once more, while uncaring shoulders of the people of Ta'ao jostled her on either side. The ringing grew louder in her ears and more of her vision whitened. Instinct battled with reason and quickly overrode it.

Rynna bolted.

She crashed her way through the crowd and ran, oblivious to the where, simply focusing on moving and escaping the never ending hordes of people. The months of walking meant Rynna was in the best physical health of her life. Her legs went at a speed that was both impressive and a little unbelievable. As such, it was a very far distance away and a significant amount of time later when she finally slowed with a burning in her side, and her breath coming in heaves and coughs.

Rynna bent double, put her hands on her thighs, and felt incredibly stupid. As she tried to catch her breath, she realized that there were just as many people surrounding her where she was now. The running had accomplished nothing but to tire her. Her only consolation was that she wasn't more lost than she had been before. Just equally so.

Her heaving eventually slowed and Rynna straightened. She studied the streets and buildings around her, determined to recognize something to help her get her bearings. A ridiculous endeavour. She had never been here before and it's not like she could look for which side of the people the mushrooms were growing on to know where to go.

Rynna was going to have to get help. Maybe she could find another friendly night lady. Or a friendly any type of lady for that matter. Somebody who could point a finger to the docks where the dragon was probably already waiting.

Rynna once again saw endless faces surrounding her, but this time she ignored the forest and concentrated on the trees. Suppressing her fear and suspicion, Rynna searched for compassion and soft features: somebody safe to ask for directions. Instead, it was something else that she noticed.

She frowned and shook her head, then frowned again. She could swear she kept seeing the same groups of people over and over again. At first she thought maybe they were looping back on themselves to stare at her in accusation. But, since hysteria, torches, and pitchforks ended along that line of reasoning, she dismissed it as improbable and more importantly, too scary as hell to think about.

The rational side of her brain presented an alternate solution, which was much more reasonable: it wasn't really the same people over and over again; it was simply the same features being repeated.

Rynna kept seeing identical green-grey eyes on the humans. The dwarves and elves had similarities among their respective races as well. The majestic tree and water people had mouths full of the same awkward teeth, and a pug nose was disgustingly frequent among the mountain folk.

The dragon had said the blood was stale here. Rynna then searched for another sign and found it, or rather the lack thereof. Children. There were no children. There were no littles chasing dogs, cats, and balls across the way. No happy toddlers testing out new feet on unsteady ground, no mothers rushing to kiss wounds all better, no women thick with child. Very stale blood, it would seem.

A loud giggle broke Rynna's concentration. She peered around, searching for the source. And there it was. A girl laughing at a trinket held by her father. She now realized it was the first child she had seen all day. Rynna smiled. A place needed kids. It was a good thing, this little one. The child's father began laughing along with his daughter and his face was lit with such joy that Rynna knew she had found her someone friendly who she could ask for help.

She stepped lightly towards the man, the crack of a smile sneaking on her face.

Which is when she collided with a person for the second time that day. On this encounter she did not fall to the ground. Instead, she grabbed for the person and steadied herself against him, an apology halfway out of her mouth as he likewise steadied himself against her.

The apology died in her throat. She knew this person. It was not an old hag, nor a night lady. It was a young man her own age. It was a shocked, young man her own age. A shocked young man her own age with red hair and a square jaw.

"Fik? Fik Tucker?"

Of all the places and all the people, he was one of the last she had expected to see. It was like running into an old lover in a bar at the end of the world. Or a cancer reappearing after ten years of benignity.

103

A surge of warmth almost began to dimple her cheeks and tilt her mouth into a smile of recognition. I say almost, because she did not smile, did not become happy. Rynna was too busy reliving her last memory of the town from which she had fled. The last memory of the fire. The last memory of her mother.

Her mother. That beautiful woman who had done so much for her. Who had hidden her, saved her, healed her, and loved her so many times. Her mother. The black skin and burnt hair and cooked flesh and the horrible breathing through it all. The ring of male bodies surrounding the house. The sound of wood popping. The sweat shining off of justified faces. Her mother. Smiling as Rynna finished planting her first garden ever. Laughing as they pulled weeds together. Kissing her goodnight on the forehead even when she was too old for it because they both liked the ritual of connection.

Her mother. Dead.

A feral snarl began in Rynna's throat. It was an angry animal noise that had undoubtedly been a habit picked up from a dragon. From the great beast it was terrifying and intimidating. From the waif-like young woman, it was the noise of insanity climaxing.

For the first time in her life, Rynna wanted to seriously hurt someone. She wanted to damage this person who had taken so much from her. Destroy this mean kid who had hurt innocent old hags, had laughed about it, and had probably laughed when he'd thought she and her mother were dead, too.

Rynna lunged.

As it just so happened, Fik was likewise remembering the last time he had seen Rynna. He had secretly snuck out of the house to watch the destruction of the witches' home. He remembered this particular creature standing there calmly as a thirty-foot monster ripped apart the townspeople. The monster she then left with.

Which is why just as Rynna lunged for the young man with hands outstretched ready to attack him, Fik began to shout.

"Changeling! Changeling! Help, that girl is a changeling!"

The entire street froze, including Rynna. The young woman's burning anger evaporated in an instance as every single person halted in whatever they were doing to stare at Rynna. It was a serious accusation in a city serious about its changelings. Fists tightened over weapons and feet shifted into tensed stances.

Now, as an aside, it must be said that at this particular point the situation was still salvageable. Difficult to explain, yes, and going to end up with Rynna expelled from the city, for certain, but still salvageable in a way that would mean she would be breathing at the end. After all, her eyes were hazel. If nothing else, that evidence announced her innocence.

However, as it turned out, changelings had infiltrated the city. And had coincidentally chosen that exact moment to begin their attack.

A loud gong began to boom. A warning bell centuries old that the citizens knew like they knew their lovers' bodies and their swords' hilts. A warning bell emanating from the centre of town, always expected and always dreaded. It was a dull throb that chanted, 'They're here.'

Gong.

GONG.

GONG.

Tight fists surrounding Rynna drew their blades. The changelings had come. And there was a female one right in front of them. Three deaths to destroy a changeling and there were dozens of people close enough for killing blows. No time to look closely at eye colour.

"Kill her!" came Fik's heated command.

The crowd surged towards the young woman. Rynna's throat closed in as she gave a strangled cry, and then crouched down with her hands covering her face. The resigned self defense pose of the soon-to-be dead. The world's fastest conviction and sentence had just been handed to her on the voice of a pubescent bully.

But her attackers only had time to take a step and maybe a handful of breaths in the young woman's direction when they started to bleed from stomachs and throats. Black eyes were flashing everywhere. The first cries of pain and fear could be heard drifting towards them from other streets as well.

Rynna looked up, wondering why she was still alive. And she saw it, too. The real changelings with their dark eyes and pitch smiles.

"Over here!" a burly dwarf called and the townspeople flocked to form a tight desperate group against the rush of underbeings who were appearing everywhere. Fik Tucker, so isolated in her focus before, melded into the others as the free races united against the changelings.

Bodies that had been originally intent on ending Rynna's life were now defending their own. Steel clashed while screams of pain and death could be heard. Rynna's instinctively stood up and moved towards the free race defenders. But no, they thought she was an underbeing too. She would be killed if she tried to join them.

Instead, Rynna stumbled and tripped across the street until she reached just inside a small alley. From there, she hunched down and watched the scene in horror. Changelings. Those cursed creatures created by the Prince of Dusk thousands of years in the past.

Monsters are usually exaggerated in the telling, but not these ones. What Rynna witnessed now was not a battle, a skirmish, a duel, or even really a fight. It was an annihilation. Changelings exist to destroy the free races and their god. They do not want to conquer, rule, or possess. They do not take prisoners; they do not leave the innocent. They exterminate. Man, woman, child. It did not matter. You had just as good a chance of surviving against the fabled starved rocks as you did against the underbeings. That breed of determination only succeeded in getting your hamstrings cut and your spine severed with a hand indistinguishable from your own.

Even though all she had ever considered doing was running away if she ever met an underbeing, Rynna recalled her mother's words when first teaching her about them as a child. That their survival depended on threes.

"Three bells to announce their coming, three people to form a defense, three deaths to kill a changeling."

Not that it seemed to be helping the people of Ta'ao survive. From the relative safety of the alleyway, Rynna saw men holding their stomachs as their insides fell in wet plops around them. She saw jaws and teeth shatter. Muscles, bones, and tendons were exposed. Arms and legs were ripped from sockets. She saw swords flash through the air as the changelings relentlessly killed their way through the people.

A pregnant elf staggered out near her. A beautiful, glowing, rare breed of woman full with child. She was desperately holding her hands over the gash across her throat, trying to keep her blood from dripping down her neck. A black-eyed human approached the woman from behind. Rynna watched as his sword severed the left side of the soon-to-be-mother's torso. Rynna wanted to puke.

And it was in this state that the voice intruded.

"My, my, my . . . . Is that a god I smell?"

Rynna inhaled sharply and turned around so quickly that she lost her balance. She had been so intent on the destruction in the streets to even think about the vulnerability of the alley in which she hid. Her mouth tasted of bile.

The underbeing in front of her was a dwarf with black eyes. Strong hands rested lightly on the hilt of her weapon still tucked in its sheath. She wore black leather, unadorned except some intricate golden stitching around the collar. The changeling had an extremely bold face which possessed an amused

108

smile. Her pale blond hair fell into her eyes in a messy way. It was tinted with a smattering of blood.

The creature breathed in deeply, her lips fluttering with pleasure. "Mmmm. Yes, it seems I have found myself a delicious, little god." Her smile was still amused, but now a sinister glint came into her black eyes. "What *are* we going to do with You?"

Rynna's pupils contracted with fear.

"Let's see . . . . Hmmm, I've got an idea." The creature's smile widened to show perfectly white teeth. "Why don't we-"

A tail smashed into the dwarven head. It was a thick, sharp, scaled tail that landed with the heavy crack of a spine snapping. The changeling's body crashed into a nearby wall, leaving bloodied skid marks as it sunk motionlessly to the ground.

"Human, we fly!"

It was the dragon. Somehow he had found her. But Rynna could not move her eyes from the wet, red smear marks on the rough brick wall where the female changeling's body had hit.

"We leave now. They come! On my back, hurry!"

The other changelings began sawing and hacking their way in a direct line towards her. All of them.

"Human!"

The body on the ground began to twitch. Rynna couldn't stop staring at those wet, red smear marks on the-

"HUMAN!"

Rynna looked up. She finally noticed the wall of death heading her way and that the body at her feet was starting to make ominous movements.

She ran.

The dragon's scales were rough and made easy footholds. Rynna scrambled up the side of the creature and settled herself directly above his wing joints. Then, she laid down flat against the dragon's neck and held on as best as she could. The dragon pivoted quickly and clawed his way towards the far end of the alley, heading for a space large enough to spread his wings.

When the two burst forth into the larger street there was a temporary cease of violence. Free races and underbeings paused to stare at the massive, winged creature and the girl perched on his neck. The presence of a dragon meant different things to the different species. The free races thought maybe they saw a saviour: the mythical dragons come to rescue them.

The underbeings, on the other hand, saw lunch. Manic grins already dripping with blood began spreading through the changelings. They forgot their current victims and began charging towards the dragon and his rider.

The great beast snarled. Rynna felt the dragon's neck constricting under her and then heard a clicking sound. His maw opened and pointed towards the underbeings headed their way. This time it was not clear water, nor delicate sculptures. It was spikes of ice five inches long which shot out of the dragon's maw in a straight, mortal path.

Humans, elves, dwarves, and changelings alike were shredded. Neither the dragon, nor his weapon made any distinction between flesh. Ice shards ripped through all resistance. The noise was hideous.

There was the quiet whistling of projectiles through the air. The thud and clatter of ice striking stone, wood, and brick. The sound of a drunken butcher relentlessly hacking away at meat. The screams of pain of those who took longer than half a second to die.

The changelings continued to rush towards them with death defying fervour even as the flesh was sliced off their bones. As for the free races, they were trying escape. All of them died. Those who fled, those who were attacking, those injured previously and too weak to do anything but moan. Rynna squeezed her eyes close and held on tighter. She tried to shut down her senses so she wouldn't hear the wet sounds, but was unsuccessful and each death tore through her.

Soon, the only thing left was a trail of red, pulpy bodies. No living beings were in the street anymore, just punctured heaps. The dragon ceased his firing and distant fighting was all the two could hear for a moment. Rynna tried to breathe through the horrible quiet.

When noise did return, it wasn't welcoming.

Squish. Drip. Thud. Crack. The sucking sound of wet bodies slowly getting to their feet. The changelings began to shake flesh back into place. The reanimated monsters moved in a calm, deliberate manner.

The great beast cursed, started to run, and began to beat his large leathery wings. They lifted from the ground and climbed through the air, ascending with incredible speed. Rynna was glad when she could no longer make out the individual faces of the bodies below. By the time the underbeings' healing had stopped, the two had already begun to head out to sea with the wind whipping past their ears.

The changelings watched the two grow small with distance and knew their prey was out of reach. In deference, the underbeings lifted their heads to the sky and howled. It was an eerie, piercing song that was shortly taken up by every changeling in the city. Black-eyed faces paused in their slaughter to lift their heads and join in. It was an old noise that none of the free races understood.

But the dragon did. Even with the howling of the wind, he heard the call and knew its meaning. The changelings remembered.

'Well met, Darlan. Well met, Dealer.'

When the pinprick of the dragon and Rynna's image disappeared from sight, the challenge died on the creatures' lips. Silence returned for the briefest of moments before the underbeings smiled their blood filled lips and resumed their annihilation. And then the screaming began anew.

CHAPTER 13
WORD OF MOUTH

The piece of parchment was crumpled in High Priest Oshar Lemin's left hand. His right hand shook. The report confirmed everyone's worst fears. The man's words were simultaneously anger and defeat.

"Who all knows?"

The solider who had delivered the report was blood-shot and sweating. He coughed before explaining, the phlegm in his throat rattling.

"From what I hear there were maybe a few hundred survivors total on foot. About a third the ships pulled away as soon as the attack began, but only a quarter of those lasted more than two minutes before they sank. We suspect changelings infiltrated the ships and then once the attack began . . . well . . . . . Our report comes from one of the surviving crews. They have promised to keep the destruction quiet for now, but you know Ibuza is not the only coastal city that the boats would have reached."

"So what you are telling me, soldier, is that everyone knows."

The human, to his credit, did not lower his eyes. He met the high priest's gaze and nodded. The world's saddest nod. Oshar broke the contact.

The two continued to walk in silence through the temple until they reached the Council Room where he dismissed the tired soldier to go clean up and get rest. The high priest pushed opened the doors and stepped forward.

Inside the room, there was a tumult of emotion. No laughter or camaraderie this time. Medial priests sat tensely in high-backed chairs. Low priests were seated around the room as well, looking even more shaken. The royalty and dignitaries in the room were doing no better.

Ta'ao obliterated. So many bodies of elves, dwarves, and humans. How had it happened? How had so many black eyes gotten into a city where hiding your face meant imprisonment? The changelings rarely attacked in such a direct, rash way. The Prince of Dusk usually deployed underbeings meticulously. Not this time. There were thousands of dead underbeings.

And why had they attacked a city like Ta'ao? Oshar's eyes slipped over to the priests as he continued thinking about the issue. Ta'ao had no tactical importance. Clearly the changelings had wanted something. The real question that squeezed sweat from the high priest's pores was whether or not the underbeings had achieved their goal, whatever it was.

Oshar pulled his eyes away from the priests and looked around at the rest of those gathered in the room. Sitting in two of the more ornate chairs surrounding the table were King Paelin and Queen Milla. Surprisingly, Louis was in attendance as well. It was still few years until the heir apparent would come of age. Too young for the conversation they would be having and the decisions they would be making in this room. But then again, there were always casualties in war. Maybe it was best that the young prince was informed. Thankfully, Princess

Eleanor was absent. At least House Gelda's innocence would be preserved in her.

Surrounding Paelin were the lieutenant-generals of the human forces, along with the head of the king's network of spies. It was a shifty little man who whispered with Paelin and Milla. Oshar thought the man's name was Forester. The high priest had never spoken with the man in person. Forester's allegiance went first and foremost to his own kind and all of his knowledge stayed with his own race. Paelin seemed to have a knack for finding fervent loyalty among his subjects. The clerk sitting on Paelin's right and the quartermaster on his left had similar dedication.

The high priest moved his gaze down towards the far end of the table where representatives sat in proxy for King Tolm and the elders of the Tree Dwellers and Water Weavers. No doubt word had reached their leaders and they were already on their way. Oshar had sent messenger hawks two hours previously, but the races had their own ways of relaying news. The diplomats from the elves and dwarves did have the authority to make decisions on their leaders' behalves, but most likely they would just stall. Oshar knew with certain bitterness that no real progress would be made until the council had convened in full.

Oshar shook his head, took his seat, and began speaking immediately.

"You've all heard the news?" The high priest's eyes slowly moved over each person seated around him. Some of them shifted uncomfortably. Others did not.

"Rumors have been in the city for a day. Of course we've heard the news!" King Paelin's face an angry colour of red so deep it could have won first runner up in a purple competition. He slammed his hands onto the wooden table and leaned towards the high priest threateningly.

"You've had fifteen years, Lemin. Your priests have crawled over every inch of our kingdoms and pawed at the blood of every creature with a pulse. Where is our god? Ta'ao is on your head. If you'd done your job, if you'd found the Lord of Salvation, this wouldn't have happened!"

Some of the priests looked shocked, but most were stone faced. Did they agree with the king? They shouldn't. The priests, unlike the king, knew that the Lord of Salvation was missing His memories. Any new high priest they chose would be as helpless as himself in this matter. But then again, there were more reasons for wanting to be the high priest than just finding gods. Many of the medial priests were of the ambitious type.

Thankfully, Paelin could do nothing until Tolm or one of the elves' elders arrived. It left Oshar with the smallest sliver of time with which to work. He was careful to contain his emotions as he responded to King Paelin's outburst.

"*High Priest* Lemin, if you please. I do not command our Lord, Your Highness. If He does not wished to be found, maybe He has a good reason for it."

"You have that blasted thing in your head. Find Him with that!"

Oshar became aware of the pulse thumping through his mind. A smile curdled halfway out of

116

his mouth. It was a pity the ignorant man before him would some day be in council with the Lord of Salvation. His god should be surrounded by a higher calibre.

"You know what you speak is blasphemy," the words were barely calm on the high priest's lips. "The Lord of Salvation is not to be tracked with the Eye like a thief by a hound. He is not a weapon to be summoned and used whenever it is convenient."

"Then use the weapons you do control. Or have you forgotten the army? You're our general, for Salvation's sake. Or at least until the Lord of Salvation does decide to show Himself. Where were your scouts? What of your intelligence agents? How did, by all accounts, at least three changeling legions make their way onto the southern continent completely unseen?"

King Tolm's representative crossed his pudgy arms in satisfaction, nodding at Paelin's words. It was some snivelling little dwarf with a pug nose who wore the sash of the dwarven diplomat. The elven representatives held neutral expressions, but they still leaned forward expectantly to hear the high priest's response. The medial and low priests for the most part seemed to be in varying stages of outrage. But there were still a few who simply stared at their hands thoughtfully. Oshar smoothed his crumpled report before answering the king's question.

"We don't know."

"Don't. Know?"

"Not really, no. A year ago there were several legions on the move, but they disappeared."

"How do fifteen thousand underbeings disappear?" the king's eyes bored into the high priest, but Oshar was not intimidated. If anything, he wanted to throttle Paelin and the others. This information had been relayed countlessly in earlier reports, earlier meetings. The Council Room was normally filled with yawns and fingers tapping if it was filled at all. The dignitaries and royalty, it would appear, always had better things to do than listen to priests repeat over and over again 'Nothing new, the situation is still being monitored.'

Oshar's words were clipped.

"Twenty five thousand disappeared, to be exact. There were five legions being tracked. They dispersed north of Lavanor. The bulk of our troops were moved to the area and we combed every inch of the forests from the Old Road to the coasts to the starved rocks and back again. The conclusion we drew was that the underbeings had returned to the Pit. The only alternative would have been if they had spent months slipping by us one changeling at a time. Regardless, we continued searching and patrolling. We found nothing."

The king seemed taken aback by the concise response and some of the anger receded from his face in patches. It would seem he hadn't expected competency. The room remained silent until another voice spoke up. The soft, rumbling voice of the medial priest Lo.

"So then why now after all these months?"

The high priest dragged his eyes from the king to the dwarf and his words became sharp.

"Why indeed."

The silence stretched again before a slim medial priest named Neileen spoke up. Her delicate elven face pinched as she frowned.

"They say there was a dragon there."

One of the human priests licked his lips before adding, "They say he breathed water."

Cully piped in to add, "They say he was protecting someone."

This was new to the high priest. It had to be a joke. A three thousand year old quip. When was the last time anyone had seen a dragon, let alone a waterbreather? Oshar scanned the room. The faces were serious, some intrigued even. Hope was there. In the face of the countless deaths, there was hope.

The bargain, Oshar thought, they want it to be the bargain. And if this new information was true-

With a loud bang, the door to the Council Room burst open and in staggered a breathless soldier. Sweat dripped off of him. His face was an unreadable jumble of emotion.

The council turned towards the interruption, King Paelin's face darkening as he prepared to chastise the man. The humans' king didn't have the chance to speak though.

"Pardon, your Graces," the soldier gasped for air, "but I have news."

***

The forest just off the Perranal Shore was unusually quiet considering it held almost fourteen thousand underbeings in very close proximity. But then, the Warrior Clan knew better than to make idle talk on free race territory. Making an army invisible is dependent entirely on its ability to shut the fuck up and kill any witnesses. Thus far, it had been going exceedingly well. Dried rations had been passed through camp wordlessly and the watch shifts were arranged without any instruction, just as they had every night since they had assembled on the southern continent. Plans had been meticulously created prior to leaving the Pit. Every minute of this expedition was accounted for, and every changeling knew his or her part in that accountability. Even the injured bore their stitching and wrapping quietly.

The only place in the camp where noises above a creak or a rustle were permitted was in the small tent containing the five warleaders, their battlelords, their spymasters, and the dreadpriest.

Even with the sixteen of them there was no unnecessary noise. It was a meeting held in whispers and stealth. "And the final losses are tallied at what?" Erin's words were mild. She was a human now, to her annoyance.

Alex spoke for the warleaders. After all, he represented the First Legion. The others were welcome to speak only if they had additional information. The battlelords were silent, as they would remain throughout the entire meeting. They were there merely as a contingency for a warleader's death.

"Eleven thousand, one hundred and six, sir."

"And of the remaining warriors, how many still retain all three forms?"

"One thousand, four hundred and twenty two."

Erin tapped a finger against her cheek. "Well, that number is just unacceptable, isn't it? Explain."

Alex paused slightly before answering. The black leather he wore framed his wide build. The man was short, with thick shoulders. There were none who had ever managed to knock him from his feet since he had learned his battle poses. His brown hair, slicked back with assault grease, framed a face that was surprisingly delicate in its elven form. That face was currently hesitant.

"The snake was a little unexpected."

"A - le - xan - der," the dreadpriest's mouth pulled fingernails across his name. "You forfeit a form when you lie to your dreadpriest. There are a few warleaders as effective as you, and I believe that the elf is the last skin you have. Yes, the reptile was a surprise, but Darlan is hardly enough to explain eleven thousand dead warriors."

The warleader's cheeks darkened in the slightest of blushes. He conceded and told the truth.

"The warleaders thought it was prudent to avoid injuring the god. The warriors were instructed to be selective before they killed."

"Have the warleaders become forgetful? Gods cannot be injured."

"No. However they can be made angry. We were being cautious."

Erin's mouth jerked into a small smile. "She will be angry no matter the physical violence She experiences." Her face hardened for her next words. "Do not indulge the warriors' sensibilities. You were not instructed to be gentle, you were instructed to fetch us a god. If She makes it to Lavanor, everything becomes more complicated."

121

Alex nodded curtly. The other warleaders likewise dipped their heads in assent. The stakes were well known among those in the tent.

"Dreadpriest," this voice was Issmith. Warleader of the Fourth Legion. His human form had a large scar tracing across the forehead from when a free race soldier had once tried to open his head. "Will we be allowed freedom in Lavanor as we were in Ta'ao?" His eyes twinkled in their inky depths.

"Although your eagerness is appreciated, even if our legions here were complete it would not be enough. The Lord of Salvation has given more protection to that city in the past few thousand years than we can tackle at the moment. We left the Gate for the god, not for the cleansing of the free races. That will come later. Besides, can you imagine the fury of the other legions if we were to play without them?"

Although no disagreement was made, there was a general feeling of disappointment in the air. As if fifteen wagging tails had been lowered simultaneously. Erin raised a single eyebrow and that smile touched her lips again.

"Easy, warriors. After the hunt is over we will have our fun." Then she paused before, "Any other business?"

Black eyes shifted from face to face.

"What of Darlan?" Mina this time. She was young for a warleader. But so quick. A very fun one to play Lokba with. "Should he be killed? He destroyed one of your forms. An unforgivable action."

The faces around the table were dark with ill humor. To hurt a dreadpriest was a sin near to that of hurting the Prince of Dusk.

"My, my, my, we are in the mood for blood today. The Dealer's fate is not for us to decide. That will be up to the Prince."

"Can we capture him, then?" Issmith again. "It's been a while since the Warrior Clan tasted lifeblood. It would be a pleasant reward."

A sudden attentiveness came into the battlelords. Even the warleaders themselves shifted at the idea.

Erin noticed it all and was not entirely displeased. "Very well, then. The legion which captures the god and the dragon may have a barrel of lifeblood to share among their warriors."

Were they any species but changelings, there would have been a collective gasp. As it was, eyes widened and more than a few mouths parted. Erin smiled briefly, then nodded calmly her dismissal.

The warleaders and their battlelords all saluted, then slunk from the tent. The spymasters would remain for another quick discussion but for the most part, it was done. The news was spread. The lightest of whispers buzzed as the words were passed. The quiet message travelled from underbeing to underbeing with efficiency and excitement. Although the army did not let out a 'huzzah,' a silent cheer did run through the ranks as black eyes met one another, and with wolfish teeth, grinned.

CHAPTER 14
THE WELCOMING OF A GOD

The dragon crashed to the ground, throwing Rynna down. The two had somehow reached the shore. Ever since the distant greenish-brown stretch had appeared, it had represented hope, rest, and safety.

But despite arriving, the shore was none of these things. The air was in a violent mood, and a harsh wind buffeted the dragon and the young woman who were gasping on the beach. Hideous sharp waves smashed over and over, threatening to drag them back out to the sea. Salt water stung Rynna's eyes and tried to fill her lungs.

She started pulling herself across the sand, all the while coughing until she began to gag. There was nothing in her stomach to lose, though. Rynna had already thrown up from the height and that had been twenty two hours ago. Twenty two straight hours of wind, rain, and being shot at by passing ships. Her arms and legs had no feeling, and a three-inch gash tied roughly with a length of her blouse had only just clotted.

Her body wanted to lose consciousness. Despite the loud crashing of waves, there was that special ear ringing and vision narrowing that Rynna knew all too well. She fought it. Passing out on the sand could mean being washed out with the tide. It could mean being lost and drowning, but unable to die. The thought of endlessly choking for air made her force herself to her feet. She stumbled, fell to her knees, but then pushed herself up again.

Rynna's vision was blurry but even still she could see the warm endurance of trees. Pines, firs, and maples waved at her from a distance, and it was to them that she made her way. Trees meant foliage and trunks, possibly fruit and nuts, or in the very least grubs near their roots. Food, water, rest: these are what she needed desperately.

Rynna blearily made her way forward, one shaky step at a time until she reached the tree line and fell at the foot of a large oak. Sticky, damp sand covered her. Dully, she brushed away the grains, but she gave up shortly and instead wrapped her arms tightly against her legs. The last thing she saw before sleep overtook her was a bulky shape on the distant beach being lapped at by waves.

It was morning when she woke. Of which morning, she couldn't be sure. Rynna's leg throbbed, the skin crusty and red near her gash. The muscles on her arms and legs were burning from holding on to rough scales and bending against the dragon's neck. Her throat, which was dry and swollen from the harsh sea winds, hurt the most.

Thankfully when she pried open her heavy eyelids, not only was there a rabbit roasting above a small campfire, but there was also a bucket crafted exquisitely from ice filled to the brim with clear water. Another smaller ice container held a thick, black substance. She was less enthusiastic about the contents of that one.

Rynna tried to pull herself up and collapsed, falling roughly against the tangle of roots in which she had slept. The rustling sound prompted a familiar voice.

"The buckets will melt soon. I do not have the reserve to make more. You should drink."

Rynna tried to get up again, and this time with the tree trunk's help, managed to push herself to her knees. She looked at the two ice containers and their contents uncertainly. The amount of lifeblood he had so casually given her could probably buy a good sized farm and the livestock to fill it. But it wasn't its worth that made her hesitate. She couldn't name her uneasiness, but she had no desire to repeat her first experience with the thick tar-like blood.

Rynna pushed the smaller bucket aside with her foot, and then reached for the water instead. The ice slipped from her fingers when she tried to grab for it, so she cupped her hands and drank deeply from them. The dragon watched impassively and did not comment on the smaller bucket slowly melting beside the two.

It was a few minutes later that Rynna gasped, wiped her mouth, and looked up.

"So, you kept us alive, after all." Her words were colder than she had intended them to be, but she did not warm the sentiment by adding a soothing comment or any gratitude. She was too conflicted about Ta'ao and too exhausted from the flight to do anything more than acknowledge their survival.

"It takes more than a little exercise to kill me."

Rynna shook her head. The creature was a mere three feet in length. He looked more like an oversized lizard than a mythical beast. Next to the campfire eight bloodied arrows were in a pile. The

126

dragon would have smoothed the wounds from his flesh already, but removing them would still have hurt.

"Can dragons ever really die, short of being eaten by butterflies? You seem to be able to patch yourself up no matter what happens."

The tiny dragon ran a claw absently along the scar marring the scales of his forearm before answering.

"All beasts die, human. I could lose a head. I could be poisoned by lethorsum. I could be bled out if my claws were removed and the wounds were not tended to. Too many swords stabbed into me at once. Starvation. Thirst. Many dragons now die as hatchlings because they are misborn and do not form breath. It is a sad thing, that. There are always many ways into the golden fields . . ." he tapered off into silence.

Thirty minutes went by. Thirty minutes of a strained and shivering silence where Rynna slowly unwound and sorted through the layers of her emotions as she rubbed her hands over the meagre campfire. The summer morning air was not cold, but neither was it warm enough to thaw the travel and icy ocean water from her limbs. Her sleep had not dried her out at all, and she felt greasy and damp.

As she sat hunched near the flames, Rynna watched the dragon from her peripheral. She did her best to eat hot pieces of rabbit meat broken into tiny pieces and drink a little more water, but was mostly just waiting for the dragon to resume speaking.

127

After those thirty minutes had passed, the dragon shook his tiny wingspan then turned towards her.

"The changelings will be after you now that they have caught your scent."

"I know." The wet, shuffling sound of bodies putting themselves back together echoed in the young woman's mind, as did the whistling sound of ice shards. She shuddered at the sheer volume of death. "The changeling in the alley. She told me I smelled like a god."

The dragon waited for more. When nothing was forthcoming, he spoke himself. "Not just a changeling. That, human, was one of the Prince of Dusk's dreadpriests. Quite an accomplishment destroying one of its forms, thank you. And quite an honour that it was sent to Ta'ao to partake in your capture. You should be flattered. But I digress. I see you have accepted what you are, then?"

Rynna still felt completely unimportant. It wasn't as if overnight she had grown the ability to blow things up with the wave of a hand. It was just that there was no other explanation. She spoke dully to the dragon.

"Well, why would the underbeing lie? She should have just killed me like they were killing everyone else, but she didn't. She seemed almost pleased. It was horrible."

The dragon smiled faintly. "Sure, human. You doubt my taste buds for over a year. One dreadpriest makes a passing comment about what her nostrils are sensing-"

"So you think she was wrong?" Rynna's eyes held that particular degree of desperation usually seen in chickens thrashing about on the blood-stained block or in the faces of the girls in Dompt following a particularly nasty stoning of Lady Shutba. The dragon answered her a little sadly.

"No, I was trying to joke, but I guess it . . . . Human, never mind the taste, you bleed the essence of a god through your skin. I have smelled many gods, and you are the worst, most pungent one I have ever encountered. Twice as bad as the last one. Believe me. It smells terrible and unmistakable. There is no doubt in my mind, whatsoever. You are a god."

The small dragon tried to smile at her again, "It is just that you would think living to see your third millennium would grant a little respect for your taste buds among the earth beasts is all. Or certainly more respect than a changeling's nose. It is a wonder I did not discover you sooner in Dompt. But then again, I tended to avoid to villagers as best I could, which you always did as well. And the packages you left me never really held your scent all that much for me to notice it back then."

Rynna gave a weak returning smile at the attempt to cheer her, but despite the dragon's light words, her thoughts only became heavier. Responsibility seemed to wrap around her neck like a rotting carcass. During the course of their trip across the sea, the wet, stinking mess had begun weighing down on her, and it was only getting worse.

The lives of all the elves, dwarves, and humans seemed to claw their way into her lungs and constrict her breathing. She suddenly wished the dragon had been successful in his earlier attempts to

129

elicit hidden memories and abilities. But even as that thought deflated pathetically, another rose up in her mind.

"Months ago you mentioned something. It's just with all the people killed in Ta'ao, I can't . . . . I mean . . . . You said that the Lord of Salvation could try to end the war. Were you serious when you said that . . . do you think I could get all the fighting and deaths to stop?"

"Much can be accomplished when you cherish life and control half the soldiers in the known world. But it would be difficult. The underbeings are single-minded assassins. The free races mostly fight to defend themselves. Your side of the war is not the aggressor.

"Also, you will still have to contend with the Council of Three. There are two kings, two elders, a high priest, and an entire religion who may have different opinions on the matter. Not to mention that it is highly unlikely the underbeings would honour any peace you proposed.

"Still, it is worth a shot. I say we start by getting you to Lavanor and then you can revolutionize the world after. The longer it takes us to get there, the further the underbeings proceed with their plans."

The dragon stood as best he could and Rynna followed a little unsteadily. Urgency seemed to press on her for the first time since she had left Dompt. The dragon was right. The more time they stayed- no, the more time they wasted, the more time the changelings had. Memories of the bodies in Ta'ao flashed through her mind again and the young woman forced herself to move despite her wounds.

It was good that they were not far from their intended destination, as their situation was a bit grim. Their food and water supplies were nonexistent. The dragon's reserve was depleted so even his waterbreathing could offer little. Despite the young woman's best efforts, Rynna could only go at a fast limp at best. Again the dragon offered her lifeblood, but she still refused.

Their possessions had all been lost, except the dragon's human suit, which had been saved by virtue of the fact that the beast had swallowed it before collecting Rynna in Ta'ao.

When they took a small break, the three-foot dragon unrolled it onto the ground. He stalked all up and down the human suit's length, pulling on skin here and there, and generally looking displeased. A butterfly fluttered towards him and he crushed it mercilessly. He lashed his tail in frustration.

"A hundred years this suit has lasted. And now look at it," the dragon growled. His stomach acid had clearly done a number on the hag. The clothes that Lady Shutba had been wearing were destroyed. Eroded away to nothing more than colourful scraps. The flesh itself was pock marked in some places, and very thin in others. Most the scalp was missing entirely. "Monstrous and suspicious."

Rynna shook her head. "Lady Shutba has always looked strange. You should stop bothering with a disguise."

He grimaced. "Are you forgetting about the poachers? No, it is no use. What I need is a new suit. We don't have the time though. Or the body. I should have grabbed one as we left Ta'ao. They are

131

probably just rotting now. What a waste of good flesh."

The comment did not sit well with Rynna. She shook her head again, this time with stern vehemence.

"That's not funny, dragon."

"I was not being funny. I was being practical."

"A lot of my people died."

"And a lot more will. Get used to it. The sooner we find your priests, the sooner we start making things better. Remember that."

With that, the dragon ignored her once again, and focussed on salvaging as much of Lady Shutba's flesh as he could.

Rynna watched the dragon work silently as his words blackened her thoughts. Was this what being a god was going to mean? A lot of people dead and nobody to blame but her?

Other things began occurring to her as well. More dark things. If she really was a god, either nobody was praying to her or she couldn't hear them. Could the gods ever hear their people's prayers, or was it just her who didn't know how to listen? The futility of all the millions of people whispering their hopes, dreams, and desperate pleas into oblivion bothered her.

Then of course there were other issues. All across the world throughout the three kingdoms there were temples dedicated to Rynna whose purported mission was helping the sick and needy. But her and her mother had still gone hungry as often as not. The incongruity grated. The Lord of Salvation oversaw the free race kingdoms. He (or rather She this time) ensured laws were just. So was it the fault of the king, human nature, or herself that over forty murderers had been walking free for a year now?

The dragon was almost finished with his task of piecing Lady Shutba back together. The flesh suit was considerably smaller, but also considerably less leprous. It was still a patchy thing though, and less human looking than ever. Rynna didn't point this out to the dragon. He seemed satisfied with his work and she just wanted to get going. Lavanor still waited.

Rynna had originally been determined that they would set out as soon as the dragon had repaired Lady Shutba, but the exhaustion and wounds from their trip across the sea caught up with her again. Reluctantly, she proposed a short twenty four hour reprieve so they could eat, sleep, and recover a little more. As rough as the flight had been, Rynna knew there was no way the changelings could have travelled as quickly across the water. Even resting an extra day, they should still keep well ahead of the underbeings searching for her. The dragon agreed so promptly that the young woman suspected she wasn't the only one still suffering.

The two searched until they found a small, clear stream where the dragon drank deeply, not through his maw, but through his snout. After several minutes he shook his scaly neck and exhaled slowly. Fog crept out and the tiny beast nodded to himself. He then scampered off to hunt more rodents to eat. The dragon was too small to bring down the big game and instead concentrated on rats, squirrels, rabbits, and snakes. Rynna set her mind to gathering wood for a fire and collecting nuts and other plants to round out the gamey taste of the meat.

The day went by jerkily. At times, it seemed to drag on indefinitely and at others rushed forward hours at a time with every blink. Rynna mostly sat in quite contemplation, eating, and drifting in and out of sleep. She was becoming increasingly nervous about the capital city and was at a loss of what to do with herself now that their arrival was so close. She was almost relieved when the sun settled below the horizon and the small dragon came to curl up beside her for the night.

The next morning, the dragon woke her when he yawned loudly and sneezed, sending a few snowflakes scattering to the ground where they melted immediately. The little dragon stretched and scratched himself idly under the scales on his neck. Rynna had to smile softly because as horrible and terrifying as the dragon could be, currently, the only adjective to describe him was 'adorable.'

They chatted a little aimlessly as they finished up the rest of the food they had prepared the previous day. No heavy topics: they discussed safe things like the weather and the birds they saw.

Rynna teased the dragon by accusing him of scavenging rather than hunting the game they had eaten, as his size was no more than that of a wild dog. The dragon responded by snorting more snow at the young woman. He then smugly rippled out to his usual twelve feet of length. Rynna laughed as the dragon spent a few minutes strutting around their little camp, making that deep rumbling purr.

The great beast gave himself one last shake before growing serious.

"Alright, human. Before we head out for Lavanor there is one more thing we must discuss." The dragon's rumble had quieted now and his tail was twitching ever so slightly. It reminded her of the twitching he had done on the day the dragon had told her she was a god. Rynna frowned slightly. The only consolation in her mind was that at least he wasn't pacing.

"The changelings. If I had suspected the changelings would be anywhere near us with the kind of numbers they brought to Ta'ao, I would have done many things differently. We cannot allow another close call and I cannot chance us getting separated again. Not in Lavanor of all places."

The dragon paused in his words and his reluctance to continue became a palpable thing of increased twitching. He then began to pace. Rynna's heart sank.

"So," he finally continued, "because of that, I am going to show you something. Something important that will allow me to communicate with you no matter where we are as long as the distance between us does not exceed a league. But you need to do something first. You must grant me access to your mind."

"My mind?" Rynna blinked. She watched the back and forth of the large beast, confusion dominating her expression.

"Dragons are not born with the tongue of the earth beasts on our lips. It develops only when we gain breath. During our Before, my kind uses another means to communicate. A direct input of thought from mind to mind. Thoughtspeech."

"So, you want to be able to see inside my mind?"

"No, human. I can input things into your mind, not extract. I will know nothing of what you think."

"Why haven't you told me about this earlier? We've been traveling for months with Lady Shutba the mute. You could have been speaking with me the whole time."

"There are complications. I would avoid revealing this to you at all if I could. The only other earth beast with whom I have spoken like this now owes me a lifedebt because of it. It is treason among my kind to share thoughtspeech. I break many rules."

Indeed, the dragon seemed hesitant. It was strange. She had seen every degree of anger she thought the beast could produce, but apprehension wasn't something he often displayed.

"So how do I grant you access?"

"Simply tell me to come in. Then I can show you what needs to be learned."

"That's it? Just tell you to come in?"

"Not all is skylights and thunder. Yes, godling. That is it, you just grant me permission. But you must truly mean it with all your heart or it will not work."

Rynna's mouth quirked. "Alright, come in dragon, welcome to my grand and mighty brain."

The dragon did not return the jest. His face was all seriousness.

"Brace yourself, human. This might feel odd."

At first there was nothing. Just the wind, one bird making a last ditch effort to call a mate for the season, and some branches scratching against one another above her head.

And then it happened. It was an all at once explosion that shot through her mind and infused every inch of her. A battering ram, ram! bruising her head from the inside. A violence and contact which was never usually experienced because of the thick layer of bone protecting her mind. Rynna clutched at her head and moaned. It burned behind her eyes and out her ears and through every vein and pathway in her head. And then it cumulated.

Hello, human.

"For Salvation!" Rynna swore.

As for the dragon, he was frowning and staring at her in bafflement.

"It must be because you are a god."

"What did you do to me?"

The dragon did not hear her right away, preoccupied with his own thoughts. "Strange," he muttered once more.

"You mean, that pressure, that feeling inside my head is because I am a god?"

The dragon looked up at those words. He chuckled. "No, human. That was thoughtspeech. That was normal. I told you to brace yourself." His mirth trailed off with his next words, "But there was a residual resonance, like an echo in my mind that I have never felt before. And it cannot be just because you are not a dragon, because I never experienced that with the elf girl. It must be because you are a god. How odd."

"The pain . . . is it like that every time?

The dragon's maw cracked as he nodded.

"Yes of course, until you adjust. Do you still wish we had been chattering for months? Among hatchlings words are kept meaningful. There is a price to conversation."

Rynna sighed. She slowly moved her head back and forth. The ringing had not subsided.

"I don't see how this is useful. If I'm in trouble, I'm going to get tackled because I'll be busy clutching my head in pain every time you try to contact me."

"As I said, a price." The dragon was still all amusement at her reaction and Rynna could not for the life of her imagine a situation where she would ever adjust to the sensation. But then an interesting thought occurred to her.

"Can I do it back to you? Can I answer in my head instead of having to talk out loud, too?"

The dragon frowned.

"You could try. But I have never known one who is not a dragon to be able to accomplish it. Although since you are a god, it might be possible."

"Wouldn't it be better? If I'm in danger and you aren't there, what good will it do if you can talk to me, but I can't send out a help signal or something?"

The dragon nodded. "You make a valid point. We could try. As I said, dragonkin are the only ones I know who are able."

"Well, let's give it a shot. If I can't learn then we're no worse off than we are now. Do you have to give me permission?"

The dragon's face darkened. "Permission is not needed to enter the mind of an earthwaterair beast." Then his face smoothed out somewhat and his voice calmed as he began to explain. "Let me see now . . .

138

. Make your message a living creature. Make it something solid, heavy, and breathing. Give it a heartbeat, give it wings, and make it want to soar. Then make the thought impatient and throbbing with energy. Make it want to burst from your lips, but do not let it."

There was something almost familiar in the way the dragon described what she had to do. When she was little, there had been times where she had been struck by ideas so urgent they seemed exactly as the dragon described them. Not just mild curiosities, but living things that needed to escape to be free in the world to seek their answers unhindered by her physical body. Of course, they were the thoughts of a child: questions regarding rainbows, flowers, and the magic of bread rising. In a way though, those thoughts had been more genuine than anything she had experienced since. Rynna decided she would enjoy thoughtspeech.

"So, after I make the thought alive, what do I do then?"

"Then you throw it at me."

The look Rynna gave him was long and searching.

"Throw them at you."

The great beast shrugged. "I am not sure how else to explain it. Like I said, we do not usually tell others of thoughtspeech outside of the brood. We know how to accomplish it instinctively. Describing it is odd." The dragon shrugged. "So, yes, throw words at me. Start with one word, it will be easier."

The scepticism crept up to the corners of Rynna's eyes, but when no other suggestions were forthcoming, she closed them and began to concentrate.

She decided on the word 'I' as it was the simplest one she knew. Now to make it a living thing, this word. Rynna thought about it intensely and tried to picture the word not as a pronoun that existed only in the theoretical, but rather as a substantial thing. She tried to make the word in her head become heavy, big, and real. She pictured it as a proud, vain thing that strutted around her mind and bellowed its importance.

So now this loudmouthed word was very much real to her, but how in Salvation was she supposed to throw it? The best Rynna could do was picture what it would be like if her brain sneezed. Some kind of explosion that would shoot the 'I' towards the dragon like bacteria waiting to find a fresh new place to fester.

So that's what she did. She gave a mental *achoo* as hard as she could in the beast's general direction.

Rynna opened her eyes. A slight smile of eagerness touched her lips.

"Did you get it?"

The dragon looked at her blankly.

"Get what?"

"My- I sent you some thoughtspeech. The word 'I.'"

The dragon shook his head. The corners of his maw quivered.

"Do you want to try again, human?"

Rynna's cheeks reddened slightly and she shook her head.

140

"Are you sure? Your grand and mighty brain should be able to accomplish this tiny task, should it not?"

Her words from before only darkened her cheeks further. Amusement was still leaking from the dragon, but he didn't press the issue and instead, the two cleaned up their little campsite and began the last leg of their long journey.

It was a happy trip towards the capital city. The dragon was a walking, grumbling purr of satisfaction within Lady Shutba (now wearing a skirt and top woven from reeds) and Rynna was smiling herself. The other travelers on the road seemed equally excited: beaming at one another and sharing greetings. Nobody gave them suspicious glares at all. One person even wished them a motive-free good day, an unprecedented occurrence in the past year. This alone so pleased Rynna that she wore a wide, contented grin for the next hour.

Why shouldn't they be happy, though? Lavanor. Capital city. Surrounded by towering walls that sloped outwards and were tipped with lethorsum laced barbed iron. Built on a foundation of rock that made any attempts at tunnelling under the walls almost impossible. Led by the king and queen of the realm. Home of the great temple of the Lord of Salvation. Keeper of the Bai Library, said to hold all of history since the beginning of the gods themselves. Founding city of the Council of Three and headquarters of the Free Race Alliance. It was the birthplace of culture and wisdom. This was it. They were finally here. Months of endless monotonous food, roads, and the same Salvation forsaken clothing were about to come to an end.

The sun had almost set when they were on their last stretch of road, colouring the hills and trees with bloodied light. The darkening hues of the evening sharpened contrasts and lent a surreal quality to the ditches that lined the road. The nearer they got, the more the other travelers began to quicken their pace. Some of the younger ones actually began to break into a light trot. Tension buzzed among the people on the road even more strongly now than it had earlier. You could taste the anticipation and see the coiled excitement in every face.

And then they finally arrived. Lavanor in all its glory was ready and waiting for them. They crested the final hill that barred their vision of the capital city and froze at the scene below them.

The birthplace of culture and wisdom was being attacked.

From where she stood, Rynna could see hundreds of people pressing around the city and streaming through the main gates. Ear-splitting screams could be heard all the way from where they stood. There was a loud drum booming that could only be another warning bell for the arrival of changelings. Most ominous of all, a dark, black smoke hung over everything.

No, no, no, no! Not Lavanor. Not here. Not now. They had been so close to what they wanted, and now all Rynna could see were the bodies. Flashes of the dead ones from Ta'ao merging with the endless ones converging on the city.

"Should we run?"

Rynna's voice was unsteady but she was not as panicked this time as last. The young woman was not pinned into an alleyway watching the massacre. She was still a quarter of a mile off. She could run to safety and take Lady Shutba with her. They could marshal and rally the free races from another city. One not decimated by changelings.

Then came the ram, ram! of a dragon clawing its way into her mind. Rynna dropped to her knees with her head pressed firmly between her hands. The awful invasion of heat and pain cut through her thoughts as the dragon spoke.

No.

"But . . . smoke . . . drums . . . changelings surrounding . . . city." Rynna's words were ground out between teeth.

Heat. Pressure. Pain. Ram, ram!

They are not changelings.

The true horror of the situation hit home for Rynna. Civil war. Elf against human against dwarf. It is said that long ago the free races warred amongst themselves. That was before the Warrior Clan united them.

Ram, ram!

Look around you.

With a pained effort, Rynna tilted her head to the side to see what the dragon meant. All she saw were happy travelers of the same degree they'd seen all day.

Travelers who were still happy.

Rynna's head snapped up, and with the movement her head throbbed anew. Once more she looked at the people, once more she heard the drums, and once more she saw the smoke. The black, welcoming, celebratory, *hello* smoke.

"How . . . how did they know we were coming?"

They did not.

"But . . . the black smoke . . . the people . . . the drums . . . . It's the Godnaming."

Yes, it is.

"But, if it's the Godnaming . . . . If they didn't know we were coming then why . . . ."

The free races have found their god.

"But . . . I'm the Lord of Salvation. You said . . . and the changeling told me . . . and . . . ." She started to shake. Everything surrounding her seemed to ooze, smear, and blend, swirling her vision into a hazy mist of colours and shapes.

Heat. Pressure. Pain.

I was inaccurate. I assumed you were the Lord of Salvation. The changeling confirmed you are a god, I just did not give her enough time to specify which one.

Rynna's fingers once more had a death grip on her forehead as she struggled to control the pain. The dragon's words pulsed.

Human, I do believe you are the devil.

Then there was a slight pause, a slight reprieve in the pain before,

I'm sorry for attacking your dreadpriest back in Ta'ao. My mistake.

144

CHAPTER 15
THE CONFIRMATION OF
SOMETHING UPSETTING

Night was in her full glory now. A darkness that fluttered and danced with the sounds and smells of the revelry within her. Firelight picked out the twinkle in her eyes and the thick welcoming smoke obliterated the distraction that the selfish stars and moon always present. Just night now: thick, loud, and hideous, dancing with the city in a complicated mix of glory and bloated heat.

The city itself was a seductress with people indiscriminately celebrating through her every inch. Lavish and coarse booze mixed freely along the streets as they sloshed from unsteady, jubilant hands. The buildings seem to quiver with ecstasy as the loud drums and music vibrated through the paving stones.

King Paelin and Queen Milla had opened the treasury to host the century's largest party and the people had reacted accordingly. Men and women of all breeds and types toasted glasses to their god. For He was here! The Lord of Salvation had come at last! The priests had made the official announcement earlier that day as they lit the skies with the heralding black smoke. The fact that the Big Man Himself was fifteen years late didn't dampen the mood at all. If anything, it made them all the happier. Fashionably late and just in time to save the day.

Only the tower watchmen and the guards on duty were still sober. It was a relative sober since all were still secretly celebrating from hip flasks, but they could all at least still see and shoot somewhat straight. In fact, the only two members of the entire city who weren't either under the age of eight or else somewhat inebriated, were Rynna and the dragon.

The two sober travelers were pushing and shoving their way through the endless bodies, trying to make sense of it all. They had initially made their way warily into the city to confirm everything suspected and feared by the two respectively. After the guards had carefully scrutinized Lady Shutba's eyes by firelight for several minutes, they had passed into the celebrating crowds to question the people. Every way they had turned and every person they had asked gave evidence of the now undeniable truth.

"The lights were amazing! Did you see it? Did you see Him? He was there! So powerful. Where? Right in front of the temple, I saw it myself! Did you know he's a human? So amazing! The skylights burned above the city. I saw it with my own eyes. The lights, his power! Tall. Handsome. Human. Praise be to the Lord of Salvation!"

The words were never so clear, nor so concise, but it was all basically the same. In fact, the more Lady Shutba and Rynna waded into the masses, the more they could only draw the inevitable conclusion that indeed Rynna was the devil. For if she was a god, the slot of 'good' was already filled leaving only the vacancy of the Prince of Dusk to be considered.

We will find lodging for the night. Then we can decide what to do. It is too much out here.

Shock had dulled the awful pain of thoughtspeech, reducing it to a back burning simmer that she suffered through distantly. Finding out one is the devil is hardly something that should be drank in a neat shot. The news should be diluted with sweeter things and then gradually sipped at over a long period. Taken all at once it is a heady and toxic thing. Rynna was reeling.

"How do you suppose we do that?"

Leave that to me. Follow quickly.

Lady Shutba forced her way through the people and gradually led the woman to parts of the city celebrating less exuberantly. The small street they ended up in was only partially filled and most of it inhabitants were either wrapped in a sloppy, romantic embraces or else mumbling quietly to themselves in semi-conscious states while being relieved of their money pouches by pickpockets. There were some small shops here, but they were all securely locked for the evening. Barred windows and doors guarded the abandoned buildings.

It was to one of these places that Lady Shutba slowly made her way towards. The chosen structure was guarded by a large padlock, but the powerfully built beast simply grabbed the lock with Lady Shutba's hand and crushed it. The now unrecognizable metal fell to the ground with the thunk of crumpled iron. A powerful arm then smashed a hole in the door to unbar it.

The door swung inwards. Lady Shutba shuffled in, with Rynna following closely behind. The few butterflies that had managed to trail them were soon

147

mashed into a pulpy mess, and then immediately afterwards the human suit was peeled back and the dragon once more stood in his own scales.

He shook himself a little, as if trying to slip the last of Lady Shutba's essence. When he was satisfied that he was completely reptilian again, he dug a foreclaw carelessly into a nearby cabinet and dragged it in front of the ruined door. The heavy wood would be enough to keep away errant, lonely drunks.

As the beast fluidly slipped further into the room, Rynna could only see the shadowed edges of his body as he fussed with something. Then, with the sound of a few sharp strikes, light flickered its way into the room. The dragon had found a lantern and some flint. Evidently, they had broken into a carpenter's showroom. All around them chairs, tables, barrels, and axe handles were haphazardly stacked about.

The dragon took a look around their acquired lodging and nodded once. It was a quiet, closed place where they could talk freely and sleep undisturbed. It would suffice. The drum beats and the corpulent smell of smoke, sweat, hala, and alcohol still leaked into their shelter, but at least there was breathing space. The dragon settled comfortably onto the floor.

"So, you are the Prince of Dusk. This changes things considerably."

Rynna shook her head slowly, "But . . . I'm not . . . I can't . . . I can't be the devil. I don't want to end the free races. I don't want to protect changelings. How can I be the god of monsters?"

"What else could you be?"

148

"I don't know, but I don't want to be . . . this. I don't want to see another changeling again in my entire life. Besides, what am I going to do . . . waltz in to the Gate and say, 'how do you do?' They will probably kill us on sight. Or they will kill you and try to kill me, which would be just as bad."

The dragon regarded the young woman seriously. He clacked his claws against the polished wooden floor and slowly chipped away at the smooth surface. He seemed to be weighing their different options and possibilities before nodding slowly to himself.

"Tomorrow we will go see the parade and discover what we can about the situation here. Then we will leave Lavanor."

"Discover what we can- I am not spying on my own species. I am not going to help underbeings annihilate my people more efficiently by doing a reconnaissance mission right before I ascend the throne and become the monsters' god. It's just twisted. I'm not evil."

"Human, why does being the Prince of Dusk necessarily mean that you are evil?"

"He's the leader of the changelings!"

"Yes, he is their *leader*." The dragon's eyes were tantalizing with promise and rationality. "Think about it. Think about the possibilities of being in control of the dangerous half of the war."

She did think about it. The cogs in Rynna's mind turned over, and three separate things clicked into place in a stunning display of competence. Leader of the changelings.

"Oh." Her protest deflated in a huff.

"Exactly, human."

"I could stop the war just by calling a cease fire of the changelings . . . . The only reason why the free races fight is to defend themselves. If I got the changelings to stop, then . . . ."

The dragon was grinning his reptilian smile. "Well done, earth beast. Maybe your kind has hope yet." The dragon's rumble increased. "Tomorrow. The parade. We see it, buy some provisions, and then we leave this city to find your underbeings. It should not be too hard. They are bound to be scouring the countryside for you just as desperately as the free races were hunting for their god."

"I don't know . . . . How will I possibly convince them to stop something they have been devotedly pursuing since they were created?"

"Rynna, you are their god. Before all this, before Dompt, the mobs, and your mother's death. Before . . . if the Lord of Salvation Himself had walked up to you and personally told you to stop eating meat entirely, for the sake of the free races, would you have done it?"

"Well, I guess so."

"And if He came and told you to stop killing mosquitos because He had grown fond of them, then what?"

"I would probably just tolerate mosquitos for a while."

"It is the same thing. The underbeings do not see the free races as their kin, remember? To them the free races are a cockroach infestation that needs to be eliminated. The free races also make a meal and some sport, but that is it. Food and a plague. And, who knows? Maybe they will just humour you for your hundred years and then go right back to

150

exterminating the free races when you are gone. But even one rebirth of the gods skipped would save countless of your kind. Imagine it, human. We can help so many."

Rynna could. Which is when the young woman realized that she was hesitantly okay with the idea. The dragon made sense. In fact, he was downright logical. Rynna tentatively nodded.

"You say 'we.' Are you sure you want to stay with me now that I- now that you know what I am? Like you have told me many times, this is not the dragons' fight. You have your own god."

The dragon scratched at the same spot on the floor he had chipped earlier. "I owe a lifedebt to you. My kind does not take that pledge lightly. And . . . ." He hesitated. That dark face changed ever so slightly as his eyes slid to meet Rynna's.

"I guess I have a soft spot for earth beasts that feed me." His words were still rough, but now, like his face, they too were different. The stubborn affection of a voice not used to being appreciative. "I was never properly grateful for your treatment of Lady Shutba in Dompt. Although I was always gone when you left the packages, the villagers gossiped about it. Thank you, human. I was not shown many kindnesses there."

Rynna smiled back and shrugged.

"You took me away from that place. You saved my life. In my mind we are more than even."

The dragon scowled at the praise. "You would have lived. It just would have hurt a lot more. Besides, killing a few of the villagers in that town is hardly something that caused me any difficulties, moral or otherwise. Two thousand years ago entire

151

villages like Dompt were turned over to the dragons to hunt. Convicts and captured changelings were always gifted to the dragons. The Lord of Salvation's mercy, they called it. If the convicts could manage to get one hundred feet without getting killed by us, then they were free to go, pardoned of all crimes."

The dragon barked a laugh. "Earth beasts always believe they can outrun a dragon's breath. None ever lived to see the end of the first twenty feet. Of course, the changelings always had to be killed. The Lord of Salvation insisted the Prince of Dusk's creations be eradicated whenever possible."

Rynna wrapped her arms around herself. So casually stated from the dragon's maw. The Prince of Dusk . . . that was her. She was the Prince of Dusk. God of the creations that the Lord insisted be eradicated. But leader of them, too. She could do it. Become the leader of the monsters, but not be one herself. It was possible. The scheme could work.

"Did you ever speak to me? The Prince of Dusk, I mean. In a past life."

"You mean to ask me if I ever fraternized with the devil?"

"Well, yeah."

He shrugged. "The Prince of Dusk does not leave the protection of the Menundra often. I only ever met you once during a reincarnation many, many years ago. It was a short encounter. I was young and stupid and should not have tried to meddle in wars that did not concern the dragons in the first place."

Rynna smiled tentatively at the dragon.

"Seems you haven't really learned much from then, have you?"

The dragon abruptly smiled himself. The animalistic grin lit his face in an almost charming way. Then he laughed.

"I suppose not," he chuckled again before saying, "You know, I am actually really glad that I could not eat you. A bad meal has never turned out to be this interesting before. And at my age with what I have all seen, I cannot say that too often. What are another few months of your stench in return for a little adventure?"

His smile only lasted a few more seconds before it retreated from his eyes. Then, he stretched himself out as much as he could across the rough, uncomfortable floor of the shop. Watching the beast settle in made Rynna aware of how tired she was. It had been a long day.

"We should try to get some sleep," the dragon began. "Tomorrow . . . ."

The two proceeded to discuss the details of their next few days. Nothing complicated. Basically their plan was to just get themselves caught by changelings outside the city as quickly as possible. The underbeings would be able to smell that she was a god, and they would take them to the Gate. It was pretty simple as far as plans went, but one that they still discussed for a long time as neither felt like sleeping on the hard floor when they got down to it. One last issue was mentioned, however.

"The two gods have been trying to kill each other even longer than the free races and the changelings have been. Much, much longer," the dragon explained with sleepy words. "Millenniums upon millenniums longer. You may not remember it, but the Prince of Dusk and Lord of Salvation would almost do anything to ensure the other died. Gods can kill gods. If the wrong side captures us, and you are given to the Lord of Salvation, then you might discover what mortality is after all. So, I emphasize to you that tomorrow we need to get out of here as quickly as we can after the parade is over."

Rynna agreed readily enough, and from there the conversation petered out. By the time the two finally curled up together, the carousing outside had quieted to a distant bang of drums and music. Slowly drifting to sleep, they were completely and inaccurately confident that on the following day, not a thing would go wrong.

CHAPTER 16
THE PARADED CAGE

The crowds were just as thick and just as noisy that morning as they had been the night before. They smelled just as badly, the music pounded just as effectively, and the people were just as drunk. In fact the only real difference in Lavanor from the previous evening was that there was a great deal more heat as the sun had now begun to beat mercilessly down on a city already too hot for its own good.

The parade, which was to be the crowning moment of the festivities, was to more or less follow the main street. Starting at the gates, it was to wind itself towards the centre of the city where the palace and great temple were. And it was there that the changeling was going to have its throat slit by the shiny new god.

For unbeknownst to the two the night before, the parade was not just a 'Welcome, make Yourself at home, be prepared to be worshiped and loved, oh and please do not smite us!' parade. It was also a 'Somebody caught a changeling last night and let us watch our fifteen year old god kill it!' parade.

A deep hollow growl could be heard coming from Lady Shutba when they did finally discover this little detail, and the shopkeeper that had been informing them about the day's events jumped and visibly paled when she heard the feral noise come from a decrepit hag.

"Thank you!" Rynna called to the woman's back as she retreated into her store, shutting the door quickly.

Heat. Pressure. Ram, ram!

We should leave now.

The hollow growl rattling out of the dragon's human suit increased in both pitch and volume. Rynna was gripping her head from the pain of thoughtspeech but still managed to whisper an admonishment to the dragon.

"Stop growling. You scared that woman to death."

Nothing good will come of this. Changelings should be killed quietly in the night, not blatantly with witnesses. The Warrior Clan reacts violently to being mocked.

"One look at the god and then we leave."

Lady Shutba nodded but that hollow growl did not stop. Thankfully, as inebriation was still the dominant state of mind for most people around them, this was not noticed.

Fighting their way to a good viewpoint was difficult to say the least. The dragon was bodily pushing people around way more effectively that a frail hag ought to be able to, and even still it took them forty five minutes to move three streets down. Eventually however, the two did manage to find a spot on a sloped street that allowed them to see over enough heads to give them a clear view.

The parade had all the usual parade-y things. Jugglers. Dancers. Balloon distributors. Jesters. Horses of the non-ugly-as-sticks variety. Things didn't really get exciting though until the royal family arrived.

The city loved its monarchy. House Gelda had been in power for four generations and the consensus was that they had done well by the people. All four of them were there: King Paelin and Queen Milla with Princess Eleanor and the heir apparent, Prince Louis. From Rynna's distance she couldn't make out many details, but to her they were beautiful regardless. After all, they were her royal family, too. No matter what backward village she and her mother had found themselves in, they had still always paid taxes and avidly followed the news and the goings-on of the royal family. Merchants and travellers who trickled through would always have a tale or two about the monarchy to share.

There used to be scores of human kingdoms which warred with each other for land and resources, but now it was just the one: Knaah, broken into four territories and governed by the king and his councillors. Although one territory had been abandoned with the fall of the Ice City, the other three were still devotedly supporting their leaders in Lavanor.

The territories skirted the edges of the Gossamer Forest and the Water Weavers' Lakes, and they stopped before the Ull Mountains began, lest they encroach on the kingdoms of the other races. The underground miners had their own monarchy. Currently the leader was a huge dwarf named Ga Tolm ba'Melg, which in the common tongue meant King Tolm the Rough Edged One. As Rynna recalled, his wives had borne him no children, and now the succession was a matter of much debate.

The elves did not claim royalty among their kind, despite referring to their lands as kingdoms. Instead, the elders gathered once a year to hold council among themselves, alternately hosted at the Water Weavers' Lakes and the Gossamer Forest of the Tree Dwellers. Each group of elves was represented by their Eldest, but almost all decisions were made collectively.

The royal family slowly dwindled from sight as the parade continued on. There was more of the dancing, entertaining sort of people, trying to enthral the crowd with their acrobatic feats. It was wasted effort, for everyone was getting restless. Soon, the Lord of Salvation, Himself, in person, would be in the parade. It was nerve-wracking, history in the making stuff that the viewers would tell their greatchildren about. To have been there at the Godnaming in Lavanor to see the new god in the welcoming parade. How exciting!

But first the changeling.

Rynna knew when the underbeing's cage was getting close even before she first caught sight of it. The mood of the crowd darkened and an angry murmur snuck into the festivities. Fists tightened and skirts were gripped in a sinister way as people discussed the captured monster.

Since the beast was to be killed ceremoniously by the Lord of Salvation, no citizens were permitted to throw so much as a pebble at the changeling before it reached the temple. But they wanted to. How they wanted to kill the thing that dared come after their god and their people. News of Ta'ao had already spread throughout the kingdoms, and there was murder in the eyes of the crowd. It was only out of sheer respect for the king and their deity that they restrained themselves.

A creaking of wheels and an increase in angry muttering. The cage had come in sight. It was a nasty affair of copper and iron lifted on a podium for all to see. Four strong dwarves were pulling the ropes that dragged the cage's stand on its wheels. It was dwarves who had been given the honour because their kind had been most insulted by the capture, most desiring of blood. For inside the cage sat a fifth dwarf. A little on the small side, and with a slightly matted look to his beard, but still a perfectly respectable looking dwarf. That is, if you discounted the hue of his irides. If you could overlook those pitch eyes that were currently gazing coolly out into the crowd.

Rynna inhaled sharply at the sight of the caged beast. She felt cold, and goosebumps raised on her arms. Danger radiated from that cage like rot does from a midden heap. Underlining the anger of the mob was also a deep terror. There wasn't enough metal in the world to make them feel okay about being around one of those creatures.

And it was to that dangerous thing in the cage which Rynna was headed. She was going to willingly let herself be captured by more of its kind. She would become their god. Seeing that face and those eyes brought memories of Ta'ao screaming back into her head. The death, the slaughter, the merciless and endless attack. She felt sick. The plan so meticulously and enthusiastically discussed the previous evening made her feel even sicker. The rage of the crowd sunk into her bones and she hated along with them. She wanted to see that changeling choke. She wanted to see its blood splatter. She wanted it to die painfully for the pregnant woman who had tried to run.

Rynna's thoughts were interrupted when something curious happened. The smirk dropped from the changeling's face. It rose sharply to its feet and began to scrutinize the crowd. Eventually, its search narrowed and it looked steadily in her direction. Which was when the changeling pressed its head against the bars and inhaled deeply.

Human, we must leave. NOW!

Rynna had not been expecting the dragon's words and they sliced through her mind in a brilliant and horrible way. The searing pathways in her head throbbed with his last word.

"What for?" It was a struggle to push out those words through the throbbing of the *NOW!* still ricocheting in her head.

The changeling. Can you not see what he is doing? Your scent. You bleed that scent through your skin. I should have realized this before. The dreadpriest in Ta'ao. The cataclysmic number of changelings there . . . . The underbeings must be very desperate to find their god.

Rynna's pupils dilated.

"Me. It was me. I brought them to Ta'ao. Somebody must have caught my scent in Ta'ao and . . . . Dear Salvation." Her breathing was becoming shallow and quick. They didn't attack Ta'ao and happen to smell her. They smelled her and so they attacked Ta'ao. A whole city destroyed for her scent.

People had noticed the changeling's strange behaviour. The murmuring of the crowd increased and people were starting to get fidgety. Something that they did not understand was happening and the unknown is automatically suspect. Curiosity not only killed the cat in Lavanor, but first it skinned it alive, then rubbed salt into the bared and bleeding flesh underneath.

The changeling stopped his intense scrutiny of the crowd. He pulled back from the bars and retreated once more to the exact centre of his cage. The crowd's breathing was haggard and rough. Thousands of marathons had just been run even though nobody had moved so much as an inch. There was silence now as everybody watched to see what the creature would do next.

It lifted its head in the air. And howled.

Aaaaaaaooooooooooou.

It was a lonely keen of a lion cub who is searching for its mother. It was the determined call of ship's foghorn in search of the shore. It was a man in the gallows singing the national anthem as the ground dropped below his feet. The sound of his neck snapping in harmony with the perfect fifth. It was the weirdest gods damned thing to hear.

Although many people had seen changelings, few had ever seen one caged, and none had heard one utter anything other than the screams and grunts of battle. This inauspicious wail terrified them. Then, more frightening, it got louder. But not louder because the howling creature changed volume, but louder because more voices joined the call. All around them came a growing, terrifying yell. It ricocheted off buildings as small, big, loud, and quiet voices took up the song.

It was not a 'well met' as it had been last time. The song said simply and succinctly: 'she is beautiful.'

Rynna started to breathe in ragged lungfuls of air. It was the same as Ta'ao. The howling as she and the dragon had left. If the changelings did to this city what they had done to Ta'ao-

But this was not Ta'ao. This was the capital city. Citizens didn't need to walk armed at all times. Panic had a contingency plan and that contingency plan had its own back up that involved a lot of poisoned weapons.

No orders needed to be given. The changeling was killed. A lethorsum laced arrow through his eye and the crowd watched him thrash to a leaking stillness. They also watched the twitching and reanimation begin and then there was another arrow. It didn't rise a third time and the body was still. The howling had also stilled. Where were the beasts now? Was it a trick? Were there actually thousands of them buried among their own ranks?

People glanced uneasily at their neighbours.

We leave this city now, human! We need to get witnessed being somewhere else.

"Yes."

No hesitation in Rynna. The young woman did not need the tint of desperation in the words burning through her mind to convince her, either. She did not understand the meaning of the howl, but even a blind green-bellied pot snake would realize that she had been spotted. Ousted in the worst possible way because it meant that every changeling within earshot was going to start running for the source of that howl. It wasn't getting caught that terrified her.

162

What terrified her was the exact number of innocent humans, elves, and dwarves that stood between her and the changelings heading their way.

Lady Shutba grabbed her hand and they ran.

Through the streets and past confused people, the two began to sprint relentlessly towards the

CHAPTER 17
THE EMPTY MEMORY

Rynna stumbled and fell to the ground, gasping.

"Get up, human! We do not have time for this! The patrols are only a few minutes behind us, and in another ten, other soldiers will have reached their mounts."

The young woman's chest was heaving with overexertion. The muscles on her arms and legs were burning, and every breath was violence in her lungs.

"Wh- what's . . . go- going . . . on . . . ?" she panted.

"Three quarters of the city of Lavanor is on our heels and you are making jokes right now? On your feet, human!"

"B- But . . . I don't . . . . What-"

The dragon slapped her. A red angry imprint of scales on her cheek and an almost bleeding line where the skin was cut slightly. A burning sensation of nerves screaming. Rynna cried out in pain.

"Move, human! If we do not get away now it will be too late. On your FEET!"

Rynna stumbled to an upright position. The dragon began to crash through the trees and the young woman did her best to follow him.

Her muscles were aching in a way that meant they had been running for a long time. And muscles weren't the only things hurting. Her stomach felt as if there was a small rat inside it eating its way out. The searing in her chest was probably the result of a badly broken rib. Her back was an agonizing crescendo of pain, and she could feel the warmth and wetness of blood trickling down her one side.

Her bare foot caught on a root and Rynna went down again. Where had her boot gone? She landed on the side with the broken rib and grunted sharply with the impact. The dragon heard the thud of her landing and turned around.

"Up! Get up!"

"I- I can't."

"Damn it, human!" The dragon reached under her prone body and hefted her up by the waist. The dragon visibly staggered under the weight, but then quickly re-accelerated to his break-neck speed. "Hold on however you can, human! If you fall, that is the end for both of us!"

The young woman wrapped her hands around the dragon's arm tightly, and it was only then that she actually looked at the great beast. He was in worse shape than she was. The majestic wings were just shy of being shredded. His left arm seemed to be completely lifeless at his side, and there were several places on the dragon's body where blood was free flowing.

Rynna closed her eyes and prayed for their survival. It was only after a few minutes that the hilarity of this dawned on her. Thus began a bout of hysterical laughter that lasted well into the next twenty minutes.

The running was forever. Or maybe half an hour. Or maybe three hours. Just seemingly endless bouncing, and her body throbbing painfully with every jolt and bump. A ripping of already damaged

165

flesh further apart. A hell of sorts only without the novelty of lava.

When forever (or half an hour or three hours) ended, the dragon slowed, then stopped completely. He did not set Rynna down gently. He dropped her, then collapsed himself. Rynna hadn't noticed that he was only seven feet long and had been for their entire sprint. Guilt and a feeling of incompetence leaked into her.

"We should be safe for now," the dragon eventually gasped out. "The changelings that descended outside the gates of Lavanor doubled back so they should be colliding with the army presently." Genuine worry was evident in his eyes. "I apologize for hitting you, but it was necessary. You were panicking. How do you feel?"

The young woman hesitated.

"I don't know . . . ."

Indeed, Rynna's head was in a daze but it had nothing whatsoever to do with being struck by the dragon.

"Well, here. Drink this. It will make you better."

The dragon drew forth his forearm and placed a claw against the dull scar there. As he reopened the wound with a sharpened talon, drops of blood began to form.

Rynna hesitated. Her stomach made queasy leaps thinking about drinking the lifeblood. It was the same uneasiness she had felt after their trip across the sea, only now it was there tenfold.

But her own blood was still seeping from her at an alarming rate and she knew that the human body only had so much leeway when it came to losing vital bodily fluids in large amounts. She wasn't worried about dying, but spending three months in a coma healing was not how she wanted to be exposed to the changelings for the first time. She shuddered, but saw no other option. The woman placed her lips gently against the dragon's forearm, and began to suck.

The god had only been semi-conscious the first time she had experienced drinking dragon lifeblood. She could not remember taste and texture, only that panicking feeling of wanting to breathe. Now, however, she could feel the thick, cloying substances ooze down her throat. She could taste it, not iron tinged as her own blood was, but instead it had the bitter aftertaste of unsweetened chocolate.

The blood was a heady rush of sensation as well. From her ankles to her earlobes, Rynna felt a sweeping tingle that reminded her simultaneously of being rocked in her mother's arms as well as swimming against the current of a homicidal river. A refreshing, dangerous, familiar, and safe feeling all at once.

She had not appreciated the effects of the blood the first time either. The moment it touched her lips, her health improved. Not just in that flesh began to re-knit, but also on a more fundamental level. The ever-present travel ache of her legs dulled. The tight muscles in her back which were knotted with worry began to loosen. She felt for lack of any other word, all better.

Then it became something more. There was a second wave of the rushing feeling of fighting a losing battle in a river. A second wave of her mother cradling her to sleep. It was an intoxicating juxtaposition of sensations. A hot-cold-fast-slow-wonderful-terrible feeling. An entire galaxy of love, hate, and beauty lived and died behind her eyelids.

There was a growing awareness of all the atoms in her body. Every single tiny piece of her sang and winked and laughed wildly. An undeniable invincibility flowed into her. She could do anything right now. She could be anything, see anything, touch anything. And the Prince of Dusk. She could be, see, and touch that, too.

Rynna felt a rough claw gently push her away from the dragon's arm and, with a sudden gasp, she jerked her head back. Black liquid trickled from the corner of her mouth.

"Do you see now why we are valued for our blood, human?"

The young woman could only vaguely nod. She was aware distantly that her broken rib was whole and that the wound on her back was also healed. But only distantly aware. She was lost in a wash of her own central nervous system. Because something else was starting too. This though was familiar. This was remembered. This light feeling of freedom. This insane desire to laugh and point out to the dragon that he didn't have any ears.

She snickered.

Rynna struggled to control herself. Tried to make her eyes see straight and her mind think straight. But it was no use. The whole of her vision and mind was looking through an inverted mirror to a world of hues, sounds, and feelings that were just absolutely perplexing.

Rynna giggled again.

The dragon's smile was wry. "If only people wanted to heal themselves, I would be quite happy to make regular donations of blood to the free races. Unfortunately, your kind tends to find other uses for it. All the benefit of narcotics without the hassle of destroying your kidneys or liver. Just some nausea, tiredness, a headache, and some hunger to deal with afterwards. The normal intoxicants provide those as well, but they do not also have the added benefit of removing any dormant infections and aspiring cancers."

Rynna wasn't listening. She was arranging her facial features into what seemed normal. She was having trouble remembering what normal was, though. For instance, how did her nose usually sit on her face? Where did she put her lips? How open did she usually keep her eyes? Rynna tried several combinations of all three, attempting to get the right match.

The dragon chuckled. "You are dealing with this surprisingly well, human. Must be the god in you. Most other humans would be trying to walk vertically or else taste colour at this point. And that is only with a third of what you had. Although I should not be surprised. When I healed you after the cliff incident I gave you enough blood to have put anybody else into a bliss stupor for hours, and during that incident you even managed to be upright for a bit. Although I guess by the time you woke up most of the effects had worn off."

The dragon then let her be and began the process of smoothing out his wounds. With deft movement of his foreclaws, he reattached his shredded wings and pinched cuts closed. He was a

169

sculptor reshaping the death of his body to an effortless, scaled perfection. The young woman distantly thought his words sounded like butter.

"Back when I was young," the great beast continued, "it used to be common practice for royalty to spike the wine with lifeblood before conducting any diplomatic negotiations. I remember the entire city of Olan was traded for a lifetime supply of nalaberry pie."

The dragon chuckled again, before adding wistfully. "Of course, you probably do not even know what a nalaberry is. Delicious fruit. If you crossed a strawberry with a mango you would almost have it. It never grew wild; the Oceo Tolok cultivated it back when they were still allowed to make new forms of life.

"But then, some fool of a priest insisted that changelings needed nalaberries to reproduce. Then they were all burned. I remember the scent of the great fields blackening. Such a sad wind blew that day and all the air beasts mourned. But then, maybe you do not even know what a mango is, either. They cannot grow in this northern climate."

Rynna was again only partially aware of what the dragon was saying. She had rediscovered her tongue. It felt dead in her mouth. A great, useless mass. What if she were to swallow it? The young woman took precautions, naturally. She tilted her head forwards and opened her mouth, to let her tongue hang down. As long as she could see the thing, there was no way she would accidentally swallow it. This satisfied her immensely. Now . . . if only her head wasn't so terribly heavy. . . .

It was two hours before the effects wore off. And just as it had last time, it ended with a migraine and Rynna emptying her stomach contents, along with some hardened black balls onto the forest floor. And just like last time, the dragon scooped them up and secreted them about his person.

"What are they?" Rynna asked after she had rinsed her mouth with water repeatedly, trying to ignore the pain in her head.

"The waste of healing. Dead skin of surface flesh can fall off to be replaced by new underneath. The replaced flesh inside you collects in these small rocks that your body expels."

"Why are you keeping them?"

"They have other uses as well. But that is unimportant. What happened in the forest, human?"

"What happened to me . . ." and now it all came rushing back. "Yes, what did happen? The last thing I remember is you holding my hand in Lavanor and then suddenly I'm tripping in the middle of the forest, apparently being chased by most of the capital city."

"You do not remember?"

"Not a thing."

"Are you certain? Do you not remember the changelings attacking before we were able to escape, or the army searching for us? Then the roof and the blade in your rib?"

Rynna placed fingers against her side and tried to picture the weapon which had cut her. Vaguely she recalled being struck down but even as she tried to focus on the image, it seemed to pull away from her, disappearing in the confusion of running through the forest.

The dragon's head was still cocked and waiting for an answer.

"I sort of remember, it's just- it's all a blur. I'm sorry."

"Shock," the dragon's voice grumbled. "I have seen it before. There is no need to apologize. A mind can only take so much before it shuts down to protect itself. You have done well for one who is so young. I forget sometimes that humans are weak. Especially when I hang around ones such as you. I promise that tomorrow we will get captured by the changelings and it ends."

Rynna nodded wearily. Despite being completely healed, she was exhausted and nursing a headache from the lifeblood. She closed her eyes and tried to shake the discomfort.

"So . . . what do we do for tonight?"

The dragon blinked a few times before answering. A lone butterfly flitted out of the woods towards the dragon and he lazily crushed it, his movement almost too slow to outwit the small insect. A deep yawn cracked his huge maw before he finally answered.

"We sleep, human. And hope the battle wears itself out before it gets to us."

A gnawing hunger had begun to tear at Rynna's gut, but she knew that foraging for food was out of the question for now and so despite her exhaustion, sleep would be long in coming. How she had managed to pass out the last time she drank lifeblood was beyond her. She continued speaking, trying to ignore the pain of her stomach.

"And what if it doesn't wear itself out before it gets to us?"

"Then I, for one, plan to die well rested."

The dragon's closed his eyes completely and Rynna couldn't tell whether his rumbling words had been truth or humor. As if sensing her thoughts, the great beast lifted one eye half open, grinned sleepily at the god and said, "Relax, human. The air smells of blood and defeat. There was a lot of death and then everybody went home. Tonight was not a battle. It was a messy game of hide and come seek. We are safe. If anybody is going to catch up with us, it will not be those who wish to kill us. Our enemies have taken enough beatings and worrying for one day. They will retreat and sleep.

"Instead of focussing on the 'what if,' you should focus on the 'what will be.' You must prepare yourself, godling. The underbeings are a hard race. They will want a hard god. Being strong and confident will be the best way to get what you want accomplished. Remember, you *are* their god. Be sure to act like it."

The dragon quieted after that and soon Rynna could hear monstrous breaths of slumber. None for her though. She was hungry and her head hurt. She was also feeling worried and confused. For hours she stared at the stars and listened to the dragon sleep, thinking that things were far simpler when the biggest thing she had had to worry about was accidentally killing herself.

It was only when she had laid down beside the dragon and buried herself under the warmth of his wing that she realized to whom the dragon was referring when he had said 'enemies.'

CHAPTER 18
'HOW DO YOU DO'
AND OTHER WAYS OF
INTRODUCING YOURSELF

A light prick wrenched her from dreams only just attained, and her eyes opened to see a weapon. Then she screamed.

The knife pointed at her throat was not frightening because of its length or sharpness, although those two aspects did make her want to scream as well. Rather, it was the size of the underbeing holding the knife aimed at her that was really terrifying.

He was a large, human formed changeling. No, scratch that. He was a colossal, human formed changeling. His arms were as thick as the young woman's waist, and the rest of his body was proportioned evenly. He was a creature almost too big for words or descriptions, and the closest Rynna could think was that this creature is what a homicidal ironwood tree freed of its roots would look like.

She shouldn't have been afraid. After all, she was this creature's god. His long awaited leader. But it was difficult to get her head and body to corroborate on the issue. Because regardless of the assurance of another eight and a half decades of life yet to come, she could not stop herself from staring at the weapon and its wielder in complete terror.

Upon hearing Rynna's scream, the dragon woke. A dangerous anger seared through his blood and made his tail lash as he took in what was happening and saw the blade aimed at the god.

"Release her, underbeing!" the dragon snarled.

The large human shaped creature shot his hand out, snatched Rynna's arm, and then gripped it tightly.

"No."

"No? NO? Do you have any idea who I am?" The dragon's words were spiked. He let the individual letters sink into the air and they hung there, heavy and potent with threat.

But the changeling was unfazed.

"Darlan, you are fresh meat."

The dragon growled, and his already swollen throat began to swell further. Rynna, eyes still trained on the knifepoint, hoped that the dragon wasn't about to get her run through.

"Fine, underbeing. But do you know who she is?"

Those black eyes, so very certain of themselves, really looked at Rynna now. She felt the underbeing's inky stare work its way up the length of her body, drinking in every divot and angle of her. Suddenly, something flashed in the changeling's eyes but its meaning was lost to her.

"She is either nothing or else She is everything," he finally spoke through perfect teeth.

The dragon's growl increased tenfold and Rynna heard a clicking sound that meant his throat had already constricted. The young woman closed her eyes and hoped it would finish quickly.

But her eyes popped open with a gasp when the changeling squeezed Rynna's arm even more tightly and pulled her up into a constricting embrace. Now those massive arms were wrapped around her in a crushing bear hug. She struggled against those thuggish limbs but it was useless.

From her one good ear she could hear the dragon's roar of anger again.

"Release her!"

"No," he repeated.

As the dragon continued to growl in fury, the large underbeing shifted his footing. Rynna felt a warm breath in her left ear and lips graze her skin. Goosebumps ran along the back of her neck as the ironwood changeling spoke to her in a whisper.

"Please forgive me."

Then the creature gripped her head tightly with a massive hand, and in one slick motion, sunk its teeth into her neck, and ripped out her throat.

Wet, tearing sounds and teeth flashing red.

The world paused as there was a quiet of the worst sort. One of deep breaths being drawn and pulses slowing. One of immobility at the sight of a young woman falling to the ground, bleeding hot and red over everything. The changeling spit out the hunk of flesh, and in that terrible quiet a rough, gurgling sound was all that could be heard.

The underbeing fluidly moved his knife and positioned it directly above the stomach of the body now convulsing slightly on the forest floor. The hands holding the weapon were trembling. Tears could be seen on the changeling's cheeks. Bright and shiny, they reflected the morning light and made those large black eyes seem less monstrous than before. His voice was shaking.

"Don't move, Darlan. Or I split Her."

The dragon had already ripped open the scar on his forearm, ready to feed her lifeblood, but he froze now and real fear entered his heart for the first time in millenniums.

"Why?" he hissed.

The changeling still held the blade in its threatening place, but he was staring at the ground. He couldn't meet Rynna's eyes, which were wide with terror and pain, nor look at her empty throat, which was bubbling blood and making that sickening gurgle.

When he spoke, his words were quiet and sad.

"We have to know."

"Smell her! Smell her for Salvation's sake, and you have tasted her besides! And what about your damned blood tests? There are other ways than this, you stupid earth beast!"

"He acts on orders, Dealer."

This was a new voice. It was a confident voice that made the dragon reel and snarl once more. A fourth body had entered their clearing. Another human formed one. Reptilian eyes met black eyes.

"You. I killed you once, dreadpriest. I can do it again. How many forms do you have left? One? Two? No matter. I will kill them all."

The changeling raised an eyebrow to this, but did not say anything. Her face was passionless and unruffled by dragon vengeance. The underbeing did not break their eye contact quickly. Instead, the changeling let her eyes slide away slowly with a message of dismissal. The dragon lashed his tail and hissed.

"You will not-"

"Sh."

The dragon growled at being cut off, but then quieted when he heard it, too. That subtle silence.

The gurgling had stopped.

The great beast shifted his eyes towards his little human. The bleeding of Rynna's gaping throat had slowed to a trickle. She lay on the ground, relaxed and bedraggled. And too still. A blind woman, had she chanced by, would note only three pulses in that clearing, and wonder why those ones were all thumping so wildly.

"Warrior Mitah. Report back to the legions. We were mistaken."

The tree trunk changeling sheathed his knife and bowed. His eyes were red rimmed, but relief was sharp in his features. It was a happiness so complete that his salute was more of a fist pump than a proper acknowledgement of her orders.

"Yes, sir."

"Warleader Sika will want a full report. Tell him I will be bringing the dragon shortly."

The ironwood changeling looked at the great beast possessively. He grinned in anticipation of the blood.

The dragon did not notice. He was still fixated on Rynna's body. On the young woman he had been with for almost every second of every day during the last year. He had sunk his claws into the hard ground at his feet earlier, and now his clenched foreclaws were crushing his scales with broken earth.

The hulking changeling glanced casually towards the corpse before asking one last question of the dreadpriest.

"Shall I bring the body back to the legion for examination or should we just-"

The underbeing inhaled sharply. The dragon also paused in his breathing. Even the dreadpriest's eyes widened ever so slightly as they locked on the young woman.

"My, my, my."

Re-growing on the end of Rynna's foot were three new toes. They were budding toenail-less from the skin beside the two lonely appendages already present. The new toes were like small fleshy saplings, just nubs now, but distinctly transforming into something useful. Both a disgusting and wonderful thing to witness.

Her skin was changing too. Some of her scars began to melt from her features, leaving her face, if not perfect, much smoother than it had been before. And her throat. The three in the clearing could see cartilage, muscle, and skin bridging across the gap in her neck. Like blind snakes, the strips of flesh were slowly wriggling their way over the hole.

Then, with a deep boom of beginnings, the fourth heart started to beat again.

"To answer your question from earlier, Dealer . . ." the dreadpriest looked at Rynna the same way the massive changeling had looked at the dragon earlier. *Mine* was written all over her face. "The changelings never developed resin. This has always been our test."

Explosion of motion. The dragon's throat constricted, clicked, and a hail of razor spikes shot from his maw in two short bursts. With precise reflexes, the two changelings threw themselves to the ground and rolled away from the deadly hail.

179

In that single moment of distraction, the great earthwaterair beast leapt to Rynna's side, then crouched over her protectively as she continued to heal. The dragon's neck was four times its usual size and almost bursting with swollen anger. He growled threat and promise through his teeth as fog continued to pour from his nostrils.

"My, aren't we suspicious? Darlan, we will not hurt Her."

The dreadpriest's words were triumphant. She was walking slowly out from behind a tree with hands resting lightly on her hips. As for the oversized changeling, he had collapsed to the ground and was spewing out a series of incomprehensible sentences with his face buried in the dirt. The dragon shifted his eyes from one to the other slowly.

Briefly, the great beast glanced down at the young woman below him. She seemed to be sleeping peacefully. The only hint that anything was amiss was that she was maroon with blood. He reached a claw down and gently pushed her hair out of her face. The smooth, almost unmarred skin looked different than what he was used to. The dragon turned darkly to the black-eyed humans.

"You will die, underbeings."

"Maybe." It was the dreadpriest talking. "Maybe we will die. But that is for the Prince to decide, not you. And I don't suggest you destroy any more of my forms." The changeling shifted her eyes from the dragon to the young woman. "She needs me. I am not just any dreadpriest. I am the high dreadpriest."

180

Then the underbeing's breath caught as she understood what Warrior Mitah had realized earlier. The changeling's eyes narrowed in anger. "And maybe it is you who She will want killed, instead."

The dragon snarled, but made no other reply.

The high dreadpriest snapped her fingers.

"Warrior Mitah." The prostrate changeling did not stand at attention when called, but he did stop his incessant inaudible rant into the ground. "Report to the legions. Tell them to come. Tell them we have found Her. We have found the Prince of Dusk."

181

CHAPTER 19
INSIDE THE GATE

Just under a hundred and sixty thousand changelings were crammed in front of the Menundra. Almost the entire Warrior Clan. There were maybe two dozen underbeings patrolling beyond the Gate, another twenty doing reconnaissance and undercover work within the lands of the free races, and fifty working inside the fortress itself. The elderly and the infirm were absent, as were the cubs too little to walk and the expecting too large to waddle, but other than that, every changeling that could was waiting anxiously on the steps of the great building for their first glimpse of Her.

The god was deep in the bowels of the great fortress having Her hair styled and Her face makeuped. The dreadpriests were unveiling their god's beauty. Despite the sterility and efficiency of their own clothing, they were quite adept in the arts of enhancing physical attractiveness. Powders, dyes, and polishes were all blended into Her features to emphasize and soften.

Rynna remained silent during the whole process. Not only was it quite clear that she had no say in the matter, but she had no desire to speak either. The god would say she was overwhelmed, but even that would require the clarity of mind to identify and separate her churning emotions. Instead, she spent the time staring blankly at the mirror.

Everything had shifted. It was all changed, all gone. Like when her mother died, only without a mission to sustain her or a dragon to care for her or the luxury of being able to retreat from reality for months. Just starkness and the knowledge that she couldn't run away this time.

So the woman sat silently, painfully avoiding the last five hours of her life while letting the dreadpriests do their . . . what would it be? Their worst? Their best? She didn't know. Five hours had shifted her perspective on many things.

When she had first opened her eyes all those hours ago, her emotional state had been completely different. Namely, confusion had been the overriding feeling at the time. For, she had been very surrounded by flowers, and almost naked. She remembered it clearly.

When she woke up, the only thing she was wearing was a light dressing gown. Why they had taken her clothes momentarily confused her, but it paled in comparison to the incredulity of all the flowers in the room with her. On the bed, on the floor, on the tables, in vases, on their own, hanging in baskets. Tulips, daisies, pansies, violets, lilies, buttercups, snapdragons, marigolds, begonias, petunias, baby's breath, sunflowers. Blues, greens, yellows, pinks, reds, oranges, purples, whites, golds. Flowers everywhere. The smell was overwhelmingly pungent, like a gathering of greatmothers wearing their favourite stale perfumes, or worse, a group of young boys who had been allowed to wear musk for the first time.

Getting to the door meant she was part wading, part swimming the whole way through plants. The details of the room escaped her completely. There was not proper furniture, per se. There were furniture shaped bunches of flowers. She thought some of the bunches of flowers were wardrobed shaped and maybe there was one fireplace shaped bunch of flowers, but even then she couldn't be one hundred percent certain.

A terrifying amount of flora.

The flowers had thorns as often as not, and thick stalks resisted her traveling through them. Small cuts and scrapes began decorating her body, and she became increasingly aware of the vulnerability her thin dressing gown created. She cupped hands over her breasts to protect them and squeezed her legs together as best she could while still walking.

It was with relief that she finally kicked herself free of the last of the flowers and found herself outside the room in which she had awoken. The transition from the brightly filled bedchamber to the stark hallway was a bit jarring, like stepping into a lamp lit room in the middle of the night. She had to blink a few times before she completely adjusted and as such, did not immediately see the person squatting on the floor.

Rynna started when she did finally notice the woman waiting for her.

It was an elf. She smiled a wide grin in greeting, then wordlessly handed Rynna a robe which only after a moment's hesitations, the god snatched. She wrapped the extra layer around herself gratefully and gripped it tightly for support.

Clothing restored to some extent, Rynna carefully studied the elf in front of her. She wore simple, black leather. A sturdy longsword in its sheath was strapped to her side and a small dagger which had its own little sheath was strapped along her forearm. Her short, dark hair shone with health and was slicked back carefully so that not a single stray lock poked out anywhere. The shape of the elf's arms and legs spoke of strength, endurance, and agility. A fighter, evidently. Strange. She had never heard of elven women taking up weapons.

The elf's sharply pointed ears seemed taut as if catching the slightest sounds which surrounded them. But then again, they probably were doing just that. The strange woman had a black blindfold wrapped around her head, the thick material obliterating all sight. More strangeness.

Rynna tightened her grip on the robe around her and tried to sound as calm as she could.

"Who are you? Where am I? Where are my clothes?"

The elf smiled slowly. Rynna couldn't decide if it was friendly or threatening. The blindfold was off putting. Was it for Rynna's benefit, maybe a token of modesty, or for some other unfathomable reason? The elf's answer had a slight musical quality to it.

"My name is Seina."

Rynna was rendered completely stunned. The answer was simple enough but the sound of it . . . . She looked at the elf with a strange frown on her face.

"Wait, what? Say that again."

"Seina Nakao. My name is Seina Nakao."

Rynna heard it again. The words themselves she dismissed, but they were louder than she remembered words being. More significantly, the sound of the elf's voice was very . . . balanced, for lack of a better word. Rynna cupped her hands around her head in wonder as realization filtered through.

"My ear . . ." Rynna trailed off into silence and tilted her head down just slightly. The young god stood motionless, listening. There wasn't a lot of noise in the room with them, but even commonplace things are sublime when heard in surround sound for the first time in memory.

"I can- I can hear! Why can I hear?" Rynna stuck a finger experimentally in and out of her right ear, checking the sound shift as she blocked and unblocked it.

"You couldn't before?"

"Not out of my right ear. But now . . . ."

Rynna was touching the right side of her head in amazement. The woman smiled in response to Rynna's wonder.

"If I may suggest, You should look at Your feet."

"My feet?"

Rynna looked at the woman blankly for a few seconds before dropping her eyes downwards. It took her a while to realize what she was seeing peeking out from under the dressing gown and robe, but when it finally dawned on her, her whole being lit up in a bright explosion of happy surprise.

"Toes! I have toes again. I mean, I still don't have toenails, but still! Look- Wait, what's your name again?"

"Warrior Seina Nakao of the First Legion."

"Look, Seina! I have ten toes!" Rynna began an improvised dance of jubilation that involved a lot of

186

ridiculous un-godlike skipping. "Count them: ten whole toes! Wait until the dragon sees-"

She stopped. With all the flowers and spontaneous regeneration, she had completely disregarded well, everything else. But now it all snuck back into her thoughts like a lover who had conveniently forgotten to mention he had several venereal diseases. It was both surprising and extremely unpleasant. *Warrior* Seina Nakao.

"You are a changeling and I am captured here." Her demeanour changed completely. No longer happy and inclusive, she was back to the cold suspicion that her first question to the elf creature had contained. Rynna's fingers touched her neck. There was a pang of remembered hurt that throbbed faintly.

Rynna then recalled what the dragon had told her. Strong and confident. She was their god and she would do her best to take control as much as she could. The woman again asked the question she should have gotten an answer to first. Despite her efforts to seem cool and collected, the question sounded dark and wary.

"Where am I?"

The changeling Seina was unaffected by the sudden shift of Rynna's attitude. The blindfolded woman straightened from her crouch to stand at attention. She was a full six feet of toned, elven flesh, standing a head taller than the godling. Even knowing she was an underbeing, Rynna had to admit that the woman would be considered beautiful even by the miners, who preferred their women stocky and slightly bearded. Vague familiarity seemed to nudge at Rynna's mind, but she ignored it and instead tried to assess the room in which she stood for danger and more importantly, its exits.

Hearing Rynna's tenseness, Seina smiled, then bowed deeply to her god. It was a full bow from the waist that reached a painful ninety degrees. There she held herself for ten long seconds before the elven changeling finally straightened to speak.

"Welcome, Dusk Prince, to the Menundra."

"Inside the Gate . . . ."

If the changelings had been the boogeyman of her childhood, the Gate had been the darkness under her bed, the shadows in her closet, and the black threat of moonless nights all rolled into one. It was the citadel which housed the demons who devoured the light.

The Gate was five hundred feet of wall that spanned the only traversable pass in the Kral Mountains. Whispered stories spoke of the fire trenches that lay for thirty five feet in front of the Gate. Of the free race bodies rotting on spikes that lined the top. Of the sickening stench of dried death that permeated everything.

Only once had the battle been taken right to the Gate, itself. Only once had the changelings been pushed back that far. There were books written by soldiers who had survived. Books that were later burned by the priests because recruitment for the army had dropped to almost nothing after their circulation. But some scraps had been salvaged that in turn had been sung into horror stories not meant to delight and thrill, but to warn.

Above all, the Gate protected two vital things for the shapeshifting creatures: the Menundra, the citadel and primary staging point for the changelings' legions; and the Pit, the lands which stretched beyond the Gate. No human, elf, or dwarf had ever gone and returned alive enough to report details of what lay there. None had ever come back from the Pit: the clandestine lands of the underbeing empire.

"Yes, my Prince." The changeling's voice in front of Rynna was mild. "After You passed the test, we brought You here. You have been asleep for a week and a half now."

Passed the test . . . . Rynna touched her neck again and this time held her hand there protectively. Closed throat, new toes, and the ability to hear from both ears. Two and two made four in her head and her eyes widened slightly with the realization.

"It wasn't lifeblood that healed me." It was not a question, just a statement that needed to be spoken aloud so Rynna could hear it. Of course, lifeblood couldn't erase old scars or regrow toes already healed over. The changeling nodded once curtly.

"Where is the dragon?"

Seina's face darkened slightly at the mention of the winged beast. "In the throne room with the high dreadpriest."

"I want to see him."

The changeling nodded once more, but this time it was done carefully. "As you wish. The dreadpriests will be here shortly to help You dress."

"I don't need help dressing. I want to go now."

"Well, in that case, my Prince, can I help You get dressed? The gown is a little complicated."

"Gown? I don't need a gown. Why can't I wear what I had on when I came here?"

189

Seina frowned. "They were rags. You are the Dusk Prince." The woman stated the words as if the two sentences explained everything there was to know about etiquette and propriety.

"I don't care about being the Prince of Dusk! I want to find the dragon now. I'm not going to waste time looking pretty. I'll go in this dressing gown and robe if I have to."

The changeling bowed again, and this time she smiled. "I think I am going to like the next little bit. You are going to give the dreadpriests a fit." She straightened once more and crooked a finger at Rynna. "This way, my Prince. We will find the waterbreather."

The woman turned around with very precise movements. Then, she slowly strode from the room with the young god hurrying after.

As they walked, Rynna evaluated her situation. She just needed to get to the dragon. Once she was with the dragon, then she was going to be okay. Then they would . . . she tried to remember the plan that they had so thoroughly discussed. It was only then that she realized how inadequate it was. 'Get caught and then tell the changelings to stop the war,' was not exactly clear.

A nervous feeling settled in her stomach. She was not charismatic, eloquent, persuasive, or dominant in any way. The only actions she had ever inspired in people were the ones that ended up with her and her mother being evicted from their homes. Rynna could only hope the dragon would help her control the changelings.

The route they took was a twisted one through the corridors of the Menundra. It was a massive building, bigger than twenty homes put together, but it was not excessive. Unlike palaces that were sung into bard's tales, there was no grandeur here. It was a fortress. A place of war stripped of all personality. There were no flammable tapestries, no superfluous furniture that could be tripped over, no stained glass windows that could be shattered, no statues or vases that could fall. Stability and strength were what the designers of the massive building had had in mind, not comfort and aesthetics.

Despite wide corridors and high ceilings, the place seemed closed in and cloying. The air felt heavy, and it was difficult for Rynna to breathe properly. Rather than slipping through her bloodstream, oxygen dripped and seeped into her lungs with reluctance. She felt the essence of the changelings already beginning to bleed through the stone to grate against her skin. The exposure to it all was starting to make her feel ill.

Rynna knew that if the free races ever succeeded in burning the cursed place to the ground, even in a thousand years no vegetation would grow over the foundations of the Menundra's walls. During the millenniums that the Prince of Dusk's followers had claimed the fortress as their military base, brutality and death must have salted the earth in a barren and irreparable way.

They passed a few other people on their way. Rynna couldn't get a good look at them though because even before they came within sight, the changelings were standing at the same ninety-degree bow that Seina had given her, with their faces looking at their feet. They were clothed in the same leather as Seina, but beyond that, they could have been anybody, really. With heads bowed and eyes hidden, there was nothing to distinguish them from the beings they mimicked.

The god and the elven changeling passed the bowing underbeings without comment, but Rynna could not shake the undeniable feeling that the elf, human, and dwarf shaped creatures were a plague giving kudos to the rat that bore the flea that was their mission. They were vultures bowing to the prince of rot and maggots. Her.

She shuddered.

After they passed their fifth devote group, Rynna addressed herself to the warrior leading her in what she hoped was a clear and commanding way.

"How do they know I'm coming?" It was unnerving that they were bent over before they even saw her. She doubted that was how they spent their days. Although, Rynna reasoned, the path down which Seina took them could have easily been planned in advance.

When the changeling spoke, her voice continued to hold a musical quality.

"You have a distinctive scent that . . . travels."

Rynna remembered then what the dragon had said about her scent. "Do I smell terrible to your people?"

"On the contrary. You smell good."

Rynna felt a brief flash of disappointment, but she had no time for self-indulgent pity. She had to learn as much as she could about these people as quickly as she could. She tried to sound casual, as if speaking intimately with this changeling didn't turn her stomach.

"The dragon said I smelled terrible."

"Well, You probably would to a reptile. Especially one as decrepit as the beast You decided to keep company with. No, to a changeling You smell- Well, it is difficult to describe. It is like the smell of a freshly killed lamb. And it is like the smell of fur drying in the sun after swimming in a river. Or how a body smells after a battle. And it is more, too. You smell strong. Like an alpha."

"An alpha."

"Yes. It is intoxicating. I remember the first time I ever caught that scent." The changeling smiled in memory. "Potential and leadership are unmistakeable fragrances, my Prince. Very intimidating fragrances as well."

"They are bowing to me because I smell good?"

"Because you smell right. You also smell menacing. Like a large predator. Just as God always does."

"Can anybody smell it?"

"Not the free races, if that's what you're thinking. Their senses are underdeveloped. The dragons can smell it. Us changelings, of course. And the lesser earth, air, and water beasts, I believe. I doubt you ever owned domesticated wildlife, did you?"

As an ostracized human, a pet would have been an ideal solution to console a lonely child starving for affection and acceptance. But animals had always avoided her. She had thought that they too sensed the suicidal defect in her. As it turns out, she just scared the shit out of them aromatically. Something that the underbeings found attractive.

The young woman felt no better at the thought, but tried to keep her voice light.

"The dragon said I tasted like a god. That's why he first started traveling with me."

"Your taste . . . . One can only assume it would be similar to the smell. Probably more potent."

The changeling bit her lip, and the young god darkened at the implication.

"Well, you can ask the one who captured me. He took a bite out of my neck. I'm sure he's well acquainted with my taste."

The young woman had not meant to make the words an accusation, but now they hung awkwardly between them. Rynna didn't take it back, though. They had ripped out her throat, if they didn't feel regret, then they should feel something unpleasant. She was their god after all. It should be death to attack her, shouldn't it?

The bite in her words was effective. Upon hearing the tone, there was a visible change in the underbeing named Seina. She was tenser now, and her casual stride had mutated into more of a determined stalk. The silence lasted the rest of their trip through the Menundra.

Why there was a throne room was a mystery to Rynna. As far as she knew, there was no royalty among the changelings. Regardless, there they were.

The throne room was just as severe as the rest of the fortress, despite its grand name. The 'throne' itself was made of polished rich brown maple and was arguably the most embellished thing in the whole place. There were no jewels inset into the wood, nor was there any gold or silver chasing. Instead the chair had elaborate carvings that seemed to depict a windy day in still wood. Trees leaned while ribbons of wind curled around the legs and arms of the chair. Surprisingly, it looked comfortable.

The throne was on the far side of the room, raised on a dais about five steps off the ground. It was flanked on either side by two more chairs carved of the same rich wood, although these were less elaborately carved. Standing beside the chairs was a group of ten male and ten female underbeings, all dressed in black leather with silver stitching in intricate patterns around their collars. In the middle of this group was a human formed changeling wearing the same leathers, but her patterns were made of golden thread. Rynna wondered how many changelings were allowed the golden stitching, remembering the underbeing in Ta'ao.

On the right side of the room were twenty changelings of all different forms, all standing at attention. They wore the same black leather as Seina, the prostrate underbeings they had passed in the corridors, and the group of changelings at the front. These ones had no stitching around their collars, but there were gold stripes on their shoulders of varying number and width. Rank, she presumed.

On the left side of the room was the dragon, looking just the same as he always did, albeit a little surlier. Twelve feet of relief for Rynna. The situation was already more manageable by virtue of his presence. One ally isn't a lot when your opponent has all the weapons, but it is better than facing an entire species alone. The dragon was not restrained physically, but Rynna saw clearly the ring of changelings with arrows nocked and drawn circling the great beast. She could easily guess what tipped those arrows.

Rynna took a deep breath and readied herself to make this meeting go smoothly. She stared down the length of her plain cotton robe overtop the dressing gown she wore, and her brain quickly calculated the exact amount of fibres between her bare skin and the officials around her. The number was disquietingly low. She suddenly wished that she had let the dreadpriests dress her.

Her stomach began to clench and unclench spastically, and Rynna had the sinking suspicion that walking in completely under-prepared and underdressed had been a really, really bad idea. On the bright side, no surprise registered on the underbeings' faces that their god chose to come before them wearing a dressing gown with hair matted on one side from sleep, so maybe eccentricities were allowed.

Just then, the blindfolded changeling's voice rang out in the hall.

"Warrior Nakao of the First Legion makes formal request of High Dreadpriest Valar to approach the throne."

Rynna almost jumped at the loud words in her newly acquired eardrum. The decorum thundered through her head. She could tell the beginnings of an important ceremony when she heard one. Once again she regretted the gown, but as there was no changing it now, she tried to compose herself with the confidence advised by the dragon.

A voice answered Seina's request.

"Warrior Nakao, why do you wish to enter?"

Rynna frowned. That voice was the same one she remembered from the alleyway in Ta'ao. The changeling with the golden stitching on her collar was watching the god intently, her face betraying no emotion.

"I bring the one who has passed the test."

The same underbeing continued, her voice detached and cool. "Is there a witness to the test?"

"Yes."

There was a shift in the changelings surrounding the dragon as one of them lowered his weapon and then stepped forward towards the dais. He was a large changeling who moved hesitantly. A very, very large changeling, who, as it just so happened, Rynna recognized with startling clarity. Her hand protectively cupped her throat. She tried to swallow but there seemed to be a many-legged creature trying to climb its way out of her neck.

"I am the witness. Warrior Mitah of the Fourth Legion."

That voice matched the imprint that already existed in her mind. The words *fresh meat* constricted her chest. The air became thick and gluttonous. That little-legged creature seemed to be digging at the flesh inside her mouth frantically.

"Does the witness have substantiation?"

Rynna almost understood the large word. It was something . . . something she knew. She had heard it before. Only it was the dragon who had said it-

"Will the witness please submit it to the dreadpriests?"

197

The dragon produced a small cloth bag from about his person and poured the contents out onto his hand-

"Understood." The massive changeling began to reach into a small pack at his side. He reached into his small pack for the proof of-

Rynna closed her eyes and tried to quell the fear and heaving in her gut.

She had to be a strong and hard god.

She could do this.

The whole thing would be a lot easier though if people would stop publically displaying rotting bits of herself.

With that, the young woman opened her eyes and fixed them on the dragon for the rest of the ceremony. She thought that she should receive commendation for not puking all over the spotless floor as the mouldy remains of her neck were passed around and examined by the underbeings with the stitching on their collars and the ones with the golden bars on their sleeves.

It helped to keep looking at the dragon. Too bad she had never succeeded in her projection of thoughtspeech or she could have been strategizing with him then and there. Rynna wasn't sure why the dragon didn't try to contact her. He didn't even look at her, period. He kept his eyes warily on the human shaped creature with the golden stitching. Most of the other underbeings were looking at that changeling as well, with the exception of Warrior Mitah who was watching Rynna in a desponded manner, his eyes full of sadness.

More important things were said and more important things were done. At one point she was prodded to stand in front of the throne while the changelings intoned something that was probably an oath of fealty or some such. She wasn't quite sure because the fear had threatened to overwhelm her so badly at one point that she began determinedly singing the alphabet song to avoid thinking about what was happening.

As a result, she spent much of the ceremony with her eyes glazed over and a low hum buzzing from her throat. She wasn't sure what impression it gave of her, but she hoped her nausea was not the predominant thing she was emitting. She was okay with them thinking she was strange, but if they thought she was weak, that was an entirely different and terrifying matter.

Eventually the underbeings with bars on their sleeves filed out with a salute to the changelings at the front and that same sharp bow to her.

It was then that she realized the dragon had been released and that she was alone with him, the underbeings with stitching on their collars, and Seina. The great beast seemed even warier than before, despite the fact that all the lethorsum tipped weapons and his guards had been removed from the vicinity.

A small amount of pressure prompted her to look down where she noticed Seina held a knife pressed against her stomach. The changelings were all watching intently.

The dragon snarled loudly. Fog began seeping from his nostrils as he watched Seina's hand.

"Tell me, oh exalted underbeing, is this how you make a god pliable?" The dragon's deep voice rumbled like thunder echoing the lightening in the distance.

"My, my, my. You have it all wrong. This is not how we make a god pliable. This is how we make a dragon pliable. It is simple. If it so much as gets damp in here, Warrior Nakao will open the midsection of the Prince of Dusk."

The dragon hissed at the news and his eyes narrowed, but the fog petered out and he did nothing.

"Excuse me, the dragon doesn't need to be threatened. Neither do I. We're on your side." Rynna tried to sound outraged and important. She more or less succeeded. Seina at least had the decency to look upset at and embarrassed by what she was doing, and most of the other underbeings shifted back and forth in discomfort as well.

The golden collared changeling's lips pursed, but Rynna continued resolutely. "Now, you seem to be in charge at the moment, so I will begin by telling you how things are going to be run around here. As your Prince, the first thing-"

The human shaped creature cleared her throat as she cut off the god.

"Allow me to introduce myself. I am High Dreadpriest Erin Valar. Behind me are the lesser dreadpriests. I act as Grand Warleader for the Warrior Clan and am responsible for the deployment of our forces in the pursuit of accomplishing the holy mission given to us by the Prince of Dusk. We seek the eradication of the beings known as the free races and their god, the Lord of Salvation, for the betterment of this land and all living beings."

"Okay, that's nice. Good to meet you. Anyways, as I was saying, the first thing-"

"I'm sorry, Prince, but You will 'first thing' us nothing." High Dreadpriest Valar's words carried polite disrespect, but were still brimming with command. The dragon's neck began to constrict. "Right now You are the body of our god, but in essence You are not the being we have been worshipping and serving these last millenniums."

"You dare interrupt the Prince of Dusk?" the dragon growled. "I think it would be wise to listen to your god. You do not want her to find a more suitable high dreadpriest, do you?"

The young god tried once again to sound confident.

"Yes, like the dragon said. I'm your god. If I wanted to I could end your life right now and find a new-"

"No," the high dreadpriest continued, cutting Rynna off for the third time, "You couldn't. I'm sorry to disrupt any plans You have made, but You have already told us about Yourself. You not only left detailed scriptures for all the dreadpriests to read, but You also explained all about this incarnation to me through the Eye before You entered the flesh.

"I know You have no memories of your past life. No powers. You can't die, human, but that's all You are. A human who can't die. You are as much a god as the dragon here is. Less of a god. He can at least breathe water. You told us specifically to disregard anything this incarnation said and continue on with the mission as planned. You said You would be amenable and helpless."

Rynna's face paled. Her only trump card. She had been hoping the changelings wouldn't know she didn't have any powers or memories.

After hearing the high dreadpriest's words, Seina's mouth parted in shock. So, still a trump card of sorts. The other dreadpriests did not seem surprised but at least it was not common knowledge, if the blindfolded warrior's reaction was anything to go by.

The dragon's face darkened with threat. "Just because the Prince of Dusk has not chosen to display-"

"Display?" The high dreadpriest raised an eyebrow. "Usually a fully cognitive five year old makes its way towards the Gate and begins by explaining the entire history of the war and then ends by asking to have its throat ripped out by one of the warriors.

"That is a display. That is how You usually come to us. But now . . . Prince, You are fifteen and shaking in fear because You have been raised with free race prejudice." The high dreadpriest paused. She smiled a little sadly before continuing. "And then on top of everything, You travelled here with the dragon. How . . . mortal of You."

Rynna glanced at the dragon. He had a strange expression of uncertainty on his face. Her eyes flicked back to the golden collared changeling.

"Why does me being with the dragon make me 'mortal'?"

The high dreadpriest shook her head.

They will start lying. Ignore everything!

The words hissed in her head and she almost lost her balance with the burn. The words weren't their usual self-controlled, painful invasion. They wavered and shook through her mind. She gripped her head to regain focus and saw that the dragon's eyes were bloodshot.

"He wouldn't tell You, of course. Not until he absolutely had to. How cowardly of him. I'm sorry to be the one to reveal this to You, but we can't allow our god to be deceived any longer."

High Dreadpriest Valar looked directly into the god's hazel eyes with her black ones. Many things seem to blaze there. Anger. Sadness. Jealousy. She took a calming breath and began to explain.

"Darlan Lal. Dragon. Hero. He saved entire cities by himself. Using his blood, he resurrected hundreds already abandoned by healers. The last proof of nobility. A fierce warrior with a heart of ivory."

The changeling paused in her account to make sure Rynna was paying strict attention. She was. The dragon had never spoken much about his own past specifically. The god was drawn in to the engrossing feeling of veracity.

"But there is a prequel to the story that is often forgotten," the changeling continued. "Darlan is what he was called on the day he hatched. But we changelings have another name for him. We call him The Dealer."

"Underbeing, do not speak any further. The Prince of Dusk does not need a history lesson. This does not pertain-"

"Oh, but it does. It does because She trusts you, and likes you, snake. And I begrudge you my god's affection because you do not deserve it. You do not deserve something so wonderful, you who have committed the worst of sins."

The dragon was breathing heavily as he spoke.

"This human does not have to listen to-"

"Tell me, Prince," Valar's voice now contained cold anger. "Has the dragon told You anything of the decision the Brood Mother made? Of what Darlan did because of that decision? About the bargains?"

Rynna could not find words to answer with and could only shake her head in ignorance.

"Three thousand years ago when he was barely past his Breathforming, he was sent to both the Prince of Dusk and the Lord of Salvation separately. He proposed the Brood Mother's deal. Blood for blood. Their end of the bargain had two parts. First, he gave each god a sample of the brood's heartblood. Can you guess what they needed it for? Do You know Your history well enough to know what happened three thousand years ago? The world rending things that happened at that time?"

Rynna's eyes widened and she inhaled sharply.

"Yes, You see it now. Three thousand years ago, when the Prince of Dusk only had humans, elves, and dwarves in his armies. When lethorsum didn't exist. So he gave a gift to each of the gods. Helped them each develop a weapon with the brood's essence. Then for the second part of the bargain, he promised each god that he would aid and escort them on their twentieth rebirth, the one where the gods knew that they would both be born without memories or powers and have to find their followers without foreknowledge to guide them.

"And both gods, ignorant of the deal Darlan had made with the second god, agreed."

The dreadpriest paused.

"Do You want to know what the dragons got in return?"

High Dreadpriest Valar waited. Rynna neither nodded nor shook her head. She was motionless with a dull feeling in her gut.

"Blood for blood. So the dragons were given god's blood. Or rather, the promise of god's blood once their end of the deal had been completely fulfilled. God's blood to mix with the dragons' to strengthen the brood."

Rynna frowned and did not understand the implication. She could not make the connection. But truth be told, she wasn't trying that hard. The god didn't want to know as badly as the dragon didn't want her to know. She missed the convenience of being deaf in one ear and the hard of hearing that went with it. She listened to the changeling continue speaking with a wet, thumping heart.

"Did You know that dragons are the only species that can cross-breed with that of another?"

Two and two made four again. Rynna brought a hand to her stomach.

"No. It's ... not ...."

Warrior Nakao spoke now. The changeling's voice was gentle. A soldier speaking to a small child who had witnessed its village's razing. The sensitive tones of recognized trauma. The lesser dreadpriests all wore expressions of sadness for their god as the warrior explained.

"Dragons reproduce consciously. They cannot create a child unless they purposefully want one.

205

There are no unwanted or accidental births among his kind. And they are not restricted by conventional means. Dragons can exchange any fluids to induce pregnancy if they so desire. They don't need to be the ones the rest of us rely on."

"It can't . . . ."

"When was the last time You menstruated?"

"I've been sick. I wasn't eating. There was so much walking. My courses have always stopped during times of stress and it's been a long year and . . . . I can't be pregnant."

The high dreadpriest turned towards the dragon in fury while Seina patted Rynna's head in what was supposed to be a comforting way.

"When was it, Darlan? Was it a stolen kiss while She was asleep? No, that would require you to actually bring your maw to touch Hers willingly. Or maybe . . . . Oh, please tell me. Oh, it would be too rich. Was it lifeblood? Did you tell Her you were healing Her? That you were worried She couldn't heal on her own? How badly did you have to hurt Her first to make Her think lifeblood was even necessary? How did you get Her to forgive you that damage?

"Wasn't She suspicious that you adamantly took care of Her, a human, one of the free races that you claim to have no part in? Wasn't She suspicious that you did not take Her to see any of the priests scouring the countryside for their god? Wasn't She suspicious that a two month long journey to Lavanor took almost a year? What could you have possibly told Her to justify your interest in Her and this war at all?"

She turned her attentions delicately back to Rynna.

"Make no mistake, Prince. Darlan knew from the beginning what he wanted. He never worried for You, only his offspring. Yes, dragons are quite the species, aren't they? Well, we can't fault him his word, he did fulfill his end of the bargain. The changelings were created and now he has brought us our god. That's all we wanted. Pity the free races found theirs as well without his help. And now Darlan will have what he wanted in . . . what, another five months now? Ten? I don't know what the gestation period for a snake is."

The high dreadpriest turned back towards the dragon once more.

"No, you didn't care if She was the Lord of Salvation or the Prince of Dusk. A god is a god and you had all your bases covered. Well, by all means. When the whelp is born, it's yours. As per our agreement. Unless that is, my god has anything to say about it. I must defer to Her, of course.

"Please, tell me, Prince. Do You wish to be a mother? I don't expect You planned this, and we have this wonderful midwife who has put lethorsum to a good use for the female warriors who do not wish to miss an upcoming battle. And it would be quite fitting. Both lethorsum and this child were created by Your dragon friend. One could easily solve the problem of the other.

"As it is, You are not bearing a mammal. You will show no signs of regular pregnancy, just as You haven't yet to this point. Your breasts will yield no milk, and Your womb will have no contractions when the time is at hand. The egg is nothing so

207

much as a tumour in Your uterus. A parasite that has been using You for a year. One which can be easily cleansed."

The dragon snarled and fog began to leak from his nostrils. His claws were trembling, though. There was desperation underlining his usually powerful stance.

Rynna was frozen, and her arms had clenched around her stomach violently. It was even worse though, because something else had occurred to the god among all of these terrible revelations.

"Dragon," she said, her voice shaking. "Is what she says true?"

The dragon could have denied it. Denied it all. But the incontrovertible proof of a hatchling was going to be forthcoming soon. When the word came, it was with a harsh and reluctant breath.

"Yes."

Rynna closed her eyes. Her arms were trembling with an emotion that was either anger, outrage, sadness, disappointment, or a horrible combination of them all. When she opened her eyes, the mess of emotion had culminated into one question. The 'worse' of Rynna's thoughts.

"Did you let my mother die?"

The question bounced off of every surface with a promise of violence. It was accompanied by the heavy breathing of a terrified and devastated fifteen year old human. The dragon took a deep, laboured breath, which sounded suspiciously like plans collapsing.

And amongst the echoing question and the vicious silence that followed came the condemnation.

"Yes."

CHAPTER 20
THE LEFTOVER SCARS

Rynna saw herself in the mirror and barely recognized the reflection. The dreadpriests were all smiling in satisfaction, wolfish teeth peeking through everywhere. Even Rynna was impressed through the layers of her frothing emotions. She was pretty. It was a prettiness that leaned a bit on the night lady side of things, but still, nicer than she'd ever seen herself before.

The young woman was wearing an exquisite silk dress that was a bright green. The stitching was elaborate and the material probably cost more than Dompt made in a year from selling sheep. It was fit for a princess or a queen. Rynna's hair, usually matted and greasy, was now clean and styled into ringlets that fell across her shoulders in beautiful symmetry. Her eyes had been lined in brown makeup to make them large. And her lips. They looked soft, pouty, and very feminine. Even when her mother had dressed up, she had never seemed so grand.

Rynna touched her face just above her right eyebrow. The skin was completely smooth. Her fingers traced and retraced the spot where previously there had been damaged and puckered skin. Other scars were missing as well, but the one above her eyebrow had always been particularly obscene, and now it was completely gone. She presumed it had disappeared the same time she had regained her toes and her hearing. When she had healed herself.

She reached back and touched a spot just below her hairline where she knew another scar had been. Her fingers brushed ruined skin. Where the scar still was.

Her thoughts were interrupted by one of the dreadpriests.

"You are beautiful, my Prince. The warriors will love You."

Rynna gave them an indifferent shrug and the three dreadpriests glowed under the bare acknowledgement of their work. The ego stroking of the Warrior Clan was the least of her concerns. Simply maintaining her sanity was more important. And right now it took everything she had to keep herself from hysteria.

Even though the dreadpriests had finished with their work, she could still feel their fingers where they had touched her. Like a greasy layer of violence to taint her humanity. But then, the dragon had already altered her.

After the horrible truth had been revealed in the throne room, after she had asked the high dreadpriest to get rid of the waterbreather, after the dragon had been dragged away by warriors called in from the corridor, after she had heard the dragon scream those desperate, pleading words through her mind, *You cannot kill the hatchling, human! Let it live!*

After all of that, Seina, the blindfolded changeling whom Rynna could almost pretend was a real elf, had gently guided her back to her bedroom to explain a few things.

"Soon will be the formal presentation of the Prince of Dusk to the changelings. After, You can rest. For now, the dreadpriests want to dress You so that the legions can know how beautiful You are. This time I can't keep them back short of killing them. Did You want me to kill them for You?"

The question had been asked so nonchalantly that Rynna almost didn't notice it. She managed to shake her head in a distant way.

Seina shrugged. "Of course. The offer always stands, however. Is there anything I can get for You in the meantime?"

"No . . . just, leave please."

The blind warrior nodded and bowed deeply.

When the underbeing turned to leave, Rynna said one last thing quietly.

"Seina, I'm pregnant."

"I know, my Prince."

"What am I going to do?"

The changeling's voice was burnt and sticky as if her teeth glowed hot as the words slipped through them. "Abort it or keep it, and either way, have the dragon's veins ripped out one by one and then fed to him."

Hours later, the young god was looking at the beautiful creature in the mirror whom Rynna did not recognize at all. The creature whose only friend had let her mother die. She touched her stomach again.

The dreadpriests who had dressed her led her through a series of stark corridors and stairways, and finally they ended in a room where Seina, Warrior Mitah, and the high dreadpriest were waiting to begin her formal presentation to the Warrior Clan.

"Ready, Dusk Prince?" Seina asked. The blindfolded changeling had burst into a wide smile upon sensing the young god's presence.

Rynna just stared blankly. Seina continued speaking.

"Here is Your knife, and the balcony is just through those doors. All You have to do is acknowledge Your warriors and then kill Warrior Mitah. Mitah, the human is your last form, correct?"

"Yes, Warrior Nakao."

A knife hilt was placed into Rynna's palm. She did not close her fingers around it, and instead dropped her hand away. The blade clattered to the floor.

The high dreadpriest's eyes slid slowly from the blade on the floor to the upset and confused young woman. When Valar spoke, her words were cool.

"Every time our god has walked in the flesh, He has killed the warrior who tasted His blood. This is not something optional. It is a sin which means death to hurt or taste You."

Hadn't she had that same thought earlier? The young woman closed her eyes and breathed deeply before opening them again. Warrior Mitah had ripped out her throat and he was a monster, but the problem was he wasn't being a monster now. He wasn't attacking her or hurting anybody nearby. He was just standing there quietly, looking at her with those same sad eyes from earlier.

"Please, my Prince. I am the witness. I tasted You. It would be sacrilege for me not to die. Hurting You is a sin. Tasting You- please, my Prince. You must kill me."

She shook her beautifully makeuped head and managed to get out some words.

"I . . . can't."

Seina and Warrior Mitah exchanged confused looks. The high dreadpriest merely asked, "And why ever not?"

She shook her head again, trying to figure out how to explain.

"I don't know."

The high dreadpriest look unimpressed. Rynna flinched at the expression on the woman's face and tried to look away, but High Dreadpriest Valar reached out, grabbed her wrist, and forced the god to face her.

"Until this past week, did You not consider the changelings evil?"

Rynna said nothing. The skin under the dreadpriest's fingers was hurting.

"And You hate us. We disgust You, and violate everything You hold dear."

Rynna stared at the high dreadpriest and finally mumbled her assent. The god could see the disappointment in Seina's deflated shoulders upon hearing this. Warrior Mitah also seemed crestfallen and the other dreadpriests were looking at their boots.

"Do You remember Ta'ao? Remember the killing that happened there? Do You think that the changelings responsible for that slaughter would deserve death?"

Rynna tried to tug herself out of the high dreadpriest's grip. Her arm was pale with pressure and lack of circulation.

"Warrior Mitah killed . . . how many did you say it was?"

"Thirty two, sir."

"Thirty two. This single changeling killed thirty two 'innocent' humans, elves, and dwarves in Ta'ao. Tell me, Warrior Mitah, how did those deaths make you feel?"

"Inadequate. I should have killed more."

High Dreadpriest Valar turned her full attention to Rynna once more. The god could see herself in the underbeing's dark orbs. Her reflection in them looked scared. The high dreadpriest let go of her with a suddenness that left her wrist aching.

"This is an important tradition for our kind. It also coincides with Your beliefs. There is no reason to resist. So, what is the problem?"

Warrior Mitah perked up and added, as if clinching the argument, "I would be honoured to be Your first kill, if that is why You hold back."

Rynna stared blankly at Warrior Mitah's open and friendly face. Happy, willing, and honoured. And not to mention a deadly, abhorrent monster.

Seina crouched down to pick up the fallen blade. She once more put it into Rynna's hands, only this time she closed the god's fingers around it.

"Don't worry. It's easy. Everybody is a little nervous their first time."

Rynna stared at the blade. Too much had happened since she had woken up. The handle in her hand felt heavy and awkward. Her body felt heavy and awkward, too. The dress had too much material and her head felt weighed down by pins. She thought about kneading dough with her mother and laughing because it was always too crumbly no matter how she worked at hers. She thought about sneaking cheese and bread to a lonely hag by the lake.

She was half guided, half pushed towards the balcony. Rynna did not resist, and truthfully, didn't even really understand what was happening until she heard the cacophony of welcome as the changelings saw their god for the first time.

The cheer started immediately. A rushing onslaught of sound that began the moment the underbeings got a good long look at Her. It was obscene. The noise was the crash of trees falling, of pots and pans banging together, of angry bees screaming, and of deer stampeding through the underbrush. It was part howl, part laughter, part roar of pride, and all noise. From every throat sang out welcoming and joy.

From where Rynna stood, the god could only see an endless blanket of black-leathered bodies. The height made her dizzy and the air was too hot.

Suddenly, there was breath on her neck. A mouth near her shoulder and a body inhaling deeply of her scent.

"I liked it, You know." The voice was no longer willing, no longer happy, no longer honoured. It was heavy with conceit and sinister in pitch. "I liked biting You. And Your blood. I liked that too." The body inhaled once more. "Do You want me to describe how You tasted?"

Rynna closed her eyes and shuddered, but said nothing.

"No? How about children, would You like me to describe how delectable elven infants are?"

She could not-

216

"They are plump and so juicy. The meat is one of the most tender. Falls apart in your mouth. And when you first rip your teeth into them, the way the blood drips everywhere is . . . mmm divine."

Rynna swallowed. Her throat was dry.

"Please, just be quiet. I can't-"

"So juicy, but nothing compares to human children in terms of taste. Especially if you can get them within a week or two of being born. Did You know that if an underbeing eats the intestines of four human infants every year then they will never die? Of course, it is just cub tales but still, fun to try. One year, I managed to eat three and a half. Half of course because the mother held the other end of her child as I ripped it in half with my teeth and ran off with-"

"Shut up."

Rynna could see the crying mother in her mind vividly. The terror and sadness pained her thoughts.

"Oh, no, Prince. How can I stop? How can I stop when Your kind are so wonderful to kill? Ta'ao was the single greatest moment of my life. There was this old man whose arms I severed and he just made the funniest noise when he bled . . . screamed like a foal being hamstrung . . . made me want to do it again and again and-"

"Shut up, shut up, SHUT UP!"

Three inches of blade in the changeling's chest, piercing his body, going through the skin like putty. Was that her hand holding the handle? So soft, so biddable that flesh was. So welcoming to the metal. Glorious rushing red running down the length of the blade and twining through her fingers. Her gown

217

was ruined. Absolutely ruined and after the dreadpriests has spent so much-

Rynna was breathing hard and her head was spinning.

No, no, no, no, no, no, no-

"My name . . ." the changeling's voice was strained when he spoke his last words. "My name is Eli. Eli Mitah. I am so, so very sorry for hurting You."

Then the tree trunk changeling took a step back and fell backwards off the edge of the balcony.

When he hit the ground he was torn apart by the crowds below. Every changeling within reach was desperately ripping at the body, just trying to get a bite of the underbeing who had tasted their Prince. One by one, the pieces of his flesh were torn off and shoved greedily into mouths. Even bones were crunched between strong teeth. A matter of a few minutes and all there was left of Warrior Mitah was the blood still hot on lips and that which had ruined her dress.

From behind, she heard the approach of bodies. Seina clapped her hands together.

"Well done, my Prince! You're a natural."

The high dreadpriest likewise came forward. She did not cheer the god. Instead, Valar simply said, "Welcome to the Warrior Clan."

CHAPTER 21
WOLF'S CLOTHING

Rynna didn't remember being escorted to her room after her official introduction to the changelings was over. She was too tired. Her emotions had consumed her, while the dull implication of everything had drained her. It was a bursting empty feeling. It did not take her long to fall asleep. There was no lazy gradual progress towards unconsciousness. Her transition from awake to dreaming was a sudden and immediate change born of exhaustion.

Her dreams were of blood running through her fingertips and the tangy metallic taste of red on her tongue. She shuddered awake and dropped back into sleep many times that evening. Gold stitching, a hatchling egg, rotting flesh, and always more blood. Human blood, elf blood, dwarf blood, changeling blood. Rivers of wet, sticky blood.

When she did open her eyes with full awareness it was early morning. Lying alone on her huge bed, the god willed existence to alter or at least for her senses to shut down a little. She touched her stomach where the egg was. Could it even be called pregnancy? Turtles buried their clutches of eggs and let the earth incubate their young until they were ready to hatch. Chickens did not give birth, they laid their eggs, then sat on them in nests.

Whatever it was called, there was life growing in her now. Pregnant or gestating or incubating, she would have offspring that shared her blood.

Rynna closed her eyes but could not sleep again. The smell around her was too distracting. The blossoms and bouquets from the previous day were just as opulent, just as obnoxious as the previous day, only now they had begun to wilt the unstoppable death march of cut flowers. The beautiful scents undercut with oncoming rot. The gift of the Warrior Clan to a sentimental god.

It was with this that Rynna began her first official day as the devil. This time, it was not Seina waiting in her sitting room. It was the high dreadpriest. She was slowly eating breakfast at a small table. There was a second chair across from her and a no nonsense expression on the underbeing's face.

The god sank into the seat and mechanically picked up a fork near the plate in front of her. She wasn't hungry. The girl god was still overwhelmed, which combined unpleasantly with her kinked hair and groggy sleep eyes. How could she do something as simple as eat breakfast when yesterday she had killed someone, been betrayed by her only friend and, oh yes, also happened to discover an egg was being kept warm by her flesh?

She tried to clear her head. She tried to face High Dreadpriest Valar with as much of a commanding presence as possible. She failed miserably at both of these things and instead, the god ended up gripping her fork like a weapon rather than an eating tool.

"Good morning, Prince," Valar greeted her curtly. "We will discuss Your duties and schedule for today. Beginning tomorrow, lesser dreadpriests will go through this with You, but today You get the pleasure of my company.

"You will visit Warleader Sika's legion, then Warleader Dober's legion, and finally Warleader Kent's legion. Bless them, but do not take too much time because You must finish all three if we are to stay on schedule. Then tomorrow You will proceed with the next three, until the entire Warrior Clan has been able to meet you personally and receive Your blessing. Afterwards, You will visit the nurseries and bless the expecting and the cubs. Then the ill and infirm. Finally, the elderly. Once every warrior has been seen to, You will begin again."

She ticked off the items on her fingers as she spoke. A mental checklist and a to do item scratched off of it.

"That's all well and good," Rynna tried to sound as controlled as possible, while still maintaining her vice grip on the fork in her hand, "but when do we begin preparations for the invasion? Will I be meeting with the war planners before or after the blessings take place?"

High Dreadpriest Valar looked at her stonily.

"We covered that yesterday and the discussion is not to be reopened. Anyways, continuing on, each morning You will allow yourself to be dressed by the dreadpriests so that You are appropriately attired. The Prince must always look dignified. Likewise Your-"

"The war, High Dreadpriest. What's happening? Tell me now," once again she tried to imbue her voice with command.

221

High Dreadpriest Valar sighed and closed her eyes for a moment. Then she opened them and met her god's eyes squarely.

"Tell me, Prince . . . . Did Your memories suddenly pop back into Your head?"

Rynna stared at the other woman, then reluctantly shook her head.

"In the night did You remember any of your miraculous powers other than healing Yourself? Do You have any type of working knowledge about weaponry, battles, or death?"

"Well, no, but-"

"Then, Prince, Your tactical usefulness goes as far as slitting the throat of the Lord of Salvation should we get our hands on him. Until then, I respectfully ask You to keep quiet, look pretty, and leave the war to us."

"I'm your god. I am the Prince of Dusk. I lead this war and don't think you can tell me-"

"We're not ending the war," the high dreadpriest's eyes saw deep into her mind, plucked out what she found there, and then cast it aside. "We are not stopping our mission. Please keep in mind that You have already warned us about this body's intentions. Why would I give leadership of the Warrior Clan to a free race youth bent on seeing us destroyed based on the lies of Her childhood? A free race youth bent on seeing the humans, elves, and dwarves succeed in this war? Isn't it a little odd that the Prince of Dusk still utters prayers in Her sleep to the Lord of Salvation? How could we let somebody like that start making all of the decisions for our entire way of life?"

She continued sadly. "Please, human. If You want to think us evil, go ahead, but don't make the mistake of thinking we are naive. Being wrong on two accounts is just embarrassing. Until I know without a doubt that You really are the Prince of Dusk in heart and mind, as well as body, You will know nothing of what the Warrior Clan plans or does.

"Killing Warrior Mitah sealed us to You, but nothing You have shown me seals You to us. Eventually You will learn and maybe even remember why we do what we do and who the true evil in this world is. But until then, You will stay on the pedestal where we put You and You will play nicely. Either that or You will spend Your hours in voluntary seclusion. The choice is Yours, Prince."

Rynna looked back at the high dreadpriest dully. She wanted to laugh. Or maybe cry. The dragon's assurances that she would be in control of half the war rang hollowly in her mind. But then, she guessed he would have said or done anything to stay with her. She wondered how many lies she had been swallowing over the past year. Why hadn't she been suspicious of all those things High Dreadpriest Valar had mentioned yesterday? Maybe the lies she had been swallowing had been her own. She finally let go of the fork and set it down quietly on the table.

"So what am I supposed to do?"

The high dreadpriest watched the young woman carefully. She licked her top lip, then closed her black eyes as if she was loath to say the next part. When she finally opened them again, her face was clenched between two conflicting emotions.

223

Which two these were, Rynna was unsure, but the contrast of the two caused deep creases to form in the middle of the high dreadpriest's forehead.

"The changelings . . . we . . . love . . . You," she finally sighed. "The warriors have always loved You. We know how worship is among the free races. Lip service at the temples and some coppers tossed to the poor. Some people are devout, but for the most part, they only do what they absolutely must and then get on with their day.

"For us, we have no temples or places of worship because worship happens every second of every day within ourselves. Even me. I have no real respect for You with the free race mentality that You have, but Your essence still calls to me. I scorn who You are but cannot stop myself from loving *what* You are. We have always needed the Prince. Not as a leader, but as a being who loves us unconditionally, whom we can love in return.

"So that is what You are to do. We love You and You are to love us back. And You will love us back."

The last part hit Rynna particularly hard and the young woman swallowed deeply. She swallowed air and her retort and the threat all in one go. It was a big mouthful which stuck in her throat on the way down.

The situation was quite clear to her. Rynna knew she would never be allowed to leave the Menundra. And unless she could somehow convince this woman that she truly was the Prince of Dusk, she would never be anything more than a glorified mascot. The gilded bars surrounding her were cold, jagged, and shiny.

The conversation more or less ended there. The high dreadpriest continued eating, and the god continued not eating. Ten minutes later with a bow, High Dreadpriest Valar was replaced by lesser dreadpriests who, as they had the previous day, painstakingly washed, dressed, and dolled her up, clucking amongst themselves the whole time. It wasn't the pleasant clucking of mother hens, it was more like the dry clucking sound a tarantula's pincers make when they rub up against one another. A dry, hissing, but nevertheless, pleased sound.

An hour of rich oils and thick powders. More layers of cloth that she usually wore in a year, a hairstyle that could be used as a weapon, and slippers made of silk. The god shook her head at the sculpture she saw in the mirror, touched her flat stomach briefly, and mentally braced herself.

Warleader Sika's legion did not react when she arrived, but you could feel the excitement as a palpable thing in the air. It bristled and pushed against training, and was only just restrained. The warriors were standing in formation just outside the Menundra. Two underbeings stood in front of the rest: Warleader Sika and the battleleader whose name the god did not yet know.

A drawbridge had been lowered so that Rynna could pass the trench that was filled to an indeterminable depth with dark oil. The young woman crossed it flanked by two dreadpriests who sported possessive faces, daring the changelings of this legion to be disrespectful to their Prince.

Rynna stepped uncertainly down from the bridge onto the hard ground. It looked burned and ruined for miles in every direction. Crunching under

225

her unsteady feet was flat earth that could hide nothing. An empty land kept pacified for strategic reasons. Among all the sterility she felt like a garish trinket in her ridiculous getup.

There was silence when she looked out at the changelings. None met her eyes, and instead they stared straight ahead at some point behind her. The young woman was unsure of what to do. She was supposed to bless them, the high dreadpriest had said. Love us, Valar had commanded. She tried to remember what the priests had said the few times she and her mother had received blessings.

May the Lord of Salvation shine His everlasting light on you.

Those words had been wonderful at the time. She had been able to feel the Lord's love flowing into her through the old priest's calloused hands. Rynna tried to remind herself that this is what she was to these creatures. The bringer of happiness and love.

But, what was she supposed to say . . . 'I, Rynna, shine My everlasting light on you?' Ridiculous. Sacrilegious. She would feel like she was playing make believe. Even in her mind, it sounded insincere and hollow. If vocalized, the words would only depreciate further.

Rynna wished she had been given a script or something. If she was going to be a puppet anyways, at least they could have made her a decently prepared puppet. Disgust at the whole situation rose up. She wanted to be elsewhere. Someplace where she could contemplate the enormity of all that had happened to her recently.

There was nothing she could do though but trudge on. Voluntary seclusion was not an appealing option for her. There would be no hope at all if it came to that. Hope of what, she was not quite sure, but hope of anything was better than endless days locked in a room with rotting flowers.

So, the god swallowed, raised her right hand, and waved.

"Hey," she greeted them.

Some of the changelings struggled with their faces and a few broke out in grins at the sight of her uncertain greeting, but nobody moved and there was more silence. Rynna was relieved when she heard the clear, commanding voice of a dreadpriest behind her.

"The First Legion will show their respect to the Prince of Dusk."

Seina's Legion. Rynna wondered if she was somewhere among the thousands of changelings present. Warleader Sika barked a command, and then the underbeings bowed deeply. It was the same painful, ninety-degree bow that everyone had been giving her recently. After they straightened, the god was once more presented with the awfulness that is uncertainty of action and a stretching silence full of expectation.

One of the dreadpriests eventually spoke.

"Prince, You may now give them a blessing which You feel best suits the situation. Or if their greeting displeased You, we may leave now."

Rynna almost jumped at the voice in her ear. The dreadpriest's eyes were hot with fervour, and his tone said that he thought something had been flawed about the impossibly deep bows, and that no changeling deserved Rynna's blessing except maybe the dreadpriest himself, and even that was only a maybe. Rynna didn't know how to react to what she heard in the voice. She thought the dreadpriests knew the truth about her. Weren't they supposed to be resenting her free race upbringing like High Dreadpriest Valar did?

The girl god just waved the dreadpriest's offer away. If she deemed this group inadequate, Valar would probably reprimand her later. It would be best to just get it over with. She coughed to clear her throat and then spoke as loudly as she could to the underbeings in front of her.

"Good job, everybody. Keep up the good work and kill those . . . ." Those what? Evil humans, elves and dwarves? Mosquitos?

"Well, kill the enemy for us."

It would have to be good enough for now. The whole process still felt incomplete though, and the underbeings continued to look at her expectantly. So, because she couldn't think of anything else to do, she loudly kissed her palm and blew one of the most exaggerated kisses of her life out to the warriors of the First Legion.

There, she thought wearily. A blown kiss. That ought to do for a blessing.

Pandemonium ensued.

The changeling that was closest to her leapt into the air, reached out, extended a hand, and closed it around empty air, only to be tackled from behind by four separate underbeings. Behind those four rushed the thousands of others who were apparently all after the same thing. It took exactly five and a half seconds for the entire legion to devolve into a giant brawl. No weapons were used but even from her vantage point, Rynna could see teeth fly, necks wrenched at wrong angles, and bones shatter. Fingers were snapped off of hands, and lips were torn from faces. It was a violence that consisted of a lot of grabbing and a frenzied search.

Rynna was shocked. "What's happening?"

The two dreadpriests looked at her curiously. The male one spoke, "Well, Prince. You chose to bequeath upon them one blessing. They fight for the honour of it."

"They're fighting for the kiss? That's just an imaginary- They're killing each other!"

"But You only blew one blessing from Your hand. I don't understand why this situation confuses You so."

The god's eyes widened in disbelief as she turned back to the First Legion. Bodies had begun to litter the ground. Some of them were sloppily shaking flesh into a new form, but others remained still. She had just ended the lives of more changelings with a kiss than the free race army had ever done with weapons in the same time span.

The carnage continued. One of the changelings was trying to run as another one latched itself onto her arm with his teeth. Rynna felt the bile rise in her throat. The underbeings were pulling each other apart like wet clay dolls because they were fighting for her love. Sure she could wipe out the First Legion like this, and maybe even the next two before the high dreadpriest found out about it. But then she would never be allowed out alone again. She would probably spend the next eighty five years in a locked room playing cat's cradle and posing for portraits with important underbeings.

In a panic, the young god bunched up her dress at her knees. Holding the thick material in her fists, she began to run towards the carnage. The underbeings closest to her ceased their fighting the moment she got close, and dropped face down to the blood-muddied dirt. She flew past them and ran towards where the fighting was the most brutal, hoping that they would notice her before she accidentally got torn to shreds.

They did.

As her scent wound its way through the fighting, the changelings all prostrated themselves on the ground. The young woman continued to run around in loops through the underbeings until every last living, conscious member of the first legion was lying down and breathing steadily.

Eventually, Rynna found herself in the middle surrounded by black-eyed bodies with downturned faces.

"Alright, who has it?" she asked, trying to sound angry and disappointed rather than afraid. "Who has the kiss?"

One lone changeling near the southern edge raised a fist in the air that he then opened and laid flat. The god stalked over to him and looked at the empty air above his hand.

This is insane, she thought.

But she made a great show of pretending to peel something off the surface of the changeling's hand. Pinching two fingers together as if holding something between them, Rynna shook her hand in a circle so that all the changelings could catch a

230

glimpse of her kiss. How the changelings themselves had kept track of who had the thing was beyond her.

Rynna's slippers were wet with gore and the hem of her dress was bedraggled. She simply shook her head then walked back to the end of the drawbridge.

"Now everybody stand back up and- and get into lines again."

She was obeyed. Seconds later, once more the changelings reformed into ranks. There were holes here and there that showed evidence that there were many unconscious or lifeless bodies. The god swallowed.

"Okay, now nobody move, please." Granite would have been more pliable than the warriors became at her request. Rynna walked until she was at the edge of the first row. She took a deep breath and then began to walk along the length of the changelings, gently cupping the face of each underbeing as she passed.

They didn't tackle each other this time, and instead shared looks of pure joy as they touched their own hands rapturously where Hers had been.

She continued through the ranks, cupping wrinkled faces, scarred faces, dark faces, and light faces. Thousands of mouths were smiling thousands of smiles as her hand became increasingly greasy. It took an hour and a half and her fingers were numb by the end of it, but finally she pushed her hand against the cheek of the final warrior.

The changelings were ecstatic. Off the wall, jumping euphoria thronged in them all. The warleader and battlelord didn't bother keeping order. The warriors were still bloody and bruised from the earlier brawl, but now they were also smiling, laughing, and hugging each other. All of them were filled with wondrous joy, for each had been touched by the Prince for a brief moment.

Rynna trudged back to the dreadpriests.

"Was that okay?" she asked. Her voice was weary. She felt tired.

The dreadpriests looked hurt. Their eyes were still hot with fervour, but on the edges of said zeal you could also see traces of unhappiness.

"It was acceptable Prince. You have bestowed a great honour on the worthless warriors by allowing them the friction of Your skin."

The god frowned. What had she done wrong?

Then she saw it. Their faces had been immaculately scrubbed since she had last left them. Rynna almost wanted to laugh. Almost. Instead she sighed and felt even wearier.

"Did you want the . . ." Rynna tried to remember what the dreadpriest had called her blessing, "friction of my skin, too?"

The dreadpriests looked severe, but there were traces of nervousness there now, too. They did not answer, but they leaned forward in anticipation. Rynna solemnly pressed her hand to their faces.

As soon as she touched them, the young god could see the same elation that had swept the ranks of changelings blossom in the two dreadpriests' eyes. It was wonder at something that they had not dreamed to experience in their lives.

For them to dress and ready the god was one thing, but for Her to touch them of Her own free will? Bliss.

Rynna turned back to face the First Legion.

The underbeings had calmed down somewhat, and now the warleader led them in another painful bow, before turning and filing out. The dead and unconscious bodies were carried away quietly by their fellow warriors. She shook her head in disbelief and waited with the happy dreadpriests for the next legion to arrive.

The rest of the day passed by in much the same way, except she didn't blow any more kisses. To see these horrible nightmares from her childhood simpering at her was confusing. Monsters whose teeth had bitten into more people than she had ever met wept when her fingers grazed them slightly. Beasts who, for the sheer fun of it, would have pulled her mother's eyes from her face while she was alive and screaming, collapsed from excitement as Rynna approached.

During the next few days as she 'blessed' the legions, she came to realize that what Valar had told her was true. The jealousy and rage she had seen in the high dreadpriest's eyes when speaking of the dragon, the reluctance of Warrior Mitah to reveal her flesh, the slaughter to reach her blown kiss with the First Legion, the lesser dreadpriests' hurt expressions . . . all of it was simply because they loved her.

When the god finally gained the courage to question Seina about it, she had explained enthusiastically. And Rynna could only close her eyes and try to breath evenly at the answer.

Even the best of the free race soldiers were weak. Their love was a faceted thing divided by degrees among many. Threaten a mother, a sister, a

233

son, a friend and suddenly you have somebody willing to open a backdoor in the defenses. Higher earth beasts are social creatures. The instincts to seek approval and affection as well as the instincts to gather, protect, and love are impossible to quell from a body.

Even when the underbeings were created, the Prince of Dusk could not get rid of this need from the stock he used to create them. Affection is dangerous is war, though. The changelings were supposed to be the most effective soldiers ever, so this unavoidable flaw needed to be bypassed somehow. And it was. All vulnerable feelings were transferred onto the Prince of Dusk. The changelings were only allowed to love one creature, but She they were allowed to love with all their hearts.

Rynna was their love. She was their mother, sister, niece, aunt, greatmother, lover, friend, and soulmate. Only better than all of those things because She couldn't die and She couldn't be used as bait nor as blackmail nor as a bargaining chip. It was for this reason that the changelings were always strongest when their god walked in the flesh. They could slit the throats of a hundred dwarves and that of the person they'd just been fucking with equal ease. They could kill effortlessly, safe in the knowledge that their true love waited for them in the Menundra.

This time though, their god didn't love them. She couldn't. The woman felt only revulsion around them. Although she smiled at them and appeared to appreciate their devotion, she couldn't love creatures who so devalued the lives of her species.

234

She couldn't love monsters that had been used to terrify her into good behaviour as a child.

On a fundamental level, it's impossible to love the boogeyman, no matter how sweetly he sings to you.

But if there was one thing that High Dreadpriest Valar had made perfectly clear to her, it was that until she was convinced Rynna was the Prince of Dusk through and through, the god would never be allowed to be anything more than a empty figurehead. Even though her stopping the war had just been a pretence of the dragon's to inspire her to continue traveling with him, Rynna still believed in the idea. Because it was either that or give up and she was done letting someone else control her life.

She would get the changelings to trust her, and they would one day attack and retreat when she commanded. Ending the war was the last thing she had and gods damn it, she was going to do everything she could to accomplish it. She held onto her purpose fiercely and as a result, even though she could not love the boogeyman, she did what all people do when faced with Rynna's situation in a relationship.

She faked it.

Rynna began her days smiling and benevolent, and that is how she ended them. She cooed over the changelings, praised the dreadpriests, and blessed the protruding faces of the underbeings as they stood rank on rank adoring her. After she had finished with the legions, she visited the nurseries, and there it was cubs and women bloated with pregnancy that she kissed, touched, and blessed. Newly born black-eyed babies looked at her with large, adoring eyes, and she smiled sweetly as she stroked their small, fragile heads.

Whenever she heard of a legion who had suffered bad losses from a skirmish or a battle or whatever it was they were up to, she would visit them. Sometimes she would even help wrap wounds and set bones with the other healers. She had years and years of training in keeping herself from dying and now she applied her arts to the underbeings.

Sometimes, she would just sing to the wounded of the decimated legions in order to strengthen their spirits. She learned the blood lullaby and sang it often.

"Fresh blood, warm blood, red blood, please, please, please. Plump helpless mammals with their backs to me . . . ."

True to the high dreadpriest's word, the god was kept away from the war, and ignorant of all its tidings. She knew nothing of the battles between her people and her species. Whether the free races were winning, losing, or just sitting still scratching their asses she couldn't have said. The only thing she could say for certain was that no fighting had reached the Gate, and also that Lavanor still stood.

She also knew that there was a lot of dying taking place on both sides of the battles. A legion would sometimes stagger back in hundreds where it had left in thousands. As for the free races, she had evidence of their deaths in a more tangible way. Sometimes when the god visited a legion unexpectedly she could see the scurry of bodies being dragged out of sight. Other times they were not fast enough and she saw the still corpses with their bright-hued irides.

Sometimes she saw other things. Bloodied tools. Sharp butcher knives and smaller skinning blades. Piles of freshly prepared meat. Skin stretched to dry, waiting to be bleached or dyed in liquid filled pots. It did not take Rynna long to discover the materials used for the ubiquitous black leather and for the stew and dried meat that were the primary staples of the legions. Rynna spent a lot of time gagging and never ate a bite when she visited any of the underbeings, but still managed a happy face for the beasts who loved her.

And how Rynna was loved. The god who had spent her entire life as an outcast was now the definition of social inclusion. She would never be outside the loop again. She was the loop, and all the underbeings sought to latch on and be a part of it, be a part of Her. Their god, their Lord of the Underbeings, their beautiful, beautiful Prince of Dusk.

When she finally decided that she would not abort the egg incubating inside of her and the word spread that she was going to bear a god cub, the devotion the underbeings felt for her intensified. They loved her more than they had before, which was almost impossible but somehow not. The little hatchling, the little god cub would now be theirs to love as well. One who shared blood with their god. A niece or nephew, a little brother or sister, a son or a daughter that they could have as their own in a way they never could for their own offspring and blood relatives. The woman god began letting the changelings touch her abdomen for a blessing, and Valar nodded in approval.

And so it continued on for months. Rynna visited, smiled, sang, hugged, and was exactly who she was told to be, all the while entrenching herself deeply into the trust and confidences of the underbeings.

The only problem, the only flaw with the whole situation, was the same flaw with which every person is faced when faking it in a relationship.

You forget what it feels like to not fake it.

CHAPTER 22
A SMALL MATTER

It had been over four months since her arrival. Now that her emotions were beginning to work themselves out, a routine of sort was in place, and she finally knew how to get around the Menundra without help, the god's natural default setting kicked in.

And so Rynna tried to drown herself in the tub.

Seina pulled her out in a timely fashion, but it was just a happy coincidence that the woman was there. The god tried to placate the warrior's concern by clarifying the situation.

After her brief explanation, Seina's facial expression spoke only of disbelief.

"You repeatedly try to kill Yourself?"

The god winced. Nobody likes to hear that their deity is suicidal. Wringing out her hair into the tub, Rynna tried to frame it in a positive light.

"Yes . . . but only accidentally."

Seina frowned.

"So . . . You accidentally repeatedly try to kill Yourself."

"Yes."

"Why? Is it because of the hatchling?" The god saw the worry in Seina's eyes at the thought of the hatchling causing her stress. Or maybe of her causing the hatchling stress, the young god wasn't quite sure.

"No, it's fine. It's nothing to do with the egg. This is something else. I've had it my whole life. I

239

have no idea why it happens. I know it doesn't make sense but it's always been this way. For as long as I can remember."

Rynna surveyed the features of the changeling before her as the other woman thought about the problem. The god's gaze passed over the fold of cloth that covered the woman's eyes. She no longer really noticed it anymore. At first, the young god had thought it was strange that the woman went around constantly blindfolded, so after a few weeks she had asked about it. Seina had frankly and unashamedly explained to her.

She was blind. She had been since birth. Rynna had felt awkward when her question was answered. She hadn't wanted to bring up a sensitive issue. But unexpectedly, Seina hadn't minded at all. In fact, she was proud of it. Born blind meant eyes clouded over with cataracts, hiding their true colour. She was one of only three underbeings in the entire Warrior Clan without black eyes, making them perfect for infiltration. Few people suspect a blind night lady.

Rynna supposed that, like people missing their eyes, the blind had to be watched constantly in the beginning to ensure they weren't secretly underbeings. How long had Seina been undercover that she was free to come and go, practicing her arts and collecting intelligence as she pleased?

This was part of the reason that Warrior Nakao was in the First Legion. Her ability to insinuate herself with her prey was unparalleled. Not to mention that she could hear the individual heart beats of hummingbirds, feel the distinct ridges in fingerprints, and identify the dinner last eaten by her target by smelling it's leavings. She could taste the air and know more about her surroundings than many two person scouting parties could with ten minutes of careful study.

Back when Seina had first explained it to Rynna, she had shrugged before concluding, "Besides, eyesight is a changeling's weakest sense as it is. The free race types rely way too heavily on theirs."

It was at that moment that the god had figured out something that had been bothering her since the first time she had poked her head out of her flower filled bedroom and seen Seina waiting for her.

"I know you."

"Thank you. It has only been many weeks since You came here. Can I start saying 'hello' or something?" The warrior had been smiling playfully.

The god had shaken her head. "No. I mean, before I came here. I've seen you somewhere else . . . ."

She had tried to think of where she could have possibly seen a blind changeling before. She hadn't been able to place it and still hadn't been able to place it, but then suddenly she had. The realization had been ice slowing her blood and clogging her veins with clotted truth. Her voice had gone very quiet when she spoke.

"You were beautiful as a human. In Ta'ao."

The light blue-eyed woman with the bodyguard giving her a coin. Telling her that she was not beneath others. The night lady's words had seemed so utterly personal at the time. But the eyes hadn't been light blue. They had been the clouded eyes of the blind. And the god's scent must have identified her immediately to the creature.

"Earlier, when you told me that you remembered the first time you ever caught my scent . . . . It was you. It was you in Ta'ao just like it was the caged changeling in Lavanor. You were the one who first knew I was a god and called the others."

Seina had responded with a voice that regretted the tale of the tragedy, but not the tragedy itself.

"I was wondering when You were going to remember that. I am told You didn't enjoy the cleansing of that city. It was why I was given the honour of escorting You to the throne room. I found You first."

"Did not enjoy- Seina, you killed them. Killed them all. Everybody. And I was there and-"

"Shhhh." Seina had then placed an arm on the god's shoulder. "It's okay. It was necessary. They were poisoned. A cancer that had to be eradicated. It's just better this way. Trust me."

Rynna had roughly pushed the woman's comforting arm away.

"Better this way?" She had clenched her teeth and made to speak but the only thing she had been able to do was repeat her earlier words. "Better this way? You think that it is better this way? With less people? In what world can you justify a city's massacre and say that the world is better off afterwards?"

But Seina had not answered her questions. She had gently touched the young woman's face and frowned, reading deeply into the set of Rynna's cheeks. Then, she had spoken quietly.

"You've forgotten so much. I wish You could remember. There would be so much less pain that way."

Now months later as the changeling faced Rynna, she was frowning again, trying to decipher the riddle that was her god.

"Have You tried not killing Yourself?"

It was the Prince of Dusk's turn to wrinkle her brow.

"We . . . . I have tried everything, trust me. I'm not looking for you to find a solution, I'm just asking to have a companion, somebody to stay with me and keep an eye out for it. The incidences are always lowered when there more people paying attention than just me."

Seina chewed her lip as she considered this, and finally stated, "Well, we'll have to consult with Erin."

CHAPTER 23
TIDINGS, OR WHAT RYNNA WASN'T ALLOWED TO KNOW

The Lord of Salvation's hand shook as He read the reports. He had been leading them for what was it now, four months? four and a half? and the death toll was already in the tens of thousands, not including the massacre of Ta'ao. The Lord of Salvation stared at His young hands. If only . . . . But there were so many, many dead.

The Lord of Salvation clenched His teeth at the thought of the Prince of Dusk. That bitch who would see them all perish. There was nothing He could do about her now. There was little He could do about anything now, really. They had already exhausted most options. The dwarves had even hunted down the fabled dragon brood and asked-no, begged them for help. It would seem the dragons were having problems of their own, however, and no winged warriors would be joining the fight. Tolm's messengers had returned singed, traumatized, and empty handed.

The entire council waited for His words, His divine, holy words, and all He was accomplishing was to shake with the sheer volume of death racing past Him into the golden fields. The god stilled His limbs and attempted to speak with a clear, steady voice.

"And you're sure these figures are accurate?"

Lemin's face sagged.

"Do you think the lieutenant-generals would lie? Surely of all people, You would know that wouldn't be the case."

The Lord of Salvation made sure to include anger in His response. "Forgive Me, priest, for hoping there were more of us alive than what is indicated in these reports. Tell Me now, what cities *do* remain?"

High Priest Lemin glared before motioning Lieutenant-General Pak forward. The dwarf was squat for her species, standing no higher than four feet.

The dwarf bowed deeply to her god before answering the question. "Things are not good where we stand now, my Lord. Lot still holds, but only barely. Dall, and the remainder of the residents of the Old Road have been annihilated. Port Algin took to the sea. The ships had landed at Fisherport last time we verified. Gravestop was evacuated to here and the Water Weavers welcomed the people of Ibuza before sealing the Open Shore. The starved rocks are still protecting the Gossamer Forest.

"But basically, my Lord, other than us and Lot, the entire Aat Territory has been destroyed, abandoned, or both. Other than us, Lot, the Dwellers, and the Weavers . . . well, the northern continent is lost."

"Thank you."

The dwarf bowed again, and then sat back down. Immediately, King Tolm, chimed his bell roughly and the Lord of Salvation nodded once to acknowledge his turn to question the woman.

"Is there any good news? We must have something to send back to our people. We need something to give the soldiers. They are dying. If we tell them the fight is hopeless then . . . well, how the hell can we possibly keep sending them to battle?"

Here the lieutenant-general spoke again in a tired voice.

"Other than Ta'ao, we know that there have still been no forays to the south. The watchtowers still stand so everything beyond them is protected, making the west coast completely impenetrable. I guess the she-beast wants to finish us off in the north before she tackles the problem of moving down. If it wasn't for that ancient technology . . . if it wasn't for the watchtowers, who knows where we'd be."

Another chime sounded. This time it was the Tree Dwellers' Eldest, Mikkella. She was a thin, frail elf who already had over a hundred and fifty years to her name, yet looked no older than sixty. Longevity as a result of techniques borrowed from their cousins. The elf nodded to the Water Weavers' Eldest before speaking.

"What of the Prince of Dusk? Any new tidings of her?"

The lieutenant-general dipped her head in apology.

"None, Eldest. But at least there is still no evidence of the god leaving the Gate."

King Paelin's turn. "And captured changelings? Have we been having any luck with them?"

Once more the lieutenant-general looked exhausted.

"They're all still empty mouthing before we can get any information."

High Priest Lemin cursed, "Lavanor is going to come under fire if we don't take drastic action soon. What can we do about this?"

Thankfully, the Lord of Salvation did know what to do about this. He took a breath and dropped His voice into the deepest register it could reach as He spoke His next words. The god only wished it was His idea and that He hadn't had to memorize a speech in order to prepare for this council meeting.

"We move all the supplies we can into the city from the unburned granaries of the abandoned towns around us. Next, we evacuate the people of Lot to join us here. Then, we simply close off Lavanor and wait. This city cannot be tunnelled under nor crawled over. It can be starved out but we have independent wells and enough food stored for a decade of siege. We send a third of the army to Watchtower, a third to Fisherport, and a third to the Gossamer Forest to reinforce the south gate of the starved rocks. The watchtowers will guard the west completely, and with two thirds of the army blocking the north roads then at least the southern continent is airtight. The last third protects the Weavers and the Dwellers-"

"So we wait to starve to death?" Lemin's words had just the right amount of disrespect. An outrageous high priest is so very effective. Lemin continued his accusation, "The changelings have been patient for thousands of years. Another ten until this city runs out of food will not daunt them. You'll lead us to our deaths!"

"You forget yourself, Lemin." King Tolm huffed. "Although you may be second to our Lord, you are not a god, Lemin. You will show respect or we will find a new high priest who can." He then turned to the Lord of Salvation with a seated bow. "Please, continue, my Lord."

The Lord of Salvation's teeth dug deeply into each other. Now all they had to do was break the last truce the two sides had ever agreed on.

"We will recommence some of the projects of the Oceo Tolok," he finally announced. That title alone made the entire council either flinch or gasp, priests included. "My beloved people, we cannot win this war anymore by numbers. There simply aren't enough soldiers to be had from the free races, even with conscription. We are going to lose, and the free races will be no more.

"But, if My plan succeeds, ten years will be more than enough time to finally end this conflict. We will wipe both the Prince of Dusk and her cursed underbeings from the face of this planet. The Oceo Tolok are our last and only option. We are faced with the end of the world. We can no longer afford to be picky about our morals."

The Lord of Salvation took a deep breath, and then counted to five before continuing.

"This cannot just be the decision of the Lord of Salvation. This is a decision that must be undertaken by all the free races willingly if we are to break the truce. As such, I call a vote of the Free Race Alliance . . . ."

The Lord of Salvation finished His speech with all the proper decorum. It was only twenty minutes later, as He heard the 'aye's and caught sight of Lemin's pale, frightened, but determined face, that the fifteen year old god of the free races wanted to throw up.

CHAPTER 24
A LADY'S FAVOURS

"That's right. Quickly but deeply. I know the last thing You want is for it to bleed out slowly and thrash more than strictly necessary. Although for the record, the meat tastes much better if it experiences a lot of pain and fear in its death."

The calf, currently struggling pointlessly against its bonds and making terrified mewling sounds at the sight of her shaking hands, evidently disagreed with Seina's enthusiasm for pain. The god nodded anyways, then brought the knife down and tried with one smooth motion to slice it across the neck of the immobilized animal.

'Tried,' of course, being the operative word.

It was not smooth, not quick, and her blade stuck in the muscle as the cow's flesh resisted death. The noises coming from the beast had become interspersed with gurgling blood and pain. With two hands now, she dragged the blade across the creature's neck, tearing skin and veins in rough jerks.

Seina listened to the pitiful thing thrash messily against its bonds, then eventually still as too much of its life fluid dripped onto the ground.

"Well, it's not the absolute worst quick death I've ever heard," the warrior tried to offer in consolation.

Rynna sighed. At least this time she hadn't nicked herself. She stuck the knife into the wooden board on which the calf's body was splayed out, and then wiped her hands carelessly at her sides, smearing the expensive dress with red palm prints.

Seina patted the god's shoulder comfortingly upon sensing the woman's mood.

"You'll get it, I promise."

'Get it.' As if it was like learning to ride a bike or weave hair into plaited braids. Just a knack to be found, then after that, easy as accidentally trying to kill yourself. At least she could do the butchering part well enough.

The idea to have the god learn to harvest meat was the high dreadpriest's, naturally. Rynna wasn't sure if the purpose had been, as she had claimed, to reward the Warrior Clan or if it was really just to toughen the god up. Either way it was successful on both accounts. Her gag reflex had certainly been dulled, and the Warrior Clan was ecstatic with this new development.

Three times a week, a select few of her changelings who had honoured themselves on the battlefield were allowed the privilege of coming to the throne room and watching her kill and butcher an animal. Then, the changelings were not only given some of the more succulent pieces from the fresh carcass, but they were also later given a strip of her ruined dress to wear as favours on the battlefield.

It was a surprisingly effective system.

Now she just had to worry about killing some poor deer, cow, pig, or rabbit every few days. But she was getting used to it. After a few weeks she now only lamented the beautiful dresses constantly ruined.

250

The god carefully gripped the knife in her hand, spread the calf's legs wide apart, and began to saw around the stomach, being very careful not to rupture the animal's bowels.

As always, Warrior Nakao listened to her work carefully, especially now considering she was wielding a knife. Usually Dreadpriest Aoa participated in these events as well just to be safe, but she had been missing for a week. One of the first accomplishments Rynna had achieved in her mission to ingratiate herself with the underbeings was to learn as many names as she could. The dreadpriests were so happy when she stopped referring to them as 'you' or 'the one with the scar.'

"Why has Jeni been skipping these sessions lately?"

Warrior Nakao grew an overly innocent face.

"I don't know . . . maybe she's making a fresh supply of assault grease. Or binging on elves. How am I supposed to know? I'm only a warrior after all, even if I am the Prince of Dusk's Companion."

The god frowned and pointed a bloody finger in mock threat at the warrior's face.

"Tell me the truth or I'm withholding from killing anything until she gets back."

Seina's lips stuck into what was a feigned pout, and then laughed.

"Alright, I'll spill, but You can't say that I was the one who told You . . . . Jeni is on a mission with the Ninth Legion to get You a birthday present."

Rynna was dumbfounded.

"A . . . birthday present?"

"Yes, Dusk Prince. Your birthday is May eleventh, is it not?"

"Well yes, but-"

"So the Warrior Clan is getting you a birthday present. It's not that far away, as You know. And sixteen is the coming of age year among Your kind. So Dreadpriest Aoa was sent personally to make sure that it arrives in time."

The god hadn't even known that her changelings were aware of when her birthday was. It made sense though. The Prince of Dusk was always reborn on the same day, with only the year differing. But still, a surprised smile began to creep across her lips. She had never had a proper birthday present before.

"So, um, where exactly is Jeni going to get-"

"Oh, no You don't, my Prince." Seina shook her head vehemently. "You're not going to sucker that out of me. I'm not ruining all of Your surprises." Seina's smile returned to her lips easily, and Rynna chuckled before returning to the task at hand.

The calf was quick work from there on out for the god. Quick, but still difficult, and it soon had her sweat running down her neck and shoulders in rivulets that paled the blood splattered there to a pinker colour.

The half dozen privileged warriors inhaled deeply the scent of their god butchering. Her sweat blended pleasantly with visceral fluids.

There was a small cub in among the six today. Rynna watched him surreptitiously as she worked down the length of the calf's body. She wasn't sure what a child must merit to attend one of her sessions. For that matter, she didn't even really know what an adult needed to accomplish, but all the same, it had been the first time she had ever seen one of the little ones in attendance.

Of all her changelings, she liked the cubs the best. She had learned to her surprise that underbeings age more quickly than any species of the free races. They reached maturity at the age of eight, and under times of duress, could be bred as early as seven and still produce strong cubs. The infancy and toddler years of humans were passed in mere months by the changelings. The god didn't understand the biology behind it, but could only assume it was the result of necessity during one of her past lives.

This particular cub looked like a ten year old elf, which meant it was probably only four or five years old in reality. She liked the little ones because innocence had not been trained out of them entirely and she could almost see village youngsters in them as they pounced on, wrestled, and chased each other, laughing all the while.

The god turned her eyes back to what she was doing as she sliced through the last of the meaty joints. She nodded in satisfaction to herself at the precise sectioning she had done. The young woman backed up a few paces and her changelings bowed deeply to her before surging forward to fight over their favourite parts.

After a few minutes of watching the growling dwarves, humans, and elves shoving pieces of carcass in their mouths, Rynna shifted her eyes from the carnage and noticed the cub standing aside, watching her quietly. The young god walked over to the little elf creature and crouched down to its eye level. She saw that his golden hair was a curly mess, and his nose was a little stubby.

"Hello, little one. What are you waiting for? Don't you want some of the meat?"

The little cub listened to her question carefully, and then shook his head.

"Why don't you want any of your reward?"

"I only wanted to come see You. I don't care about the meat." Then, the little elf's chest puffed up. "I killed two whole rabbits all by myself last week. My name is Chi."

"Well, Warrior Chi, how about you lick the blood off my fingers instead? If you promise not to bite, you can at least have that."

The cub nodded his curly head ever so slowly just in case the Prince wanted to take Her offer back. The god, seeing his hesitation pushed her bloodied hands forward, sticking the tips of her fingers under the little cub's nose.

The young changeling's body lit with happiness and he began to lap up the blood in earnest. Rynna smiled at the creature. The god was so involved in the whole process that she didn't notice that every changeling behind her had stopped eating.

One of the adult changelings snarled.

The god jerked her head up just as the young cub shied away from her. She stood slowly to face her followers whose faces were now contorted with anger.

"Seina, what's wrong with everyone?"

Chi fell to his belly and was wriggling away from her with small whimpers of, ". . . sorry Prince, sorry lovely God, sorry, sorry I . . . ."

"Seina?"

254

There was a rush of violence surrounding her and a strangled scream. It lasted mere seconds, and then the wave of bodies receded. The god was left standing beside the little cub, now crushed and limp, his light curly hair damp with his own blood.

Rynna frowned. "Seina, what was that about?"

Her Companion was busy preening herself. She was licking blood from her hands, her tongue sliding carefully along the ridges of her fingers. She paused long enough to comment.

"It is a sacrilege to taste You. A death is necessary. You already know that tradition. Remember when Warrior Mitah tasted You?"

Rynna's frown deepened. "But, I told him to. He killed two rabbits just to see me."

"Rabbits?" Seina chewed the words slowly in her mouth before smiling. "Ahhh, I see . . . . Rabbits. The cubs have renamed their kills because of Your human body."

The god waited for the small underbeing to reform itself. She decided that she was going to kiss the undersized changeling all better once it shook its flesh into place. And damn if she wouldn't let him lick her fingers until they were raw.

A few minutes passed as Rynna continued to wait, but nothing was happening. The little body did not move.

"Why hasn't he assumed a new skin, then?"

Warrior Nakao had resumed grooming herself, but paused to listen carefully to the clearing. She was counting pulses.

"Ah, that's right. The cub lost two forms killing the humans. That was his last one. Pity, he was quite fierce. He would have made an excellent warrior."

The cub's last form. Which meant . . . . The young god suddenly felt a little tired.

"Well, then. Let's get that dress off of You." Seina's voice was chipper as she licked the last drop of blood from her hands. "The changelings are eager for their favours, Dusk Prince."

The god shook her head, then raised her arms in the air and thought in a detached way about another ruined dress.

CHAPTER 25
COMMITING

The Lord of Salvation stood nervously beside His high priest. Lemin seemed less nervous, but maybe it was just because his desperation was bleeding so thickly through everything else that it drowned out other emotions. A grimace to his god was all Lemin was able to give Him.

The Master standing in front of them was smiling smugly. He was holding out a document that just needed a holy signature to get the work started. The Lord of Salvation swallowed deeply and began to sign His name in a hand that shook only a little.

"Excellent, my Lord. We will begin immediately. Thankfully, many of the original theories used in our works have been preserved. There will be no need to restart from the beginning. We can have a working prototype of the weapon within a few months. Of course, it will take a few years before all the problems can be worked out, but the other Masters and myself are confident that with a little study and experimentation we can avoid many of the issues experienced with past models."

The Master was almost bouncing in anticipation and satisfaction. What he had just admitted to would have meant a death sentence twenty four hours ago. Now it was to their benefit that the Masters had been lying and deceiving the Council of Three for thousands of years. What other projects were waiting to be restarted?

The Lord of Salvation wanted to punch the man in the mouth, but not only would it have been hypocritical of Him, but at this point in events He didn't have the energy to do more than feel a lurch in His stomach.

Nevertheless, the decision had been made and there was nothing left to do but follow through and face the consequences of their course of action. There would be time for regret and remorse after the war was won. Either history would forgive them or there would be nobody left to write one. Beside, disturbing tidings from the center of the southern continent had Him even more terrified and angry than He had thought possible. It some ways it made what they were doing now easier. Only in some ways, though.

When He had finished signing and initialling the document, the Master snapped the roll closed quickly. He then bowed in an oily way and the Lord of Salvation acknowledged the old creature with a nod. The Lord then turned and left the room along with His guilt, followed quickly by Lemin and the guards. For better or worse, the decision had been made and lingering now would only delay progress, and ultimately, what little victory they could hope to claim.

CHAPTER 26
THE GESTATION PERIOD OF A SNAKE

The young god was worried. And it wasn't just because of the fact that she was incubating a two fist sized egg rather than a mammal attached by an umbilical cord, and that when it was time for the egg to hatch, the dragon would claw its way through her stomach to freedom rather than instinctively travelling along the birth canal. Although this was quite unnerving in her mind, what really frightened her was that she just didn't *feel* like she was going to be a mother.

Eight months had passed since the Induction Ceremony, and there was still no physical evidence that Rynna was going to be bearing offspring soon. No swelling, no extra weight gained, no bizarre cravings for pickles dipped in chocolate. She didn't cry when she accidentally put her socks on the wrong feet nor did she tell people to go to hell for forgetting the slice of lemon she liked with her tea.

Rynna, the poster child for inferiority complexes and bad self-image, had in the very least been hoping to go up a few cup sizes. But no, as the high dreadpriest had predicted, her breasts stayed identical to what they had been before. She wasn't bearing a mammal, after all.

Her mother had given her a thorough run down in terms of a sexual education. After all, should Rynna follow her into the night lady business, she would need to be able to protect herself. So, the god knew all about which herbs discouraged implantation, and which ones could either delay her courses or help them arrive earlier than usual. She knew about the danger signs of bleeds, the importance of avoiding intercourse on days fourteen and fifteen, and about spreading infections. She knew about semen, ovaries, and most of the tubes, whether of the fallopian or urethral variety.

Of course, she'd never experienced any of it. Writhing bodies, the exchange of fluids, and engorged organs were completely academic. Just a series of lesson drilled into her head that had a two-dimensional quality about them. They were true, and perhaps useful in some vague future, but utterly flat and surreal to her at the moment.

After the initial shock and sense of betrayal had passed, she had decided she was tentatively happy about the egg. Pregnancy was a rare thing. Successful ones even more so. Free race couples were lucky to have one child, and two were almost unheard of now. It was for this reason she couldn't have killed the egg in her. Life was difficult enough a thing to come by that she would not rid herself of it so lightly. Particularly since she had never thought she would *ever* have offspring. To do that would mean finding a mate, and frankly she had usually been happy finding a warm place to sleep at night. A warm body with whom to share said place had seemed an impossible thing.

When she had been young, the god had enviously watched other women as they exclaimed over their bulging bellies, commiserated over swelling, and looked fondly at hands placed over stomachs feeling tiny kicks for the first time.

It was this kicking that most fascinated her about the whole thing. The little feet and hands reaching out to freedom, testing new muscles, and stretching small bones, only to be hampered by the thick flesh in the way. That didn't stop them trying though. Still they reached, kicked, and proclaimed that they were alive through their small, growing bodies. Determined little things, those prenatal beings are.

Which is why stillness in an unborn is terrifying. Too much stillness for too long usually means that once again the mother's body only holds one heartbeat. Then the bleeding would start and the healers would be called and valiant efforts would be made by all. But usually there was nothing to be done and a small, wet, half formed lump would be buried in woods while everyone hoped the mother would pull through.

By all accounts, she had been harbouring the egg for almost two years now. And although she knew logically that eggs don't kick, she couldn't stop that little niggling voice in her mind that told her there was nothing but rotting shell hanging out in her midsection.

Which is why it was such a resounding relief when the physical evidence did finally appear.

The god had been eating breakfast at the time with Warrior Nakao and Dreadpriest Thorren. Seina was quietly keeping an ear on the knife the young god was using while the dreadpriest was going through the list of wounded they were to visit that day. It was then that the Prince of Dusk felt a painful brush against her mind.

Earth-Mother.

261

The god choked. Seina whacked her on the back and Rynna took a gasping breath as the food dislodged.

"Another attempt, my Prince?" Dreadpriest Thorren asked, looking up from his tally. "The warriors can always wait. Even if some die in the meantime, I believe most on the list have more than one form remaining."

Rynna nodded ambiguously, not wasting time with a proper response. Instead, she bent her head towards her stomach and was staring at her own mid section. The young god was waiting, hoping, and praying that-

The softest of violent pushes in her head.

Hello, Earth-Mother.

A grin erupted on Rynna's face and lit her entire being.

"What is it?" Seina's voice was steeped in curiosity, sensing the change.

"Just a minute," Rynna whispered and the two underbeings fell into an expectant silence.

The god's head was still straining towards her stomach to hear-

I am afraid.

She could feel the light voice curling through her mind. It was shaking slightly. A small, unpractised voice that didn't hurt near as much as the booming, invading tones of its father. No permission had been given to access her mind, but maybe once you shared a body, permission wasn't necessary. The god continued to listen.

You are breaking.

Rynna could feel the voice pause in her head as it gathered its remaining energy to send one last

262

message. The Prince of Dusk touched a hand to her lower stomach. Still no movement. No kicks. Just the little scared voice with the terrible message, its worry, and-

Not . . . alone.

Every vein, pathway, and nerve in her mind around which the voice was curled suddenly lit with terror. It burned through her head and seared her heart.

The god moaned and cradled her head with her arms.

"Dusk Prince, please! What is it? Tell us!"

"It's. The. Hatchling," the god managed to get out between her teeth. It felt like there were six sets of claws gripping her skull.

Seina slipped an arm around her back with one hand and slowly probed her god's forehead with the other, searching for discrepancies.

"Brenn, get the high dreadpriest. There is something wrong with the Prince of Dusk."

Rynna's head throbbed in a painful and systematic way. Was it time? Was she soon going to feel the pressure that would end in a little dragon ripping her open? She shuddered to think that this is what it felt like before she had blood falling in rivulets down her abdomen.

Then, Rynna's body inexplicably steadied. The god felt the threads of thought slipping off her mind, and the fear along with its pressure relaxed. Her head again felt normal-ish, if somewhat swollen on the inside. She pulled her hands away from the sides of her face and looked up into Seina's concerned features. She spoke in a voice that was supposed to be reassuring, but came out a little too tight.

"I . . . I think I'm okay."

"Are You sure?"

"Yes. For now . . . but I think there is something wrong."

Seina pursed her lips. Hers was a face not placated at all. "Well, yes. We know that already. You keep trying to kill Yourself. But we're dealing with that and-"

"No, something else. There is something else wrong with me."

Worry sunk into the blind warrior's cheeks. At that moment the doors of the god's room were opened and the high dreadpriest walked in. Her footsteps were even and her face was the picture of calm, not a single drop of sweat marring the perfect edges of her face. But the god knew with certainty that the high dreadpriest had been in the War Room, which was three stories up and two hallways over. She must have sprinted for the entire trip. Dreadpriest Thorren did not return with her.

Erin Valar didn't bother to greet her god in any fashion. No bow, no nod, not even a courtesy throat clearing to announce her presence.

"What's wrong?" she asked.

"The Prince of Dusk thinks there's something happening with the hatchling."

The high dreadpriest crossed her arms.

"Does it get more specific than a hunch, or are we just going to force feed Her every concoction that the healers possess just in case?"

The god got to Her feet unsteadily. The high dreadpriest saw the tightness in Her face and the

264

strain in Her eyes. One of the Prince's hands was shaking, too. Valar's confidence slipped and her voice lost its edge, replaced with reluctant concern. "What's the problem?"

The Prince shook Her head.

"I don't know. She . . . ." Rynna knew it was a she. The voice had been so little, so fragile, and most of all, so feminine. "She said that I was breaking and that she was afraid. She was terrified, I could feel it. Something's wrong."

The high dreadpriest's eyes went flat and her expression stilled. Her words came carefully and a little too lightly. "What do You mean, 'she said'? You mean You spoke to the hatchling?"

"Just- never mind that. Maybe there's something in the scriptures about this. Or maybe some changeling lore that has been passed down. The dragons helped make you. Shouldn't there be something about dragons in your histories that we can reference?"

Valar shook her head.

"No. After You were given heartblood that was the end of our contact with dragonkin. The books say nothing about this sort of thing. And I personally know too little about reptile progeny. We would have to speak to a dragon directly to learn anything useful."

Rynna cringed at that. She didn't want to speak to any dragons. She had been strictly avoiding thinking about Darlan and the betrayal. It was already difficult enough considering that she had his child inside of her. Seeking out dragons would only bring back painful memories.

"I don't want to go looking for dragons."

"Well, of course we won't," the dreadpriest's words were dry and brittle. "We have a perfectly coherent and mostly intact dragon in the dungeon. Why on earth would we waste time finding another one? We'll just torture the answers out of him."

This took a bit for the god to process. During that time, the high dreadpriest did not alter her expression in the slightest. The young god's words were careful.

"What do you mean, there's a dragon in the dungeon? Which dragon?"

"Why, the Dealer, of course. What other dragon would it be? We haven't exactly started a collection and the choices have become rather limited in the last few centuries. The waterbreather should be able to answer our questions well enough."

There was a pause before, "Wh- why do you have him in the dungeon?"

It was Seina who answered. She was smiling ever so sweetly while her teeth ground together in what could only be described as a satisfied gnash. The warrior's voice was husky as she spoke.

"So we can hurt him, my Prince. We've been tearing out his veins and feeding them to him, of course. Like I told you earlier."

Rynna felt a sticky electric sensation spreading out from her chest. A convoluted mix of dread, pain, and justice. Her face paled. The blind changeling tasted the air, frowned, and shifted to the high dreadpriest.

"Erin? Why is She upset?"

266

High Dreadpriest Valar's response was ridged. "Evidently, She suffers from a malleable conscience."

The young god's reply came in a whisper.

"I told you to get rid of him. Not to hurt him. Not to torture him."

"Prince, he ended Your mother's life and raped You. What did You think we would do? Pack him a lunch and send him home?"

The god shook her head in denial. "He didn't rape me. He never touched me like that."

Seina spoke up again. Her cheeks were uncharacteristically dark. Anger was as plain on her face as disappointment and disbelief was on the dreadpriest's. She bit her words.

"But he did. He put something in You without Your knowledge. There was no consent asked for. Just because the dragon didn't use reproductive organs doesn't change the act. He deserves every hurt he's gotten and more. What he did to You is worse than hurting or tasting you. Far worse. He used Your body, lied to You, and manipulated You for . . . ."

Rynna stopped listening as a thought occurred to her. She had begun thinking about dates and the terrible number eight was humming in her mind. Eight as in eight months. That is how long the young woman had been in the Menundra, and that is how long they had been hurting her dragon. Eight long months.

"Take me to him."

The dreadpriest's reply was curt.

"We will question the waterbreather. There is no need for You to-"

267

"Take me to him, now."

Valar shook her head slightly, and then bowed stiffly, "As you command. Prince."

Seina was not so acquiescing, her voice heating with each additional word as she addressed her god. "You're pitying him? No. You can't! The snake is nothing but-"

"Warrior Nakao. Our god has spoken. We will oblige Her wishes and take the Prince to The Dealer. You will withhold your opinion."

Seina did. Her cheeks tinted again, but the blind warrior said not a word. A dangerous tilt entered her cheekbones in the absence of speech.

The high dreadpriest made another bow to the Prince of Dusk, and then left the room. Rynna followed anxiously with Seina stalking her heels, a whisper of a tail lashing behind her.

The hallways and stairs separating the god's bedroom from the dungeon were thereafter permanently seared into the young woman's retinas as she steeled herself for the encounter. She knew seeing the great beast again would mean losing her tentative see no evil, hear no evil, speak no evil status. The 'I know you know I know but I'm pretending not to know' existence that only barely conceals that protective level of ignorance essential to keeping one's sanity intact. But she went anyways. She felt a guilt-infused need to witness this being whom she had inadvertently condemned to months of torture. Rynna shivered and readied herself for the stench of blood.

She didn't prepare enough.

It clouded around her the moment she entered the room. Not just blood. No. There were other aromas, too. Urine and fecal matter being among the more pleasant ones. Under any other circumstances, the changelings would have seen the god lose the contents of her stomach despite all the strengthening that the tri-weekly slaughters had done for her. However, the smell was the least of the distractions in that dungeon, and shock froze even her stomach.

Torches lit around the room rippled across the distorted body that lay in the middle. There was no cage. They maintained their captured earthwaterair beast with weapons lodged in the prisoner's vital organs. The dragon was surrounded by no less than ten underbeings. Upon seeing the new arrivals, the guards parted for the high dreadpriest, the Companion, and the Prince of Dusk. The three walked until they stood within an arms length of the restrained beast.

This closer inspection of that tortured flesh made Rynna feel even worse.

When the young woman was later to think about the mangled body of the dragon, the one thing that she always pictured first was his foreclaws, or rather, the lack thereof. Where there should have been reptilian hands with three inch claws on their ends, there were now only stumps: dark, crusted stumps that bespoke of a dull hacksaw and many hours of blunt sawing. Beautiful dragon forearms ending in rough, ruined flesh.

Presented with this horrible sight, one hardly noticed the other scarring details. The barbed wire wrapped in a tight muzzle around the dragon's maw. The pus filled eyes. The scales dulled to a sick grey, having lost almost all their green beauty. The iron hooks that were dug deep into his hind legs. The thick rope threaded through a series of tears in the dragon's wings and hooked onto pulleys.

Rynna felt dizzy and tried to work saliva into her mouth as the dragon pulled unseeing eyes in the young god's direction. Seina's words snuck back into her head. *You have a distinctive scent that . . . travels . . . .*

The high dreadpriest snapped her fingers at the changelings who were holding the ends of the flank hooks. They jerked their holds and then the sound of flesh squelching could be heard. The dragon grunted and stood taller, but beyond that, did not react. Two other changelings approached the captured beast. They were wearing gloves fashioned from links of metal intended to keep hands safe when handling sharp iron roughly.

The changelings worked their fingers under the tight muzzle that muted the dragon, then wrenched on it.

More ripping and the dragon's maw was free. A bleeding mess of broken teeth, swollen tongue, and wrecked jaw. The underbeings retreated away from the dragon, bloodied muzzle in hand. Then, there was a long silence of crackling torches as the high dreadpriest waited.

When the dragon remained quiet, she snapped her fingers once more, and the hooks in the dragon's hind legs were wrenched violently.

"Greet the Prince of Dusk, snake."

The dragon coughed and then spoke.

"Greetings, oh Lord of the Underbeings."

The god could say nothing.

"What, no conversation? You have just come to point and laugh at a caged animal, then."

His words were hoarse, slurred, and violent. There was no submission in them, nor questioning. But they were words thick with pain. The pity that Seina dreaded slipped into the young god's heart. When Rynna responded her voice was very small.

"No."

"You have come to kill me, then."

"No!"

"Then, why have you come?"

A legitimate query. She could not focus on the questions she had wanted answered earlier about the hatchling. When she had first felt that terrified voice in her thoughts and the high dreadpriest had been sent for, there had been thousands of concerns crammed in her mind. But now . . . . Now, she could only concentrate on the smell, the sights, and the sounds.

"They will stop hurting you. I'm- I'm sorry. I didn't know they were. I'll make sure that you are let go and allowed to leave the Gate unharmed."

Those pus filled eyes blinked slowly.

"So I am to be banished. My presence is too heavy for your conscience?"

The smallest amount of anger flared up with those words, accompanied with a thimbleful of justification. "Well, yes, I want you gone. Can you really blame me? My mother was everything to me. And when she was gone, you were everything to me. But then . . . everything was . . . . ." She swallowed, closed her eyes, and then spoke quietly again. "I don't want you tortured, but I still never want to see you again. I don't know what you

271

deserve, but whatever it is, I don't want it being meted out near me."

As she finished speaking, the little fury she had marshalled slipped away and Rynna shivered. She could find her answers somewhere else. The young god turned to leave, but before she could take a step the dragon's stumped forearm shot out to across the space that separated them to bump sloppily against her stomach.

Changelings in a hiss of motion. The pulleyed rope was heaved on and the lacing tightened in the beasts wings, forcing him back. The underbeings manning the hooks also pulled so that already deep iron was driven deeper. A beast on a leash pulled in to heel. The high dreadpriest barked her order.

"Remove your forearm, waterbreather, or we remove your head."

The dragon did not remove it. Despite being yanked backwards, he was still maintaining the barest of contact. Concern outlined his already pained eyes.

"There is something wrong with the hatchling isn't there?"

Silence.

Rynna nodded shallowly. "Yes. There is something wrong."

Wide eyes all around. New and terrible information being revealed to the guards. Their god cub was in danger.

"What did it tell you?"

The dragon's voice was like butter. It sounded exactly like it had the night after they fled Lavanor. When she had been healing and he had described nalaberries.

272

"She said 'Hello.' She called me Earth-Mother. She said that she was afraid, and that I was breaking, and . . . she said 'not alone.'"

The dragon frowned. "Not alone . . . ." His eyes widened and his stumped forearm shook.

"And what have we realized that makes us so jumpy, waterbreather?" Valar's words were dangerously mild.

The dragon ignored the changeling. His focus was all on the god's midsection. The great beast's words were strangled.

"What else other than the flight from Lavanor?"

"What do you mean?" Rynna replied in bewilderment.

"Important things taste the best. What else is missing? What important thing is missing?"

"What is he talking about, Dusk Prince?" Seina's words reflected the worry in all the warriors' eyes. Instantly, the god was forgiven Her dragon pity, forgiven Her affections, forgiven everything as Seina begged to know what was wrong and how she could fix it. Valar watched the whole exchange with dark, piercing eyes.

That was when a horrible realization dawned bright and ugly in the young god's mind. The beginning of fear was starting to creep into her. Things that were missing. Like the flight from Lavanor. Tears began to tumble from her eyes as she figured out the important, delicious thing that was missing.

"My mother's name . . . . Dear Salvation, my mother's name!"

The warriors were confused and looked at one another uneasily. They snuck looks at the high dreadpriest for confirmation, information, or in the very least some instruction. However, the high dreadpriest's eyes were still locked on the dragon and she did nothing but wait.

The dragon began to growl. He growled at all the warriors, at all the underbeings in the Menundra, and at all the changelings in existence.

"Oh you miserable little earth beasts . . . . Not alone. The hatchling is not alone inside of your god's body because there is another being in there."

He growled even deeper, his clouded eyes passing over every creature in the room. "Your god has a bellanus in her head which is even now eating her mind. She's going to die."

CHAPTER 27
DARLAN LIVES UP TO HIS NAME

The high dreadpriest's voice was dismissive and sharp.

"The Prince cannot be killed. Besides, the bellanus is nothing more than a myth. The dragon lies. And I expected so much better this time. Huh. Well, re-muzzle the waterbreather. His usefulness has ended. We are done here."

The warriors had no idea what a bellanus was. But they did know that the Prince of Dusk was shaking, which was enough for them to know that whatever the dragon had said, it wasn't completely untrue. Warrior Nakao moved to the young god's side and the others hesitated.

"I said we are done here. Warriors, muzzle the beast immediately."

Valar's words were still mostly controlled but the edges of them were just a little shakier than they had been previously.

The dragon hissed.

"You will not ignore this! You can't. Her heart cannot stop, but if you do nothing her mind will be as useful as that of a corpse. Do you know what happens when a bel butterfly lays eggs in its host? Do you want me to describe to you how the skin bubbles when the caterpillars hatch?"

"Tales of a dragon's nightmare are not going to get you out of this prison, waterbreather. Besides, I am not so gullible as that. What of the permission? You forget that little detail? History is clear that

275

butterflies cannot enter an earth beast's mind unless asked to enter."

He growled deeply. "I don't know when she gave permission. Maybe that, too, is something that gods are-"

"Dompt."

Both the black-eyed creature and the scaled one started and turned towards the god. Her face was a mess of bloated sadness and Her words were choked, but She said it again.

"I once invited a butterfly into my head in what I thought was a dream. Back when we were in Dompt. I thought- I thought it was just a dream, but I guess I was just under the effects of lifeblood. I didn't know . . . ."

The dragon's eyes narrowed at that news. The warriors continued to look uncertainly between themselves. Whatever was happening involved their god and it was bad and so they wanted to kill something and make it all better. Like the dragon. He would be a good dead body to start rectifying things with.

As for the high dreadpriest, she made her decision right then and there. A rabbit is a rabbit is a rabbit until the day it grows to ten times it size, gains claws, and sprouts a longer tail. Then, it is a panther. You don't question why the rabbit is now a panther, nor how it came to be so. You simply accept it, adjust accordingly, and extract your larger knives.

"Release the dragon. Remove the hooks, the rope, and then file out. Speak of nothing that has happened in this room. Warrior Nakao, please escort the Prince of Dusk to Her chambers. If I hear even the whisper of the word 'bel' or 'bellanus,' then everybody's remaining forms are forfeit and your names will be stricken from the roll. Move. Now."

It was done with quiet efficiency and the desolate god didn't resist being ushered out of the room by Seina. The warriors removed the restraints from the dragon with rough jerks then left with only a few anxious glances to the high dreadpriest. A few minutes later, the dreadpriest and the dragon were alone in the dank room.

Erin was calm as she spoke.

"How do we get it out? Legends say the dragons had a method. Tell me."

The dragon said nothing. After being freed, he had moved his stumped forearms to push tenderly on the holes in his flanks where the hooks had been. The beast stood warily and strained to see the underbeing through his filmy eyes. Finally he shook is head.

"The only way we have requires an airbreather. There are none alive that can use that method to remove the bellanus."

The dreadpriest's face whitened ever so slightly. Nevertheless, Erin's voice remained smooth. "Fine, we will rip it out of Her head. She is a god. She will live. We should be able to simply crush Her skull, then reach in and pluck it out."

The dragon growled at the suggestion. "Simply reach into . . . you are a fool, underbeing. Who knows what the result of completely ripping apart a mind would be. You may end up with a drooling infantile creature or a complete personality change or worse . . . . Her body can't die, but her mind can only take so much abuse before drastic, irreparable things occur. That method is out of the question if you still want your god to be intact mentally at the end of this."

The high dreadpriest paused for a moment to think about the options. Finally, all she could ask was, "What is the longest time a dragon has ever remained coherent with a bellanus butterfly eating its mind?"

The dragon did not respond and instead brought his stumps up as if willing them to be whole. Erin's voice cooled threateningly.

"I said, what is the longest time a dragon has survived mentally?"

The dragon's growled. "Give me my claws first."

The high dreadpriest smirked. Other than that, she did not acknowledge the demand.

"My hands. My foreclaws," the dragon reiterated with a hiss. "Return them to me, or I'll stop answering your questions."

The high dreadpriest tapped a finger against the side of her cheek. "No, I don't think so. That won't do at all. You see, if I give them back to you, then you can heal yourself and change your size to become just another little snake slithering through the cracks to freedom. Then I lose my leverage. And the torturers lose sport. Instead we can just wait here together and wonder if the bellanus caterpillars can burrow through the shell of an egg."

The dragon's already angry face darkened and twisted even further. But he conceded.

"Thirteen months. It was over thirty years ago. Another waterbreather. One of the strongest of the brood. In the end he was nothing more than a husk of his former self. There was not a spark of thought left in that body when it did finally perish. Dompt, the village your Prince spoke about, was almost two years ago. Do the arithmetic, underbeing. Can you really afford to waste time? Now that your precious Clan loves that unborn hatchling, now that you love your godling, now that you need her to keep being your Prince, you have no leverage at all."

Erin pursed her lips. Irrefutable was a word that didn't usually sit well with her.

"I believe," the high dreadpriest finally stated, "this is what they refer to as an impasse. Well, what is your solution, waterbreather? Obviously you have a bargain in mind, and I'm just tickled pink to hear you tell it to me."

The dragon growled at the tone, but he did tell her his idea. The dragon explained the terms. Gave his proposition. Put forward the deal. It was simple, to the point, and to start immediately.

At the end of it, High Dreadpriest Valar smiled.

"My, my, my. I never knew you had it in you. Sounds divine. I'd suggest we shake on it, but well, that's just a bit insensitive right now, isn't it?" She paused a moment before adding, "You know, I've always wanted to see the Gossamer Forest burn."

CHAPTER 28
EVERYTHING YOU EVER WANTED TO KNOW ABOUT THE BELLANUS BUTTERFLY
(AS DESCRIBED IN "THE HISTORY OF THE GODS, PART I" COMPILED BY CHALAD NARUMANDER)

Important things are the most succulent. As such, the first losses of the mind manifest differently in each creature affected, depending on what they value to be the most important. In some beings, it is a precious memory. In others it's an attribute or a skill. Sometimes it is as complicated as losing language itself, and other times it is as simple as losing a single word.

Regardless of the order, all things are affected eventually. Memories are the only immediately quantifiable aspects that are consumed. Others, such as creativity, intelligence, libido, musical talent, wit . . . these things are more difficult to measure. Usually, they are eaten so carefully that at first it is impossible to be sure that anything has been removed at all. The last things eaten are always the basic functions of the human body.

The bellanus butterfly above all else is an expert chameleon. Detection is often delayed until very large pieces of a being's mind have already been consumed. In this way, a bel butterfly's offspring are usually well on their way before the bellanus is even suspected.

The butterfly's breeding habits are similar to those of vanas ticks. The butterfly mates prior to entering a host. Then, once it has consumed enough sustenance, proceeds to lay eggs into the bloodstream of its victim. The stronger the host, the longer the new insects will remain in egg form, and the stronger the resulting butterflies will be. When the eggs hatch, the bellanus will have entered their second stage: the caterpillar. The caterpillar stage lasts exactly thirty two days. These caterpillars are about the size of a maggot, and can sometimes be seen wriggling under the skin of the victim during this part of the cycle.

Finally, the caterpillars migrate to the mind of the host to spin their cocoons. At this point in time, sufficient space will have been hollowed out by the adult butterfly, as it will have continued a steady consumption of the host. The silk used to spin the bellanus butterfly's cocoon is corrosive. Therefore, three weeks later when the butterflies begin to emerge from their cocoons, the victim's skull has usually been reduced to a thin, soft layer, easily penetrated by the insects. After a bit of work, the head of the victim will burst and dozens, sometimes up to a hundred small bellanus butterflies will emerge to seek victims of their own.

It is for this reason that persons very late into the infection are usually beheaded, and both their bodies and heads are burned. It is only in this manner that the butterflies can be conclusively eradicated. Often, the host will notice that they have been infested before it becomes apparent to others. Some creatures, knowing the fate that awaits them and the pain that they will face when the butterfly continues to feed, will choose to kill themselves early on. This is seen in most communities as an honourable death.

There have been no documented cases of a bel butterfly being forcibly removed before the victim's mind has been completely consumed. Even if it is male or has not mated prior to entering its host, after the butterfly has departed the body to seek a new one, the resulting shell dies of starvation or thirst, lacking even the aspect of its mind that knows how to digest food, that is, if the bellanus has not also eaten the part of the mind that tells the heart how to beat and the lungs to breathe.

It is said that later in their susceptibility, dragons developed a way to remove the bel butterfly, but their secrets are not known to any outside their species.

The bellanus butterfly was originally developed as a weapon by the Oceo Tolok* during the fifth rebirth of the gods. The Warrior Clan had just been delivered a devastating blow by the Allied Kingdoms of the South. Having been caught away from the Gate, the army had been split, and almost completely destroyed. Wanting to give as much advantage to his remaining warriors, the Prince of Dusk was testing different substances on his soldiers, hoping to open new pathways in the brain and free their minds from the earth beast limitations. Indeed, some speculated that he wished to allow his warriors to evolve into the first sentient earthair beasts.

Much of the data on which he was basing his experimentation had been stolen from the Oceo Tolok themselves. Angered by the breach of security, they sought to develop a weapon to use against this new threat, should the Prince of Dusk ever successfully accomplish his research and experimentation.

The Prince of Dusk succeeded. The Oceo Tolok however, did not.

The insect served as an effective weapon, but it was not as particular about its victims as the Oceo Tolok would have liked. The bellanus butterfly had a taste for the mind of earthair beasts, but the Prince of Dusk had not altered enough of his warriors by the time the bellanus butterfly was released to satisfy their hunger. Since the bellanus was a voracious parasite with a strong will to live, it began to settle for less delectable options once the preferred prey had been entirely wiped out. The minds of lesser beasts did not contain enough sustenance, so the butterfly's survival depended on higher beasts.

It did not take long until the epidemic began. The Prince of Dusk's sentient earthair beasts were rendered extinct, and then the sentient earth beasts became targets. There were hundreds of thousands of casualties per day. The Second and Third Continents were abandoned completely as the populations there were wiped out. Nothing could be done about the insects. Wearable protective netting and meshes were devised but none were successful in stopping the bellanus, although it is said that towards the end of the epidemic, new materials with significant potential were in development.

Both the Lord of Salvation and the Prince of Dusk suffered heavy losses in their followers and the Oceo Tolok were almost credited with the apocalypse.

And so it came to be that the Lord of Salvation** approached the dragons to ask them to make a sacrifice. Until that time, they had been the only creatures unaffected. As higher earthwaterair beasts, their minds were too strong for the bellanus butterfly to penetrate. The god's request was simple. He would use a portion of His powers to alter the higher earth beasts so that it would be impossible for the bellanus to enter their minds without being invited in by the host of their own free will. A solution to the destruction of the sentient peoples of the world.

There was a catch though. Once this measure was enacted, the bellanus would be forced to adapt in order to overcome the previous barrier that kept the dragons safe from the deadly insects. The sentient earthwaterair beasts would become the new vulnerable species. Also, the god needed heartblood in order to accomplish His goal, and asked for the Brood Mother to give it willingly.

The dragons nobly accepted.

During the last hour of the gods' one hundred years, the Lord of Salvation sacrificed some of His own abilities to change the laws of creation, making it thereafter necessary for the predator to ask permission before attacking its prey. The minds of every human, elf, and dwarf were altered to give them an extra barrier of protection against any invasion of the mind.

In every subsequent rebirth, the Lord of Salvation has always been slightly weaker than His counterpart, but in doing so, saved the lives of every higher earth beast in the world.

As predicted, the butterfly adapted. Dragons began to die in scores. The Oceo Tolok, in an attempt to rectify their horrendous act, taught the dragons the secret of weaving water, so they could fortify themselves against the butterflies. Even the waterbreathers, already adept in the manipulation of water, benefitted from this information. The dragons also found that once in their earth beast suits, they were safe from penetration. Many in fact, chose to live the rest of their lives buried in the form of a human, elf, or dwarf in order to escape the terror that was the bellanus.

As a result of the creation of this parasite, the Oceo Tolok were forbidden to ever dapple with the genetic structure of any living organism again. Those beings that had already been altered were allowed to continue with their life cycles, but no new meddling was permitted. This was unquestionably supported by all factions, and a truce was struck between all sides in the war to refrain from allowing the Oceo Tolok to experiment on life.

Since the sacrifice of the dragons was made, the bellanus has been reduced to a very small population, surviving only off of unwary dragons and sentient two-legged earth beasts stupid enough to let one in.

Editor's notes:
**There has been some debate regarding the identity of the god who altered the minds of the sentient earth beasts, saving them from the bellanus.

Although most factions agree that it was the Lord of Salvation who was responsible, for many years there was support among scholars that it was the Prince of Dusk who became the weaker of the two gods after saving the world. This idea has since become heresy.

*The name for a group of elves known today as the 'Water Weavers.'

CHAPTER 29
ONE LAST LOOK

There was peace that day. Not peace because there had been an armistice struck with the underbeings who sought to kill the free races. Instead, there was peace because when the soldiers wearily got up from their bunks, when they exhaustedly walked patrols around their camps, when they listlessly rebuilt fires that would reheat last night's supper gruel which was to be today's breakfast gruel . . . when they did all of these things there were simply no attacks to be had. No throats were slit, no enemies were seen, no guerrilla tactics were used, nor did any lethorsum tipped arrows rain down. There was nothing but silence and the first true rest they received since before the gods had been found.

The dwarves, humans, and elves were confused by this turn of events. There was no reason for the changelings to withdraw. What need had the wining side to stop pressing forward? Clearly there was something else at work. Was it some ploy to lure them into a trap? Was it a retreat so the underbeings could attack from a new angle? Lieutenant-generals consulted with the Lord of Salvation and tried to deduce the meaning of it all, but nothing made sense, and they waited fearfully to see what the she-beast was scheming.

The reason was nothing so complicated as the armies of the Free Race Alliance feared. The reprieve in the attacks was simply due to the fact that a week previously, all the troops within a reachable distance had begun to sprint as fast as they could back to the Gate. Even those who hadn't been able to make the Prince's formal introduction, even those who had been undercover for years and deeply entrenched into free race society abandoned their posts to go home.

The Prince of Dusk was leaving.

Their god, their Lord of the Underbeings, their benevolent, lovely Prince was going on a mission. The nature of that mission was not important. Warriors did not receive the same training as the dreadpriests. It was only the most intelligent underbeings who were selected for the upper echelons of the changeling society. The dreadpriests were trained to command, the warriors were trained to obey. The dreadpriests were privy to the truths and fictions of their society, while the warriors were privy to the thirteen ways you can sever a spinal column with nothing more than a pointed stick and an apple core. The warriors were not meant to know why. They were meant to kill, kill well, and not ask questions.

But this did not mean that they were not allowed to know that there *was* a mission. And for that reason, they had gathered to see Her off, see their lovely and beautiful and so deliciously smelling god off. So the dreadpriests called them home. All of them. Come see Her leave, see Her for the last time for a while and no, we don't know how long that will be but we trust Her and She will love us even if She can't be with us because She's magnificent that way.

288

So the entire Warrior Clan still possessing a pulse who hadn't been a month-long journey away was waiting to see Her. The cubs were held high to see better and changelings further back stood on one another's shoulders. There was no pushing, nor shoving. Every underbeing understood that She did not belong to one, but to all of them, and every warrior had the same right to watch Her embark.

The Prince crossed the bridge over the oil moat then immediately waved to Her people. A cheer roared through the crowd. Incredibly, She was not wearing the usual lace and frivolous garb She usually sported. Instead, the Prince wore the Clan's black leathers with weapons strapped to Her sides that were identical to the ones worn by the warriors themselves. Likewise, instead of curls, bows, and ribbons, Her hair was braided and slicked with assault grease.

There were no dyes worked into Her flesh. God stood proudly, simply bedecked as all Her creations did when heading to battle. Although the changelings had always appreciated the beauty of their poised Prince, there was something much more satisfying about this determined, real god. This was not God giving supine inspiration, this was God in action.

Beside the Prince walked Warrior Nakao, the Companion chosen by the Prince of Dusk. Warrior Nakao did not wave to the Clan. She knelt and laid a palm to the earth. She was unconcerned with the tumult of leave-taking. As always, she was searching for danger to thwart, both from the bodies surrounding her and attempts from the Prince, Herself.

Behind the Companion, two dozen warriors from the First Legion stood in dark stances. The elven, dwarven, and humanoid bodies were as wary as Warrior Nakao. The personal safety of the Prince of Dusk was now their responsibility, and they would allow nothing to happen to Her.

Finally, out came High Dreadpriest Valar and Darlan. There were low growls heard at the sight of the waterbreather. There were whispers that the reason She was leaving was because of something the reptile had done. They said the scaled monster had brought an evil with it. All knew The Dealer was a snake, but they had thought it a toothless one. It seems there had been venom buried in the creature's gums against which they should have been vigilant all along.

For the most part, the Warrior Clan knew nothing of the eight months of torture, the bellanus, nor of the Greatest Sin, but they saw the determined way with which the Prince avoided the great beast, and that was enough for them. The dragon had travelled with Her before She had come back to them, but whatever good the waterbreather may have done during that time meant nothing to the warriors, now that it no longer held Her sacred favour.

Why the beast had been included in the mission was unknown, but they had faith that High Dreadpriest Valar would only include the monster because it was essential. But the mission would have to end sometime, and then The Dealer would be dealt with.

There was no parting speech. The Prince of Dusk smiled fondly at them all, then turned and began to head east. Warrior Nakao walked confidently beside Her. The other warriors saluted the remainder of the Clan before fanning out in every direction and disappearing in the distance, scouting the way for Her. Next, the waterbreather growled deeply, and then slunk off after the departing god. The last one to remain was High Dreadpriest Valar. She watched the chosen bodyguard of the Prince disperse, nodded crisply, and then stalked languidly after God, passing the waterbreather to join the Prince and the Companion.

Within a few minutes, none of the party could be seen. Yet the changelings quietly kept vigil until the Prince's scent disappeared from the wind. It was late when that time finally came. The sun was nothing more than a golden splash of colour in the distance, and a bruised sky began to ooze blemished stars which were immediately suffocated by dark clouds. When the last of their god's smell had left them, they said goodbye. That is, they lifted their heads, and howled together.

The deep, sad keen travelled across the entire northern continent. Rynna heard it as she walked in leathers towards the Tree Dwellers. The lesser beasts heard it and either burrowed deeper or scurried up higher. And the soldiers heard it. Those soldiers who had been waiting for the changelings to descend. They heard it, and those who did not shiver, wept.

CHAPTER 30
FLAMMABLE BREECHES

The black leather she wore was uncomfortable for many reasons. The first and most obvious being that she felt strangely naked in them after having gotten used to the excessive layers of petticoats and undergarments which the dreadpriests had thought necessary for their woman god. The second reason was that, undoubtedly, the leather used to belong to a creature with hopes, dreams, and most likely a biological resemblance to her. The tailor's expression 'like a second skin' was disturbingly accurate in her case.

It was quite sturdy, however. Sturdy yet pliable, which she would not have expected. But then again, thin clothing that ripped easily or else rubbed and blistered were not very practical for an army.

The god also found it strange to be carrying weapons. Of course, she was not expected to use them and they were only dull practice blades. The woman had neither the coordination, the training, nor the self-confidence (in that, she did not have the confidence that she would not try to kill herself) to use the weapons, but in the very least she could give the illusion of being her own last line of defense.

Seina walked beside her, navigating the woods far more easily than the god who had the use of both eyes. Every now and then, the warrior would smile at her god briefly before returning to her careful scrutiny of the area surrounding them. The Prince of Dusk was glad Seina had been allowed to come along. It was nice to have a familiar face to reassure her when terror threatened to overwhelm. The terror was justified, mind you, but still, the god did not have the luxury of letting her fear get out of control.

The bellanus. It was the source of her justified terror. Now that she knew of its existence, she could feel the bel butterfly in her head as a physical thing. The god could sense the insect flaking away slivers of her mind on which to feed. Her self was slipping away in incremental amounts. She remembered when the dragon had told her that his people would claw at their heads and dig gouges into their flesh upon learning of their infestation. The woman understood the desire now. She longed to ram a finger deep into her head to extract the thing.

At least with the dragons, death would welcome them. But she was a god and her body couldn't die. So she would end up as a shell. An empty god shell. No thoughts, no basic motor skills, no drive to eat, nor the ability to shit. When the butterfly was done with her, she wouldn't be able to digest food even if it was force fed down her throat.

As the god walked through the forest, she continued to do the same thing she had been doing almost every five minutes since the moment the dragon had brought the information to her attention: combing through the seconds of her childhood trying to remember her mother's name.

There was nothing there. Not a first letter, nor a rhyme, nor the shadow of meaning. Rynna felt as if something terribly vital had been ripped from her, and indeed it had. But not ripped. Eaten. Just like everything in her mind would soon be.

What else had she already lost? Maybe . . . maybe she had picked out perspective names for the hatchling but had had that taken from her in the meantime. Maybe she had lost her favourite tastes. Lavanor was a significant gap, but even now as she racked her memories, other than her mother's name she couldn't detect any other rifts.

And the worst thing of all: was the bel butterfly eating her mind alone, or was the hatchling being affected as well? That lovely little hatchling who, according to the dragon, was near its hatching.

She didn't even want to think about the other issue. The 'what if the butterfly had mated' issue. The god could hardly keep herself from compulsively running her fingers up and down her neck, her closest exposed skin, searching for any small caterpillar sized lumps wriggling underneath.

Seina. Dependable Seina. She had simply leaned in to confide. "Of course we'll get it out. No worries at all." As if that 'of course' solved all of the world's problems. But unfortunately, the other items on Seina's 'of course' list were not reassuring. 'Of course' raw meat tastes better than when it is cooked. 'Of course' victims beg for mercy, that's the fun of snapping off their fingers one at a time. 'Of course' the free races will be eventually eradicated. The inevitability was all just a matter of time.

The god shuddered and wished the efficient leather came with a cloak she could wrap around herself for warmth.

The now twelve-foot long dragon smoothly stalked about twenty paces in front of her. Twenty paces in front of everybody. His wounds were all healed. She hadn't watched, but Seina had and then had reported it all to her in vivid detail. How the dragon had lined his stumps up with the withered foreclaws, and how upon contact the flesh had begun to reattach itself. How the dragon had proceeded to smooth out all of his wounds and reform his wings.

It had made the warrior angry having all that lovely torture be for naught. Especially considering she still felt that the only appropriate punishment for the dragon was to have him tied to a rock and his liver eaten daily by birds of prey. If the Warrior Clan hated Darlan with an undying fury, then Warrior Nakao was doing a splendid job representing them. Seina's sole regret was that this mission needed him, meaning that a messy accidental death was out of the question.

For once, Rynna agreed. Not with the birds of prey or the messy death part, but she wished the dragon was not here with them. Seeing the dragon had her remembering the talks, the food, the adventure, and the roads. It made her throat feel dry and scratchy.

He had tried to get close to her when they had first headed out. He hadn't tried to touch her, or talk to her, or even walk beside her. He had simply attempted to come within her vicinity. Seina, hearing the anger and wariness build in the young god, had immediately and soundlessly let fly a small dagger which landed with a thick 'chunk' as it buried itself just under the dragon's left eye. The great beast had snarled and snapped his teeth at the blindfolded warrior, but had still grudgingly slunk to the head of the column, where he had stayed ever since.

His presence on the trip unavoidable because of his association with Lira Spencer: an elf that owed the dragon a lifedebt. The three thousand year old beast was going to call in that debt to gain access to information regarding the Oceo Tolok.

It was almost eight thousand years ago that their experiments and projects had been stopped. Not only stopped, their research had been all but destroyed. Laboratories gutted. Textbooks burnt. Tools shattered or melted beyond use. Although the elves of the Oceo Tolok had agreed to the truce, nobody had really trusted them to keep it. The purge was so complete and had happened so long ago that the only information left about the ancient people and their works were to be found with scholars of the free race variety who had access to the personal records and dealings of the Lord of Salvation with his pet scientists. The Bai Library wasn't an option as it was being protected happily in Lavanor. They would need to search elsewhere for their answers.

Enter Lira: one of the Water Weavers' librarians. Hypothetically, she would either tell them what they needed to know, or else bring them to where they needed to be. The ancient woods that made up the Gossamer Forest and from there across the Crystal Bridge was the only access to the Water Weavers' island now that the Open Shore was closed.

"You actually believe she will honour the debt?"

The high dreadpriest's words had been full of scepticism when the dragon had first suggested it.

"She will, if we are also threatening the trees of their precious forest."

Their backup plan. Well, actually, it was their coinciding plan. If the elves were feeling uncooperative, or even just not moving quickly enough to suit the underbeings, then they would hold the woods hostage until the needed information was handed over. The trees had been the ancient home of the elves for longer than the war had existed. Rynna saw the calculated brilliance of the plan. She knew how painful it was to watch your home and everything you love burn.

So there it was. A plan perfectly packaged, tied with ribbon and a bright pink bow on top. All to get information that would somehow save the devil from losing her mind. And a plan where the dragon was fundamentally necessarily and therefore, whose death for the moment was completely unacceptable.

The only problem with the pink bowed package, the only solution the dragon could not provide, was the one for the starved rocks.

The starved rocks. Another atrocity of the Oceo Tolok. The woman god grimaced at the thought of them. Like the watchtowers on the southern continent or the indestructible Crystal Bridge connecting the Gossamer Forest to the Water Weavers' Lakes, nobody knew for certain what the original intent of the starved rocks had been, but they served their current purpose well.

She was told that the staved rocks looked innocent enough. They were supposedly a small, four-foot high stone wall that completely encircled the Gossamer Forest. There was an eight-foot gap in the south end and another where the Bridge began. Those gaps served as the only two entrances to the woods, and other than that the rocks formed a complete loop.

Allegedly, the wall looked sloppy in its construction, some of the foundation blocks being uneven and badly cut. Certainly the stones were nothing to cause any alarm at a glance, unless you were aesthetically minded. However, unlike most innocent four-foot walls, this one was rather more dangerous.

It was carnivorous.

The hows and whys were lost along with the rest of the details about the projects of the Oceo Tolok, but the result was a four-foot wall that consumed any meat that touched it as effectively as a vat of sulphuric acid does cotton candy, or sordid gossip does social circles.

And it wasn't just the stones themselves that ate. Although the physical wall stopped after four feet, its mouth continued up, up, high into the air. The dragon had revealed that in his youth, on a dare, him and five other dragons had tried to fly high overtop the cursed earth. Even at ten thousand feet the waterbreather had not been able to get past the invisible barrier. Moreover, before he had been able to extricate himself, he had developed a thick rash on his toughened scales as those hungry stones pulled meat into themselves even at that height.

Living or dead, the rocks ate any flesh they could find. And the starved rocks were very good at finding said flesh. In what was known as the Last War of the Free, a particularly clever and ambitious human king built iron contraptions that were essentially a series of large, metal boxes connected to pulleys. It was inside these that his soldiers stood while hundreds of feet of thick cable hoisted them well above and across the hungry stones. The king's brilliant plan was that the layer of iron would protect the soldiers. After all, the wall liked meat, not metal. Flesh, not steel. What interest would hungry stones have for more earth?

The result of this simple experiment is possibly one of the more gruesome events to ever occur on that little planet. Because everything has holes. Even if it is simply the barest of rifts between two atoms, that space exists. Infinitesimal gaps.

And the stones pulled their victims through the very walls of those iron boxes. Ripped the soldiers' meat out of the sealed metal contraptions and ate them piece by tiny piece. The king went mad with the screaming. By the time they got the boxes back on the ground, there was only discarded armour and some partially dissolved bones rattling around inside.

The elves in the Gossamer Forest have not been successfully attacked, ever.

The god shook her head. At least the starved rocks weren't her job to deal with. Her job was to be pregnant, give birth, and then let the butterfly be pulled out of her head. All the uselessness of her time in the Menundra with a slightly better view and no dreadpriests trying to pretty her up in the morning. All in all, if she didn't have a an insect in her head eating her memories, a carnivorous wall to surpass, and a daily reminder of her dead mother, life would have been an improvement over what it had become over the past few months.

The god was the most relieved about the fact that they hadn't left her back in the underbeings' fortress. They could have easily come to the conclusion it was safest to keep her locked away and bring the solution to her. Thankfully it was decided that every part of her mind was precious. Once the method for saving her was discovered they couldn't afford to waste time before implementing it, even if it was just for another few weeks.

Meaning she was allowed to come along for the mission. She wasn't sure if it was a sign of their increasing trust in their Prince or else if they just didn't want to deal with her protests, but either way, the woman god was supremely relived that Valar and the other dreadpriests had reached the decision to bring her along.

They set up camp when the sun had set completely. The day had been long and hard because there was no allowed conversation to hasten time or lighten hearts. Her changelings did not chat when they travelled. They went quickly and quietly. They did not talk while they made camp either. Instead, they moved in memorized silence. The underbeings seemed to frown even upon heavy breathing, and the god had spent the first few hours of their trip being painfully aware of how her changelings glided through the trees, while she went at a pace that was more of a stomping, thrashing wade.

This voyage was the first time the god had ever watched the shapeshifters travel. The last time she had been with them had been spent unconscious. And now, when she watched their lithe bodies move through the woods with grace and silence, she realized that their comportment around her in the Menundra was them relaxing. Expressionless, emotionless stalking is what they all did when on duty.

The most superfluous things she saw were when the changelings would crush any butterflies attempting to follow them, and even then it was a swift, sure movement of death. Seina, usually loquacious if a little macabre, was now straight faced and mute, placing her feet carefully one before the other and listening to the sounds of the life surrounding her to determine a path.

Her changelings had brought no tents and they made no fires. The prearranged first shift took their watch and the rest ate cold provisions, took a few sips of water, then curled up with thin bedrolls on the ground and fell wordlessly into sleep. The well-briefed and well-trained group of underbeings were all but invisible. The god alone seemed to crave conversation, but of the three she knew well enough to say more than two words to, one she couldn't stand, one was busy coordinating warriors, and Seina had been set on first watch.

The young god wrapped herself in her own bedroll and tried to find a patch of ground that didn't have too many sneaky rocks waiting to dig knots into her muscles. It was during this that the dragon approached the god again. Only this time, despite the guard set purposely to be a sentinel for her, none knew about it.

The pain was almost nonexistent as he snuck into her thoughts.

Human.

The young god flinched and the changeling guarding her opened his eyes wider in question. The god nodded to the guard reassuringly before closing her eyes. She didn't know if it had been light enough for the underbeing to see her cheeks burning.

To have the dragon in her head now after everything that had happened, invoked a basic and profound bitterness in the young woman. She wished she had never given the dragon permission to enter her head. In retrospect, many of her current problems would be eliminated if she had just had a more exclusive membership to her body.

The young woman considered telling Seina. The warrior would probably know how to get the dragon to stay out. But that would mean she would be spending the next two hours watching the dragon be tortured. The god thought about barbed wire wrapped around the scaled maw. She thought about cable laced through ripped wings and iron hooks in hind legs. No, that wasn't an option. She would simply ignore it. She would ignore the burning voice of the dragon.

Human. I must discuss something with you. Speak with me.

The god clenched her teeth. Ignore it. Show no reaction and he will give up. Or better yet, let him think she was asleep. The young woman tried to even out her breathing, and inhale more deeply. The nice in-and-out pattern of a dreaming god.

I am not asking for forgiveness and loyalty. Conversation and explanation, all provided by myself. Come. Now.

The words started to hurt more. Their presence in her head became larger and the pathways were growing coarse and raw in her mind. Maintaining the even pace of her lungs was difficult. That profound bitterness heated with anger. The god clenched her teeth some more.

Human.

Rynna's gums were numb with the pressure her jaw was inflicting on her teeth. That heavy adult dragon voice burned in her mind. The beast was making it very hard for her to regret the treatment he had endured by her people. Something in the god's head began to react. Leave. Me. Alone.

Human!

The dragon's voice screamed at her and echoed the implicit command repeatedly. Anger was poisoning Rynna's self-control.

Come speak to me NOW.

The god snapped.

FUCK OFF!

A rushing feeling. A slight sucking. Then, solitude. No trace of the dragon voice there any longer. Relief washed over the god despite the rage still burning through her. The god unclenched her jaw slowly and rubbed her gums gently to return sensation to them. She took a deep breath and opened her eyes.

Every single underbeing in the clearing had rolled out of their bedrolls, drawn blades, and was now staring at her uncertainly.

A hand lightly grazed her arm and the god sat up violently. Seina was standing there, her stance letting the god know the warrior was perplexed. The high dreadpriest was also beside them. Warrior Nakao spoke quietly.

"We heard You. Everything okay?"

Heard her? The god shook her head, not understanding the warrior's question. Valar soon clarified things for the woman. Her voice was just only audible.

"Pray tell us, Prince. Why did we all just hear You screaming inside our minds when You are not supposed to have any powers beyond that of the average human? And screaming with such colourful language at that."

The darkness of the evening was not broken by the moon or stars. The overhead clouds blotted the sky and left the figures in front of her hazy and indistinct in detail. The god couldn't see the high dreadpriest's face, and hopefully that meant the underbeing wouldn't be able to read hers either.

A small debate began to take place in the god's mind. She could tell them about thoughtspeech. An opportunity for some revenge against the dragon. Gods know the manipulative creature had earned it. But to what end? The secret of an entire species had been entrusted to her. The dragon sharing thoughtspeech had been one of the only genuine things the two had experienced together. Did she want to ruin that, too? And besides, the Warrior Clan was deadly enough as it was. Did she want them to hone their efficiency even more?

Her debate resulted in no definitive ruling either way, and everybody was still waiting for her to speak. She would have to stall for now and figure out what she really wanted to do about everything later. An explanation slipped through her lips.

"I must be uncovering some of my powers."

She hadn't bothered to whisper when she spoke and, as such, her voice was deafening in contrast to her dreadpriest's. Valar's intrigued tones spoke of the smirk she knew the changeling to be wearing.

"My, my, my . . ." Valar paused, weighing her Prince's words against a golden feather. Then abruptly, she spoke clearly. "I guess that must be the case. Well then, if You have begun to discover some abilities, maybe You could put them towards defeating the wall we'll be reaching soon."

There was some light rustling as the high dreadpriest's words were passed quietly through the small group. It was just their god being a little more Princey than usual today. No problems there and no more explanations needed. Tenseness left the underbeings, and they slipped off to resume their former positions: the watchers watching and the sleepers sleeping. Seina squeezed the god's arm once before silently disappearing herself back into the woods. The dragon must also have been satisfied because the Prince of Dusk felt his eyes leave her.

It was only High Dreadpriest Valar who continued to watch her with amusement. The god turned away from the woman's black eyes and sought the abandoned bedroll.

Rynna had barely settled in when she felt a set of fingers touch her shoulder. The god looked up to see the high dreadpriest. Valar was squatting incredibly close to her. The god had not heard her move. High Dreadpriest Valar smiled, and then whispered.

"Liar, liar pants on fire."

Then she abruptly got up and melted into the night.

The god was left staring in confusion. She shivered as a breeze prickled her skin so she tucked her blanket in tighter and curled herself up.

305

She had almost fallen asleep when she felt a gentle ramming voice, so much more welcome than the last one had been.

Earth-Mother, what does 'fuck' mean?

Despite everything, the god touched her stomach, and smiled ruefully.

CHAPTER 31
A GOOD WITCH 'SA DEAD WITCH

The attack came the following morning. The god was ripped unceremoniously out of sleep by the dragon and lifted into the air seconds later. Rough claws gripped her around the middle and the ground dropped away from her at a lurch. The flapping wings near her almost drowned the sound of clashing steel and dying soldiers. As the blood rushed into her head, realization and consciousness slowly caught up with her and a knot of frustration began burning in her chest.

When there was nothing left below them but black-eyed creatures wiping blades clean, the dragon flew back to the ground and dropped his unwitting passenger. The god landed with a grunt, rolling slightly to cushion her impact. The dragon didn't offer an explanation, but instead looked at her coolly before stalking off towards Valar and speaking to the underbeing in a low growl which the young god couldn't make out.

The god stomped right after him, but was soon interrupted by Seina, who stepped smoothly in front of her, and smiled with too many teeth.

"Good morning, Dusk Prince," she greeted.

The god scowled. "I thought you hated the dragon, and here you let him rip me out of bed and cart me through the air? What happened this morning?"

The blind woman's face darkened. Her whisper was now more gravelly in composition. "Believe

307

me, it wasn't my idea that the waterbreather should-
"

"My, we are lively this morning." The high dreadpriest smoothly cut into the conversation with her own whisper. She had evidently finished speaking with the dragon and came to join the two. As she spoke, her eyes were sharp and piercing. "That is very good. We need to make up lost time."

"Lost time. Is that what you're calling me being dragged into the air?"

The high dreadpriest's reply was just as even as her greeting had been. And it was just as quiet. "We didn't think it was necessary to let You know that our first line of defense is to have the dragon fly You to safety. You might have ordered us not to. Even though You will survive it, its upsetting to see You get hurt, Prince."

The dragon was watching the exchange with a guarded expression. As for the god, she closed her eyes and breathed deeply. *All the uselessness of her time in the Menundra with a better view and-*

"Who attacked us?" she demanded, her voice still reeling with volume.

The high dreadpriest nodded in deference, her voice even quieter still. "Who else? Free race patrols searching for us. Your departure created waves. Our adversaries are not completely bereft of intelligence and reliable scouts. They know You are on the move and they think You would make a good gift for the Lord of Salvation. Although the Warrior Clan has . . . difficulties with the dragon's involvement in all of this, it is unquestionable that the safest place for You in the event of any incursions against us is hundreds or else thousands of feet in the air, out of bowshot range."

The god's outrage wavered somewhat.

"Well, in the attack was anybody . . . did any of our . . . ."

Seina smiled and shook her head. Her voice was thick and happy even in whispered form.

"No, my Prince. After all, we brought the best. All twenty hearts are still pumping blood, and only one form was lost. The patrol was clumsy and we knew about them well in advance. We thought You'd like the extra sleep. Next time we will give You more warning."

The dragon hissed his way into the conversation. His words were dark. He, like the god, did not bother to lower his voice.

"Let us leave this place, underbeing. The bloodlust smells rank."

A nearby warrior in the human form growled at hearing those words, and the dragon was quick to snarl back.

The high dreadpriest shook her head at the offending underbeing and it immediately quieted, slinking off to the side.

"Noisy, noisy, noisy. My dear Prince, when You don't keep yourself quiet, You give all kinds of notions to the rest of those here. Maybe if You can't remember to whisper, You could use last night's method to communicate with us."

She smiled stiffly and paused a few seconds before continuing.

"No? Very well, then maybe we should get moving as the waterbreather suggested. I am sure there are other patrols and when this one is discovered missing, they will send more. Next time their numbers will not be so insufficient. Besides, the butterfly won't take itself out of Your head, will it, Prince?"

The high dreadpriest smiled again before turning to Seina and whispering to her a brief message. Then, she walked away to delegate specific instructions to the other members of their group. The dragon watched Rynna for a few extra heartbeats before turning away himself.

When Seina returned to the god's side, the young woman couldn't help but ask bitterly, "Why does she push me like that?"

"Who, Erin?"

"Who else!"

Seina paused carefully and then shrugged, "She is disappointed with You."

"Because I can't remember who I am? But Valar has made it perfectly clear that the scriptures said I wouldn't know anything. How can she blame me for that?" The god continued to speak in exasperation. "The other dreadpriests have known the truth from the start and they never had any problems with me. The warriors love me. I am the Prince of Dusk, but she still treats me like I'm just-just a human. Why?"

Seina ran a hand over the hilt of her weapon in a caress as she spoke.

"Erin is different than all of us. She knew You personally before You were born. She knew the person You were when You remembered everything. She was so excited when You left her to walk the flesh. She couldn't wait to meet You and speak to You again. But then, when she did finally meet You . . . . You had no idea who she was, who we were, why the Pit exists. You were just another member of the free races, cowering in an alleyway. The rest of us have only known You as the flesh being You are now. We love You because, despite Your deficiencies, You love us and You are God. But Erin misses who she hoped You were going to be based on the person she had been speaking to for over a decade."

"So, that's it then, she'll just always think I'm not good enough and I'll have to deal with it."

"No, Erin loves You the same as the rest of us. She has always been impatient, though. And waiting for You to become who You are has been difficult for her. Don't worry, my Dusk Prince. Your high dreadpriest's blood is Yours just as much as mine is."

With that, her Companion left to see to her duties as the group prepared to leave. The party's camp was packed away much more quickly than it had been set up. They spent more time concealing body imprints in grass and burying free race corpses than they did actually gathering supplies. One would hardly guess they had stayed the night at all, let alone that there had been an attempted ambush. They filed away quietly and continued on their way.

On that second day, the walking was just as tedious as it had been on the previous one, only this time the god had the company of a growing blister on her left heel. She briefly considered asking Seina to teach her something of the Warrior Clan's method of traveling so quietly. It would be nice to feel a little less useless among her underbeings. The initiative didn't last though because she couldn't help from wondering what the point of learning anything new was if it was just going to get eaten anyways. Her mood did not improve from there and the god continued on in stony silence.

All too quickly, the god's foot developed that wet sticky feeling which meant the blister had ruptured and she was bleeding. Calluses earned while walking the roads with the dragon had been lost in her months spent at the Gate, and her feet were no longer used to boots. Her leg now burned with each step, and she couldn't help but limp a bit.

Seina glanced at her questioningly, but the god shook her head curtly. She didn't want to be the reason they stopped early. She could last just as long as the rest of the warriors. She was not some helpless girl that needed to be flown to safety by a dragon. She was the Prince of Dusk, the powerful god of the underbeings.

However, as this is a thing much easier said than done, the god began to grunt in pain as her boots rubbed away more flesh. Her Companion tilted her head towards her often and with an increasingly worried expression on her face. The god tried to squeeze the woman's arm reassuringly, but it was a squeeze that became progressively less steady as the grating of her raw skin turned into a pulsing throb.

To distract herself from the constant sear in her heel, the god decided to concentrate inward. As much as she had abhorred the dragon's intrusion into her thoughts last night, it had resulted in an unexpected blessing. Not only had the hatchling heard her, but the little dragon had spoken back to the god as well. Certainly a little prenatal dragon would be better company than blisters, and definitely more engaging.

The young god had no desire to repeat the previous evening's performance, though. She didn't want to scream messages into the mind of everybody within a league. What she really wanted was a one-on-one discussion with the little creature growing inside of her. Did her hatchling dream of human things as borrowed images from her mother, or did she dream of the mountains and wings of her species?

The god remembered little of what the dragon had taught her about how to project thoughtspeech, and even less about what she had done in a fit of anger the previous night. She did recall something about a brain sneeze, but it didn't seem quite momentous enough for what she was attempting. She spent the rest of the day trying to send words to the hatchling with no success. No matter how fat, jaunty, or personable she made the words, they determinedly stayed in her own brain.

Unsurprisingly, all evening she was also unsuccessful in her attempts at communication. The following day the only thing she accomplished was to rub a matching blister into her right heel. It wasn't until the third day when she finally got something through. And curiously enough, she hadn't even been trying to use thoughtspeech at the time.

Their group had reached a low ditch flooded with spring waters. The warriors were passing through the shin-high murky water in single file. Whether this was to ease passage or to hide numbers, the god was uncertain. She didn't ask, trusting in the abilities of her changelings.

While Seina whispered quick instructions as to the easiest way to surpass the small ditch, a sudden, nasty memory sprung to mind. In it she was holding her mother's hand and carrying their meagre supplies when suddenly some children, prodding one another for courage and whispering in dark voices, gathered around an old hag in filthy clothes. The memory was so real and vivid, that the god couldn't stop the twisted lyrics of the girls' song from thrumming in her head.

> *Buried in the back ditch*
> *Hot fire and black pitch.*
> *A good witch 'sa dead witch.*

The song laid heavily in her stomach. She wished she could pick and choose what the bellanus ate. It was cruel that she couldn't remember her mother's name, but could recall perfectly what vegetables they had bought that day and how tight her shoes had been. The water from the ditch through which they walked squelched between her toes as it soaked down into her boots. Wet feet would make for a miserable evening and her mood did not improve.

She continued to fixate on these things until her attention was broken when an unmistakeable voice echoed in her head.

You were so little.

The god's eyes widened and her heart wrenched. The little female voice was full of so much beauty.

Seina turned her head towards the god. She had felt the shift in her Prince and was certain that passing minnows were not the things eliciting the strange reaction.

"It's the hatch- the god cub. It's the god cub speaking to me," she whispered quickly to the elven woman leading her.

Seina smiled and nodded. No interruptions from her.

A second question rammed itself into her mind.

Who is the woman being hurt?

So . . . the hatchling had not only heard the chant, but she had seen the memory, too. The dragon had never mentioned the possibility. Maybe he had thought that she wouldn't have been able to survive something that complicated. Or else maybe this was only something that hatchlings could do.

The young god's happiness at hearing the little voice mixed sourly with the bitter memory of Lady Shutba's stoning. Although she loved the idea of communicating with the small being, she didn't want the hatchling exposed to such violent thoughts. Her life would undoubtedly be savage enough as it was without prenatal trauma being tossed into the mix. The god carefully phrased her next thought, making her words thick and substantial enough to push towards the little being incubating inside her.

Somebody who was waiting to be paid.

And who is the woman you are holding?

The god again thought back to what she had been picturing. The young girls singing, the boys throwing stones, Lady Shutba stumbling along as she tried to get past the group. And her mother. Her

315

mother had been holding her hand, and then had quietly led her away from the local sports team.

She struggled to keep her response firm and vivid in her head so she could maintain this tentative connection with her daughter.

It's my *mother.*

The god felt a smile poke out with the next question that squeezed into her head.

Great-Earth-Mother?

The young woman couldn't help but grin at the excitement in the voice. Her response was light and playful.

Yes, Great-Earth-Mother.

The voice bubbled golden through her thoughts. Even the water squelching in her boots could not dampen the optimism of the giggling, exuberant voice.

Then abruptly, it all changed.

What is Great-Earth-Mother's name?

An incredible pain throbbed in the woman god's chest, and the connection between the two of them snapped. Seina felt that break like you would feel icy river water being splashed against the person next to you. It raised bumps on the warrior's skin, and she reached out to touch her god comfortingly.

"What is it?" she asked softly. The Prince of Dusk pushed away Seina's concern and her hand.

The dragon, still walking in front of everybody, was glancing around and caught sight of the god. He saw the expression on her face and growled in the warrior's direction as if he thought the situation was somehow the Companion's fault.

"How long."

316

Seina tore her attention away from the dragon to focus on the god once more. "Until what, Dusk Prince?"

"Until I can get the butterfly out," the young god whispered in a volume that would have satisfied the high dreadpriest's strictest evening regulations. "Until this is over."

"As soon as we get to the Gossamer Forest, we can find the solution. At most it will be only fifteen more days until we reach the starved rocks. As soon as Erin finds a way to bypass the wall, it will be no more than days after that until you are cured. The elves won't refuse us."

Warrior Nakao smiled reassuringly after she was done speaking. Dreadpriests were infallible, of course. As infallible as gods were. The Prince of Dusk clenched her hands then opened them again to stare at her palms. Just over a fortnight to calmly figure out something that had never been done before. She wondered how many names could be eaten in a fortnight.

The dragon was still watching the two of them darkly. This time, the god noticed as well. She glared at the dragon in return, and her voice was messy with feeling.

"Fifteen days. Good. The sooner this is finished, the better. Let's just break the stupid walls or feed them or do whatever ingenious thing Valar is planning and then get back to the Menundra."

Nothing more was said for the rest of the day, and nothing much for the rest of the week for that matter. There were no more attacks. Some of the scouts for their group left for long periods of time, but they always returned with only minor quantities

317

of blood on their black leather. The hatchling did not speak any more to the god, and so the Prince of Dusk kept quiet with her thoughts buzzing.

It would be another nine days until a dragon attempted to initiate contact again. It was evening at the time, and the stars were playing chase across the sky as the moon looked at everything fondly. The god had been sitting beside the fire trying to make the flatbread she was eating taste like anything other than the same flatbread she had been eating ever since they had left the Gate when suddenly, her mind burned fiercely.

Human.

His words were sandpaper on her thoughts. Fine grating that tore away at the skin to leave exposed raw muscle. The god grunted at the feeling which had taken her unawares.

The god had neither the energy nor the ability to respond with anything else but,

Go away.

Her eyes stole over to where the dragon sat, hunched with his back to a thick tree. The beast wasn't looking in her direction. His eyes seem to be staring into the shadows beyond the camp, perhaps either tracking the changelings on patrol or else searching for fluttery predators.

You have been practicing.

His voice in her mind was dark. The hint of a threat was there as well, and the god felt as though she should brace herself for some reason.

I said go away. You have no right to be in my head.

You invited me. You wanted me to come into your great and mighty brain, so here I am. What I

318

want to know is with whom you have been practicing.

What do you really want? I'm sick of all this.

The dragon sobered at her directness. No games. Just a statement of business so she could get on with resenting him.

You have been speaking with the hatchling. What have you told her of me?

Worried about her finding out the truth?

If it were the truth, yes. But now my worry is that a hysterical human will tell lies to a small, impressionable being.

What lies? You admitted you let my mother die. You stuck this egg in me without telling me. I haven't told the hatchling anything, but if I wanted to, I wouldn't need to lie.

As I once told you, greatmothers are very important to my kind. Very important. I need you to understand what happened before the hatchling hates me for something I had to do.

Something . . . something you . . . had to . . . had to do-

That thought was the last coherent one the god had. What followed was what one might call an explosion of thought. A hydrogen bomb of the mind whereby the god blindly reached out and dealt a crushing blow to the dragon's central nervous system.

The great winged beast went limp and collapsed in a pile of rubbery muscle. His bulk twitched for a while before it finally stilled. The underbeings who were eating their own dinners looked up questioningly at their Prince, who wore a face of retribution and fury. They nodded in satisfaction, gave her covert thumbs up signs, and then returned their attentions to what they had been doing previously. Although they tried to conduct their affairs with the same seriousness as before, you could see pricked ears and toothy grins everywhere.

High Dreadpriest Valar raised an eyebrow in her direction, the waterbreather still spasming occasionally behind her.

"One more thing You are beginning to remember, Prince? You seem to offer more surprises every day. Do play nice, though. The reptile is the only one with the ability to hold the elves accountable."

The Prince's anger quickly petered out as the shock of what she had done began to sink in. She could still feel the violence of it in her head. She hadn't meant to do . . . whatever it was she had done. Something had just taken over for a few seconds. Something violent, terrible, and powerful.

The young woman spent a while trying to decide whether or not she regretted the action. If nothing else, the god thought with a shake of her head, she couldn't deny the effectiveness of it getting the dragon to leave her alone.

CHAPTER 32
MEDIUM RARE

Erin Valar, high dreadpriest of the changelings, marvelled at lesser earth beasts. There was such a fascinating dichotomy between the complication of their instincts and the simplicity of their minds. Take the rabbit currently thrashing violently and trying to escape from her hands. By all rights, the hare had no reason to be afraid of the starved rocks. It had never heard of the Oceo Tolok, didn't have a brain big enough to process the idea of them, nor what they did. But still, this little lesser earth beast was scared senseless at the sight of that short wall.

Erin cleared her throat, indicating for Seina to come forward. The blind woman picked her way easily towards the high dreadpriest. Erin watched the warrior's nostrils flare.

"What do you smell?"

Seina considered carefully before she spoke in crisp tones.

"The rocks don't smell like anything else I've been around before. And they don't smell like the watchtowers either. This resembles more like the smell of the sea at high tide during a lunar eclipse."

Erin hefted the rabbit in front of the female warrior's face.

"And the bunny?"

Seina's mouth curled upwards into what was undoubtedly bliss at the creature's smell. She licked her lips and then her face flushed.

"I thought so." Even with Erin's own muted senses, the rabbit smelled delicious. Unadulterated terror was the most sublime of culinary aphrodisiacs.

"Can I have him after you're done?"

"Are we craving fresh meat or is it the fear we want to taste? You have been deprived of sport ever since you were made Companion."

Seina shook her head eagerly. "No, the Prince of Dusk has never eaten raw meat before. Can you imagine? I've been waiting for the right way to introduce it to Her and the rabbit is going to taste exquisite."

Ah, so that was it. The high dreadpriest was highly amused for a few moments, but then she quickly shifted her eyes back to the wall and sighed. Dreadpriest Thorren would do an adequate job at the Menundra in her absence, but even still . . . the starved rocks were supposed to be her crowning checkmate, not some paltry rook castling technique.

The idea of the Prince of Dusk as a shell was unthinkable though.

Erin frowned. Worse, she needed the dragon. The Warrior Clan had not needed the aid of another species since the underbeings were created. The whole situation made Erin's flesh rank with dissatisfaction and anxiety. Not for the first time she wanted to be nothing more than a warrior, responsible for death dealing and not for keeping a god's mind alive.

Erin once again looked at Warrior Nakao and assessed the careful way she evaluated the squirming lesser earth beast with all but one sense.

"You may have it after I kill it."

Seina bobbed her head quickly. "Thanks, sir."

Erin tensed the muscles in her arm to get a firm grip on her victim. Those delicious little instincts kicked in and the rabbit squirmed even harder, sharp toenails driving long scratches down her arm. Erin let the beast have its last glorious moment in life. She did not resist as the rabbit tore up her skin. Then, the high dreadpriest brought her hand back, and tossed the hare towards the stone wall in front of her.

The rabbit did not hit the starved rocks themselves, but the unseen wall above it. There was a hiss of dissolving flesh and the small mammal screamed. The two underbeings watched the animal fall along the lengths of the barrier, leaving a dark red, almost black streak behind it until it landed on top of the stones themselves.

Interestingly, the creature was still violently alive. The rabbit kicked out wildly against its pain in the hopes of removing itself from its predator. Flesh still dissolving, animal still screaming, the hare thrust its legs around haphazardly. Its foot somehow caught on an edge and the mostly consumed thing rolled away from the stones. However as too many of the rabbit's insides were no longer on the inside, four shallow, panicked breaths were all the beast had left before it died.

Exactly six seconds had lapsed since Erin had thrown the hare. The high dreadpriest calmly walked over, picked up the rabbit, and then handed its remains to Seina.

"For the Prince."

Seina nodded. Erin could see the wheels twisting in Warrior Nakao's mind, as she no doubt wondered where they could get their own pet carnivorous stones. Now if only they did not have to scale this lovely wall, Erin would have been quite satisfied with the day. She wondered if the dragon had any ideas. As amusing as the Prince's performance had been, it was really too bad he was still unconscious.

"After you have fed the Prince, return with an update on the," her lips thinned, "waterbreather's health. The Prince has been moping long enough. The longer the snake is unconscious, the more he dilutes Her beautiful wrath."

"Yes, sir." The warrior's salute came quickly and then she turned to trot away. Her steps contained a bounce of excitement for being able to bring the Prince of Dusk the delicacy of raw, frightened meat.

The high dreadpriest watched her go with more amusement. Reckless Warrior Nakao, she thought, is going to lose herself a form.

Erin turned back to the starved rocks and watched as the last of the hare's blood was absorbed into the stones. It was then that she recalled something the god had said in passing to Her Companion, which Seina had so dutifully reported to Erin, just as she had reported every word which had crossed their god's lips. It was something which gave the high dreadpriest a tantalizing idea. Even if it didn't work, in the very least it would be incredibly amusing.

"Seina!" Erin called after the retreating woman. Warrior Nakao paused, ears perking to catch the dreadpriest's words. "Disregard my earlier orders.

Instead, be a dear and collect the Prince of Dusk's birthday gift. I've had an interesting notion."

Warrior Nakao's face broke into one of the largest grins it had ever sported. Eagerness nestled into her cheekbones and she inhaled deeply with in a mix of pride and excitement.

"Really?"

"Yes. It's a little early, but you may be the one to deliver them to the Prince."

"Where will She be when I return?"

"Here, with me. And do hurry. You and I both wish to cure the Prince of Dusk as soon as possible so we can end The Dealer's involvement with all of this. It shouldn't take you long. It wasn't that big of a village. Bring a legion to help you, The Second Legion will do. Now run."

Warrior Nakao smiled once more.

"With pleasure, sir."

CHAPTER 33

The dragon groaned as consciousness returned to him. The thinness of his blood told him it had taken a lot for his body to heal. It had possibly even been an entire system renewal. Bested by somebody not even into their third decade of life. It hurt, that. His only consolation was that the bester in question was a god, which mollified his pride if only by just a little. The dragon shook his body, letting his scales settle comfortably around him. There seemed to be no lasting damage, at least.

But how had she been able to do it? No memories, no powers, no nothing for almost sixteen years and then she runs a power rod through his skull and fries his system like he was a hatchling barely finished with his Before. The dragon shucked the thought aside as he had the wound to his nervous system. There were more pressing things that needed to be addressed first.

The dragon had to close and open his eyes rapidly to clear his vision before he took in his surroundings. The god was close by, sleeping up against a tree with one hand on her stomach and the other laying by her side.

Her hair fell messily across her face where it continued down her shoulders in the wild whorls of their traveling days, when regular hygiene had not been possible. She still had the remnants of the assault grease she had been wearing when they had left the Menundra. As such her hair was now clumped together in thick, knotted chunks. Her head and neck were at angles that implied sleep had not been her initial goal. When she woke, she would have the sore muscles of the inept watchman.

The dragon reached over to brush the greasy hair from the god's eyes, and then he tucked it behind her ear to reveal the soft skin of her face.

When the coarse feeling of his claw brushed up against her, the young woman stirred and the dragon quickly retreated a few paces back and watched as she slowly unglued her eyes from sleep to look at him.

"You're awake," she stated with slumber still crackling in her voice. Slumber and guilt.

The dragon nodded carefully.

The god's brow puckered slightly. "Are you okay? I'm sorry. I didn't mean to do that to you."

Her voice was almost soft with empathy. The dragon chose his sentences carefully.

"I am fine, human. I misspoke and you got upset. It is understandable. I should be more careful with the words I choose when speaking to you."

The young woman's eyes clouded.

"Yes, because I am just a silly earth beast, right? Far be it for me to actually understand something a mighty dragon says." Although the words were harsh, they were lacking any true bite. She shifted her legs to get blood flowing and numb limbs to function, but other than that there was no effort given by the god to move from her position.

The dragon spread his left wing and curled it towards the god.

"Please, human. Let me talk. Give me five minutes to speak my peace and I will never bother you again. If you ask, after I help you remove the bellanus, I will leave these lands entirely. All I ask is for the opportunity to explain my actions."

The dragon's voice was strained and the god was not meeting his eyes. She braced her arm against the trunk of the tree and made to stand. The dragon withdrew his wing carefully and said just one more word.

"Please."

She still said nothing, but did slowly pull her hand away from the tree.

The dragon took a deep breath and began.

"You asked me if I let your mother die. And I said yes. Which is true. I did let your mother die, but I never lied to you. I told you that your mother's spirit was broken and that her soul had died. What I did not tell you is that yes, I could have continued healing your mother's body, I could have made her live, but it would have only been her body and mind that lived."

The god kept quiet as she listened. She began to shred an errant piece of grass that had found its way into her hands. The dragon continued as gently as he could.

"Losing your soul is worse than losing your mind. Because the body is completely capable of surviving and even procreating without a soul. Squirrels do not have souls. Neither do frogs nor rats nor cows nor sheep. And that is what your mother would have become. A lesser beast. No speech, no lasting memories of you. No fine motor skills. She would have been an animal that urinated whenever her bladder was full and rutted whenever she was in heat. And worse . . . only beings with a soul produce offspring with a soul. What if your

328

mother had started giving you half sisters and half brothers without souls? Little naked piglets grunting and squealing and eventually probably impregnating each other or their mother because animals do not remember lineage."

"Could you have helped her live?"

The dragon shook his head sadly.

"Not as the person you knew. And you are not selfish enough for the other kind of life she could have had. If your mother was beside you now, mindlessly gnawing at an itch on her leg, you would regret it."

The dragon could see reason working its way through the god's head. But he could also see it being resisted by anger. Her words, when they came, were less sharp than before, but the difference could only be measured with grains of sand.

"Why didn't you just tell me the truth? Why lie about it? You could have just told me then and there rather than me finding out at the Induction Ceremony that you let my mother die."

The dragon shook his head again.

"We had to leave those woods surrounding your village. For me to explain all of this to you then when you were so distressed? Would you have listened? Would you have truly thought through the consequences?"

Reason sank even deeper into the young woman, more grains of sand trickled through, and her voice dulled further. She sounded more sad than angry now.

"Okay. You had to let my mother die. You still lied to me, and then impregnated me, and then led me across two territories so your unborn child could keep baking. Why keep me ignorant of that?"

The dragon paused before responding, feeling the sudden hollowness of his bones and the brittleness of his scales. His voice quieted as he answered. "Did you ever wonder why most earth beasts remember dragons only in song and story? We're all gone, human."

"What do you mean, 'all gone?'"

"I mean all gone. Done. Dying out. Where once we numbered in the millions, now there are two hundred dragons. Maybe even less. The poisons of your kind and the bel butterflies have killed us. Less hatchlings are born, and the ones that survive the egg are weaker than they once were. There are no airbreathers. I am the last waterbreather. There are a few dozen earthbreathers. The rest are the weak flamebreathers. That is, if they actually form breath at all and don't just die during their Breathforming."

More silence followed this. A light flapping of wings in the distance. A lone cicada. The distant rustling of wind through the new buds on the trees. The ever-present sound of lost words. The dragon breathed deeply again.

"Whether it is the changelings who win this everlasting war or the free races, the dragons will still disappear. Nothing but bones to be studied by the Water Weavers.

"There is a comfort knowing that even when your own breath fades, the heartblood will continue on in others. There is also a tragedy in watching nine out of ten of your children not make it past their second year of life. And the one who does survive is misborn with stunted wings and has barely enough flame to heat its body. Pain, sadness, and death were the future of the dragons.

"And then suddenly, we had our answer. Believe it or not, it was not the dragons who approached the gods, but the gods who approached us. They wanted heartblood and promised us the world in return.

"In that moment, we saw our salvation. We saw a way to renew the brood. We could make the blood strong again and continue on as a species." The dragon paused once more and looked up at the sky. "So three thousand years ago, the Lord of Salvation agreed, and so did you, the Prince of Dusk. It was all supposed to be simpler. Blood for blood.

"But then you did not remember anything. And in the years since the bargain was made, even more of us had died. So when you were alone with me in the woods I made a rash decision which I came to regret almost immediately. But the egg was created and it was done. What was one human's opinion of me against the fate of an entire species?

"Besides, I thought given enough time I could invoke the memories in you. Fair is fair after all, and once you remembered who you were and to what you had agreed, of course the whole matter would be cleared up. And then maybe the dragons would live. But you never remembered who you are. And now I am not a partner due his share but a lecherous beast who took advantage of a disturbed young woman.

"But I promise you, if I could rescind my actions, I would."

There was a pause as the dragon's words dispersed among the underbrush. The god frowned deeply.

"So now," she asked quietly, meeting his eyes for the first time since the dragon had began, "this speech is supposed to excuse everything?"

"No," the dragon shook his head slowly, "it is supposed to excuse nothing. You do, however, deserve the explanation. My actions were monstrous. But at least now you know why I did them."

When it was clear the dragon had nothing more to say, the god got to her feet. She didn't say anything else either. The young woman did not seem angry anymore, but neither was she granting him forgiveness. The god turned around, and this time the dragon did not try to stop her from leaving. He simply watched her go.

The Prince of Dusk had almost entirely disappeared from sight before the beast spoke again. As such, she did not hear the dragon's final words, whispered so softly, so gently, and ever so sadly.

"I'm sorry."

Then in the distance, the god screamed. She dropped to her knees, gripped her midsection violently, and started convulsing on the ground. The dragon cursed and began running.

CHAPTER 34
IMPORTANT THINGS ARE THE MOST SUCCULENT

_____

_____

_____

_____

_____

_____

_____

_____

_____

_____

_____

_____

_____

_____

_____

_____

_____

_____

_____

_____

_____

_____

_____

_____

_____

CHAPTER 35:
THE BODY OF THE LITTLE VOICE

The god blinked twice. There were tears in her eyes. She had been crying. The young woman shook her head, trying to clear her eyes and to get a sense of what was happening, and where she was. The tears didn't stop though. Not had been crying. She was crying. Present continuous.

"Are you well, Prince?" came the soft tones. She didn't immediately recognize to whom the tender voice belonged. "Your skin has healed completely. Is there any pain remaining?"

The god sat up and looked down. Her leather clothing was in tatters around her and fresh blood decorated her skin in copious amounts. She couldn't remember what had happened though. The god noted the sun's position. How much was missing from her memory this time?

The tears kept falling.

"You're okay, Prince. It's over now."

The god finally noticed who held her and spoke to her with such tenderness. It was Erin. The high dreadpriest had never seemed so genuine in the entire time the young woman had known her. It was strange, but also nice. The god smiled weakly. There were other warriors surrounding her, too. Strangely, the dragon was there as well. His eyes held the same depth of concern as Erin's. There was a fierce pride in the great beast's features.

"What happened?" The god licked her lips which she had just noticed were dry and cracked. "I don't remember."

Instead of derision or sarcasm, the high dreadpriest smiled as did all her changelings. For that matter, the dragon's maw was parted in a toothy grin as well.

"May I introduce," the dragon's deep bass voice vibrated in her chest, "our daughter."

The god paled slightly as the dragon touched a foreclaw gently to her abdomen. A tiny dragon scampered towards her while a little voice burst in her head.

Earth-Mother!

The god's eyes widened and her mouth parted ever so slightly.

Some women are born mothers. They climb out of their own mothers' wombs ready to take care of others, and they spend their adolescences alternately caring for others' children and trying desperately to find themselves husbands so they could get started on their own procreation.

Other women feel it as they get older. It comes on them one night while they are sleeping, and with a great boom their biological clocks start ticking and they begin to think that settling down might be nice.

Other women are like the Prince. Convinced they will never have children or become a parent. For these women, motherhood does not hit them until the moment they first look into their child's eyes.

And even if those eyes were reptilian, the instant bond still slipped into place.

The god kept crying, but she was smiling, too.

Somebody had carefully cleaned the hatchling of blood, eggshells, and whatever else it would have gotten covered with during its journey from her gut to the outside world. And now it sat, a little bundle of silver-white scales. A beautiful creature. The god reached out and let the small dragon slowly crawl into her hand. Its claws dug into her skin not unlike a kitten's are wont to do. Not too painful, just tiny pin pricks.

The god could hardly breathe with wonder. The young woman curled the hatchling towards her chest and lightly kissed its small head. The joyful voice sang in her mind once more.

You are so pretty!

The little dragon crawled further up the god's body, cuddling into the side of her neck. The creature began to emit a stuttered rumble from her chest in an attempt to purr her happiness.

The high dreadpriest and the changelings who were not on guard surrounded her in a polite circle of curiosity and affection. The god looked up from her daughter and smiled at them all.

"Well," High Dreadpriest Valar commented, trying hopelessly to suppress a smile, "at least she isn't as ugly as her father."

With a pang, the god looked at the dragon. She still didn't know how she felt about what he had told her. She remembered it more clearly than she did the wondrous and disgusting birth of her daughter, that was for sure.

Affection bickered with resentment in her mind, and she quickly looked away from the beast to concentrate on the silvery dragon purring against

337

her neck. The high dreadpriest's voice came gently, although it still contained the demand which her voice always carried.

"And what is our god cub to be called, Prince?"

Good question. She couldn't very well call a part god/part dragon 'Sue.' It was too common. Joan? Anne? With out without an 'e' it still seemed inadequate. The underbeings were looking at her expectantly and she was at a bit of a loss what to say. The dragon's voice hummed through the air.

"Vyvi. She will be named Vyvi."

Confusion flared in the god's chest. Not that there was anything wrong with the name, but what right had the dragon after all he had done to be the one to name the hatchling? In the very least the decision should be made together.

"Vyvi." Erin scoffed at the name. "Where did you drag that from?"

The dragon smiled smugly. "It is the Prince's mother's name."

The god's voice was touched with awe.

"My mother's . . . ."

"Yes. Your mother's. You spoke of her often when we were traveling together to Lavanor." An unreadable expression lidded the dragon's eyes. "I thought that it would be a good name for our- your daughter."

The god took a shuddered breath. Vyvi. There was no ping of her memories coming back. There was no clicking into place. The young god did not recognize those four letters at all. She tried to feel out the name in her mind. She silently formed the name on her lips, searching for some kind of familiarity, but it was futile. The name had no connection to her.

I like Great-Earth-Mother's name. Please, can it be mine?

The god's eyes shot away from the twelve-foot dragon to fixate on her daughter. The little silver-white dragon was looking at her eagerly. Was it convenient timing and a conspiracy, or a little earthwaterair beast who was just that good at reading her? Were emotions blood, her heart would have ruptured with the excess. As it was, the heavy feeling of uncertainty beat frighteningly.

Please?

Vyvi . . . that name bounced in her mind. It did not latch, but now that her daughter's voice asked again, the four letters began to brush lightly against memory in an almost familiar way. Was it imagination or hope or-

Please?

The god shook her head.

Finally, she decided that if nothing else the hatchling did need a name. The god closed her eyes.

Vyvi will be your name, then.

Elation bubbled through the veins of her head in a heady whoosh of little dragon emotion. It was raw happiness at having a name by which to be called.

Vyvi . . . . If it was true then she owed the great dragon something. She owed him for the borrowed joy she felt dripping down into her toes. The ground seemed to slowly tilt with the conflicting chemicals fighting in her head.

The expectant pause, which had begun with the revelation of the Prince's mother's name, continued

for a while as the underbeings waited for their god to speak. As for the dragon, his eyes were still rimmed with that same unreadable expression from earlier.

"Her name is Vyvi," she confirmed to those around her. Then, she sent another private message to her daughter.

The large dragon. That's your father. His name is Darlan.

The little hatchling seemed to perk up in her hands as she saw the older dragon in a new light.

What's he like, Earth-Mother?

The god looked into her daughter's eyes. She smiled at the little dragon, took a deep breath, and then responded.

He's like all dragons. Noble and brave. Just like you will be.

CHAPTER 36
HUMAN, WITH A SIDE OF GRAVY

Two hundred and thirty eight pairs of eyes looked at the god and they all hated her. Every last pair of colourful irides bore down on her with the force of anger and disgust so strong that she felt it as a solid wave against her chest, battering at her lungs in the least pleasant way possible.

"What?"

"I said, 'Happy Early Birthday!'"

"You brought me a village? Why?"

Seina was perplexed.

"Well, it's not like it's just any village. It's Dompt."

The god blinked violently, then turned her eyes once more to look at the humans being held firmly by the Second Legion. Seina was right. There was the mayor, and one of the Tuckers, and there was the whole clutch of the eyelash-batting girls. She didn't know if everyone was present. She hadn't associated with the village at large enough to know them all by name, but there certainly seemed to be a lot of them, and the god doubted her changelings would have left any behind.

The Warrior Clan had given her . . . a village. The last village in which she had lived.

"Why would I ever want to see these people again?" The god's voice suddenly became edged.

"Because," and it was here that Seina's smile become quite beautiful, "You get to decide how they are to die."

There was a quiet moment after this as the god processed what the warrior had told her.

The dragon was standing off to the right. Currently, he was growling as he looked at the group of villagers. The god wasn't sure whether it was the concept of murder that upset him or the villagers themselves. For that matter, she couldn't decide what her own opinion about that was. For lack of anything else to say, the god turned to Warrior Nakao.

"Thank you?"

Seina smiled widely and bowed.

"The entire Clan did it."

"Then everybody, thank you."

The warriors all beamed. Even the ones who were holding prisoners in death grips managed to grin and still look terrifying.

Vyvi, still curled against her neck, nudged her gently, asking,

What are they?

A gift.

Why would you want a village as a gift?

They are the ones who hurt Great-Earth-Mother.

Heat flickered along the edges of her memory.

The little dragon tried to growl in the direction of the villagers, but only managed in making it as far as the gggg before she ran out of breath and had to stop. The god smiled at the effort, but then frowned again as she returned her attention to Seina.

"So why have you brought them to the starved rocks?"

The wall was off to the right, innocently guarding the old woods. The god could sense

342

nothing unusual about them. If she hadn't been repeatedly told about their horrendous properties, she would almost be tempted to clear them in a single jump.

The high dreadpriest was the one who responded.

"Ah, don't You remember? You wanted to . . . how did You put it? 'Break the stupid walls or feed them.' Well, I see two birds and one stone. But Your gift is Yours to do with whatever You will."

The god did remember. It had been the day of crossing the ditch. The thought had been an offhand, flippant one. But here they were. An early birthday present. Walking, talking meat who, as it just so happened, had committed the sin of crossing the Prince of Dusk when she was young and impressionable.

The young woman turned to face the group of villagers and eyed them carefully. They were less afraid that she thought they should be. Maybe they had been held captive too long and had gotten weary of terror, who knew? It was the men she looked at first. Men whose faces she tried to recognize from that night. She knew some of them from village events, but couldn't remember specifically who had attended the fire. They were none and all guilty. Maybe if she saw sweat glisten off shiny faces they would be made more recognizable. Maybe if they were reeking of liquor, power, and maleness then familiarity would settle into place. An old hate began to reawaken in the young god.

There were children among the group. Little girls and boys were clutching skirts protectively as some of her warriors gripped their shirts or hair to pacify them. The god thought of her own child, little Vyvi, who was trying and failing to purr on her shoulder. There were older children among the captured villagers, too. Ones on the cusp of adolescence who were too young to be brave but too old to allow themselves to be cowed. In front of her was a past of sorts and a future as well, and she suddenly felt the enormity of her clout.

But children held hands of mothers who protectively supported their husbands who gallantly rid the village of witches, demons, and lonely mothers with sick children.

"Do you know who I am?" The god addressed the entire captured village in a loud, clear voice.

The villagers' hateful glares did not alter in the slightest. One of them spit at the ground however, and she took that as an affirmation.

"Do you know what I have the authority to do?"

"Burn in hell!" came defiance from the back. There was a heavy thud followed by a scream that turned into a groan.

The god shook her head at the stupidity of the villager who had spoken.

"Anybody have something constructive to say?"

More angry glares.

"They hate You," Seina supplied helpfully. "You are the Prince of Dusk."

High Dreadpriest Valar strode over to her god with careful steps, and now stood tall beside her. She was an elf currently, and she matched Seina for height. It was strange to see the dreadpriest as

344

anything but a human. But Valar was the same creature. Although the bones in her face had become finer and her eyes now tilted upwards somewhat, that same self-controlled smile possessed that overly handsome face. For once, her dreadpriest didn't deride the god though. She said nothing and instead waited patiently for the Prince of Dusk to react.

"Erin, I don't think I can order the death of all these people."

"And why ever not?"

"They're . . ." she couldn't finish the sentence.

"What? Innocent? No, You don't believe that."

Valar was right, they weren't innocent people. Well, at least not all of them were. But even still, she felt uneasy and unbalanced.

The high dreadpriest's voice spoke in her ear yet again.

"If You free them, they won't spread tales of the Lord of the Underbeing's unending mercy, if that's what You're considering. I'm sorry, Prince, but redemption is only a luxury for those who repent their actions. And even if You did, the world does not forgive its tyrants easily, innocent though they may be."

The god, still feeling horribly unstable, spoke hesitantly. "I . . . can't kill them . . . ?"

The high dreadpriest nodded to her seriously.

"You know, the free races used to kill each other before we started killing them. If we left them alone, how long do You think their peace would last before somebody got greedy again? They are a destructive infestation, Prince. Either we kill them or they kill each other. It's much simpler this way, don't You agree?"

The young god looked at the dreadpriest. There it was once more, THE MISSION, stamped in angry violet ink across logic. Brainwashing at its finest and ignorance at its worse. But what bothered the young woman is that for once she didn't know if it was her or the dreadpriest to which those things applied.

"Why do you hate the free races so much? Why did I give you a mission to kill them? I'm not going to suddenly remember it one day and I'm tired of not knowing why you think it is the free races who have to die."

The high dreadpriest tapped a finger against her cheek. Then she nodded once to herself and smiled a little. There was nothing mocking about that smile. It was one that was full of cautious hope.

"My Prince," Erin told her quietly, "If You watch these villagers be killed and You still want to be our god afterwards, I will tell You everything You want to know."

"There's always me," the god suggested. "If we think the walls can be satisfied given enough food, then I could just stand there and regenerate over and over again, letting the walls strip off my flesh until they get full. Then nobody has to die."

The high dreadpriest shook her head, her cheeks darkening slightly. "These people do not deserve to be saved at the expense of Your sanity, Prince."

The god looked at the wall to which the high dreadpriest was pointing. That simply constructed stone wall. She then looked at the villagers. The ones who hated her every fibre with their every fibre. The ones who would kill her if offered the opportunity, give her to their god, laugh at her death, kill her people and her child and . . . .

The high dreadpriest watched her god, and then smiled once more. It was an older sibling congratulating the younger one for receiving an A plus after much studying and hard work. "Just give us the word, my Prince. We are ready when You are. Just give us the word."

Then the dreadpriest strolled away just as lazily as she had approached the god, only now was humming a tune languidly. *Hm, hm, hm, hm, hm, hm, please, please, please. Plump helpless mammals with their backs to me . . . .*

The dragon had watched the underbeing speak with the god, had seen her features contort in uncertainty, and now snuck into her thoughts.

What are you going to do, human? You are not a murderer.

What am I supposed to do?

With those words ricocheting in his mind, the dragon strode across the ground to stand directly beside the young god, shrinking to seven feet in the process. The warriors watched the waterbreather's movements carefully.

For one thing, you could refrain from mass killings.

The god shook her head, now looking away from his eyes. The high dreadpriest's words were gooey and trailed through her chest. *Just say the word, my Prince . . . .*

We have to get by the rocks. Her response in the dragon's head was cool and only a little defensive.

This was survival. She was the leader of her changelings and there were things that were unavoidable.

I get to choose how these people die, not whether. If I spare them the rocks, then it only leaves me. I don't want to let the wall eat me, and I don't want to lose Vyvi to the bellanus. I can't do it. I'm not that good. Not to people who killed my mother. Not to the people who did what I hated you for. Why do I have to be the saint? You've killed people. The free races have killed people. If you have a problem with this, then you can turn away, dragon, but I can't-

The dragon brought forth a claw and brushed the hair from the god's face, tucking it behind her ear. With the contact the god flinched and stopped sending her thoughtspeech justification.

Then, the dragon took that same claw and gently lifted the young woman's chin until she was looking directly at him and he was looking just as intensely back at her. No dispute, no accusations, no guilt-ridden statements. He simply said,

"Then let's kill us some earth beasts."

The god was a little surprised by his response, but she was beginning to regain her earlier lost balance and for the first time in months- no, for the first time in years she felt a sense of stability. The god was still white with the decision, but she nodded.

The warriors had all heard the dragon's words and for it, hated him slightly less. Vyvi, sensing the decision, tried another abortive purr as she scampered from her mother's shoulder to her father's and curled around his neck instead.

348

Then the Prince of Dusk gave the high
dreadpriest of the changelings The Word.
And the people began to die.

CHAPTER 37
MEASURES OF THE DESPERATE VARIETY

An uneasy peace seemed to reign in the woods just on the other side of the starved rocks. The monkey and the weasel giving up the chase momentarily because all around the mulberry bush there was now an army of fire ants ready to help them lose weight, and imminent death is always more pertinent than fun. Or, more specifically, the high dreadpriest and the dragon were tolerating each other's company momentarily because the bel butterfly had to be dealt with, or else a god forfeited.

The changeling had brought nothing but a single match, and the dragon had brought nothing but his breath. They were unconventional tools for unconventional comrades. But really, what else did they need? A third of the free race army was waiting somewhere in those woods. A thousand knives wouldn't stave off death against those odds, even with a waterbreather to punch holes into them. Two beasts can sneak in much more easily than a dozen, and it only takes one woman to light a match.

It was an eerie forest that they walked through. Despite there being no wind, the branches rubbed up against each other, chortling about the intruders. Erin wondered if the trees themselves were manipulated beings, like so many of the things the Oceo Tolok interacted with. Erin tried to ignore the unnatural movements of the greenery around them, and instead concentrate on what they were going to do.

Eventually, signs of civilization could be seen. Small cottages with gardens began to dot the way, grey smoke from their chimneys twisting through the branches above them. The beautiful homes looked like extensions of the trees or else trees themselves. Erin found it contemptible. Higher beasts were supposed to be above the earth, stone, and water survival stages. Great civilizations were never marked by their ability to camouflage well.

The homes grew progressively closer together, progressively larger, and progressively more intricate in their design. The silent movement of the two travelers was slowed and then halted as it became impossible to continue without incurring detection. The dragon looked to the high dreadpriest who tipped her head forward. Erin then backed away and buried herself among the root structure of a crippled and knobbly old tree.

When Erin had finished concealing herself, she watched as the waterbreather enlarged himself to thirty feet and stalked away from her position. When he stopped he was barely still in sight, but she could still make out his body. She was glad about this. It meant she got to watch.

And watch she did. She watched Darlan lower his maw to the earth below him. She watched his neck constrict and click. And finally she watched the damage unfold.

Frost tipped the dragon's nostrils as a hazy substance leaked from his jaws into the earth below him. The moment the mist touched the ground, a dry cracking sound could be heard as ancient soil froze and fractured. The patch of earth beneath the waterbreather's feet lightened in colour as the cold spread like a festering wound corrupting the flesh surrounding it. Deep into the earth the cold penetrated while its burning touch crept along the forest floor. Animals living below ground burst from the undergrowth as they fled the bleak ice that consumed their burrows.

The rustling, chortling, whispering trees from before began to thrash. Erin watched as the bark cracked and the leaves shrivelled. Lush, brilliant trees shrunk before her eyes and were prematurely thrust into dormancy, then death as sap froze, then burst, and roots were numbed and shattered. The frostbitten ground spread in every direction, the furious ice ravaging the earth in an ever-widening circle.

Thousands of leaves dropped to the ground as trees tried desperately to conserve energy in their cores. As the piles of fronds, needles, and petals grew on the ground, Erin nodded appreciatively. So much lovely tinder. Who knew it was possible to kill a forest with cold and heat simultaneously?

She readied herself and waited for the next part of the plan to unfold. Somewhere ahead, she knew The Dealer would be clawing his way into the air to begin circling the blemished woods, and then the real fun would begin.

"Tree Dwellers!" screamed the dragon in what was part address, part command. His voice boomed and Erin nodded appreciatively once more. "I am Darlan of the clutch Lal. I have come for the elf known as Lira."

Still hidden, Erin heard the sounds of alarm begin to spread. From the panicked quality that those noises contained, it seems that news of the dragon's affiliation with the Prince of Dusk had spread. Either that, or the damage from the waterbreathing was realized. Both ways, the effect suited the high dreadpriest.

Somewhere, some elf must have replied to the dragon's demand, as he quickly howled an answer.

"I cannot thaw the earth. But I can promise not to start a blaze that will destroy your homes and scour this land to its rawest form. Lira owes me a lifedebt. I have come for payment."

Once again, Erin reasoned that somebody with a strong voice had passed a message to the air bound waterbreather, as he soon replied.

"My allegiance is to the devil, you insufferable earth beasts! Do you really think appealing to my mercy will achieve anything?"

Erin could hear nothing for a while, and she spent the time systematically clenching and unclenching her different muscle groups. She though it wise to keep herself prepared for sudden action in case the elves' response was a violent one.

It was unnecessary. Erin soon felt the whoosh of air and the heavy thump of a body landing which meant the dragon had returned, now just four feet long from nose to tail. From the lack of pursuit, it seemed cowardice and compromise were still the free races' default solutions.

The dragon's greeting to her was clipped.

"Let's go, underbeing. They will meet us in the clearing."

"'Let's'?" The dreadpriest's words were a whisper, "My, aren't we thinking highly of ourselves today. Unless of course you are not referring to the royal 'We' and intend me to go with you. Which I highly doubt since the mental capacity of your species is supposed to be higher than average, and that plan is nothing short of asinine."

The dragon growled. The changeling looked at him calmly, then spoke again.

"If they kill you I can still quell these woods."

The dragon's growl deepened. "How will that save your Prince?"

"If we cannot find a way to get that butterfly out of the Prince's head, she will appreciate us demoralizing half of the known population of elves. It wasn't our side that created the anathema."

"So you leave me to do the real work while you hide and destroy a people."

"If only it were that easy. I'll settle for these woods, though. And if you didn't want the 'real work' maybe you shouldn't have got Her infected in the first place."

Valar's smile was all teeth. Then with the satisfaction of licking the last bit of batter off the spatula, she added,

"Do hurry. Before she forgets your little reconciliation and remembers exactly what kind of snake you really are. Because that would be such a tragedy."

Darlan growled again, but said nothing else as he turned and stormed away. Erin noticed with particular satisfaction that he did, indeed, hurry. She settled down and prepared herself for the wait. Self-control had been schooled into her limbs for years,

354

so it shouldn't have caused her any trouble. But her veins still pounded with the thought of an empty god, and despite all the composed derision of her words, she was a little afraid.

Erin wanted this insane plan to work so badly that the only thought in her mind was one that was as improbable as abstinence on a stud farm: she truly wished The Dealer well.

CHAPTER 38
THE MANY WONDERFUL
MIRACLES OF THE OCEO TOLOK

The dragon left the underbeing with anger seething through his veins, but there was also guilt there, lacing his mind with the burn of moonshine and sour wine. He tried to push the thoughts aside and concentrate on his task, but it was futile. The dreadpriest's words sat in the back of his mind staring in accusation and smug self-righteousness. As he expanded his essence to twenty feet, he couldn't help but wish he could alter his thoughts as easily as he could his body.

As he approached a cluster of homes, the dragon began to see elves. The graceful people were watching him with either wariness or fury, depending on whether they knew about the extent of the irreparable damage he had done to their trees.

It had been a while since he had visited the elven people. He had not missed them. Even with the destruction of the equipment and the knowledge, the evidence of meddling could be seen. The faces of the beings who now surrounded him were proof enough of that. Those pointed ears, those pinched cheeks, that unnatural height, the longevity . . . the elves were an entirely different species than they had been before. Only slanted eyes and the predominantly brown or golden hair were unchanged from the Oceo Tolok his greatfather had described from thousands upon thousands of years earlier. The dragon wondered if they altered their young at conception or birth and how much it hurt to do so.

The elves around him were getting angrier. Good. News of the attack on the ancient woods was spreading. It meant they would take his threat more seriously and less time would be wasted.

Ahead there was a group of people towards whom he made his way. Among them was a man wearing the robes of the elders. The old elf had thin skin that was a sallow yellow colour, and he seemed even more ephemeral than the rest of his kind. The clothes marking him as one of the leaders of the Tree Dwellers sagged on his thin form.

Darlan joined the group and waited in tense silence. After hours had passed, fifty elven defenders and one woman arrived.

"Elf," he growled when she came to a halt beside the elder, and the defenders took up their positions. "I have come for the lifedebt."

"Why have you hurt our trees, Darlan?"

He shot back a reply, crisp and sharp.

For insurance purposes.

Then, in a loud, angry voice, he said,

"That is, if your kind still honours your lifedebts."

The elder was the one who replied. His words were just as wrinkled as his body, just as stiff as his joints.

"Aye, dragon. We do. Even with one who has chosen the company of underbeings. I thought your kind took no sides in the war. Will we soon need to fear hordes of dragons flying in over the starved rocks?"

The dragon narrowed his eyes at the elf. He felt no need to correct their assumptions.

"All I want is information on the bellanus. Take me to the Weavers' library and help me find my answers, and then your woods will be harmed no further."

With the utterance of that sentence, the entire mood of the encounter changed. Hostility and anger from before became nervousness. Both Lira and the elder eyed him cautiously. A fringe of onlookers had accumulated by then and they began to whisper amongst themselves. The defenders raised weapons and aimed them at the intruder.

The dragon knew a chord had been struck and he wished he could hear the tune to know whether it was one with which he was already familiar. The dragon growled at the thought of innuendo. He only wanted his answers and then he would take the godling and the hatchling back to his people, where they could finally take to wing and be free of earth beasts.

"We have no idea what you're talking about."

The dragon scowled at the elder's statement. He aimed his words at Lira.

"There is a changeling hidden ready to start a blaze. If that happens, most the forest will die, not just the ones I've already frozen. Either you take me alone to the information I want, or the trees burn. If the defenders shoot so much as a single arrow, the trees burn. If anybody follows us even a few paces, the trees burn. Decide quickly. I have little patience for your elder, elf, and I am inclined to eat him if he does not start providing what I want."

Lira closed her eyes.

"Petty threats? Do we mean so little to you now? Once we were good friends."

"Once the situation was different. I still wish no harm to come to your people. Give me what I need and I will leave peacefully."

There was nothing for a while. The elder was waiting calmly. He was content to postpone. After all, a messenger hawk had been sent. The army would be galloping their way as they spoke. Let the great beast take forever with banter if he pleased.

As for Lira, she was staring at the dragon intently. Her cheeks had coloured in an emotion that was unreadable for almost everyone in the clearing. Her words were the barest whisper.

"Two hundred years is not enough, but a hundred is?"

The dragon snarled.

"Enough, earth beasts. This is your last chance."

Murder. Hatred. Rage. The elves weren't sure what they were seeing in the dragon's eyes, but they didn't like it. They were a frail bookish people grown lax and indifferent behind their starved rocks. The elves were the planners, thinkers, and inventors. War machines and more effective arrows were the tall people's contribution to defeating the evil changelings, not hearty soldiers as the mountain people and the humans produced in droves.

Their defenders were a defeated skeleton crew. A living breathing, furious dragon was too earthy, too fleshy, too here and now for the elves to do anything about except hope that the army was moving quickly and wish the present soldiers were not shaking quite so blatantly.

The elder deigned to speak again. His voice would have been calm and soothing if the dragon had been a hatchling waking with a nightmare.

"The Oceo Tolok were disbanded. Everything was destroyed. We kept no records of anything. Surely the dragons remember this."

The dragon growled. His Before had ended before this elf's greatparents, as ancient as the elder seemed, first met. And the dragon had never had nightmares. So he did something he had not tried to do since a small clearing two years ago when he first met the devil.

The dragon ate him.

The elder didn't taste terrible. He tasted light and the great beast had forgotten how sweet higher earth beasts were. His twenty feet of bulk had no trouble in crunching through the soft bones of the old elf, and the small body slid down his throat like pudding. He only lamented that the man had not been naked at the time. The garments were certain to cause heartburn later.

The elves were frozen with terror.

"Does anybody else think that the knowledge is gone?" the dragon hissed, spraying elder blood through his teeth as he spoke. A panicked silence met this as hundreds of people calculated the distance between where they currently stood and the south gate. Prayers began to stutter through lips. The prayers grated against the dragon's scales like a de-boning knife against rocks.

The dragon began to growl.

"Darlan, please. I'll take you."

Lira was beside him now and had placed a hand on his large flank. The dragon shifted ever so slightly from the familiar forgotten palm. Anger flared up at the contact, but he allowed his form to melt, to shrink down to a conservative five feet of less vagrant conspicuousness.

Lead the way.

The female elf nodded slowly. She paused to speak briskly with one of the defenders, and then began to walk with the dragon. They left the centre of the forest-bound city and headed towards the Water Weavers' Lakes, the remnants of the Oceo Tolok. After a few minutes, that elven voice spoke once more.

"You're going to burn the trees anyways."

The dragon thought of a high dreadpriest waiting with nothing but her pride, conceit, and love of her fading god to keep her company. The waterbreather finally answered when they had left the last of the trees behind. And to his credit, there was even a hint of reluctance there.

Probably.

Nothing more passed between the two until Lira had taken him to his answers.

Across the achingly beautiful and indestructible Crystal Bridge, over the meadows surrounded by sheer cliff drops and interspersed with the towers usually manned by the defenders, past the closed Open Shore, through the submerged city of the Water Weavers, below the bedrock of their civilization, they had arrived.

They were in the old labs now. Or what was supposed to be the old labs.

The room was white. It was too white, too new, and conspicuously not a collection of burnt ruins. Test tubes glittered around the room in their shiny

361

upkept glory. The laboratory was rebuilt or never destroyed in the first place, and either way a violation.

"Why are you showing me this?"

The dragon's words corroded through pretence to drip on exposed ideals. Lira shrugged sadly.

"You would have figured it out if I gave you access the information you want. I know you, Darlan. You would have seen through any explanation or excuse. Thought this would waste less time."

The dragon's neck began to swell.

"What have you been doing, earth beast?"

"We're trying not to die."

"By breeding new creatures again? That worked out so well last time."

"If you really have decided to side with that she-beast, then you know as well as I do that we're losing. The Lord of Salvation issued a command. The Masters were thrilled and the rest of us did what we were told."

The size of the dragon's neck did not decrease in the slightest. More anger bubbled out of the winged beast and he gnashed his teeth with rage. The elf's pinched eyes met his directly. Then she broke the stare, and looked down. The dragon inhaled her scent, tasted the fear, and he could feel the drudge of compromise on her skin.

The great beast hissed. He shoved the elf aside and stalked to the back of the room where a door marked 'Authorized Personnel Only' barred his way. A quick constriction of his neck and a sharp click preceded the fog that rolled from his nostrils and the liquid ice that poured from his maw. His breath shattered that which it touched. The door splintered and crashed to the ground, revealing the room behind it.

Five scientists nearly fainted when he burst through the doorway. They cowered away from him in fear. But the terrified elves were not pertinent to the dragon. What were significant were the anatomy diagrams tacked to the walls and the glass containers filled with twitching creatures. But upon closer inspection, Darlan's gut wrenched. The twitching creatures weren't 'creatures' at all. Or at least not yet.

They were cocoons. A throbbing, multitude of cocoons encaged in seamless glass cases. The cocoons were an unbearable onyx colour. They were black as the sky after all the stars die and there is nothing to reflect the cold surface of the moon anymore. Not the black of evil. Evil black is a black of hatred, anger, murder, rape, and petty malice. These cocoons, these pulsing living things were the lonely black of emptiness.

"This is not the bellanus."

The hollow-eyed elf had stepped up beside him to rest her gaze on the same glass chambers that the dragon now watched.

"They call it the milatta butterfly. Bellanus' cousin."

"You're going after the dragons?"

"Never. It's for the changelings."

"Useless. No beast, no matter how tampered with, can enter the mind of a higher earth beast."

Lira looked away. She couldn't answer him with any kind of conviction. When the words finally stuttered out, they sounded just as empty as she felt.

"It- It doesn't eat the mind."

"So what does it eat?" he hissed.

And so Lira answered.

"The soul."

The dragon could have uttered stock phrases at that moment. He could have screamed 'why' or 'no!' or 'what have you done?' and peeled some answer or explanation from the elf. But this situation was beyond that. This empty creation was beyond speech itself. The milatta was not the end of life. No, this was much worse than that. It was the end of sentience. It was the end of all the higher beasts. They would become chattel. Empty beasts, fucking for the sake of replicating DNA and survival instincts.

The dragon grew. He was ten feet, fifteen, twenty, twenty five . . . he continued to swell, filling the room and beginning to crush sensitive materials.

"How do I remove the bellanus? The one that kills my people, the one that your people made, the one that is eating the Prince of Dusk's mind as you sit here and breed another, worse version of that parasite. How do I remove the bellanus before her mind dies?"

"You can't," Lira yelled back.

"You lie, earth beast!"

"Cut off her head, rip open her mind, burn the body. You can kill the butterfly before it infests others, but you can't get it out and her be intact. Think, Darlan. The gods couldn't figure it out and you expect us to have? And *if* we had, we would have shared it! I would have told you if I had known any way of saving Fenon, you have to understand that!"

"On your life, elf! On the debt you owe me for every breath you take, tell me."

"Darlan, I'm sorry. There's nothing you can do," there was barely room to move or even to breathe. The dragon filled the room with his presence and his body. He filled the room with his accusation and wrath.

"But it's better," she pled. "Better that it is the bellanus. Better that it is not what they're making now. At least she will still have her-"

White rage to match a white room with white jackets worn by the Oceo Tolok. There was a noise, a click, a cloud of fog, a lake above their heads, and a waterbreather at work. Then, the world went an off-white that clashed with all the sterilized absence of colour from before. The labs, the people, the dragon, Lira, all of it now a mushroom cloud of evaporated anger, flesh, and an almost completed experiment.

Outside, above the lake, beyond the meadow, across a Crystal Bridge, through the clusters of elven homes, sitting hidden in the middle of dying, frostbitten trees and dry leaves, a high dreadpriest heard the explosion. With the precision of a chain smoker with a habit or an arsonist with an orgasm, she lit the match against the leather of her sleeve. The small but sturdy flame flickered to life with a hiss of air being consumed and the slight hint of sulphur.

CHAPTER 39
THE SECOND LEGION FAILS

The death of the village of Dompt was not as bad as the god had thought it would be. Once it had begun, she had become curiously detached about the whole thing. Don't be mistaken, it was still more disgusting than anything she had ever seen before. Watching hundreds of people being pulled into the rocks was obscene. Their defiance and cursing had all too quickly devolved into a group of humans soiled with fear and urine, begging to be spared. But even still, the god didn't cry. She didn't even turn her head away. She simply watched it all dispassionately.

Some of the villagers had prayed to the Lord of Salvation. Old devotions that all youngsters must memorize. The god felt her lips tracing the words along with them and she had to forcibly still her mouth to get herself to stop. The young woman again wondered about whether gods could hear prayers when they walked in flesh. Before she had assumed it was a deficiency in herself that prevented her from hearing. But perhaps, the simpler explanation was that her changelings didn't need to pray.

So yes, not as bad as she had thought. And there was even a consolation of sorts. They had started with the men and the rocks had had their fill before all of the children had been killed. Presently, Seina and the original guards who had accompanied her from the Menundra were making the trip back to the Gate with the remainder of the prisoners. The lucky ones, or maybe the unlucky ones depending on what their new situation would be like. The god hadn't bothered to ask.

After Seina and company had taken the survivors and herded them away, the dragon and the high dreadpriest likewise left her, slipping over the wall in search of a solution for the thing eating her. The god and Vyvi were left to wait and be protected by the entire Second Legion, now numbering at three thousand and sixty.

The god had grown comfortable with her little contingent and missed them. The First Legion warriors she had known by name. The dragon had finally started to be redeemed in her eyes. Seina had become her closest friend. She and Erin were getting along much better than they ever had. In fact, the high priest had promised that when she returned from the Gossamer Forest she would explain their mission and the history of their people. An unprecedented level of trust and inclusion for the god.

For now though, there was nothing for the god to do but wait, feeling a little lonely.

There wasn't anything wrong with the Second Legion. They were also her people and she was glad she could give them the comfort of her presence. She just wished there were at least a few dreadpriests around to gossip with.

Thankfully she had Vyvi with her. Glorious, playful Vyvi, who was angered by the fact that she could not fly like her father, nor speak the earth beast tongues like her mother. Vyvi, who skittered along the ground stalking crickets and beetles, trying her best to crush them. Vyvi, who begged to know when she was going to develop breath (your father says not until you are two years old).

The Prince of Dusk marvelled at having a daughter only weeks old who could communicate in fully formed sentences, support her own neck, and bang her head up against anything she wanted without immediately caving in her skull.

Sometimes, looking at the foreign little dragon the god had difficulty reconciling the idea that she had helped create it. Vyvi was beautiful the way a waterfall is beautiful. It was a cold and distant beauty. Vyvi was not the typical round face, rosy cheek, gurgling mammal, incapable of so much as rolling over if a predator came a-calling. She was a dragon with agility, strength, claws, and teeth ready-made for protection and survival. It was watching Vyvi cavort across the ground that made the god finally understand why the dragon viewed the free races as such base species. It was because they were.

Currently, the little dragon was playing pounce with one of the underbeings. She would take turns sneaking towards the changelings, and then try to attack them before they knew she was there. She only succeeded maybe once in twenty, but this was actually quite an accomplishment since the Warrior Clan didn't give wins. To watch Vyvi's repeated failures and see her tail droop in sadness was heartbreaking, especially considering that if the warriors caught her, they pinned the little dragon to the ground and swatted her across the snout for failing.

The first time she had seen this was right after they had fed the starved rocks. The god had been about to intervene and berate the offending warrior when the dragon had invaded her thoughts instead.

Let them be, human. They make her strong. If she were with the brood it would be no different. Dragons do not survive long if they cannot learn stealth.

And so she let the mild abuse continue. On the up side of the whole things, Vyvi, who had quickly discovered that she wasn't to be coddled, was very happy when she did successfully catch a warrior unawares. Seeing the little dragon dancing and roaring triumphantly made her smile every time.

"Pardon me, Dusk Prince."

The god tore her eyes from Vyvi to look at the changeling standing awkwardly in front of her, nervously gripping the blades sheathed at his belt. She didn't know his name, but he was currently a human. The being was thick, but not with fat. It was muscle that corded heavily along his form.

"Yes?"

"Warleader Dober wishes to speak with You," the underbeing whispered.

"Mina?" Seina had spoken often of the Second Legions' warleader and always with pride. The youngest to be appointed in two generations. The god had only met her officially twice: the first time she had blessed the Second Legion, and five minutes before the dragon and the high dreadpriest had left. Other than that, she had only ever seen and spoke to the warleader in passing when she went to visit the Second Legion.

"Yes, Dusk Prince."

"Okay, tell her I'm on my way, then."

The changeling's eyes widened. His words tripped over one another in their panicked rush, "No! No! There is no need, Dusk Prince, the warleader was just asking for permission to approach. There is no reason for You to have to move. I will go get her now."

And with that, the underbeing bowed deeply before quickly scurrying off lest God decided his speed did not satisfy Her and that She had to exert Herself.

The god shook her head and smiled.

Soon enough, a pleasant seeming dwarf was walking her way. Her form was a little small and awkward, her shoulders being a bit too narrow to be aesthetically pleasing, but her black eyes smiled in a way that made up for deficiencies elsewhere.

"Hello, Dusk Prince. How is the Lady today?"

"The Lady?"

"Vyvi, the god cub. The Warrior Clan has received news of her birth and calls her the Lady, after The First Lady."

"The First Lady?" the god smiled at the affectation, "Who is 'The-'"

Warleader Dober's head whipped towards the trees and her eyes narrowed. The god was watching that direction as well.

There it was again. The sound of a Zzali. Only there is no such thing as a Zzali. Which meant that there were currently many changelings fighting to the death. And that the numbers were too overwhelming to send a messenger. Only enough time to send a signal to be passed down among the scouts before racing to the battlegrounds. The signal meant two things. First, it meant *Pass on message, then come*. It also meant *No chance of success. Evacuate the dreadpriests*.

Only there weren't any dreadpriests. There was a god.

They were found. If the odds were overwhelming against the Second Legion, it meant that the free race army thought to be guarding the south gate of the starved rocks was almost within throwing distance of their current position.

"Third File take the Prince and make for the Menundra. Everyone else, fastest forms, now!"

The shifting took seconds. Everybody who could took elven form, and barring that, the human one. Then, the changelings were one and all running. Vyvi was grabbed from the ground and pushed into the arms of the god, who was then hoisted over a sturdy shoulder. It reminded her of the first time she had been carried away by the dragon as Lady Shutba. This time she did not struggle. Instead, she made herself as pliable as possible, got ready to be carried to safety, and did her best to reassure a terrified infant.

Earth-Mother, what is happening?

The little dragon was quivering in the god's hands, confused at the suddenness and roughness of the past five seconds. The underbeing carrying them was prioritizing speed over comfort and the two were being bounced violently.

We're running away from the bad men.
Do the bad men want to hurt us?
Yes.
Will the Warrior Clan protect us?

371

The woman shuddered. The fear leaking from her underbeings was so strong that she found the terror slipping into her as well. The god swallowed deeply, and was finally able to reply to her little dragon daughter, barely keeping the fear from seeping through her own thoughts.

They   *will*   *try.*

CHAPTER 40
THE BASKET IN WHICH ALL
THEIR EGGS HAD BEEN PUT

The limp form was dropped carelessly at the edge of the crater. At first glance, she seemed dead, but shallow breaths were still being pulled into the chest. Lira had been beautiful to the dragon, once. Now the only emotion he could elicit was disgust. He spoke to her unconscious form.

"Your lifedebt has been filled, elf."

The great beast glanced behind him at the crater that used to be the almost completed milatta. He brought a claw forth to graze his neck. It felt empty and broken. Never before had he wrought destruction on such a large scale. He had pushed it too far, he knew. Would his breath ever return or had he done irreparable damage to his glands? It would be a long time before he would be able to use his waterbreathing again, if ever. Claws and teeth would have to suffice for defense.

There was nothing he could do about it for the moment. He could only return to where the Prince of Dusk protected Vyvi and somehow explain that, despite his desperate effort, they had failed and the god was going to have her mind eaten after all.

The dragon noticed the flames in the distance. A shame, that, but not too surprising. He had known the temptation would get the better of the dreadpriest. The only good thing he could see in the situation was that he would be able to safely fly out now. There would be no arrows to pinhole him when the entirety of the army stationed here, all the defenders, and most of the civilians were busy in passing buckets of water hand to hand to save leaves, bark, sap, history, and culture.

Although with so many working, the dragon wondered how they hadn't at least killed the flames somewhat. The winged beast could see the tall fire still leaping and hissing even from his distance. Regardless, it didn't matter. Getting Vyvi to safety was all that mattered now. The blood would rally once he took the hatchling home.

The dragon was still his thirty feet of bulk and he shrunk down to a shameful three feet. It had been centuries since he had had to restrain his size and now he had done so twice in as many years. He truly was getting old. The dragon started to smooth his claws along his wounds, willing his flesh to soften and seek wholeness. The tough scales did not react to his weavings. The dragon frowned and once more he pulled at a gash along his right flank against which glass cases and instruments had been crushed. Instead of melting flesh back into place, the gash widened from his rough treatment.

The dragon shivered. It seemed his breath was not the only thing that had been damaged. The dragon gave up on his efforts and resigned himself to healing like an earth beast. As ragged as his flesh was, at least none of the wounds were actively bleeding. The golden fields beckoned lazily, but the thing was not yet done and death would have to wait.

The dragon stretched his wings briefly and nodded to himself when he caught the wind enough to indicate flight was still possible. He prepared himself to launch from the ground, but before he did he glanced behind him briefly into the crater that had once been a lake, an underwater city, and a people. Elves had surfaced from the second lake to stare blankly at the gaping hole that had been their neighbours.

The elf Lira, if she lived, would be able to tell them of it. Of how the Water Weavers' Lakes became the Water Weavers' *Lake*. Their abuse of life no longer warranted them the plurality of people, or of waters. The dragon's anger still burned hot. But he was tired now. He felt old, and spent. First the permafrost and then imploding the lake . . . a toddler with a sharp stick could probably kill him now, and he decided that a quiet exit would be prudent.

The dragon spread his wings wearily. He shrunk still more until he was one foot of lightness. Less energy to fly meant more for later when who knew what awaited him. He and his daughter would be of size now, which he knew the hatchling would enjoy. He smiled fondly at the thought.

The small beast wondered briefly if he should try to extricate the dreadpriest, but then dismissed the notion immediately. It wouldn't be the most terrible turn of events in the world if the smug underbeing had been lynched. With that, he flapped his wings and began to ride the currents of air which danced above the sea.

It took the dragon an entire day to arrive at the little camp where The Prince of Dusk and the Second Legion had been left.

Had. Been. Left.

The dragon felt his blood cool frighteningly. Where there had once been a legion, there were many, many bodies there instead. The high dreadpriest stood among them, alone.

The dragon landed quickly and sloppily.

"Where is she?" he snarled, whipping his head around. There was death here. A lot of painful, violent death. It had evidently been a short, rough fight.

The high dreadpriest had noticed his approach and now she turned towards the dragon. The rocks must have still been sated to allow her to pass back over them. Vyvi was wrapped around Valar's neck.

"She was taken," the high dreadpriest's words were quiet and she avoiding looking the dragon in the eyes.

Young one. Where is Earth-Mother? he shot the question to the small dragon. This was a mistake.

The hysterical voice that now latched onto his mind was fierce in its turmoil and desperation.

I don't know. Bad men came.

A series of images flicked through the dragon's mind. Playing, then rough hands, then fast movement, then so many dying bodies, then Earth-Mother pushing, and looking into eyes, and saying *Hide Vyvi! Make no sound and hide!* and trying to be smaller, and being so very afraid-

I hid. I did what Earth-Mother said.

Another series of images. Earth-Mother screaming, strong arms pushing Earth-Mother to the ground, Earth-Mother keeping her eyes away from the tree where Vyvi hid, her hands being tied tightly, her hands paling under loss of circulation and weight of other bodies pressing down against-

Bad men took her. I did what Earth-Mother said. Where is Earth-Mother? Where?

Another series of images. Earth-Mother hurt and bleeding while thick fingers were probing. There was laughter, unending laughter-

The dragon wrenched his mind free from the panicking one of the hatchling with an effort and put up blocks against her.

"How long ago did she say it was?"

The high dreadpriest had watched the dragon's concentration slip from herself to the hatchling, and then back again. The beast hissed in anger. The dreadpriest knew the what if not the how. One of the last secrets now exposed. But of course there were more important things. More important by far.

The dragon sifted through the series of images to search for a perspective of time. Sixteen hours. It had been sixteen hours ago that she had been taken, when he had been somewhere between here and there taking his time because he was old and tired and he had used too much breath and-

The hatchling's emotions were seeping back into his mind. He struggled to shut her out again.

"They are not yet a day gone. We can still catch them."

The high dreadpriest was pale and she was looking at the ground. Maybe thinking about where she had been sixteen hours ago. Maybe considering how she had dawdled.

"No, I really don't think that's a good idea."

"What do you mean, 'no'?"

"I mean that it's you and me against whatever force was strong enough to wipe out the entire Second Legion."

"For Salvation . . . all of them?" It was not the slaughter of the underbeings that made him pause, but rather the numbers and strength capable of doing it.

"Yes. They were wiped out to the warrior."

The hatchling, still panicky and perched on the shoulder of the high dreadpriest, began to shake. Vyvi curled her head towards the warmth of Valar's neck for comfort. The changeling leaned her head just a fraction of an inch to return the affection. The dragon caught sight of that and growled.

"Give me my daughter."

The high dreadpriest's voice was blank.

"She will be our surrogate god now that the Prince of Dusk has been taken."

"You were going to kill the hatchling before she was even born and now you claim stewardship? It was your guards who lost the god. You will not touch Vyvi for another moment."

"My, my, my, are we jealous? She finds comfort in flesh, dragon. Your cold-blooded indifference is hardly warm and cuddly. The Prince is human, after all. Maybe the god cub prefers us."

The high dreadpriest's gaze finally met the dragon's. Her words were flippant and mocking, but her eyes revealed something else. Devastation played there. She had lost the Prince of Dusk. They were godless. She would have to break the news to the Warrior Clan. The brilliance of funnelling all love into one person was that emotion couldn't be used as a weapon against your soldiers. If that person went missing, and there was nobody else to fill the void then very, very bad things could and would happen.

But the dragon didn't give a flying fuck. He wasn't losing another woman to two-legged earth beasts.

One, two, three, four. The dragon shot four of his most powerful images associated with the high dreadpriest at his little hatchling. They hit her like a physical blow.

In a city alley, the dreadpriest standing in front of a terrified Earth-Mother-

Earth-Mother lying motionless, a large piece of her throat newly healing, Father crouched protectively over her while the dreadpriest watched with triumphant pleasure-

The dreadpriest at the Induction Ceremony, telling Warrior Mitah to proceed with the submission of evidence, Earth-Mother looking pale and upset-

And finally . . . .

Father in the dungeons, bloody and hurt, and the dreadpriest giving orders to have his claws removed-

Vyvi screamed with little dragon fury and sank her small teeth into Valar's neck. Nothing more than a pinprick for the changeling, but enough pain that years of training and reflexes took over before she could help herself. Her hand came around and made to deal a crushing blow to the attacker, but even quicker, the little dragon lighted from her shoulder and flew in choppy, unsteady wing beats to the safety of the older dragon.

She landed on his back, quivering from the tip of her snout to the end of her tail in shock of her virginal flight, but she still managed a little Vyvi hiss. There was barely enough room on the dragon to support the hatchling and his weakened form almost shook with the effort.

You are safe with me, little one. The dragon smeared the thought with a mental nuzzle. Then he bared his teeth which, despite his diminutive size, still promised threat to the underbeing.

"Not jealous, changeling. Never jealous of you and your kind. Wary is more accurate. You do not have the best track record with me and this one's mother."

The dragon took a steadying breath before continuing.

"I will fly her to my people. Alone. I want none of your minions knowing the way or getting in mine."

The high dreadpriest stared at the hatchling. She seemed to be . . . at a loss. Her voice, when it came, was gravelly and tight.

"So you will take her and leave us then? You know what they will do to the Prince of Dusk. They will do to Her everything we did to you and more. She is a sixteen year old young woman. There is so much more that can be done.

"But then again, that's right. Your kind removed themselves from the petty war of the earth beasts. The bargain has finally been fulfilled and you are finished with us. Take your fresh blood and go. Leave Her. Leave the young god to Her fate. She's just an earth beast, after all. A stupid, naive earth beast who had begun to once again trust an old beast with an agenda."

It was meant to burn and it did. The words sank hotly into his heart and the dragon's eyes narrowed.

"Two weeks, underbeing. If I fly directly it will take me two weeks to take the hatchling to my brood and return to the Gate. Then I will go with you to retrieve her. That should be enough time for you to come up with an excuse for losing your god."

He didn't wait for an answer to his statement, but instead turned and beat his wings unsteadily against the weight of the hatchling on his back. The dragon refused to look at the underbeing he had left behind. He couldn't bear the accusation he knew would be in the dreadpriest's eyes. Two weeks was a long time to be held prisoner. But there was nothing else that could be done. He had to keep Vyvi safe. The hatchling was the most important thing, wasn't she? For thousands of years he had been working towards this goal.

The dragon soared high above the treetops. His thoughts chased him, speeding his flight along. They followed him the entire way and threatened to dampen the joy he felt at watching Vyvi spread her wings and successfully fly alongside him for stretches of time. The little one's elation of soaring through the air was projected so strongly that the dragon could feel it leaking through his scales.

This is where his kind belonged, he thought roughly. In the air. In the mountains. Away from the earth beasts. With the brood.

We go home, little one, he shot into the mind of the small flyer beside him.

The response was an image of Vyvi cuddling beside the older dragon, the two surrounded by other dragons. The purring rumble, so absent of late, began to vibrate through the old dragon's bones at the joy of youth, fatherhood, and flying. It darkened however, when the image in his mind shifted to that of the god: bloody, exhausted, and with that ridiculous grin on her face as she saw the hatchling for the first time.

What of Earth-Mother? Vyvi pushed into his mind.

The dragon did not answer that, and spent the rest of the trip avoiding the subject.

CHAPTER 41
TWO GODS MEET

Somebody kicked out the god's legs and she collapsed into a heap before both her gag and blindfold were ripped from her face. Harsh, unpitying light flooded her sight and her pupils dilated in a painful way.

She tried to get her bearings but she was disorientated and her thoughts were messy. They hadn't bothered to feed her on the rough journey here. Always starving but unable to perish from it. They had given her water, plenty of water, forcing her to drink. But that was only for the pleasure of seeing her piss herself, as they did not allow the devil the luxury of privy breaks along the way.

She hurt. Her body could heal, but she could not control when and regardless she still felt the pain. For the first time, she wished the butterfly would eat her memories more quickly. At least that way she wouldn't have to remember the fists, the feet, and everything else. The god barked a bitter laugh thinking about Seina's ardent claims that the dragon had raped her. She knew now how untrue that was and wondered in a dull way whether she had stopped bleeding there yet.

The room in which she had been dumped seemed garish to her. A real throne room perhaps? Opulence overflowed around her as she saw lurid tapestries, brash vases, and a disgusting overuse of gold. The god wondered if she would have thought the room beautiful before having witnessed the stark simplicity of the Menundra. She wondered if she would have found the room beautiful if she had not arrived in chains.

In front of the young woman stood about . . . one, two, three, four, five . . . more than five people at least and she couldn't muster the concentration to count past that. It seemed full in there. She knew that some were soldiers and the others were important people. Which ones were which was impossible to tell as her vision blurred one body into the next.

The god held no illusions about what was going to happen. She was the bad guy. These were the good guys. She only hoped that they wouldn't parade her in a cage like they had the last prisoner she had seen in Lavanor.

It took her a while to realize that a man standing in front of her was speaking. Angrily. She got the feeling that he had been repeating the same thing over and over again. The god struggled to pay attention.

"If you won't admit it, then we will use our own methods to prove it to everyone. Now, I will ask one last time. Who are you?"

There that concept was again. Proof. Every time she met somebody new they seemed to need to throw that around. How she was beginning to hate the idea of concrete knowledge.

The god's tongue felt heavy as she tried to speak.

"I'm Rynna."

She felt the fist hit her teeth without seeing it come. There was a crack and there was an iron taste in her mouth. The god coughed and red leaked out from between her teeth.

"Your real name! What is it?"

"Just- just Rynna."

The fist came again.

More blood.

"Who are you? Say it clearly for them all to hear!"

A ringing in her ears and the room becoming blurry-

The phrase, *we will use our own methods* droning through everything else-

Buried in the back ditch, hot fire and black pitch, a good witch 'sa dead-

"I am," she coughed more blood onto the floor and wondered whose job it was to clean it, "I am and always will be the mighty and terrible Prince of Dusk."

A hush met this. There was an awkwardness and uncertainty that the councillors and priests felt upon hearing the pathetic little creature say those words. The she-beast and her changelings were a murderous terror. But this girl, here? This human girl just coming into womanhood? They could not corroborate her with the fire and brimstone, red-eyed, powerful, deadly Prince of Dusk they had been fighting.

Finally, a sad looking man just past his prime spoke.

"King Paelin, are we sure that this is really the Prince of Dusk?" So, it had been King Paelin who had been the one hitting her. The god had just enough young girl left in her to feel honoured to finally meet her monarch. She had always loved the royal family. No matter what backward village her and her mother had found themselves in, they had still always paid taxes, and avidly followed the news and the goings on of the royal-

"I am sure, Lemin. *I* recognize her."

This was a new voice. A deep voice of command and power. After these words were spoken, everybody in the room went down to their knees or else sunk into deep bows and curtsies.

"Prince of Dusk," the same man past his prime addressed her with a tired voice, "meet the Lord of Salvation."

The bruised god raised her eyes slowly so that she could see this new arrival, see her nemesis. Although he was the same age as her, he was much taller and had filled out into manhood quite well. He was swathed in rich velvets and purples, and he wore a large ruby on a pendant around his neck. The young woman's eyes focused on his face. His aesthetically pleasing, familiar god face.

"Fik?" incredulity rang in the god's voice.

Then, she began to laugh. She couldn't help herself. The red headed, mean tempered, square jawed bully was the free races' god. Somehow, it seemed entirely fitting. She felt a deep contempt for these people. A deep contempt for all humans, dwarves, and elves for putting their fates into the hands of so unintelligent and simple a being. At that moment she was supremely happy that she had fed the starved rocks with their hometown. At that moment, regardless of the original reason for it, she hoped her people would succeed in their mission to wipe every elf, dwarf, and human off the face of the world forever.

The god was still laughing and Fik's face began to burn with anger. He made a motion with his hand and somebody slapped her. She didn't know who it was, but this did not stop her mirth. On came the gales of side heaving laughter. A small slap was nothing. How often had she tried to kill herself, slicing flesh with a blade? How often had she felt the cut of sharpened stone and destruction of hungry flames as a child?

And what can a slap compare with seeing your mother burn alive?

This slap, this pitiful defense for a god who was even more pitiful himself made the situation all the more hilarious. The god's empty stomach hurt as she continued to screech and cackle with laughter.

But then they slapped her again. And again.

And again.

Only they weren't slaps any longer. They were blows that used fists, and defiance in bondage cannot win out against unrestrained fury.

The last punch landed in her stomach and the tied up woman doubled over in pain. She was no longer laughing. She was dizzy and her body throbbed.

Fik's voice was calm. Towering over her as he did, all broad shouldered, deep voiced, and clothed in glorious fabric, he was holiness itself.

"You are going to hurt. Hurt for all the people you have killed and all the people your underbeings have killed. You are going to hurt until I close My eyes and no longer see the ruined streets of Dompt."

The young woman watched as pain wrinkled Fik's brow and darkened his eyes. He licked his lips and then added one last thing hesitantly.

"Tell Me one thing. There were no bodies. Not even charred bones. What did you do to the people? To My family?"

The god managed one last smile. Her lip was puffy, and wet blood still covered her teeth. It was a broken smile, but one that still expressed sick joy.

"I think it is better if only you hear this, Fik," she gurgled as her grin widened.

Fik eyed her wearily but eventually leaned his head down so that his ear was a mere inch away from the woman's lips. The god explained in clear detail exactly how the starved rocks had been fed. Happy birthday to her.

The Lord of Salvation's face paled to a deathly white.

"You will die for that, bitch."

Then the Prince of Dusk began to laugh again. Only this time, she was not silenced until they had rendered her unconscious.

CHAPTER 42
TORTURER STU

The floor looked like another floor. It had been a floor where a dragon had lain with forearms ending in rough stumps. Only this time there weren't any guards manning a series of restraints. The free races didn't need them for one powerless god. Basically a child, too. All they needed for her was a strong set of chains, some manacles, a room with a lock on it, and a floor with a drain in it.

Torturer Stewart was thrilled.

He was a good guy, that Stu. Always paid his debtors, never cheated on a woman, donated handsomely to at least three different charities. Maybe he was a little too picky when he ate out at inns, but he always tipped well and never sent food back more than once in the same night.

He was an all around nice person for somebody whose profession involves a lot of other people's blood and pain. But he couldn't help his job. It was a calling. He could no more resign from the torture gig than a musician can stop playing or a dancer can stop moving. He was just thankful that Royal Torturer was a legitimate profession. He had tried being a mass murderer before, and it was just a lot more stressful, what with how suspicious the general populace was getting of late.

When he first heard the news that he was going to be receiving a project that was impossible to kill, he immediately realized that he had won the sociopath lottery. How many times had he had prisoners where his art had been restricted? 'Make sure this one survives,' was a sentence he was particularly loath to hear. Even worse was 'He must not sustain any lasting damage from his treatment.' Seriously, how can one expect the best results with such strict specifications? And no lasting damage? That takes away most of the really fun things you can do with a crowbar!

Which is exactly why Torturer Stu was so thrilled. They were giving him a certifiably evil person to torture who could definitely feel pain, but was incapable of even the smallest of scarring. He wondered excitedly if when she bled she would eventually run dry and he would have to wait for new blood to form, or if the blood would just keep coming, restocking itself instantaneously. Torturer Stu imagined showering in a never-ending stream of arterial fluids.

Even better, there had been no finish date. No deadline, no end point, no stopping in the conceivable future. Just the endless opportunity of ruining nerve endings.

And the Prince of Dusk of all people! He, lowly Stewart Lomat, was going to get the opportunity, no, the honour of administering hurt to the devil! The baddest of the baddies. The archetype of suffering and hatred. Why, why, he was rendered speechless at the mere thought!

When they brought her in, Stu was standing in the middle of the room fretting with his hands. He was too excited for words and instead just pointed to the stretch of chain he wanted them to hang her wrists from. He would adjust the bindings to her size and height later.

He wished he had been given more specific details in advance. He just felt so, so, unprepared. And he hated being unprepared. For reassurance, he glanced at all his instruments neatly hung against the opposite wall. They were all there, freshly cleaned and waiting for his skills to use them to their full potential.

The two guards dragged the unconscious god to the centre of the room. Not carried, mind you, dragged. Torturer Stu could see scratches that traversed the length of her body from where they had passed over gravel on their way here. Injuries obviously incurred on her trip to Lavanor could be seen as well. Torturer Stu *tsk tsked* in his head. He hated amateurs. The beefy men seemed to barely notice the young woman's small weight and simply dropped the body when they reached their destination. One of them lifted the young woman's limp arms and secured them one at a time into the manacles that he looped around the chain.

"Yes, that's fine," he muttered as the two guards finished their work. He shooed them from the room and then quickly locked the door behind them.

Torturer Stu turned his attention to the comatose young woman. Considering she hadn't been fed in a couple of weeks, he was surprised she did not seem completely emaciated. Maybe it was another perk of being a god. Perhaps there was a minimal level of muscle that was always retained despite a lack of sustenance. Enough to function, in the very least.

Stewart carefully readjusted the bindings and hoisted on the chain so that the god's feet were only just touching the ground. Currently the weight of her body rested largely on her wrists and shoulders, and Torturer Stu watched the skin there strain with satisfaction. This was going to be everything he had ever hoped for and much, much more.

The pain of her weight pushing against the manacles soon brought the god to consciousness.

"You're awake!" Torturer Stu exclaimed with an enthusiasm that did not bode well for the god at all.

The god moaned. In her warped, disorientated state she knew nothing except that she had to relieve the pain in her shoulders. She sloppily tried to stand on her toes to shift the weight of her body off her wrists.

She could only succeed if she concentrated and balanced carefully. The man watched the god's efforts with barely controlled excitement.

"My name is Stewart," he told her. Then he wrung his hands and took a few deep breaths before bursting out, "Okay, I'm so sorry. You know, I promised myself I wouldn't do this, but can I just say . . . wow. I mean . . . . Wow. The things you do . . . the things your people do well . . . it's a privilege. A real privilege to meet you and work with you."

The god's foot slipped and she collapsed with a gasp as her shoulders once again wrenched at an awkward angle. She regained her toehold with a painful effort.

"I mean," the happy man continued, "the whole empty mouthing concept was brilliant. You have no idea how many times I have been thwarted by your followers when they used that little technique." He chuckled to himself, as if appreciating that he was at the butt of a good-natured joke. "The dedication is just marvellous."

That was when the man's face became completely serious. A professional being professional.

"I just want to put this out there," his words were just as measured as his face. "If you have any criticism for me, any at all, please let me know. I'm always looking to improve myself and I realize that there is just so much I could learn from you because you are the master. You are . . . wow . . . just wow."

The god lost her balance again. Immediately her shoulders burned and the manacles began to cut into her wrists. She struggled desperately to regain her footing. Completely ignoring the torturer, her only concern at the moment was being able to stand. She felt sick and still hurt from what had been done to her over the past two weeks.

"So I was thinking," the man continued, "I might start on your thighs. These days the thighs are neglected when it comes to torture. Of course, I don't know how fast you heal so some of my usual techniques may have to be tweaked a bit, but I'm sure we can come to some sort of arrangement."

Tentatively, her toes took the weight from her once more, but her body shook with the effort. She had been in the little room for less than five minutes and already she in agony. Tears began to stream down the god's face.

"Thighs, then? Right. Well, I'm just going to jump right in."

Torturer Stu hummed to himself merrily and he reached for one of the instruments that hung on the wall. The piece of metal he settled for looked like an eleven-inch fork with barbed points. Then the man looked at the god with all the earnestness he could muster.

"I won't let you down, Miss Devil."

He wiped his hair back from his face, secured his glasses in place, and then began.

The   god   screamed.

CHAPTER 43
THE CENSORED VERSION

It is difficult to describe what happened to the young god in that locked room. It hurt. Hurt a lot. And it lasted a long time. The god told Stu everything she knew about the changelings and everything she knew about herself. She told him things she didn't know too. She screamed that she was not evil, that she was not this person he thought she was. She talked for a long time before she realized that it changed nothing. Stu did not care about intelligence she carried, nor about the revelations she could make. That wasn't the point of it all.

The only thing that the free races wanted accomplished with the Prince of Dusk's capture was for her to feel a lot of pain. So she did. She felt it in every way imaginable. All the instruments on the wall were used. New ones were added. It was torture for torture's sake, meant simply to break her. And it did. It broke her completely and unequivocally. But even then, it did not stop. During it all there was little coherent thought in the god's mind.

There is one curious thing that occurred during Stewart's work. And it is worth noting because it was something he had never experienced before in all his days of torturing. It surprised him even more than the resiliency of the god's body did. And it should also be noted because it was the last time Stu laid so much as a finger on the young woman.

It was eleven days into his acquisition of the god. He had been using a large mallet at the time, taking it in turns to crush the god's knees, feet, and hands. Watching the bone knit was something that brought him a lot of pleasure, and he always enjoyed the convulsion that a body made when its legs were being ruined.

The god herself had been unconscious at the time of the occurrence. That was okay. The pain of awakening to a knife working its way through your intestines or having your chest cavity open is a horror all on its own.

As he worked that mallet up and down, crushing the young woman's skeleton, he suddenly had a thought. A thought about something that had always been taboo in his profession due to the tendency it had to irrevocably end the prisoner's life. A thought about the god's head.

Why the heck not?

Almost reverently, Stu placed his feet solidly and raised his large hammer in the air. Then, with that same respectful attention, he brought all his strength to bear that mallet down onto the young woman's skull. With a heavy crack, he heard the bone splinter. Ever so carefully, the torturer stepped towards the ruined scalp. The head had partially collapsed, and Stu bent down and began pulling away large pieces of bone, skin, and hair until the back of the woman's head was completely open before him. There was little blood compared with other areas of the young woman's body, so it wasn't even all that messy.

Stewart inhaled slowly and smiled.

He tenderly began to dig his fingers into the soft tissues there, feeling for the first time the fleshy rivulets and folds of a living soul's mind.

It was beautiful. Warm, oh so warm. And wet, the way a woman's body is wet. The mind was smooth like the keys of a piano, but more efficient and not restricted by two dimensions of playing space. The torturer smiled with newness and the feel of fingers buried in the warm insides of the young girl.

Which was when something bit his hand.

With a small grunt that was more surprise than pain, the torturer jerked his hand out of the god's head. There was too much blood already covering him to be able to see how bad the bite had been. Probably nothing. It had hardly felt any worse than an ant bite. That wasn't the point. The fact that something had bit him at all was what made him pause.

Stu considered for a few minutes, his lust now abating slightly with the cold return of curiosity. Then, with a nod, he placed his fingers to either side of the god's brain matter and gently parted it. He stretched it so as to be able to see deeply in. Once the folds had ripped and pulled themselves into two clear halves, the torturer was quite surprised as he discovered his attacker. For right in the middle of the god's head there was an engorged butterfly.

Disgust twisted Stu's stomach at the sight of the thing. It was unnatural. He knew that for certain without ever having heard even a whisper of the bellanus myths. He reached over and pulled a pair of tongs off the wall. Then, once again parting the

397

folds of flesh, he carefully extricated the insect and held it at eye level an arm's length away.

It was a nauseating thing to look at. First there was its size. It was a corpulent, swollen creature whose abdomen was much too large for its thorax and head. Then there were the wings. They were a harsh pink swirled with shades of dull yellow-green. He could see the small, black legs wriggling frantically but Stu kept the tongs clamped shut tightly, not daring to let the abomination free.

Instead, the torturer reached for another instrument from his wall, this time just a small knife. With it, he skewered the small insect, sticking the blade deep within its body. He did not remove the knife until the bloated butterfly was completely still, deciding that he didn't care what the abhorrence was, Stu just wanted it dead.

Strangely enough, when he removed his knife from the now limp insect, what covered the blade was not blood, pus, or crushed innards. Instead what coated the blade was a liquid comprised of the most powerful colours he had ever seen. Reds, blues, purples, greens, yellows, they were all there. It was a cosmopolitan of hues that swirled with an inner harmony completely unknown to the man. They were pigments so beautiful that they made his lovely locked room drab. They made his life drab. And he knew without a doubt, without an iota of uncertainty, that the colours had come from the wrecked and unmoving god still hanging from her wrists.

Stewart touched the blade of the knife and watched as some of those wondrous tints transferred onto his fingers. He felt them seep into him, leech into his bloodstream. He could see the colours now, just below the surface of his skin. Then they began to move.

Slowly, the colours shifted up his arm along his veins. The torturer no longer watched the colours with awe, but rather with a combination of intense curiosity and a little bit of fear. The colours began to race towards his shoulder and a masochistic pleasure-filled terror was creeping into his mind. All of the veins along his arm were soon livid with a polychromatic brilliance, and it was engulfing his shoulder and neck as well.

The occurrence stopped being enjoyable when the colours reached his head.

At that point the torturer dropped the knife and the butterfly, then quickly crushed his hands against his face and moaned. Words and images crammed themselves into his mind and a jumble of emotions not his own coursed through his veins. Stu gasped, shuddered, and then convulsed as fragments, conversations, and entire episodes of a girl's life rammed themselves into his head. Lightening was flashing behind his ears, frying essential things, and replacing them with bloated memories that were not his own.

When it was finished, Stu was laying facedown on the ground, shivering. All he managed to do for the next forty minutes was hold himself and try to forget. The man was gripped with an emotion he could not understand because he had never felt it before.

Stewart did not hurt the god again. He wanted to get away from the small, destroyed woman. He wanted to get away from the locked room with the drain in the floor. Not only did he want to leave, but he never wanted to return to this dungeon again. Instead, he wanted to see the god whole. He wanted to see her walking, talking, and not ruined by what he had done.

Stu unlocked the manacles, gently lifted the young woman down from the chain, and laid her carefully on the ground.

Then he fled.

Remorse. The new emotion which he had felt had been remorse. He cried for a long time that night, alone in his small quarters.

Back in the room with the drain, scalp, hair, bone, and flesh made themselves whole. The god's mind did its best to reassemble itself, but there were holes, rips, and tears both physically and mentally so it took a very long time for this to happen.

When all was said and done, for the first time the god knew the answer to why something had always been fundamentally wrong with her.

And as it just so happens, when her mind was through the reassembly process it succeeded in fixing it.

CHAPTER 44
TORTURER STU REMEMBERS 'A SMALL MATTER'

"Have You tried not killing Yourself?"

It was my turn to wrinkle my brow.

"We . . . I have tried everything, trust me. I'm not looking for you to find a solution, I'm just asking to have a companion, somebody to stay with me and keep an eye out for it. The incidences are always lowered when there more people paying attention than just me."

Seina chewed her lip as she considered this, and then finally stated, "Well, we will have to consult Erin."

It took us only a few minutes to walk the halls of the Menundra. When we finally arrived at the War Room, the high dreadpriest was bent over a series of maps, many of them clearly out-dated as they still showed the tactical positions of armies surrounding the Ice City. Others were far more recent, and held large stones placed at strategic points both around the Gate and Lavanor, with smaller stones seemingly placed sporadically elsewhere on the map.

"Erin, the Prince of Dusk needs your advice," was how Seina introduced us.

The high dreadpriest looked up from her maps to stare at us.

"Whatever it is, I am sure you and the Prince can adequately handle it yourselves."

Seina saluted the high dreadpriest and stood straight and unmoving with her arm at her forehead until the Valar finally sighed.

"And we are waiting for what, exactly? A more direct dismissal?"

The elf lowered her arm, but did not leave the room. Instead, she simply proceeded to explain my revelations with much more detail than I, myself, had used. The high dreadpriest's face drew darker and darker with every word.

"My, my, my, now this is no good," her words were perfectly calm but a disturbed expression cut her features.

"I just want you to know that I should probably have company. I mean, I guess it doesn't really matter since I'm a god and I can't die anyways, but the changelings are going to get upset if word gets out that I'm slitting my wrists every other day. So all I am asking is that Sein- Warrior Nakao be allowed to just keep me company."

"But that's just the thing," The high dreadpriest's dark eyes began to sweep along my body. She reached out a hand. Delicately, she slipped it around my neck and touched the scar at the base of my hairline.

"You can die."

I flicked the changeling's hand away.

"Oh, yes, because the Lord of Salvation is going to slip into my room in the middle of the night and smother me to death."

Seina was staring at me in horror, evidently having realized something I had not.

The warrior whispered, "Gods can kill gods."

I rolled my eyes. "So, what?"

402

"So? You're a god. If You kill Yourself, well . . . ."

My eyes widened and I placed my fingers on the same scar that Erin had touched earlier. I remembered how I had gotten it. It had been the time I had thrown myself off the roof and a fence had sliced open my scalp. And my toenails. They still hadn't grown back. The lost toenails were from the time I had slowly walked towards the fire and-

"Like I said, Prince," Erin's voice made me want to shiver. "This is really no good."

CHAPTER 45
THE WHY

"... their twentieth rebirth, the one where the gods knew that they would both be born without memories or powers ...."

***

"The lights were amazing! Did you see it? Did you see Him? He was there! So powerful. Where? Right in front of the temple, I saw it myself! Did you know he's a human? So amazing! The skylights burned above the city. I saw it with my own eyes. The lights, his power!"

***

"Human, never mind the taste, you bleed the essence of a god through your skin. I have smelled many gods, and you are the worst, most pungent one I've ever encountered. Twice as bad as the last one."

***

"But there was a residual resonance, like an echo in my mind that I have never felt before."

***

"The two gods have been trying to kill each other even longer than the free races and the changelings have been. Much, much longer," the dragon explained with sleepy words. *"Millenniums upon millenniums longer. You may not remember it, but the Prince of Dusk and Lord of Salvation would almost do anything to ensure the other died."*

***

After all, she didn't mean to keep trying to kill herself. It was something that happened when she wasn't paying attention.

***

"Who knows what the result of completely ripping apart a mind would be. You may end up with a drooling infantile creature or a complete personality change or worse . . . . Her body can't die, but her mind can only take so much abuse before drastic, irreparable things occur. That method is out of the question if you still want your god to be intact mentally at the end of this."

***

In the quiet, desecrated emptiness that is a torture chamber at rest, a god's eyes shot open.

Abruptly, she began to giggle.

CHAPTER 46
WHAT HAPPENS WHEN A GOD
HAS A GRUDGE

There was a very quiet knock on the door. The rap had been so soft that almost nobody in the Council Room heard it. But Lieutenant-General Pak heard the little sound coming from the door, then cleared her throat loudly until everyone in the room stopped speaking to see why the dwarf was drawing attention to herself. And as silence descended upon the room, they all heard it too. That persistent, tap, tap, tap.

King Paelin's face boiled into hard veins and redness.

"Well? Somebody get the damned door."

It was some nameless priest who went for the door. Poor kid. Never knew what hit him.

The priest had just put his hand on the door handle when the thing exploded inward sending thick pieces of wood to sever his spinal column. He flew back with the impact and landed on the ground, blood trickling from his mouth. Now just a footnote in history, with no cross-references in life.

The rest of the priests, all of the councillors, the elders, the kings, Lemin, Pak, and Fik Tucker stood up immediately at that. Some screamed, but for the most part the people controlled themselves. They watched as the dust settled and a woman wearing ragged black leather stepped into the room.

406

"Oh, hello," the Prince of Dusk greeted. Her eyes were unfocused. "I'm not interrupting anything, am I?"

Fik walked out from behind his podium and stalked down to the centre of the room to face the intruder. His voice was full of outrage.

"How did you escape?"

The Prince of Dusk smiled beautifully.

"I woke up, blew open my prison door, and killed a lot of people. The real question, Fik, is how was it that you escaped?"

"Escaped what?"

The woman kept flashing those pearly white teeth.

"Detection."

Nobody really understood this statement except for two people in the room. The first was Fik himself who stared at her in panic. The second was Oshar Lemin who closed his eyes wearily, ready to face the consequences for the desperation of past actions.

"Seize her!" King Paelin ordered and it was Fik who reacted first. Fik who pulled the knife and lunged for the woman. The god did not move, and simply smiled wider as the young man raced towards her, aiming the weapon at her throat threateningly.

"Speak one word and I kill you."

The Prince of Dusk focused her attention on Fik, and said quite simply.

"The problem with that, is a knife is only a real threat to me if it's wielded by a god."

The woman, still smiling, always smiling, walked into the blade at her throat. She kept walking into it until the metal was sticking out the back of her neck and blood was dripping down her shoulders. Then, just as slowly, the god walked away from the blade. She walked away until the knife wasn't touching her at all and was only supported by the shaking hand of a scared young man.

The woman slowly moved her hand to wipe the blood free from her neck. There was no wound, not even a mark. It had healed instantly and completely. She smiled again.

"It might be wise for you to use some of the blood on that knife and conduct a test with the sacred resin," she spoke clearly in a tone loud enough for everybody to hear. "Also," she paused for a moment to look carefully at Lemin. His eyes were full of apology and regret. He did not fight the judgement he saw in his Lord and instead, closed his eyes and accepted his fate. He collapsed to the ground.

"Also," the god continued, "I'll be needing a new high priest. Seems the current one has had an unfortunate brain aneurism. Pull the Eye from his head and give it to somebody more adequate, if you would."

Nobody moved or said a word, and finally Fik spoke.

"But . . . you're the devil. You killed all those people. You're evil."

The god nodded knowingly to this. "And you are absolutely correct, Mr. Tucker. Turns out I'm just really good at multi-tasking. It seems the Lord of Salvation and the Prince of Dusk were reborn into the same body." She mused for a moment before adding. "You know, remind me to tell the dragon that it *is* all humans who are stupid, and not just me."

The entire room stared in disbelief and shock, eyes jerking between the dead high priest, the terrified Fik, and the blazing Prince of Dusk. One and all refused to accept the truth until a terrified voice asked a question.

"What are you going to do with me?" Fik's voice cracked. Evidence that puberty wasn't as long past as he would have had people think. Nerves, youth, and even still the vestiges of innocence. That crack said oh so much about that silly thing called truth. The entire council went either white or green depending on whether they currently wanted to vomit or pass out.

"Well, I'm not sure about that. There are two people advising me now, as you know, and they both seem to be giving me very different advice. Edmund wants me to kill you. He wants you to die as all usurpers of the holy throne have. Painfully and without mercy. Thom, however, disagrees."

Fik realized he was still holding the bloodied knife upright. He lowered his hand, and the weapon along with it. His voice was shaky. "And what does Thom say?"

"He keeps telling me to kill myself." The woman scrunched up her face as she thought while that luminescent smile faded momentarily before brightening again. "But then what would be the fun in that? Right. Death for you it is, then."

"Wait! Please! Wait! Don't kill me! I'm useful! I know things. We had plans. Secrets. If I die you won't- please, I'll show it to you!"

409

The god paused. She tilted her head and stared directly into the former's Lord of Salvation's eyes.

"Go on."

"Just let me live. I'll do anything."

The woman blinked twice and then she grinned, her eyes still unfocused. "Well, looks like I wasn't the only one with a malleable conscience. Okay Fik, you and I are going to have a little talk together. Does anybody have a problem with this?" The last question was asked offhandedly to the room at large.

Nobody reacted at first. Not an eyelash shifted for a full ten seconds. Then King Paelin, who was the smartest, the quickest, and the most informed of those still alive in the room and not being threatened with death, kneeled.

"Anything You say, my Lord. Provided the priests can confirm the blood tests, my people's and my family's loyalties are absolutely Yours."

The others quickly copied the king's actions with words either very similar or exactly the same as what he had just said. You don't fuck with the god you just ordered tortured for the past weeks. You pray She doesn't want to wear your intestines for a necklace and you agree with whatever the hell She says.

The woman poked Fik in the chest.

"Well then, now that that's settled, let's go see these secrets of yours. Oh, and you. You come with us as well. I can't be bothered to watch Fik carefully. So, if he escapes, you die."

She had been speaking to Lo. The dwarven priest jumped at the command and hurried over to join the two by the door. And together, the three left the rest of the councillors and the priests alone with her blood to confirm the truth.

The god hummed as she walked along the corridors of her new home. It was a half remembered ditty that was half popular half a lifetime ago. All cacophonous 'C' sharps and 'E' flats that jarred the ears and set teeth on edge. There were no words that she accompanied it with, just a corpulent melody. An ugly, mutated song which Lo and Fik listened to with terror.

Eventually they came to a door.

They were deep in the earth at this point. Deeper than the kitchens, deeper than the storage cellars, deeper than the prisons, deeper than the room with the drain in the floor. They were as deep as the place went short of being in the cisterns.

"Secrets?" The woman tilted her head, still a vague smile on her lips, indicating towards the door.

Lo looked helplessly to Fik, who in turn spoke hesitantly.

"I- I don't know exactly what it is. Lemin said it was a weapon that we were going to use. But that it was not quite finished yet."

The woman nodded seriously at this. Yes, I understand. But if this room is empty and you were lying, I will bathe in your blood. The god began humming again. Her eyes focused then unfocused once more.

Fik opened the door.

Inside the room were cocoons. Hundreds, thousands of cocoons. All of them were thick, corpulent, and twitching from restrained movement on the inside. The cocoons were a kaleidoscope of black. An unbearable vacant, swirling pitch colour.

411

The gods both knew what it was and that knowledge made her mouth twist into a shortly-after-sucking-on-a-lemon shape. A sour crinkly expression full of vitamin C.

A small giggle escaped the woman's lips.

"What- what are they?" Lo's voice was barely audible. An instinctive reaction made him shy away from the creatures and step back from the door. Fik, dulled to their presence, did not step back, but he too was nervous. The skittishness that a deer has around a lion. Prey acknowledging a being higher up on the food chain.

Only the woman was calm. Which is why she was able to calmly reach over and calmly rip one of Fik's arms from its socket.

The young man screamed and immediately brought his other arm to clutch at his unbalanced side. Red poured through his fingers and his voice took on a shrieking quality that was ever so annoying to have to hear.

The god turned to a pale, motionless Lo. His thick dwarven hands were gripped together to a near whiteness of blood restriction.

"If Fik survives that," she said nonchalantly, "he is allowed to live." The god then gently wiped her soiled hands onto Lo's robes, ridding them completely of visceral liquids.

"Oh," she added as almost an afterthought, "when you're done dealing with him, I would like you to tell the Council of Three that we will be convening shortly after supper. I believe that the entire Warrior Clan is on their way here, probably planning on killing everyone and everything, and I haven't quite decided yet whether or not I want them to succeed."

Lo's bow of acquiescence was impeccable. Fik had actually gone all the way down to the ground when he bowed. Although, he was probably fainting from blood loss at the time, which ruins the credibility of the whole thing just a little.

CHAPTER 47
HER ID

She was drinking wine and wearing repaired black leather made originally from bleached and dyed human skin. She was a rough iron body, drunk with beauty and fermented grapes. Her eyes were glazed over and she was lounging on a seat that didn't exist, rather it was reality bunching itself together to hold the god just so.

The seven-foot dragon didn't recognize the woman. He knew the curve of her legs, the sweep of her hair, and the shape of her eyes, but still he did not know this creature of power. This was not the young woman who had been captured. This was not the young woman who had mourned a mother and watched a hatchling cavort.

The high dreadpriest recognized her, but it was a recognition that came in and out of focus. She had known this creature since before the body lying on the non-existent couch was born. The voice in her mind which had guided, pushed, advised, and whispered. The voice which had disappeared sixteen years ago. It was that voice which was now stronger, now weaker when she looked at the woman.

As for Seina, Seina recognized nothing. Neither the curve of the leg nor a presence long absent. But Seina heard a heartbeat and a chest rise and fall that were utterly different from the woman who had been the Prince of Dusk. And that constricted her lungs with worry.

The three who had entered the clearing were unaccompanied. The Warrior Clan was a day off. These three alone had been chosen to represent the underbeings at this meeting. They all had their reasons for wanting to be included, and collectively had the authority to deny any wishes otherwise.

So there they were. Three who were so familiar with a woman whom now none of them completely recognized. They wondered uneasily about this foreign lady before them.

The woman smiled. She set down her glass on more substantial nothingness, the air struggling not to spill a drop. Then, the woman stood. The fluidity of it was that of water and oil slipping together in a dance that was not unlike gentle sex. It was a grace that had been borrowed from souls practicing it for longer than the sun burned, and would for long after the sun died.

She was alone and not alone. She was there and not there. She was everything that is and is not all wrapped up in a skin that was taut and elastic.

"Prince?"

The high dreadpriest's voice was uncertain.

The woman's teeth showed and her mouth curled. Her voice was silk on silk.

"Erin, I now have a working knowledge about weaponry, battles, and death. It seems my tactical usefulness has changed?"

The high dreadpriest's face was unreadable. She watched the god carefully and said nothing more. Those foreign eyes focused and unfocused, then settled on Warrior Nakao. The god showed her teeth again.

415

"Seina. Pretty Seina. If I were to tell you to stop killing mosquitos because I had grown fond of them, would you?"

The blind warrior did not understand the question, but familiarity wrenched itself into place as that voice, that same Prince of Dusk voice spoke. Seina replied plainly and firmly.

"Come, Dusk Prince. We need you in the Menundra. Let's go home."

Seina held out a hand for her god to take. But the body's eyes unfocused and refocused once more.

"It's of fundamental importance, Seina. The fate of the mosquitos must be decided. Please answer me. Would you stop killing mosquitos if I asked."

"Do mosquitos pose any kind of a serious threat to you?"

"Yes. They want to hurt me very badly. And they did hurt me very badly, now would you stop killing them?"

Seina frowned. "Then of course not."

The woman god closed her eyes and breathed in the world with a great sigh of satisfaction.

"You see, Darlan," her eyes were alive with instability. "You were wrong. From the start you were wrong. You wanted me to end the war. Or you wanted me to believe you wanted me to end the war at one point. I find it difficult to keep it all straight now. Who said what when. Hows and Whys and Wheres and Becauses. But I do believe at one point you spoke about the unfortunate mortality rates, so yes you wanted me to end the war.

"But the mosquitos will die. They will die and I never had any chance of ending anything. The free races and the underbeings. I am both and neither

416

and it hurts to be in the middle when daddy and mommy are fighting.

"But then again, I never knew my father. And my mother was a drunk, stoned whore. So there goes that analogy."

Then the body laughed. "Actually, it fits quite well now that I think about it. Can you guess who you are, Erin? Are you the defeated matriarch, or the unknown body abandoned in the night?"

"Human, that is enough," growled the dragon.

"Ah, but I'm not human. And you, Darlan. Strong. Patient. Old. I begged pretty please for them to tell me why the two of them have been just hanging around, fucking about for all this time. But they wouldn't tell me. Do you remember? Does Maulo know? For that matter, why were you fucking about for all that time? How did the great and mighty gods not know where I would be, but a dragon was waiting patiently to scoop me up?

"You were so offended when I thought you were a changeling. I believed you hit me and then threatened to tear something out. But the underbeings, they were made from your species. I would doubt if the differences outweighed the similarities. Seems the abuse was a little unwarranted, but then again that pretty much sums up your entire existence, doesn't it? You were right though. Despite what I thought, I never did outrun your breath."

Seina walked forward. Her steps were careful not because she was afraid, but because she was concerned for her Prince. For the young woman who obviously needed her Companion now more than she ever had.

417

"My Prince," Seina placed her hand on the Prince of Dusk's shoulder soothingly.

The god calmly reached out, grabbed Warrior Nakao's hand, and then pulled the other woman's wrist against itself until the dull snap of bones breaking could be heard. But she didn't stop there. The god kept pushing on the hand until blood poured onto the ground, and the back of Seina's hand was flat against her arm, the appendage now completely useless.

"No thank you, Seina. Your presence is no longer comforting."

Warrior Nakao did not cry out. She did not yell, plead, or scream. She simply kissed the palm of her whole hand and then moved it to touch the other woman's cheek. The god slapped it away.

The warrior collapsed and started convulsing. The woman god kicked herself free of the blind underbeing now struggling to hold on to consciousness on the ground.

"Erin, what is that law again? About tasting me? About hurting me? What is the penalty for breaking it? A death, if I remember correctly. I find Warrior Nakao's touch to be painful now, and tradition must be upheld."

The woman showed her teeth for the third time and she began to move her hand towards the hurt warrior on the ground.

"Rynna!" the dragon called.

The woman froze with her hands only inches away from the bleeding and barely conscious Seina.

"Rynna, stop it!"

That name. The woman hadn't heard it in over two years other than when she had spoken it herself upon first meeting Seina and then when reuniting with the free races. Two years is such a long time to go without hearing your name. It is such a long time to be only addressed as a species or a title or an assumption.

It had been such a long time since she had been addressed by the five letters her parents had given her.

"Rynna, please." As the beast approached, the dragon's voice caressed the name. He wrapped his tongue around that name.

Rynna's eyes opened and through all the ruptured damage done by a madman with a sledgehammer, familiarity and sanity peeked out. Rynna shook her head and looked at her people, the ones who had come to save her. The young woman was fighting through the folds of her mind, struggling to seize control of what was happening, of who she was, and of what she was doing.

"Rynna, look at me."

She did. Comprehension, horror, and focus came into her eyes.

"Dragon?"

The great beast nodded slowly. Tears began to well up in her eyes. She reached out to touch the scaled creature who was now right beside her.

"Why did you come here?" her voice was almost silent as she felt the warmth of the dragon's body beneath his scales.

The dragon shrank to Rynna's height, shedding feet and weight as he became the same size as the broken god. The waterbreather carefully lifted a claw to brush the hair from her eyes. Gently. Tenderly.

His eyes and voice were dry, but soft.

"My lifedebt, Rynna. I swore I would protect you. A life for a life until the sun dies."

The young god shook her head. Her voice was small and uncertain "And that's all? That's the only reason why you came?"

"Of course it isn't, Rynna. How could it be? The hatchling needs you if she's going to survive long enough to reach her Breathforming. You know. So that the blood will rally and the dragons can survive."

The dragon kept smiling, but the god's eyes slowly began to empty out. Then there was a pause as a giant fist closed around something small and fragile fluttering in a girl's chest.

The high dreadpriest was the only one who immediately understood what had happened. She had always understood. Since before the Induction Ceremony. She had known in Ta'ao even if the dragon still did not. Only Erin Valar felt the full devastation of what had just happened to her god. Her god who was only sixteen. She was sixteen and too young with too much power to deal with such a staggeringly simple thing.

Reality lost its grip on Rynna's wine glass and there was a tinkling sound when it landed.

Then the cracks began to form. Cracks around Rynna. Cracks that were not in the leather, or in the earth, or in the dust at her feet. They were cracks in something deeper and bigger and older. They were cracks that began to spread.

A pressure began to build in the air. There was a burst of flapping wings and scurrying in the leaves as birds, squirrels, and racoons got the hell out of there. Those lovely lesser earth and earthair beasts' instincts were kicking in even though their brains weren't big enough to understand what was happening.

The cracks went deeper still, further still, and started to bleed light and darkness into the woods, twisting and warping whatever they touched. Trees, ferns, and wild flowers burned indigo and fluorescents as creation itself slipped through gaps to fuck with the rules of nature.

Rynna doubled over and began to cough blood onto her shirt. A crimson heart colour shining on the black leather.

The cracks widened further. The land began to waver as the fabric of the winds and water shivered. It was not because of a shift in tectonic plates, nor of an epicenter vibrating its effects, but rather because of this god right here, in agony. A mind patched and destroyed who had almost found what she was looking for. A mind fighting desperately, and losing to something that had finally seized on a chance for which it had been waiting for a long time.

And of the three who had come that day to see a god, one could feel the wind howling through his wings, one felt the scream of the earth's pain, and one was struggling to speak.

"Dusk Prince . . . I just . . . why?" Seina whispered through the delirium of lost blood and a ruined wrist.

The young god's eyes were unfocused once more. Her answer was jagged, and came through lips sullied with her own blood.

"Because on a fundamental level, it's impossible to love the boogeyman."

Something broke.

It was not the world. A god did not end everything that day. The only thing a god ended was one weak young woman in a lot of pain.

There was a perceptible snap, and then the god's body calmed down. The world relaxed as well, and those cataclysmic breaks in the world quietly melted away, leaving only the evidence of wrong coloured greenery to mark their presence.

Then, with a smile, something bigger, older, and more powerful than a scarred sixteen year old spoke through soft, female lips.

"Well, that was just a little too close for comfort."

Seina had finally fallen completely unconscious while the dragon and the high dreadpriest were dizzy with what had almost happened. The powerful god figure stretched her arms above her head in a lazy way as she continued to speak, regardless of her listeners' states of being.

"I'm glad it's all over. The young are so dramatic. Darlan, you are a lifesaver if there ever was one. First the butterfly, and then that beautiful performance at the end. Really, this whole thing wouldn't have been possible without you. Of course, I will have to remember to thank the torturer as well. If he hasn't gone mad yet."

The high dreadpriest regained enough control to speak. Erin's face was white. White, angry, and very afraid. This wasn't the voice that had left her sixteen years ago. This wasn't the Prince of Dusk either.

"You're the Other God," the high dreadpriest's words were shaky. "What have you done to the Prince of Dusk?"

"Which one? The hormonal drama queen or the hypocritical pacifist?"

The dragon was the one who answered. He constricted his throat, but there was no click and no ensuing fog. A dry rasp was the only thing heard. He shook his head violently, then flexed his sharp claws and roared.

"What did you do with Rynna?"

The god chuckled lightly at the emotion. At dragons. At beasts. She curled her fingers upwards and the waterbreather's claws began to burn a black stench. The dragon howled and thrashed his foreclaws against the earth.

"Do you realize how difficult it is to take control of a body? I mean look at that, I almost tore this place apart. As an aside, I'm quite happy that didn't happen. Hm. You know, it's funny. For all Thom tried to kill us, *she* never wanted to die."

High Dreadpriest Valar reached down and slid her sword from its sheath. Erin's black eyes were glistening. She mirrored the dragon's words, only hers were darker and tinged with more hate.

"What. Did you do. With Rynna?"

"Down girl." The young woman flicked her finger casually and the impotent weapon shattered in the underbeing's hands. "Tell your precious Clan that their god is nice and safe up here." The young woman tapped her index finger against her head twice. "The real Prince of Dusk, I mean. Not that twit of a girl who has been parading. She's gone."

"What do you mean, gone?"

"I mean, she's no longer an issue of contention, let's put it that way. And now, if you'll all excuse me, I've got a populace to win back. This body has been the devil for quite some time and if I want my followers to ever really trust this girl, I've got my work cut out for me.

"You, underbeing. I'll leave you your life. The last thing I want is to have to kill the entire Warrior Clan and if you don't return, I'm sure they'll go swarming over the walls of Lavanor to acquire this body. No, I will let you live so you can go explain everything to them.

"And you, Darlan. You, too, I will let live. It amuses me to do so. I know about that hatchling though. I will find her, don't you worry about that. I always wanted a nice little daughter to mould in my image. Although I always thought I'd be the father in that situation. Oh well. From what I've gathered, the mother has all the sway when it comes to your kind anyways."

The dragon snarled, and his throat expanded to a violent thickness of anger.

"You will not touch her."

The old presence in the woman's body smiled once more.

"Yes, I will. And now I bid you farewell. This has been a great pleasure for me." Then the god grabbed the bleeding, comatose Seina, and in one smooth motion hefted the underbeing over her shoulder. "Oh, and I'm taking her. With such soft flesh . . . well, a god has needs."

The high dreadpriest had not dropped the ruined weapon and she raised it now, the blade only one foot of jagged metal.

"You will not take Seina!"

The god repositioned the limp body on her back so that it was in a comfortable position. She graced the high dreadpriest with her attention just long enough to say firmly and decisively,

"Yes, I will. Now, goodbye."

Fury boiled across Erin's face and she tore across the ground, closing the distance between her and the god in seconds. Erin's muscles coiled in preparation to strike.

The god smiled and flicked a finger once more. The high dreadpriest was thrown to the side, her shattered blade singing through the air to touch nothing but the wind. The god's grin widened and she moved her finger again, sending the dreadpriest flying once more. You could hear Erin's neck crack when the tree that she hit ripped into her. The changeling's dead body dropped heavily.

And with that, the old god began to calmly walk away.

The dragon choked out a desperate question after her retreating form.

"What are you going to do?"

The god paused. Paused, turned around, and then smiled. "A friend gifted me with something called the milatta."

The dragon paled.

"Ah, then you already know about it. Well, the cocoons are probably hatching as we speak. They will be hungry, Darlan. And you of all people know the precedence that survival takes over all else."

Quietly, the dragon's last words came.

"Just, tell me. Did you destroy her soul?"

The presence in the woman smiled.

"You'd think after three thousand years you would have gotten over sentimentality. If I were you I would breed that hatchling of yours as soon as she's physically able. Because I am coming for her, Darlan. Coming for this body's daughter."

Then the being walked away.

When the last traces of the woman had gone, the forest was still cowering from its near rendering experience. Because of the earlier exodus, now the only living things left near the spot where gods fought were the ones rooted to the earth, a changeling, and a dragon. Without the chirps, croaks, and snuffling of lesser beasts, there was an unnatural silence broken only by the sound of the Erin Valar's bones snapping back into place as another death echo was added to her heart.

But the dragon didn't notice any of this. Instead, he was staring at emptiness and wondering why he couldn't stop shaking. He was wondering why he couldn't stop thinking of tucking hair behind a soft ear. He was wondering why for the first time since his Before, tears were brimming in his eyes.

CHAPTER 48
THE SIDE WHERE GRASS IS GREENEST AND GLASSES ARE HALF FULL

Thousands of butterflies flew above the battlefield that day. Both the changelings and the free races saw it as a sign from their god of an assurance of victory. Because they were not ordinary butterflies. They were glorious butterflies coloured a bright golden-white. It was an awe-inspiring hue that reflected the sky with an undeniable brilliance. The creatures were light itself, each one born of the sun. They were bringing that fiery, almost painful heat and radiance down to earth to favour the higher earth beasts there.

Proudly, gloriously, and confidently the armies ran towards one another. Screams could be heard from the bottom of the Pit to the tallest tower in Lavanor. As the battle began, the world rocked from the pure noise of conflict resolution. It was the beginning of the beginning and the end of the end all in that one beautiful moment of violence, clashing bodies, and golden butterflies.

Far away, two gods were having a conversation of sorts as they watched the battle begin.

Are you happy now? the voice was bitter.

"I couldn't have planned it better if I had been controlling this body all along," the reply was in the gentle tones of a sixteen year old girl. It was going to take Edmund a while to get used to hearing himself as a female. He grinned as he ran a thumb along the curve of his breast. At least, he thought mildly, there were some fascinating compensations.

The other voice was silent for a while. Then, it finally stated.

Why don't you call a stop to all this?

Laughter barked from the young woman's lips.

"I'll tell you what. You give me the code to call off your pet changeling so I can see what you've been hiding in the Pit all this time, and then we can end the war together." There was a slight pause before, "No? I thought not."

The voice became unexpectedly smug.

Erin knows better than to let you have access to it, especially after that little stunt you pulled with her littermate.

"Unless I can get the dreadpriest to defect. The girl did a fantastic job making your little pets love her. Maybe I will have my own army of changelings soon. The war would end quickly enough then."

You are not that young woman. They would know the difference. You could never be what she was. The voice then became more subdued as it added, *You should not have done that to her. She deserved better.*

"It's not my fault that you didn't press the advantage and do something similar. And since your first act upon acquiring this body would have probably been to kill us, I think its best that things played out as they did."

Darlan is not finished with her.

The body frowned.

"There is nothing that the dragon can do. I am a god. I can incinerate him with a thought if I wanted to."

Could you? I am not so certain . . . the breathers were Maulo's first and favourites. Remember, you could not take the heartblood. You had to bargain for it. You would think that a powerful god such as yourself would not have to strike deals with beasts to get what he wants.

The creature's shoulders shrugged.

"I guess we will just have to see, now won't we?"

If a disembodied voice were said to have lips, Thom would have been chewing his at the moment. Edmund listened to it with amusement and wasn't surprised by what the voice said next.

Why are you letting this . . . milatta . . . free? You can't have forgotten what happened last time.

"Because I finally realize the ingenuity of some of the things you did. There was lingering sympathy among my people for the so called Prince of Dusk for generations after you ended the threat of the bellanus."

You think that this parasite can be so easily controlled?

"You did with the other one."

I sacrificed much.

"I guess you did, didn't you? Good thing too. Otherwise, I would probably have a daily struggle to keep you from stealing this body from me in my sleep. Then where would we be? The devil in control? No, that wouldn't do at all. But I'm not worried, I'm sure I'll figure out something."

And what if you don't figure out something, and thought dies?

Edmund mused on this for a while before shrugging once more.

"Then I guess we can play cards or something for the rest of eternity, or until father finally remembers where he threw us."

There was a sudden flurry, a sudden burst of energy inside the young woman's head as another soul struggled for control. Because Edmund had not been expecting it, his hand jerked towards his own neck and made it halfway there before he was able to stop it. The voice known as Thom snarled.

I fucking hate you.

Edmund fingered the scar on the back of the young woman's neck and thought about how this body could no longer grow toenails. Finally he said a little wistfully,

"You always did, brother."

He tilted the lips into a smile and added. "Cheer up, though! Think about the pandemonium that is about to ensue! Premium entertainment doesn't really get any better than this."

With that, the body formerly known as Rynna turned itself back towards the battlefield, where the two gods watched the first of the butterflies begin to land.

THE END